UNDER THE APPLE TREE

A Paranormal Tale of Love and Suspense

by

Kathleen J. Easley

Published by Ames Lake Press

ISBN 979-8-9917310-0-3

Cover art by Dar Albert, Wicked Smart Designs

"Don't Sit Under the Apple Tree (with Anyone Else but Me)" was a popular song during World War II, made famous by Glenn Miller and the Andrews Sisters. The melody was written by Sam H. Stept, with lyrics by Lew Brown and Charles Tobias.

Also by Kathleen J. Easley

SIBLINGS and SECRETS

A Brenna Wickham Haunted Mystery

(Book One)

FAMILIES and FELONS

A Brenna Wickham Haunted Mystery

(Book Two)

Praise for Siblings and Secrets:

"A slow-burning contemporary mystery using red herrings, psychological insights and clever twists. The intricate plot, nuanced relationships, and well-hewn characterization are among the book's major strengths."
> —**Pacific Book Review**

"The book kept me turning pages one after another to find out what happens next."
> —**Richard G. Hunter, author of *Lamplight Declassified***

"The characters are very real, and the story is so touching ... Don't miss this lovely book."
> —**Regina Duke, USA Today Bestselling Author**

"This story is about reconciliation, love lost yet found again, misunderstandings, and revealing the truth. If you want a great book to curl up with, look no further than Siblings and Secrets."
> —**Readers' Favorite Book Review**

Praise for Families and Felons:

"A light and easy read in the cozy mystery genre. It flows seamlessly, keeps the reader guessing, and the characters are easy to connect with."
> —**Readers' Favorite Book Review**

"The book's vivid descriptions, unexpected twists, and well-developed characters keep readers on their toes, making it a perfect read for those who love a good, eerie mystery."
> —**Amazon Reviewer**

"Easley's skillful storytelling weaves together a compelling blend of mystery, romance, and supernatural elements that keep readers engaged from start to finish."
> —**The Book Maven**

Dedication

To Jim, aka Gizzard — poet, artist, musician, biker, Viking warrior, little brother.

Chapter One

"Whoa, Kate, this would make one hell of a haunted house!" Jared rolled up the car window and unfolded himself from his battered old Toyota, shaking his head in amusement as he surveyed my newly purchased home.

I glowered at my brother. "I warned you it needed work. How do you think I got it so cheap?"

He strode up the walkway to join me on the veranda. The boards creaked and sagged as he mounted the steps.

I ran a possessive hand along the porch rail. It wobbled and bits of crumbling paint rubbed off on my palm, but I didn't care. "They don't build houses like this anymore," I said, giving my hand a furtive swipe on my jeans. "It just needs us to rescue it."

From the moment I saw it, I knew this moldering old mansion was meant for me. Its dark, empty windows and faded siding spoke to me, not of age and ruin, but of hidden grandeur waiting to be coaxed out.

"Kate, you said it was a little run down. This place looks like something right out of *Tales from the Crypt.*"

I punched him playfully in the arm. "It's over a hundred years old," I said. "What did you expect?"

Three stories high, the imposing Queen Anne Revival boasted all the opulence of a nineteenth century show piece with its decorative excesses—wide veranda, steeply pitched gables, patterned shingles, and miles of elaborately carved gingerbread. A tall round turret rising from the front corner evoked images of a fairy tale castle.

I had to admit the place *did* look a bit Halloweenish with the remnants of a thick morning fog clinging to the overgrown weeds in the yard and a dreary leaden sky casting a pall over the desolate façade.

"I know, I know," Jared said, a teasing grin spread across his face. "It was owned by a little old lady who only lived in it on Sundays."

I paid no attention to his gibes. For all his teasing, I knew my brother was a romantic like me. I knew he would recognize the underlying grandeur, the potential. My fingers traced the scrollwork on one of the porch columns. The artistic detail fashioned into the wood was exquisite despite the layers of grime.

"Okay, it has possibilities," Jared conceded with a sly wink. He ran a hand over his jaw. "A couple of nails, a little paint . . ."

The house sat in the middle of an acre of land facing east toward the Cascades, a scant mile from the town of Salmon Falls, Washington. Twin big-leaf maples stood like gigantic sentinels on either side of a long gravel driveway. Grass and weeds grew knee high. To the right stretched a thick, woodsy tangle of trees and underbrush separated from the yard by a wooden fence, part of which had fallen over. To the left, over the fence, stood a neat white two-story house bounded by trees and rhododendrons. Here and there across the road, several homes clung to the outskirts of town.

Jared cleared his throat noisily. "So, are we going to stand around out here all day or do I get to see the inside?"

"Keep an open mind," I warned as I turned to lead the way.

The hinges squealed a protest as I swung the door open. Dust motes stirred in the dim light as we traversed the broad entryway; the air smelled musty and stale. Proudly, I pointed out the classic architectural features, the extravagant woodwork, high tray ceilings, and wide staircase that ascended into darkness. Flocked velvet wallpaper, faded and worn, adorned the walls.

It appeared the style and décor hadn't changed in over a hundred years, but, sadly, as the previous owner aged, she had become frail and eccentric, lacking the resources to keep the property maintained. The house had literally deteriorated around her.

"Like Miss Havisham's mansion," I murmured.

"What?"

"*Great Expectations . . .* never mind. What do you think? Won't this make a great bed-and-breakfast? Once the remodeling's done."

Jared strode under an archway into the living room. He set down his duffel bag and guitar case, nodding his approval. "It's impressive, I'll give you that." He took a moment to gaze around. "Looks like you even got the furniture."

"Some of it." I glanced at the haphazard assortment of chairs, lamps, and bric-a-brac. Tucked in the recess of the front bay window, a single chair and small round table looked forlorn as though waiting expectantly for a long-overdue cup of tea.

Relics of a simpler way of life, I thought wistfully, *and I love every grimy, cobweb-shrouded inch of it.*

"After the owner died," I said, "the house sat empty for years. I bought it as is, along with whatever was left inside. Got the whole thing for a steal."

Jared cracked a grin. "Probably because nobody else wanted it."

I ignored him and went on. "Of course, I'll need to spend time sorting the random dust catchers from the genuine antiques. Some of them will need refurbishing, but it'll be worth it to have authentic period pieces throughout the house."

At last, I'd be able to use the knowledge I'd acquired working seven years in an antique shop in Seattle. Daniel, my ex, hadn't liked the idea of me working after we were married, but I had insisted, learning from every appraisal, every transaction, intrigued by the function and history of each unique item that had passed through the store.

"Awesome, Kate," Jared said. "No joke. It really is awesome. Where do you want me?"

"The library. Through there, to the left. I spent all day yesterday sweeping out the dust and spiders."

"Sounds good." He picked up his sparse belongings, pushed open the solid wooden door, and looked around. The wallpaper was gray with age. One window was broken and boarded up, blocking out a portion of the natural light, giving the room a gloomy cast. A faded wingback chair stood to one side accompanied by a small end table on which stood an old glass hurricane lamp. Two of the walls were dominated by imposing floor-to-ceiling walnut bookshelves laden with rows of musty hardbound volumes.

"All the books are still here," Jared said with surprise.

"I know. I'm hoping there might be some good first editions hidden in there."

He frowned, fingering his chin. "It's strange . . ." His voice trailed off.

"What?" I looked at him curiously.

"I don't know, I guess I'm just amazed the place wasn't trashed. You said the house stood empty for years before you bought it, right? Usually, abandoned old houses like this are targeted by vandals and teens looking for stuff to steal." His lips tightened and I wondered if he was remembering a time, not so many years ago, when he might have been one of those delinquent teenagers. "But other than a couple of broken windows and a little bit of graffiti on the wall by the front door, there really isn't much damage."

"You're right," I said. "I got off lucky. It could have been a lot worse."

Then his gaze came to rest on the cot I'd purchased from the local thrift store. His mood bounced back to its habitual good humor. He tilted an eyebrow. "That looks comfy."

"Sorry. It'll have to do for now. At least you're up off the floor."

"Don't worry about it."

"The upstairs bedrooms aren't fit to live in right now."

"Kate, I said don't worry about it." He grinned. "I've slept in lots worse places than this."

I nodded and brushed back my hair with my fingers. "Anyway, if you get bored, I brought along a box of my own books which you're welcome to read."

I never went anywhere without an armload of books.

He chuckled. "I might have known. I don't suppose you've got any good techno-thrillers or sci-fi?"

"No, but I've got a couple of Sherlock Holmes mysteries you might like."

"We'll see." He sounded doubtful.

"I'll be in a sleeping bag in a room just off the kitchen. There's a couple of rooms back there that I'm guessing were for the housekeeper. I'm planning to convert them into a suite for Amy and me." I smiled at the thought of my fair-haired, eight-year-old daughter, an angel with soft pink cheeks and bright blue eyes. "Once school is out, I want to bring her here.   She's staying with Mom during the renovation."

Jared looked around again and shook his head.   "I can't believe you want to live here in the middle of all this mess. Is there even a functioning bathroom?"

"There is now. That was my first priority. I had the contractor and plumber working non-stop for a week replacing the pipes and water heater running to the kitchen and main floor bathroom." I laughed. "In the meantime, they installed a porta potty in the back yard."

"Great." He grimaced and dropped his belongings on the cot. "Okay, let's see the rest of the place. I want to see what I've gotten myself into."

He was not one to waste time standing around.

A throwback to the 60s, Jared was a musician, an artist, a would-be hippy. At thirty-four I was a year older, but as children we had often been mistaken for twins with our straw-colored hair and cornflower blue eyes. Now, tall and self-assured, a braid down his back, Jared resembled a Viking. He had never been one for the nine-to-five lifestyle, but preferred the meager living he made selling hand-crafted jewelry and tooled leather goods, though he sometimes tended bar at a friend's tavern downtown. In his free time, he wrote songs and played guitar with his friends. When I had proposed giving him room and board, and the basement as his own private workshop in exchange for help around the house, he had jumped at the offer.

Turning toward the door, I suddenly halted and put up a hand. "Do you hear that?" A lonely melody drifted on the air, suffusing the very atmosphere with a yearning despair.

Jared paused and listened. "Sounds like someone playing a piano." His nose wrinkled in distaste. "Can't say I like their choice of music."

"Must be the neighbor," I said. "I'm surprised we can hear it all the way over here."

"Sounds close," Jared said. "Like, in the next room. Do you have a piano?"

I frowned. "There *is* a piano, but there shouldn't be anyone else in the house."

Cautiously, I pushed open the door and peered into the living room. All was gloomy and hushed as before. The music had stopped.

I exchanged a glance with my brother.

"Weird," he said, shrugging his shoulders.

"*Had* to be the neighbor," I said. There was no other reasonable explanation. "These old single-pane windows aren't exactly soundproof."

Moving across the living room and back into the cavernous entry hall, I pointed through a wide arch beyond the base of the stairs toward a room in which stood a magnificent grand piano. "I call that the music salon."

"*Gee*, I wonder why." Jared's deadpan expression was betrayed by the smirky twinkle in his eye.

"It's a Steinway," I said, ignoring him. "A gorgeous piano."

"Looks old," Jared said. "Cleaning and tuning will probably cost you a fortune." He approached the piano and plunked a couple of notes. The tone was clear and resonant. "Doesn't sound too bad. A bit dusty maybe, but it seems to be in pretty good condition."

That's when I saw the sheet music propped on the rack above the keyboard. Had that always been there? I hadn't noticed it before. *Beethoven's Moonlight Sonata.* A galactic leap from the beginner piano lessons I'd taken as a girl. The complicated splatter of notes across the staves made my eyes blur. I cracked open the piano bench and slid the pages inside.

I turned then and led the way through the dining room and down a short passage to the kitchen. In traditional Victorian fashion, the kitchen lay at the back of the house sequestered behind a sturdy door lest unwary guests be offended at the sight of the cooking staff.

I loved kitchens in old houses and this one in particular. Besides being enormous, it featured a brick fireplace and an old-fashioned butler's pantry. It needed renovating to make it functional for modern living, but I was adamant about keeping the charm and character of the original architecture.

At the moment, things were in disarray. Portions of the walls had been removed to allow access to the plumbing, and in pulling up the old linoleum, the contractor had discovered a patch of dry rot. This had necessitated tearing the floor down to the joists in front of the sink. Like the rest of the house, the kitchen was dirty and drab; the smell of old grease permeated the air and mice infested the cupboards.

Being Sunday, there were no workers in the house. Our footsteps echoed off the walls as we walked through the empty rooms.

Just inside the kitchen, a door opened to a stairway leading down to the basement. I gave Jared a sheepish smile. "I'm afraid I've only been down there once and it was pretty bad—full of dirt and spiders and junk. But there *is* electricity, and I *am* planning to have a bathroom installed."

He gave a short laugh. "Well, I wasn't expecting the Ritz. Let's take a look."

I flipped a switch on the wall. A lightbulb suspended from a wire in the ceiling over the stairs made a lackluster attempt to dispel the gloom. As we descended, a hodgepodge of random shapes materialized out of the dark—a discarded trunk, a rusted bicycle, various garden tools, and heaps of forgotten household items dumped here out of the way. Along one wall were an ancient washer and dryer and washbasin, plus a shelf full of empty canning jars. A large oil furnace hulked like a great troll in the shadows. The floor was concrete, smooth and gray and water-stained. A door to the outside was set unobtrusively in the wall near the back corner.

Jared stood for a few moments on the bottom step sizing things up.

I repressed a grin. "Nothing a big, strong guy like you can't handle, right?"

"*Geez*, Kate. There must be a century's worth of crap down here. I'll bet if we dig deep enough, we'll find the Lost Dutchman mine, D.B. Cooper, and the Holy Grail."

I swept my hand in front of me, encompassing the contents of the room. Cheerily, I said, "Anything you find, it's yours. When do you want to start?"

He wrinkled his nose in an unenthusiastic grimace. "Let's see the rest of the house first. I'm going to have to work up to this."

We tromped back up the stairs to the kitchen. In the far corner by the back door another narrow stairway led up.

"Where does that go?" Jared asked.

"That's the back staircase for the servants. There are maids' quarters and a nursery on the third floor."

"Cool," he said. "Let's go see." Stepping around the carpenters' tools, he headed up. I followed on his heels. I hadn't been to the top floor since my first visit after the papers had been signed. All I remembered was a big dark space that had obviously been used for storage.

At the top of the stairs, the door opened onto a wide room with a pitched ceiling matching the contour of the roof. A brick fireplace against the wall shared a chimney with the kitchen fireplace below. I figured this must have been a common sitting room for the maids who had once lived here. Four other rooms opened off of this one. I planned to eventually reconfigure them for guests.

"*Cripes*," Jared exclaimed, staring around. "There's almost as much junk up here as there is in the basement. You could make a fortune just holding a garage sale."

"Sure, if I can find anything of *value*." I flicked my fingers lightly at the shoulder of a moth-eaten dress form, raising a puff of dust. "I'm guessing there isn't much demand for this sort of thing."

I moved on a few steps and considered a slightly lopsided three-legged easel splattered with dried paint, underneath which was tucked a box of petrified oils. "I'm sure someone would *love* to have this."

Jared conducted his own investigation. He examined a small wooden table. "Why do you suppose this is up here? Looks like a perfectly good nightstand to me."

I looked up from a box of old clothes I had discovered. "If you like it, take it. You can use it in your room when you get it fixed up."

He didn't respond but kept fiddling with the table.

Finally, I said, "What are you doing?"

"I'm trying to get this drawer open. It's stuck."

"It's probably locked. You'll have to break it to get it open."

"No, there's no lock. It's just stuck." He gave it a couple of good whacks with the heel of his hand and tugged on it again.

I went back to digging through the musty garments. I could probably sell them to a vintage clothing store. I knew there was a market for authentic period fashions. The stirred up dust made my nose tickle.

"Ah-ha!" Jared said.

I saw he had gotten the drawer open and was rifling through it.

"Hey, Kate, look at this." He held up what looked like a book.

"What is it?"

"A family Bible. It was in the drawer. There's a picture inside. Here, take a look."

He pulled a small black and white photograph from the front of the Bible. He handed me the worn photo and I found myself looking at a picture of a pretty, dark-haired young woman sitting in a straight-backed wooden chair with a toddler on her lap. Behind them an older man stood with his right hand on the woman's shoulder. The picture appeared to have been taken on the front porch of this house. Judging by the grainy quality of the picture and the clothes worn by the subjects, I guessed it was taken sometime in the early part of the last century.

"Sometimes these old Bibles have a page to fill in your name and family tree," I said. Taking the heavy book, I flipped curiously through the first few pages. "Yes, here it is: *Blossom Elizabeth Thatcher, born December 8, 1919, daughter of Morgan Virgil Thatcher, born February 2, 1880, and Angela Rose Wilkins Thatcher, born June 5, 1898.*"

"Blossom Thatcher," I repeated slowly. "That was the name of the previous owner. This is probably a picture of her as a baby with her parents."

Jared's forehead creased as he considered this. "She had to be over a hundred years old when she died."

I nodded. "I talked to some people in town when I first came to look at the house. They said she was kind of eccentric and lived alone here most of her life."

Immersed in this lonely tale, it didn't take much to convince my imagination it heard the soft sounds of a woman's sobs emanating from a corner of the attic. An icy shudder rippled down my spine. I turned, my eyes straining to pierce the shadows, but saw nothing. Jared appeared oblivious. Strangely shaken, I hurried to the door. This dark, stuffy garret was giving me the creeps.

Chapter Two

"What's wrong?" Jared called.

"Nothing," I lied. "I've got to go downstairs. Daniel will be here soon. He had Amy over the weekend and agreed to drop her off here. She's been dying to see the house. I'll take her over to Mom's later."

"Daniel's coming here?" His face went rigid. "Great. I'll be in my room. With the door shut."

Twenty minutes later, my ex-husband pulled up the driveway, revving the engine on his muscle car just to show off what a macho guy he was. His reaction to seeing the house for the first time was predictable. To him, the whole thing was a foolish waste of money, a bad investment. I clenched my fists and forced a smile. I didn't care what Daniel thought anymore. The divorce was over and done, the final papers signed. This was my money I was spending now, my decision for better or worse.

"So, this is your dream house, is it?" Daniel's voice oozed derision as his eyes raked the front of the weathered old mansion. He stood half in, half out of his polished silver Jaguar as if poised for a hasty retreat.

Trust Daniel to see only the age and rundown state of the grand old Victorian. It had never been in his nature to see the romance of a thing, or to visualize the inherent beauty of an object hidden beneath layers of tarnish just waiting to be restored. He saw only costs and liabilities. Ambiance, character, and historical significance were lost on him. Daniel liked all things modern—glass and steel and straight lines.

I ignored his remark.

"Did you have any trouble finding the place?" I stood on the porch speaking to him over the tops of the unpruned azaleas that sprawled in front of the railing. Afternoon shadows were beginning to stretch before the house, dimming the sun's light and creating a cool, dark swath across the yard. I shivered and pulled my sweater tighter around me.

"Hardly. I just drove into Salmon Falls and asked the first person I saw to point me in the direction of the biggest, ugliest old house in the vicinity. Funny—he knew exactly what I was talking about."

I kept my gaze steady and held my tongue, refusing to be drawn in by his sniping. Fortunately, at that moment, the back door of the Jaguar swung open and Amy scrambled out.

"Mommy," she cried, running toward me. "Is this whole house *ours?*"

"Every last inch," I said, a smile bursting onto my face at the welcome sight of my daughter. "Do you like it?"

"It's so big," she breathed in wonder, gazing at the turret towering above.

"Wait till we get it all fixed up and painted," I said. "It's going to be beautiful."

Amy joined me on the porch. She pointed to a pane of glass in the front door. "Mommy, that window's broken."

"I know," I said regretfully. "There are lots of things that need fixing. We'll probably replace all the windows. These are real old and drafty, and they rattle every time the wind blows."

Daniel snorted. "Sounds expensive."

"But in the long run it will save a fortune in heating bills. I'm sure you can appreciate that." I smiled sweetly.

"Can I go look around?" Amy asked.

"Yes, but don't go inside. The workmen have their tools spread all over the place. You can go check out the back yard. I'll take you on a tour in a few minutes. Here, let's zip up your jacket. It's getting chilly."

Amy fidgeted while I fastened the front of her pink hooded jacket, then she dashed off the porch, running to explore the expansive gardens.

"Please tell me you're not letting Amy sleep here tonight," Daniel said. His face knotted with disapproval. "The place is probably teeming with mice."

"Of course not." I pressed my lips together and folded my arms in a defiant posture. "She's staying at my mother's till the renovations are complete. Mom will drive Amy to school so she can finish out the year with her class. The work here should be done by the end of summer." I swung my arm toward the front door. "As long as you're here, would you like the grand tour?"

He remained where he was, one hand on the roof of his car. "No, thanks. I've got to be going." Then he looked around again, taking in the flaking paint and sagging shutters, and shook his head. "I can't believe you think you can manage this all on your own. Is it even safe?"

I gave him a cold look. "Don't worry, I've hired an experienced contractor. He assures me the house is sound. And I won't be all alone. I've hired Jared as a live-in security guard-slash-handyman."

"Your *brother?*" He rolled his eyes for effect. Daniel and Jared had never had much use for each other.

"He's inside," I remarked casually.

Daniel's gaze slid to the rusty red Toyota parked unobtrusively alongside the fence. "I *thought* I recognized that heap of junk."

My eyes narrowed. "Didn't you say something about leaving?"

He got the message. Turning, he yelled, "*Amy*, I'm leaving! Come kiss me good-bye."

Amy came running from around the side of the house, blond curls flying. In her hand she clutched an early daffodil plucked from among the weeds in one of the overgrown gardens. She presented it to her father as she hugged him good-bye.

"I'll see you next week," he said, tousling her hair. "Be good and work hard at school."

"I will, Daddy."

Daniel straightened and gave me an earnest look. "Seriously, Kate, I worry about you out here. Call me if you get into trouble."

I nodded. When pigs fly.

"Bye, Daddy." Amy waved as the Jaguar purred to life and began backing down the driveway.

I grabbed her hand to prevent her running alongside the moving vehicle. Daniel waved the daffodil out the window by way of farewell. The little flower would probably be tossed in the ditch before he reached the end of the road.

"Come on, Amy," I said. "Uncle Jared's waiting inside to see you."

Amy's hard-soled Mary Janes clicked and echoed on the oaken floor of the entrance hall. Eyes wide, she twirled this way and that, trying to take it all in. Her dazzled reaction was understandable. Before moving in with her grandmother, Amy's entire eight-year life had been spent in apartments. First was the trendy downtown Seattle three-bedroom with its elegant furnishings and sweeping fortieth floor views of Puget Sound. Daniel and I had lived there for eight of the ten years we were married. After the divorce, I'd rented a modest flat north of town. Neither could compare to the sprawling enormity of this house.

Jared must have been listening for us because he emerged from the library and approached with a wide grin. "Hi, Squirt," he said to Amy, leaning toward her attentively. "What do you think? Pretty awesome, isn't it?"

"Yeaah," she said, stretching the word out. Her eyes were round with excitement.

My brother's tall, brawny figure silhouetted in the dim light of the hallway beside that of my slight, elfish daughter created such an incongruous image that I couldn't help but smile. *Beauty and the Beast? The Lion and the Mouse?*

"Come on, Amy," I said. "Let me show you around." I led the way through the archway into the main area of the house. "This is the living room, and down this hallway is the kitchen."

As we moved through the house, I saw Amy's nose turn up slightly and her lips scrunch in distaste as she caught whiffs of stale odors. Her forehead puckered as she noticed the grimy carpets and ran her hand across the flaking wallpaper. Overhead, tattered strands of cobwebs hung from the ceiling like gauzy streamers.

I hastened to reassure her. "Don't mind the dirt, Sweetie. Remember, we've only just started cleaning things up. There's a lot of work to be done before the house will be ready to live in."

She nodded, her face betraying doubts.

Maybe letting her visit the mansion so soon had been a mistake. I didn't want her going away with a negative impression. If she told her father she didn't like the house and didn't want to live here, Daniel wouldn't hesitate to make trouble. He had not kept his opinions secret regarding what he called my "questionable judgment." To Daniel, the idea of living in a "rotting old derelict" was unfathomable.

Then Jared chimed in, his jovial voice full of enthusiasm. "Hey, Amy. You know what's so great about an old place like this?"

She shook her head.

"You get to take out all the old yucky stuff, then fix the house up any way you like. New floors, new wallpaper, new rugs, new lights . . ."

Amy pressed her fingertips to her lips as she considered.

Jared continued. "Same with the furniture, the cupboards, and even the paint. You can make everything any color you want."

Amy's eyes widened as she caught on to the possibilities.

"And this is a grand old house," Jared said, spreading his hands wide. "A real mansion. Just imagine—once everything's cleaned up and polished, the whole house will be practically new again, only bigger and fancier than any other house you've ever seen."

"Like a *castle!*" Amy squealed excitedly.

I gave my brother a grateful look as I pushed open the door to the kitchen. "And wait'll you see this," I said to Amy. "There's a fireplace in the kitchen. We can roast marshmallows in here on cold winter nights."

Her happy gasp was heartfelt as she ran to examine the cozy brick recess in the wall. Shaped like an arch, the hearth was built two feet above the floor so that you could sit in a chair and look directly into the flames. Underneath was a built-in wood storage compartment. On one side, a wrought-iron hook was fastened to the brick so that a pot or cauldron could be hung over the coals. Of course, I reminded myself, there would be no fires until the chimney had been inspected by a qualified technician. I had no idea how long it had been since the chimneys in the old house had been cleaned.

I glanced at my watch. It was getting late. "We'd better get going, Amy. Grandma's expecting us for dinner."

As I reached for the door to go back the way we had come, I suddenly stopped. "Listen. There's that piano again."

I cocked my head trying to pinpoint its origin. The soulful notes seemed to issue from the very core of the mansion—close, yet somehow distant, a heartrending dirge ebbing and flowing on a melancholy tide. Whoever it was, they sure had depressing taste in music.

"Wait here," Jared said, pushing past me into the hall. Stealthily, he edged along the wall toward the front of the house where the piano sat secluded in the music salon at the base of the turret. The music faded away.

Moments later, he called, "*Kate!* It's okay. There's nothing here."

Amy and I hurried to join him. My heart hammered like I'd run a mile. I took several deep breaths to banish my jitters. *Really?* Had I actually imagined an intruder had broken into the house to play the piano? I almost laughed at the absurdity. Yet Jared seemed to have had the same idea.

"It has to be the neighbors playing their music real loud," I said. "They left their window open and these old walls aren't enough to block out the sound."

Jared scratched at the stubble on his chin. He flipped a loose tendril of hair behind his ear. "Right," he said. "Of course. What was I thinking?"

Mystified, Amy simply looked around, her eyes drawn in wonder to the huge grand piano dominating the center of the room.

That's when I noticed the sheet music. I would have sworn I'd put those pages into the piano bench earlier that morning. I grabbed them off the rack. *Chopin's Funeral March.* Different music. I rounded on Jared.

"Did you put these here?" I demanded. Once again I thrust the papers inside the piano bench, letting the lid slam down with a resounding bang. "Very funny."

His mouth dropped open in consternation. "I *didn't*," he protested. "I don't know how those got there."

My lips compressed and I exhaled sharply through my nose. Jared's sick sense of humor could be so exasperating sometimes.

"Fine," I grumbled. "They crawled up there by themselves." I turned to Amy. "Come on, honey. We're going to be late, and you have school tomorrow."

As we headed out the door, I called back, "I'll be staying at Mom's tonight, so I'll see you in the morning."

Glancing over my shoulder, I saw Jared give the piano a reproachful look.

Chapter Three

I buckled Amy into the back seat of my Subaru and started down the driveway, tires crunching in the gravel. I paused before turning onto the road and waited for an approaching truck to pass. That's when I noticed a stranger standing on the shoulder facing the house. I hadn't seen him earlier; he'd been hidden behind the brambles that grew wild and neglected along the front of the property. An old yellow Volkswagen Beetle sat parked on the grassy margin nearby.

My eyes narrowed as I scrutinized him. He was tall and thin, clean-shaven, and dressed in jeans with a brown suede jacket. He appeared to be holding a cell phone in his hand. He turned toward me and smiled, raising his free hand in a little wave.

Alarmed, I stared back. What was he doing? *Casing the place?* Or merely taking pictures of the old house? Admittedly, the hundred-year-old Victorian architecture was unique and exceedingly photogenic.

"Who's that?" Amy asked curiously.

"Nobody," I said. "Just some guy looking at the house."

I chewed the inside of my lip. No need to jump to conclusions. He didn't look sinister, and he wasn't exactly trespassing. *I suppose when a person lives in a historic landmark, gawkers are bound to be expected.* I didn't like it, but figured there was no law against taking pictures by the side of the road. I returned the wave with some misgivings. If I'd had more time, I might have stopped and talked to him, but I was running late.

As if sensing my unease, the man gave me a nod, turned, and strode to his car. He pulled a U-turn and drove back toward Salmon Falls. I watched him go, then shrugged and steered my car toward the highway, heading out of town.

* * *

Staying at my mother's was like stepping back in time. The old split-level had barely changed since Jared and I were kids, except that his room had been converted to a sewing room, and mine was now reserved for guests—certainly neater and more tastefully decorated than when I had lived there.

The old Seattle neighborhood hadn't changed much either. It had seemed an idyllic place to grow up. I could still picture all us kids tearing up and down the streets on our bikes, laughing and calling to each other as our parents mowed lawns and weeded gardens. The fort Jared and his friends had built out of scrap lumber in Ledbetter's back yard was gone now, but a remnant of the old rope swing tied to a branch of McGinty's giant maple could still be seen. Peter Wilson had tried to climb it in fifth grade and fallen off and broken his right arm. He had strutted around in a cast for a month like it was some kind of trophy. Peter had always been such a show-off.

I smiled. I hadn't thought about Peter in a long time. For all I knew, he was a tycoon on Wall Street. More likely, he'd taken over his dad's sporting goods store. All of the kids I'd known from the neighborhood had grown up and left, leaving the place quieter and a bit timeworn—like the people who still lived here, most of whom were grandparents now.

My father had passed away a few years ago, and I sometimes worried about my mother living alone, but she insisted she was fine and refused to consider moving. I knew who I'd gotten my stubborn streak from.

As I pulled into the driveway, my eyes fell on the wooden sign carved and painted years ago by my father and mounted proudly above the mailbox. *Thorson*, it said. I remembered my father explaining how our ancestors had come from Sweden, and how our name meant *Son of Thor*, god of thunder. Twelve years old at the time, I had exclaimed indignantly, "What about Thor's *daughter?*" After all these years, the memory still made me smile.

"What's so funny, Mommy?" Amy asked from the back seat.

"Nothing, sweetheart. I was just remembering your grandpa." I felt a brief pang of loss. If not for Amy I would gladly have taken back my maiden name. But for her sake I chose to keep our last names the same, and I remained Kate Ecklund.

I stopped the car and my mother hurried out to meet us. Dusted with flour, the blue gingham apron draped around her stout figure perfectly defined her role as grandmother, yet her energy and rich brown hair with its mere trace of gray, strove to deny it. She had taken a leave of absence from her job as a nurse at the local hospital to help me out with Amy. Though she had the means to retire if she wanted, she scoffed at the idea. Her job gave her something to do.

"Grandma," Amy cried, flinging open the car door. "Wait till you see our new house! It's *huge!*"

"Can't wait," my mother said with a broad smile. "Why don't you run and play with Taffy in the back yard until dinner's ready."

Taffy, Mom's amber-colored cocker mix wriggled and cavorted about our knees. Amy called happily to the dog and together they ran around the side of the house. I followed my mother inside where I was immediately engulfed by the warm, sweet aroma of baked cinnamon and apple.

"Mmm . . ." I murmured. "You've been baking."

She smiled and gave a dismissive little wave. "Just a little something for dessert. Now, tell me about this huge project you've undertaken."

I pulled out my phone and showed her a picture I'd taken of the front of the house. "Naturally, it's going to need a lot of work. Everything's old and covered with dust and grime, but the contractor assures me the bones are good. It just needs cleaning and updating. He's already started in the kitchen and I've spent hours scrubbing and sweeping."

My mother frowned, the lines deepening around her mouth. "I don't know, Kate. Sounds like an awfully big job."

She pulled a package of hamburger out of the fridge and began browning it in a large skillet. Then she opened a cupboard and pulled out a jar of ready-made spaghetti sauce.

"I'm enjoying it, Mom," I said. "I really am. And I'm optimistic. Once the remodeling is finished, I can just envision people flocking to stay there. It's the perfect place for a vacation. Salmon Falls is a quaint little town surrounded by mountains. It's full of restaurants and antique shops, plus there's fishing, swimming, and hiking at Angela Lake just a short way up the road. In the wintertime, there's marvelous skiing only a mile or so away."

I smiled as I got caught up in my imagining. "Besides, the Victorian architecture is amazing, like something right out of a gothic romance novel. If I didn't own the place, *I'd* love to stay there. You know I've dreamt about doing this for a long time."

She quit stirring and let out a sigh. "I know you've always loved old houses." She looked me in the eye and laughed softly as though caving to the inevitable. "But then, you always did take after your father."

An armchair historian, my dad had always preferred the flourish and charm of antiquity over modern plainness and sterility. As far back as I could remember, he and I had shared an affinity for all things classic, whether it be medieval castles, tales of ancient civilizations, or flickering black and white movies starring forgotten actors of a bygone era.

"Remember when I worked in the antique store downtown?"

She snorted. "I'll say. You drove us all crazy with your 'Rococo this' and 'Renaissance that.' I still can't look at a stick of furniture without hearing you describe the differences between Queen Anne and Chippendale. Even now I can tell Depression Glass from Carnival Glass."

I laughed. "Nice to know you were listening. But seriously, I loved that job. And now I get to put some of that knowledge to use. The house may be old, but it's beautiful. I want to bring it up-to-date but, at the same time, restore its intrinsic character. I've hired an architect and a contractor experienced in renovating historic homes. They'll do most of the heavy lifting."

"Still . . ."

My smile dissolved into a somber pout. "I feel like I'm finally accomplishing something for myself without anyone criticizing me or telling me how I ought to be doing things."

Mom sniffed and cocked one eyebrow. "*Anyone* being Daniel, I take it." She set a large pot of water on the stove to boil, then opened a can of green beans and dumped it into a small saucepan.

"He would never have let me do this," I said heatedly. "*Or* he would have taken over and done everything *his* way because everything *I* did was *wrong.*"

My mother kept her eyes fixed on the water simmering on the stove. A mixture of emotions clouded her face. She found the subject of my unhappiness and divorce distressing.

"Don't mind me, Mom," I said, fanning the air to cool the flush in my cheeks. "I'm just tired." I took a deep breath and let it out again.

Just then Amy came running up onto the back deck with Taffy beside her. The little dog panted blissfully, tongue lolling to one side. Amy pounded on the sliding glass door. "Is dinner ready yet?" she hollered. "I'm starving."

I slid the door open. "Go wash up. It'll be ready in a minute."

Later that evening, after Amy had gone to bed, Mom and I sat in the living room conversing over a glass of wine. Above the fireplace hung a large painting depicting a grove of palm trees beside an impossibly blue ocean—a memento of my parents' visit to the Caribbean the year before my father died.

Leaning back in her chair, Mom brought up the subject of the house again. "So, how did you find this place?"

"My friend Julie is a real estate agent," I said. "I told her I was interested in buying a historic home I could run as a bed-and-breakfast. She started watching the listings for me, but all the nice ones were way out of my price range. So when she saw this one, she called me and we drove right out to Salmon Falls to see it. It was love at first sight."

"Of course it was." Mom smiled indulgently.

I gave a little laugh. "We had lunch at a café in town, and when we told the waitress why we were there, she and several other locals were only too happy to jump in and tell us all about that 'creepy old house.'" I emphasized this with air quotes.

Mom made a grimacing face. "Oh, dear."

"They said the old lady who had lived there was kind of strange, a little demented. But considering she was over a hundred years old it's probably no wonder. They told us she died in the house and now—get this—according to local legend, she *haunts* the place. The kids in the area won't go near it."

"Oh, for heaven's sake, you surely don't believe that."

"Of course not. But you know how kids love to scare themselves." I paused. "On the other hand, owning a haunted house might be kind of cool. Think of all the old houses in Seattle that are supposed to be haunted."

"Kate . . ." The disapproval in her voice left no doubt as to Mom's thoughts on the matter.

"Come to think of it," I continued slowly, tapping a finger against my lips, "I have been hearing some strange noises . . ."

The expression on my mother's face cracked me up and I couldn't help laughing.

"Anyway," I continued, "I did a search online and it turns out the local Salmon Falls Historical Society has a blurb about the house on their website. It's something of a local landmark. They call it the Thatcher Mansion, built in 1914 by Morgan Thatcher, one of the early settlers in the area. He was some kind of lumber baron. His daughter's name was Blossom, and she lived in the house her entire life. According to the history, she was the oldest person ever to have lived in Salmon Falls."

"Didn't she have any family?"

I shrugged. "I guess not—not around here anyway. The website said she was a recluse. She never married and eventually died alone in the house."

"That's sad," Mom said.

"The court did somehow manage to locate her next of kin, but they never did anything with the house. It just stood empty until they finally decided to sell it."

"So that's where you came in."

"And just in the nick of time," I said. "That beautiful house was being ravaged by neglect."

"You know," Mom said, "I was just thinking, if you're going to run a bed-and-breakfast in such a prominent old house, you ought to print up a brochure or create a website to tell people about its history. People love that sort of thing."

I grinned. "That's a good idea. When I have some time, I'll see what I can put together. Jared and I found an old family Bible in the attic with a photo of Blossom Thatcher as a baby with her parents sitting on the front porch of the house. That would add a real personal touch. Maybe I'll look for members of the Historical Society and pick their brains. It's a small town; there must be people around who still remember Blossom."

Mom leaned toward me then, concern casting a shadow over her features. "Won't you be lonely out there, Kate?"

"Oh, *no*," I said with feeling. "I'll be far too busy. Besides, I like the solitude. It's such a relief after that rat race in Seattle."

"But you used to have so many friends."

I shook my head. "Friends of Daniel's, you mean. Hoity-toity wives of businessmen he wanted to impress. I don't miss any of them. I'm starting a whole new life. I can hardly wait. Besides, I'll have Jared. He'll be working for me as a handyman. I'm giving him the whole basement for a workshop. He's pretty motivated."

Mom chuckled. "That old house of yours must seem like a palace compared to some of the places he's lived.

Remember after high school that house he shared with those guys in Ballard?"

I clapped my hands together, grinning as I recalled images of my brother at nineteen thrashing vigorously on his guitar, shaking his long hair to a thunderous beat. "His rock 'n' roll days! It's a wonder they weren't evicted."

"You'll be a good influence on him," Mom said with a contented nod.

"You know," I added thoughtfully, "they actually weren't half bad."

* * *

When I woke in the guest room the next morning, I lay in the big double bed for several minutes just admiring my daughter as she slept beside me, listening to the sound of her gentle breathing. She looked like a porcelain doll, all pink and smooth, hair curled on the pillow. Out of nowhere, a thought intruded of the poor old woman who had spent her entire life in the house I had just bought. Had she always been alone? Hadn't anyone cared? An air of sadness seemed to surround her.

I had a sudden urge to wrap my arms around Amy and press her close to me. Instead, I just watched until her lashes fluttered and she woke.

"Hi, baby."

"I'm not a baby," she protested.

"To me you are." I leaned over and kissed her on the forehead, inhaling the sweet scent of her strawberry shampoo. "Are you ready to get up?"

As we ate breakfast, I reminded her, "I'll be at the new house all week, so Grandma will pick you up at the bus stop. I'll call you tonight before bedtime. Now hurry up and I'll drive you to school."

Chapter Four

By the time I got to the house, the contractor and his men had already arrived. I had warned them my brother would be here, and I was pleased to see that amicable introductions had been made and work was in progress. The plan was to continue working on the floor in the kitchen, removing the old linoleum and replacing the rotted subflooring. I left them to it; they knew what they were doing and I didn't want to impede progress.

"I'm going into town to get some supplies," I told my brother. "Shouldn't take too long. I've got an ice chest I want to stock for later."

"Okay," said Jared. "Get some beer, will you? I'll need it once I start sorting through the junk in the basement. There's a place in Monroe that recycles metal, and I want to rent one of those big dumpsters from the garbage company."

As I turned to walk away, he added, "Could you leave your phone? I want to call Gary and see if he'll bring his truck out."

Gary had been Jared's buddy since junior high. They did everything together: hung out, drank beer, picked up girls, played guitar, and occasionally got into mischief. He could be a little coarse, but he was a good friend and I liked him. Plus, he came with the added bonus of owning a big pickup truck.

"What's wrong with your phone?"

He gave a short coughing laugh, then ran his tongue sheepishly back and forth over his lower lip before confessing. "I forgot to take it out of my pocket last time I washed my jeans. It hasn't worked since." He smiled crookedly and shrugged. "I haven't had a chance to get a new one."

I rolled my eyes and let out a sigh. The only real surprise here was that he had actually washed his jeans.

I left Jared and went to get my purse out of the room I had assigned myself. Located in a hallway just off the kitchen were two rooms I felt certain had once been the housekeeper's quarters. The larger room contained a classic vintage iron bed frame, while the smaller had only a dilapidated old chair and had probably been used simply as a sitting room. It occurred to me that the elderly owner might have used the bedroom as she'd gotten older and could no longer manage the stairs.

The fact that the mattress was missing suggested the old woman had died in bed in this room. There was no telling how long she might have lain there before being discovered. If indeed that were the case, the mattress would by necessity have been removed and discarded. Hence my sleeping bag on the floor. I suppressed a shudder. I had considered disposing of the bed frame as well, but instead decided to clean and repaint it. It would be beautiful once restored.

I handed my phone over to Jared, then left for Salmon Falls. As I neared the town, the clouds parted and the sun shone through in patches. Along the road, groves of budding alder and cottonwood lined a narrow river that wound lazily back and forth through the valley. Spring grass grew lush in the meadows while legions of dandelions lined the road in masses of brilliant yellow.

The Salmon Falls Cemetery was located at the edge of town on a tree-lined lane surrounded by a high wrought iron fence. On a whim, I pulled in, parking the Subaru and walking across the verdant, well maintained lawn. A group of three gray-haired women moved reverently among the tombstones, stopping here and there to leave bouquets of fresh flowers.

I made my way toward a gravesite marked with an imposing black granite obelisk, six feet high. As I neared, I saw that it was engraved with the word *Thatcher*. Under that were carved the names *Morgan Thatcher* and *Angela Rose Thatcher* along with the dates of their births and deaths. Doing some quick calculations, I noted that Morgan had been nearly twenty years older than his wife, and that, sadly, she had died quite young.

I thought about the picture in the old Bible and felt pity for the little girl who had lost her mother at an early age. Beneath the names of her parents, the daughter's name had been added to the stone, along with the date of her death just a few short years ago.

Curiously, I was not the only one interested in the grave. A man close to my own age stood nearby studying the obelisk. At first, I thought he was the stranger I'd seen in front of my house taking pictures, but on second glance I saw that he was a different man, darker complexioned and not as tall.

When I looked in his direction, he met my gaze and smiled. Embarrassed, I quickly averted my eyes. A moment later, I sneaked another look.

He had a slender face with a thin aquiline nose and neatly cut brown hair. He wore jeans, a light blue shirt unbuttoned at the top, and a fawn-colored sports jacket. One side of his mouth quirked up impishly when he smiled—which he did again when he caught me looking at him for the second time. I responded with a smile of my own, then turned my gaze back to the grave marker.

As I considered how I might introduce myself, I was suddenly descended upon by the three elderly ladies I had seen earlier. I glanced around for the attractive stranger, but he had slipped away.

"Hello, dear," said a stout woman with mousy gray hair, "we were just putting flowers on some graves and saw you standing here. Did you know Blossom? Are you a relative?"

"We didn't think she had any family close by," said another.

"Was that your husband with you?" said the third. "He seems to have left in rather a hurry."

Startled, I shook my head. "No, I don't know who that was. I'm Kate Ecklund. I recently bought the Thatcher house—"

"Oh, you're the one who bought Blossom's house," the plump lady with the mousy gray hair said with enthusiasm. Her face lit up as she grasped my hand. "It's so nice to meet you. I'm Mildred Birch. My grandmother used to be Blossom's housekeeper a long time ago. I spent many happy hours in Blossom's kitchen as a child."

"Esther Wick," the second lady interjected, stepping forward to take my hand. Her voice was thin and reedy, much like herself. "It's a pleasure to meet you, dear."

"I'm so glad somebody bought it," the third lady said. Her puffy mound of white hair made me think of cotton candy. "I hated seeing that lovely house get so run down. My name is Opal Johansson. My father worked at the old sawmill. I remember having picnics on the lawn at the mansion when I was small. It was quite a place in those days."

The first woman nodded, speaking wistfully. "Yes, it used to be so fine and elegant. I hope you're not planning to change it too much. It's a true piece of this town's history."

"No," I said, feeling slightly overwhelmed. "I love the house the way it is. I want to restore it as authentically as possible but also bring it up-to-date."

The lady with cotton candy hair pressed her hands together and leaned toward me, her voice reverent as though confiding a great truth. "It was built by Morgan Thatcher, you know. He was an important man in these parts back before the war. World War II, I mean. Blossom was his daughter. After he died, she lived alone there for the rest of her life."

"How sad," I said. "I wish I could have met her. I would have loved to talk to her about the house and its history. I'm sure there's more to her story than what I read on the Historical Society's website."

That set the ladies to nodding and chattering at once.

Finally, the woman who had introduced herself as Mildred Birch said to me, "There's a kind of local museum run by the Historical Society at the Senior Center in town. There are lots of pictures on display that I think you would find interesting. You really should come by some time and take a look."

"Thank you," I said. "That sounds wonderful. I definitely will." Then I bade each lady a genial good-bye. I needed to be going; Jared would be wondering what had happened to me.

When I reached the parking lot, the stranger in the fawn sports jacket was leaning against an old Ford Bronco. His tight blue jeans accentuated the lean lines of his body. I controlled the urge to study him up and down. He smiled and straightened when he saw me.

"I thought you'd never get here," he said.

I cast around for something to say. Finally, I glanced at his battered old vehicle and blurted, "I took you more for the sports car type."

He grinned and patted the fender. "She may be old, but she's still got a lot of spunk. Kind of like those women you were talking to." His mouth tilted up in that crooked smile I found so intriguing.

"They were here putting flowers on some of the graves and saw us standing by the Thatcher monument. They thought we might be relatives of Blossom Thatcher. *Are* you a relative?"

He nodded. "Her grandnephew, actually. My name is Dillon Thatcher. My grandfather was Blossom's brother."

"Really? So, your father was her nephew. We were under the impression she didn't have any family around here. I'm Kate Ecklund. I recently bought Blossom's old house. I'm hoping to renovate it and run it as a bed-and-breakfast."

"Nice to meet you." He extended his hand, surveying me with eyes the color of dark chocolate. "And I'm *not* from around here. I only arrived in town two days ago. This is my first trip out here. My grandfather left Salmon Falls a long time ago and never came back. I was born and raised in Ohio. I never met Blossom and doubt she even knew I existed."

I shook his hand. It was warm and uncalloused. "So what brings you here now? Did the court's investigators track you down as next of kin?"

He nodded. "My dad got a letter from some attorney telling him he'd inherited this rundown old house in Washington State. He held on to it for a while, but ultimately realized he couldn't afford the taxes and didn't know what to do with it. He finally contacted a local real estate agent and told them to just sell it for whatever they could get. I only came here now out of curiosity. My grandfather used to tell me stories about this grand old mansion his father had built." He smiled again. "I was hoping maybe you'd let me come out and see the place."

"Of course," I said. "Any time, although I must warn you it's in pretty bad shape at the moment. I hope to restore it to its original grandeur, but it's going to take some time."

"That's all right," he said. "Why don't I come by tomorrow afternoon? You can show me the house and then I'll take you to dinner to show my appreciation."

His smile was irresistible. I fervently hoped I wasn't blushing.

"Okay," I said. "Then you can tell me all the stories your grandfather told you about the house."

* * *

All the way to the store I kicked myself for being a weak-willed ninny. A complete stranger smiles at me and I'm ready to go out with him? What was I thinking? I knew nothing about this guy, and the absolute last thing I needed in my life right now was any sort of entanglement.

After my oppressive ten-year marriage, I was eager— no, *determined* to make it on my own. I finally had a clean slate and I was bursting with creative energy. The old mansion was my fresh start. I knew it would be a huge job, and starting a business was daunting, but I had been dreaming about this for years.

I could scarcely wait to start decorating, to scour the antique shops for precisely the right furnishings. In all my years of marriage, I had never been allowed to pick out a single piece of furniture, carpet, linen, or china without first having it approved by Daniel's mother. How easy it had been to leave it all behind. I had felt no attachment to anything. My clothes, a few personal items, and Amy's things had all fit in my car. I smiled grimly. My whole life in the back of a station wagon.

After a quick stop at the hardware store to pick up some mouse traps, I pulled into the grocery store and began circling the lot for a parking space. I did a double take as an old yellow Volkswagen approached on the road. It didn't turn in but continued into town. I rolled to a stop and stared. It had to be the same guy I'd seen in front of my house yesterday. I chewed my lower lip pensively, wondering if I had reason to be concerned, or if this was just coincidence. The quick toot of a horn behind me reminded me where I was. Hurriedly, I moved forward and angled into a slot facing the front of the store. By the time I exited my car, the VW was out of sight.

When I returned home, I found my brother hard at work pulling things out of the basement and piling them in the yard. It was a struggle because the outside basement access was recessed at the bottom of a steep concrete stairwell. He had already amassed quite a heap of broken, worthless objects.

"Gary can't make it today," Jared informed me, wiping a sleeve across his forehead and reaching eagerly for the cold beer I offered. "So I'm just stacking stuff out here for now. He'll try to get here tomorrow."

"That's fine, no hurry," I said, juggling grocery bags. "Wait for me on the veranda while I put these things inside, then we'll have some lunch."

Five minutes later, I handed him a roast beef sandwich I'd purchased from the grocery store deli. We ate outside since the carpenters had taken over the kitchen. Jared was only too happy to take a break.

"You'll never guess who I met in town," I said.

Jared shrugged. He tipped up his beer can and drained the last few drops. Taking a huge bite of his sandwich, he reached for a second can.

"I met Blossom Thatcher's grandnephew at the Salmon Falls Cemetery. His name is Dillon Thatcher, and he's the grandson of Blossom's brother who left Salmon Falls years ago. He came here all the way from Ohio just to see the house. He said his grandfather used to tell him stories about it."

"What were you doing at the cemetery?" Jared mumbled between chews.

"I don't know. Just curious, I guess. I stopped there on my way to the store."

"Blossom Thatcher's grandnephew? What does he want?"

"He wants to see the house," I repeated. "He's coming here tomorrow."

Jared made a face. "Tomorrow? Seriously?"

"Yes. After all, his great-grandfather built it. It's like his ancestral home." I focused on my sandwich and added quickly, "Then he's taking me out to dinner."

Jared stopped eating. He gaped at me like I'd lost my mind. "Kate, you don't know anything about this guy." His expression became wary. "How do you even know he is who he says he is? Did he show you his ID?"

"Oh, for heaven's sake. He seemed nice enough to me." I knew my brother had a point, but I refused to be lectured by him.

I glanced at my watch, signaling an end to the conversation. "It's nearly two o'clock. We'd better get back to work. I want to start pulling up carpet. I still can't believe anyone would put carpeting down over beautiful hardwood floors."

Jared got the hint. He slapped his hands against his jeans to knock off the crumbs, then shook his head and trudged back toward the basement.

Tying a scarf around my shoulder-length hair, I started prying up carpet in the formal living and dining rooms. I could tell by worn marks in the old carpeting that there had once been a heavy table and eight chairs in the dining room. They must have been exquisite judging by other random items that remained throughout the house. Everything in the mansion displayed expensive taste.

All that was left in the dining room now was an oak sideboard with an ornately carved dish cupboard above it. I wondered if the elderly owner had been forced to sell pieces of furniture in order to buy food and necessities. A troubling thought.

By six o'clock, I declared it quitting time. Pulling up carpet was dirty, backbreaking work and I was exhausted. The workmen had left at five.

Once the dust settled, I swept an area of the dining room and set up a card table, two folding chairs, and an ice chest. Then I went down to the basement to see how Jared was faring. The dank, mildewy odor was palpable, the gloominess depressing, like the dungeon in an old horror movie.

A heater down here would help, I thought. Looking around I could see that Jared had made a significant dent in the mound of junk.

"I just want to finish hauling out these old newspapers before I knock off," he said, then added, "What's for dinner?"

"I thought I'd order a pizza, but I'll need my phone back." I held out my hand.

He patted his pockets, then glanced around. "Let's see, I set it down someplace."

"*Jared*." I pushed my breath out through gritted teeth.

"Oh, there it is. On top of the washing machine." He grinned.

"You've got to get your own phone."

"I know. I will. First chance I get."

Resisting the impulse to scream, I retrieved the phone and started for the stairs. I had to argue with the man at the pizzeria about where to make the delivery. He evidently thought my request to have it brought to the old Thatcher mansion on Angela Lake Road some sort of crude practical joke. I finally suggested he call the local Salmon Falls real estate agent who had helped broker the deal on the house.

I was preparing to give him her cell phone number when he interrupted.

"Never mind," he said. "I have it. She's married to my cousin."

I shook my head. Small towns.

Chapter Five

While I waited for the pizza, I called my mother for my good-night ritual with Amy. When she came on the line, her sweet voice was like a burst of sunshine in my dreary day. She chattered about school and about helping her grandma bake a cake. She sounded happy.

I sighed heavily as I ended the call. I missed her so much. After my divorce, friends had asked me whether I would have done things differently had I known how my marriage would turn out. Tempted as I was to respond with a resounding *yes*, I had only to think of my precious Amy to know the answer was *no*. How could I possibly wish away the one thing in life that gave me such incredible joy? For all his faults, I would be forever grateful to Daniel for our daughter.

The house was eerily quiet. I scrolled through the music selections on my phone. More than anything else, I craved the noise to dispel the gloom that lay over the house. The tomb-like stillness was enough to drive a person crazy. A fire in the fireplace would have been cozy, but I feared the ancient chimney might be plugged with old bird nests. The bedrooms upstairs had fireplaces too, which added to the romance and charm, but, until I had all the chimneys cleaned and inspected, I would continue to rely on the old oil furnace in the basement for heat.

I glanced at the time on my phone. Only eight thirty. I would have sworn it was later. I was dead tired. Outside the window, a barren twig scraped against the glass like a cat scratching to get in.

A knock five minutes later signaled the arrival of the pizza. I hollered at Jared in the bathroom, then hurried to answer the door. The sun had set, leaving behind a shadowy twilight. Already, the moon had risen over the mountains, shining full and bright like a white paper lantern. A stray breeze rustled the branches of a nearby tree.

I handed the teenager thirty dollars. "Keep the change."

Without a word, he took the money and stuffed it into his pocket.

"Beautiful night," I said conversationally, taking the large flat box.

"Yeah," he mumbled, then turned and bolted down the porch steps, running for his car.

"Thank you," I called after him.

The way he took off, you'd have thought he'd seen a ghost. I laughed nervously and, without thinking, looked over my shoulder. Sheepishly, I rolled my eyes and chided myself for succumbing to superstitious rumors.

* * *

I awoke with a start. What was that? A moan? A creaking floorboard?

Nerves on edge, I sat up and peered around. The moon cast a silvery glow through the window in a feeble imitation of daylight. Scrubbed clean and devoid of personal effects, the empty room held all the charm of a cardboard box. The only furnishings were the old iron bedstead pushed into a corner and a wooden nightstand that had seen better days. Filthy curtains had once hung over the window, but I had taken them down and put them in the trash. Now overgrown shrubs in the garden outside sent shadows like bony fingers scrabbling across the drab gray walls.

I sat in the dark straining to hear. Must have been Jared. Closing my eyes, I snuggled once more into my sleeping bag trying to get warm.

Then I heard it again. A murmur? A footstep? What was Jared doing prowling around in the middle of the night? Old houses settled, though, didn't they? Wood expanded and contracted with changing temperatures. Wind whistled in the eaves. That had to be it. I tried to relax, tried to will myself back to sleep.

A breeze ruffled the branches outside my window. Occasional gusts rattled the glass. Mice made little scraping noises in the hallway. Forget it. I'd never be able to sleep at this rate. I grabbed for my phone lying nearby and glanced at the time: 3:20.

Luckily, I had my father's old flashlight with me. He had given it to me years ago and half-jokingly told me never to go anywhere without it. Now, I pulled it from my duffel bag, thinking that, in a pinch, the chunky metal cylinder would also do as a makeshift weapon. I switched it on and crawled out of my sleeping bag. My cotton pajamas provided little defense against the chill air. Rummaging again in my duffel bag, I found a sweatshirt and tugged it on over my head.

Shivering as much from nerves as from cold, I got to my feet and crossed to the door, opening it a crack. For several seconds I just listened. Not a peep. No axe-murderer, no boogeyman. Just a creaky old house. I kept my cell phone firmly gripped in my left hand; the thought of having 911 at my fingertips was reassuring.

I shined the flashlight into the hall. The circle of illumination cut a path through the blackness as I tiptoed toward the kitchen. My bare feet made hardly a sound against the smooth linoleum. A surprised mouse squeaked and scurried across the floor. With a shudder, I made a mental note to be sure and set out some traps tomorrow.

I reached the door to the kitchen and stood listening, then pulled it open. Moonlight shone through the windows, casting weird shadows over objects left strewn by the workers. The flashlight revealed a switch on the wall. I automatically reached for it, then hesitated. If I started throwing lights on, Jared would be sure to wake up and delight in teasing me. I ought to just return to my room, crawl deep into my sleeping bag, and go back to sleep. But if there *was* a prowler . . .

I knew I'd never sleep. That's what came of having a tenaciously over-active imagination. I took a step forward. The floor creaked eerily. The air was thick with the odors of sawdust and mildew. I took another step, paused, and listened. Then another step and another. The darkness was ominous, every sound portentous, but when no assailant jumped out of the shadows at me, I began to recoup a grain of confidence.

Working my way around sawhorses and carpenters' tools, I moved through the room, shining the flashlight over the countertops. I reached the opposite door and blew out my cheeks. There had been no more noises and I was feeling braver now. I pulled open the door, took a quick look around, and hurried through to the dining room. The empty pizza box still lay on the card table along with a couple of discarded cola cans.

The room was quiet, eerily dark and echoey. The flashlight did little to dispel the gloom. Through an archway stretched the living room bathed in pale moonlight filtered through dust-caked windows. Outside, an owl hooted.

I continued forward, caught between curiosity and apprehension, stepping softly so as not to disturb the fragile, ethereal quality of the night. I had never seen the house like this: at once terrifying and sorrowful, as though yearning for bygone days when it was new and rang with young voices.

I turned the flashlight to the left across the wide entryway, then continued toward the arch leading to the music salon. The room lay deserted save for the ancient thread-bare carpet, some dusty old drapes, and a large ornate fireplace. Even in dim light, the grand piano stood out as the focal point of the room.

Then I heard the music. I froze and held my breath, listening. Unlike the earlier complicated classical arrangements, these notes were soft and simple. The tune was familiar.

I swung the flashlight up, edging closer. The light seemed dimmer now. The batteries were going. I thought of my brother asleep in the library on the other side of the house. Would he hear me if I screamed?

Heart convulsing, I aimed the failing beam at the piano where a shadowy figure bent over the keyboard. To my astonishment, the light revealed a wizened old woman, thin and frail. Her white hair fell in limp strands about her shoulders.

Softly, she began to sing the lyrics to the music. I recognized it from a record my grandmother used to play. It was a lively old song, popular in the 1940s. But the old woman slowed it to a melancholy tempo, murmuring the words, changing what should have been an upbeat ditty into a heart wrenching ballad: *"Don't sit under the apple tree with anyone else but me . . ."*

As I watched transfixed, her voice faded. She stopped playing and slowly rose. A shaft of moonlight shone through the curtains just enough to illuminate a rectangular patch on the old carpet. The elderly woman drifted into the light, her pale features radiant in the faerie glow, her diaphanous gown floating just above the floor.

I couldn't move, couldn't speak. I just stood and stared at the ghostly apparition. Profoundly old, her withered skin hung loose and sallow on a frame of brittle bone. Her craggy face was etched with pain.

My breath did a sharp intake as she seemed to notice me for the first time. She stretched out her hand and took a tiny step toward me.

Before my eyes, she began to change. For a moment, her face appeared both old and young at the same time—firm, youthful skin superimposed over great age, like two transparencies laid upon one another. Then the wrinkled visage vanished completely to be replaced by that of a lovely young maid with long, dark curls. Only the doleful expression in her eyes remained the same. A glistening tear trickled down her cheek.

Suddenly, the light flared on in the hallway behind me and I heard Jared's booming voice. "What's going on in here?"

I gasped in surprise, stumbling backward till I nearly stepped on my brother's bare toes.

"Are you all right?" he said. "I heard a noise."

Stammering stupidly, I waved the flashlight ineffectually in the direction of the music room.

Jared gave me a sidelong glance. His mouth widened in a mocking smile. "You've been sleepwalking."

I turned warily to peer once more through the archway. The room was empty.

Chapter Six

March 1936

"Miss Thatcher!"

With a start, Blossom looked up. Her teacher, Mr. Bushmeyer, was standing beside her desk irritably slapping the palm of his hand with a ruler. "You've been day-dreaming in class again, Miss Thatcher. Has it become necessary for me to speak to your father?" He emphasized this remark with a quick rap of the ruler on the corner of her desk. It hit with a resounding whack.

She answered meekly, "No, sir."

He wouldn't dare strike her, she knew, but neither would he have any qualms about going to her father. Her father approved of Mr. Bushmeyer's stern methods; the educator had been teaching for four decades, and was well known for encouraging hard work and punishing idleness.

Sniffing loudly, he straightened his spine and drilled her with a severe look. "So, can you name one of the programs enacted by President Roosevelt as part of the New Deal?"

Blossom could feel her classmates watching her, holding their breath as she licked her lips and concentrated. Her friends offered silent encouragement, though she knew that certain among them were prepared to poke fun at her if she failed. Her position as Morgan Thatcher's daughter often made her a target of petty envy.

She fidgeted with her pencil, turning it over in her fingers. Mr. Bushmeyer's proximity and critical stance made her nervous. How could she think while he stood glaring at her? She thought hard as the lesson she had studied so arduously came back to her.

"The Social Security Act," she said.

He nodded. "Very good."

Turning then, he appraised the other students, searching out another victim. His glance sent tremors rippling through the class. "*Mr. Jones!* What is the purpose of this act?"

Blossom sighed heavily and looked at the clock on the wall. Almost three o'clock. Class was nearly over.

* * *

"My grandfather says the Germans have broken the treaty and marched an army into the Rhineland," Calvin Pritchard said as Blossom and her friends walked home from school. Calvin's parents rented a cottage on the Thatcher estate where Mr. Pritchard cut wood for the mill.

Blossom only half-listened. What did it all have to do with them, anyway? The Great War had been over for ages. They were sixteen years old. Way out here on the west coast of the United States, Europe's problems seemed a million miles away.

"He says the Germans are going to conquer all of Europe," Calvin continued, punctuating his remark by lobbing a stone at a passing cat. Tall and lean, he had made a name for himself on the school baseball team. It was no secret he hoped to someday play in the majors.

"Don't," squealed Shirley Brown, slapping at his arm. Calvin's opposite, Shirley was short and curvaceous with coquettish blue eyes, a button nose, and blond ringlets. She had merely to twitch her little finger and every boy at school would come running, but she only had eyes for Calvin. He gave her a foolish grin.

"Aw, what does your grandfather know?" Joey Sievers said, struggling to keep a hold on the stack of textbooks clutched in his arms. Joey was slightly built and bookish, with freckles and prominent ears. A year younger than the others, he was treated like a kid brother.

"My grandfather fought in the war," Calvin retorted. "He says that if Adolf Hitler isn't stopped there's going to be another war for sure."

Shirley looked indignant. "My pa says Roosevelt is the best president we've ever had. He won't let that happen, you'll see." Like most of the men in town, Shirley's father worked for Morgan Thatcher. He kept the books and did the financial accounting for Thatcher's vast timber holdings. Shirley stepped around a mud puddle in the road, careful to keep her new leather pumps clean.

This talk of war made Blossom uneasy. All the tales she'd heard about the European war in 1917 were bloody and terrifying. She wanted to change the subject.

The spring dance was two weeks away, and her thoughts were occupied with matters of a more immediate nature—like dresses, petticoats, and new shoes. What pleasure it would be to dress up and join her friends in a night of dancing and merriment. With her slim figure and long dark hair, she imagined attracting admiring glances as she walked onto the floor, twirling gracefully to the music.

Now, if only . . . *No*, she wouldn't let cheerless thoughts of her father intrude.

She turned to her friend, Helen Carmichael. "It's almost Easter. Have you decided what you're going to wear to the spring dance?"

Helen was an attractive brunette with a slender face and full mouth. She wore her hair short with tight finger curls like her favorite movie star, Myrna Loy. Her father was a mechanic and kept the big trucks running. Her mother cooked and cleaned for the loggers in the bachelor dormitories.

"My mother is going to alter one of my sister's old frocks," Helen said. "She'll just change the neckline and shorten the skirt. I thought if I added a bow and some lace to the front . . . *Wait,* will your father let you go to the dance?"

"I'm going to go whether he wants me to or not," Blossom declared with a vehemence she didn't quite feel. She longed to go to the dance, but her father could be so unreasonable. If he had his way, she would be locked up in the house day and night, and never allowed outdoors without an armed guard. She gave her head an impatient toss.

Helen gave her a doubtful look. "What are you going to do? Sneak out your bedroom window after your father goes to bed?"

"If I have to." Blossom set her mouth in a hard line. Billy Corwin, the baker's son, had smiled at her that day and passed her a small flower in the hallway at lunchtime.

"Are you kidding?" Shirley chimed in. "Even if you do sneak out, no boy will ever ask you to dance after what happened to Chet."

Blossom felt her face flush. Last December, Chester Mayfield had marched right up to the Thatchers' front door, determined to get permission to escort Blossom to the Salmon Falls Methodist Church Christmas pageant. Perhaps he had thought Mr. Thatcher would respect a forthright approach from an upstanding young man. After all, Chester was the preacher's son and generally well liked.

Chester had been wrong.

Morgan Thatcher had run him off the porch with a shotgun, firing a warning shot so close that if Thatcher hadn't been such a dead shot, it might have been suspected he was trying to hit the boy. Chester had run all the way back to town with Thatcher yelling threats to blast him in the backside if he ever so much as looked at his daughter. Of course, the sheriff had been called out, but Morgan Thatcher wielded so much power and influence in those parts that the consequences hadn't amounted to much more than a slap on the wrist. A few townspeople had even grumbled over who had done the slapping and who had received the slap.

The next Sunday, Thatcher had swaggered into church with his foreman and several loggers from the mill, sitting in the front row and rubbing the whole incident in the face of the minister and his son. Since most of the town folks depended on the Thatcher's lumber industry for their livelihood, no one had dared force the issue and the whole thing had eventually died away, only to be brought out occasionally and muttered about behind the hands of a few disgruntled housewives.

For a week afterward, poor Chet had been the brunt of jokes at school. The other boys had laughed and pointed fingers, furtively pinning targets to his back when he walked down the hall. Blossom herself had felt like a pariah. None of the boys would talk to her. Many had delighted in screaming and running away whenever she approached.

Shirley was right. Blossom's father would blow his stack if he caught her dancing with a boy, even at a school dance surrounded by a hundred chaperones. Calvin and Joey only walked with her because their fathers worked for Morgan Thatcher at the saw mill. They had grown up together like siblings and had been walking home from school together since they were small.

Blossom tilted her chin in the air and gave her long dark curls a defiant shake. "My father doesn't own me," she declared. "I *will* go to the dance, and I'll dance with whomever I please."

* * *

They were joined at the dinner table that night by Jed Hawkins, the company foreman, which meant that Blossom was largely ignored as the men discussed lumber prices and the acquisition of a new buzz saw for the mill. Jed was an imposing man in his mid forties, tall and muscular from years of cutting and hauling the massive fir trees felled on the surrounding slopes. No one could climb a tree or wield an axe like Jed. His ability to keep the men in line was invaluable to Morgan Thatcher's logging operation, arguments and disputes being quickly settled through the diplomacy meted by Jed's sledgehammer fists.

Blossom had once read a story about the Minotaur of Greek mythology who was supposed to have the body of a man and the head of a bull. She decided that if such a creature existed, it would come very close to describing Jed. He had dark bushy hair that engulfed his head and merged with his beard. His eyes peered from beneath a thicket of black brow, and his sizeable nose jutted like a rock formation from a craggy cliff. Blossom had never seen him wear anything but dungarees and sturdy boots.

In contrast, Blossom's father, a tall, lean man of 56 years and daunting presence, always comported himself as though he were about to meet with a room full of bankers. His gray hair and mustache were cut short and neatly trimmed. He never wore anything but a three-piece suit and silk tie with a costly gold watch chain dangling from his waistcoat pocket. When he went out, he pulled the brim of his bowler low over his eyes to give himself a more commanding appearance.

Blossom knew that in his youth, her father had labored in gold mines scattered throughout the Cascade mountain range. Drifting from site to site, he had hoped, like everyone else, to strike it rich. He didn't talk much about those days, except occasionally when he'd had too much to drink. Then he would curse the grueling privations suffered in lonely mining camps, the cramped underground shafts, and the futile dream of discovering a rich vein of ore and making a fortune.

During his mining career, he had seen countless good men killed by rock slides, cave-ins, dynamite mishaps, flooding, and infection. When gold *was* discovered, it was the mining conglomerations with headquarters in places like New York City that profited—rarely individuals with small mining claims.

Besides mining, Morgan Thatcher had tried his hand at hunting and farming, but it was logging where he had eventually found success. His strength and dexterity had made him a sought-after tree topper and lumberjack, bringing him a certain notoriety in those parts. His business savvy and dogged determination had ultimately resulted in his owning the company.

Blossom struggled to find a way to broach the subject of the school dance. She loved her father, but he was hard to approach sometimes and his mien could be intimidating. She had to join in the conversation somehow, get him to listen to her.

"I've got the men scouting trees for that road the CCC's puttin' in up by Gold Bar," said Jed. "No telling how much timber they'll be needin' for trestles and the like."

Morgan nodded, smearing butter on a piece of bread. "One of Roosevelt's better ideas. That project should keep us in business all year, plus I just signed a deal for a truckload of cedar shingles for the new school in Kirkwood."

Blossom took a breath and plunged in. "Father, it's almost Easter. School will soon be out for the year."

He turned his eye to hers, his attention momentarily caught. But at that moment, to Blossom's dismay, Martha, the housekeeper, chose to bring in the applesauce cake she'd baked that morning. Martha was a sturdy middle-aged woman with fine wrinkles and graying hair just starting to show around the edges. Bustling about, picking up empty dinner plates, she clucked to Blossom. "Honey, why don't you pour the men some coffee?"

As Blossom scurried to comply, Morgan grunted and turned back to Jed. "That reminds me, how's the water in the river? High enough to float logs all the way to Everett, do you think?"

"I'd say so," Jed nodded. " 'Specially with the rains we've been having lately. Shouldn't be a problem. Thanks," he added absently as Blossom sloshed some coffee into his extended cup.

Martha shot her a disapproving frown, then turned and headed for the kitchen with a stack of dirty dishes.

"Father," Blossom said. She had slid back into her seat the instant the coffee was served, impatient to insert herself once more into the discussion. "I turned sixteen on my last birthday."

Her father ignored her and kept talking to his foreman. "Oh, and I want you to get the vet out here tomorrow to look at my new mare. This is her first foal and I'd like him to check her out."

"Sure thing," Jed agreed.

"Father," Blossom interjected again, her heart pounding, "the spring dance is in two weeks and . . ."

"I paid a king's ransom for that mare."

" . . . I think I should be allowed to go."

Her father paid her no heed. "She's descended from one of them Kentucky race horses and bred to a son of Man o' War himself."

Blossom was getting desperate. This was not going as she had planned. Soon her father would leave the table and head either for the barn or his study, both male sanctuaries into which she was not allowed, and her opportunity would be lost. She had to get his attention.

"Calvin Pritchard's grandfather says there's going to be another war," she blurted.

Her father turned and narrowed his gaze at Blossom. "Who the devil is Calvin Pritchard?"

"You know, Father. I go to school with him. He . . . his father works for you."

"Matt Pritchard," supplied Jed. "One of the sawyers. Good man. Rents one of the houses by the river."

She gave him a grateful look then continued. "We . . . us kids were walking home from school today and talking, and—"

"Another war, eh?" her father said, leaning back and lighting a cigar. "Good. That's just what this country needs."

"What?" Blossom said. "How can another war be a good thing?"

"Get people back to work, that's how. Think about it. All them guns and supplies don't just appear out of thin air. Takes factories."

"Lose a lot of good men, though," Jed put in.

"Get people buying and building again," Morgan said, taking a deep pull on his cigar.

Blossom struggled for words. She had to turn the conversation before her father began expounding on how he could make money off a new war. Now that he had finished eating and was relaxing with his cigar, she hoped he would be in a more receptive mood. But as she prepared to speak, Martha burst into the room again, all aflutter.

"Sir," she exclaimed, out of breath, "there's a man at the door who—"

The visitor, apparently unable to wait, pushed past and approached Blossom's father where he sat at the head of the table.

"Morgan," began the man without preamble. He looked to be about the same age, but rather than being well-groomed, his appearance was shabby. The suit he wore was a size too large and hung crookedly off his bony shoulders; the knees and elbows were threadbare and the cuffs were frayed. He hadn't shaved in several days.

"Hiram Decker," Morgan said evenly, leaning back in his chair, fingering his cigar. "You've got a lot of nerve showing your face in these parts."

Chapter Seven

March 1936

Jed rose from his chair, his burly shoulders bulging like an ox. "You want me to get rid of him, boss?"

Morgan waved him back, never taking his eyes off the stranger.

Blossom froze where she sat, watching the drama unfold. Obviously, her father knew this man, but she had never seen him before. He had to be someone from her father's turbulent past.

The man, Hiram Decker, clutched a battered fedora in his hands and spoke again in a supplicating tone. "Morgan, I need your help. You know I'd never come to you 'cept I was desperate."

"Last I heard, you was living the high life off of that great gold strike of yours—the one you elbowed me out of when you decided you didn't need a partner no more, remember?"

"That was a mistake Morgan, a big mistake." He rolled his hat in his hands nervously. "The vein petered out like you said it would. You were right all along. I should've listened to you. I messed up and now I've lost everything." He pressed his face into his hat, his whole frame shuddering as he coughed, as though the effort of his confession was too much for his frail body.

"How's Regina?" Morgan said in a level voice, his gaze black as a cobra's.

Hiram looked up with sunken eyes, seeming to have aged ten years in the space of a heart beat. "She left me," he croaked. "When the money ran out, she left me."

Morgan nodded contemptuously. "She never was no good. What about Clayton?"

"He's stashed in a hotel in Seattle waiting for me."

Morgan rose to his feet, voice edged with anger. "You think I can't find him? Why, I ought to kill you right here where you stand and go retrieve him back here myself." His fist came up menacingly.

Hiram cowered back a step but raised his chin as he snarled. "You think he'd love you for that? He calls me pa, you know. He don't remember nothin' about you. To him you're nothin' but my old business partner—someone I came to for help."

"He's my *son*! You stole him when you ran off with my *wife!*"

Blossom stared, stunned, the dance forgotten. She had a brother—and her father had had another wife. Her own mother, Angela Rose, had died when Blossom was small. All she had left of her was a small photograph taken when Blossom was two years old. Morgan had never spoken of Regina, nor mentioned his long lost son. Had the heartache been too much to bear? Or was the fact that his wife had left him for his business partner too humiliating to face? Morgan Thatcher was a proud man.

"I know, Morgan, I know," Decker continued, "and I'm sorry—dreadful sorry. I wish I could go back and do things different, but I can't, and now I need your help. *We* need your help—Clay and me. I'm afraid they'll hurt him to get to me. I'm broke, see, and I've got creditors hounding me day and night." His voice had sunk to a plaintive whine.

Blossom didn't dare move or make a sound for fear her father would remember her sitting there and banish her from the room. She noticed that Jed and Martha had likewise gone quiet.

"How old is he now, Hiram? Mid twenties, must be."

"Twenty-three. He's a young man and you'd be proud of him. Looks like you too."

"So, what is it you want? Money?"

"I ain't looking for a handout, Morgan. I want to sell you something. I've got a map—a map to an untapped gold mine."

Morgan sat heavily back into his chair and rolled his eyes. "Oh, Hiram, not again. You're always falling for these things."

"This one's different. The prospector who discovered the mine died in my arms on the mountain. He'd been mauled by a bear and I found him and nursed him as best I could. He was grateful. He had nothing to gain by swindling me. This is genuine. Just take a look at it, will you?" He reached into his coat pocket and pulled out a dirty, rolled up piece of paper, extending it to Blossom's father.

Morgan took the paper and set it on the table without looking at it. "How much do you need?"

"Ten thousand."

Morgan exploded in anger, springing to his feet once more and pounding his fist on the table. His porcelain coffee cup flew off the table and shattered with a jarring crash as it hit the polished oak floor. "Ten thousand dollars? Are you out of your mind? God almighty, you've got a nerve."

Hiram quailed. "It was Regina," he cried. "She had to have all them fancy things. She just kept buying and borrowing. And I started gambling. We thought we was rich, you know? We never dreamt the mine would go bust. We never dreamt we'd run out of money. And now they're going to kill me, Morgan—they're going to *kill* me if I don't pay up by next week. Honest, Morgan, I never would've come to you if I wasn't desperate." Tears rolled down the man's haggard face as he pleaded.

"Tell you what," Morgan began slowly. His jaw was set, his eyes steely—and suddenly Blossom understood how her father had risen from a poor mining camp laborer to a wealthy land owner and lumber baron in this hostile mountainous region despite a depression that had brought many to the brink of ruin. "I'll give you your ten thousand dollars in exchange for my son. You bring Clay here and leave him, and then I don't ever want to see your sorry face around here again. Understood?"

"But what'll I tell him?" Hiram wailed.

"You tell him the truth. I don't care how, but if you don't, I will."

That's when Jed finally stirred. "Boss, *ten thousand dollars* . . ."

Morgan turned and gave his foreman a hard look. "Sell the mare."

* * *

Two days later, Hiram Decker's weather-beaten 1930 Ford Model A Coupe rattled and jounced up the driveway belching foul-smelling black smoke. Horses in the paddock snorted and flung their tails high, bolting in panic at the sight of the malodorous black machine.

Blossom ran to join her father on the front veranda. She had been waiting eagerly for this day, the day she would meet her half-brother for the first time. She could scarcely wait; her fingers twined nervously around the small embroidered handkerchief she held crumpled in her hand. She had played out all manner of scenarios in her mind, imagining how each would act and what each would say. They would be shy at first—that was to be expected—and perhaps a little awkward as they were introduced, but before long they would smile, clasp hands, and become fast friends.

She would be an only child no longer. She would have a comrade, an older sibling with whom to talk and share important moments. She pictured herself walking through town on the arm of her big brother, proudly presenting him to her friends and acquaintances.

The car stopped. Blossom could make out the figures of two men talking to each other in the front. Blossom could sense her father shifting impatiently next to her. Until just this moment, she hadn't considered how he must feel. He hadn't seen his son in twenty years. She glanced at his face. The usual stern features were unyielding, but she knew he must be as nervous and excited as she.

Morgan gave a slight nod. Jed Hawkins stepped from the shadows and approached the vehicle, handing a thick envelope through the window to Hiram Decker in the driver's seat. No words were spoken, but the opposite car door opened and a lean young man emerged and walked toward the house without looking back.

At first glance, Clayton Thatcher appeared to resemble his father. Closer examination revealed him to be a lesser copy. Tall and slim like Morgan, Clay had a broader nose, a weaker jaw, and his eyes were closer together. Where the elder Thatcher bore himself with poise, authority, and vigor, Clay seemed ungainly, his sandy-colored hair and clothes disheveled.

"Clay," Morgan said. "*Son.*" His somber expression softened. He gripped the younger man by the shoulders and studied his face. "Welcome home."

Clay stiffened and pulled back, a sullen glower fixed to his face. He didn't turn as the car engine revved behind him and began backing down the driveway.

"This here is your sister, Blossom," Morgan continued, maintaining a civil countenance despite his son's dour look.

Blossom stepped forward with a beaming smile on her face, eager to make a good impression. She had fixed her hair and worn her best dress. Martha had even allowed her a bit of lipstick with the understanding that it was only for this special occasion and not to be asked for again.

"I'm so happy to meet you, Clay," she said, her voice bubbling with delight. "You can't imagine how excited I was to learn I had a brother. I just know we're going to get along splendidly." She wanted to embrace him to show him how pleased she was but feared he might think her too forward. Instead she reached for his hand and gave it a welcoming squeeze.

"Pleased to meet you," he mumbled, his grim expression never altering.

Blossom stepped back. The look in her brother's eyes was dispirited and resigned. *He's hurting. The only father he's ever known has just abandoned him and thrust him into the midst of strangers.* How could she have been so thoughtless, to expect him to cheerfully accept the situation and leave behind everything he'd ever known? He needed time.

Again, she took him by the hand. "Let me show you inside." She smiled in a way she hoped would reassure him, pulling him gently with her. "Martha's made a feast in your honor. You can sit by me."

His face remained obdurately glum, but he let her lead him. "Thank you," he said as he followed her into the house.

Chapter Eight

My plans to sleep late the next day were thwarted by shafts of brilliant sunlight streaming through my window, along with a chorus of trills, chirps, and squawks—the kind of sounds heard only in the country. I would have reveled in it if I hadn't been so bone tired.

Rolling out of my sleeping bag, I searched through my duffel bag for something suitable to wear. I was here to work and hadn't brought along any dressy clothes, but Dillon Thatcher was coming today and I wanted to at least be presentable. I finally decided on a clean pair of jeans and a light blue shirt.

But first, I needed a bath. Once the plumber had turned the water on in this portion of the house, I had spent hours with sponge and cleanser scrubbing the antique clawfoot tub in the housekeeper's bathroom. It was tedious work, but I had achieved a certain sense of triumph as years' worth of scum yielded to my efforts. Now, I could honestly say I had never been so grateful for hot water in my entire life.

Afterward, I dressed in a hurry and headed for the dining room which had become our staging area for groceries and supplies until the kitchen was usable. Jared was already there, rummaging through the cardboard box of provisions I had brought.

He looked up and gave me a wisecracking grin. "Seen any more ghosts?"

I made a face at him. I was never going to hear the end of this.

He smirked.

"I know, I know," I conceded finally. "It had to be a dream. It just seemed so real, and I've never sleepwalked before." I still couldn't believe I'd done it, but I had no other explanation.

He went back to searching through the box. "I found a coffee maker," he said without looking up, "but I can't find any coffee."

"Keep looking, I'm sure I packed it. There should also be a package of muffins."

"I found the muffins." Agitation was beginning to supplant his usual calm. "But I can't find the coffee. You can't expect me to work this morning without *coffee.*"

I shouldered him aside and began a systematic search. The box contained all the essentials I figured we'd need for several days of roughing it. Everything from bread, jam, and peanut butter, to bottled water and toilet paper. I had apples, cookies, and paper plates, but, apparently, no coffee.

Great. Just what I needed—mutiny in the ranks for lack of caffeine. Now I would not only have to endure Jared's teasing about my sleepwalking, I would have to listen to him whine about this.

I straightened up and exhaled briskly. "Okay, so I forgot the coffee."

He looked stricken.

"I'll make a quick run to the coffee shop in town and bring some back. It'll take fifteen minutes."

As I retrieved my purse and keys, there came a light rapping on the back door. I hurried through the kitchen to open it, assuming it was the men arriving to begin work. Instead, I was astonished when the door swung open and a chubby woman bustled in. She wore black stretch pants and an oversized t-shirt emblazoned with the words, *I Don't Do Mornings*. Her dark hair was so short and curly that it quivered like a mat of tiny springs on her head. I guessed her to be about forty. A large wicker picnic basket hung from the crook of one arm.

"Yoo-hoo," she tittered as she entered. A wide jovial grin stretched across her face revealing a mouthful of large crooked teeth. "I'm Wendy Hilliard from next door. I was just waiting to be sure you were up. You can't imagine how thrilled I am to have a new family living in this old house." She set the basket on the counter. "Welcome to Salmon Falls."

"Uh . . . thank you," I said, recovering from my surprise. "I'm Kate Ecklund and this is my brother, Jared Thorson."

"Nice to meet you, Wendy," Jared said.

"I've been dying to meet you," Wendy said. Her relentless grin crinkled the corners of her eyes and gave her cheeks the look of ripe apples as she turned in a circle, taking in the disarray.

"Excuse the mess," I said. "We're in the middle of remodeling."

The old linoleum had been stripped down to the subflooring, the antiquated range and refrigerator had been disconnected and pushed out of the way, and the cupboard doors had been removed and set aside. I had opted to keep the original cabinets since they were solid wood and in good condition. They only needed to be sanded and repainted to replicate the look of the kitchen as it had been in 1914.

Wendy peered into every corner with obvious curiosity. "It's quite a house, isn't it? A shame it was allowed to get so run down." She made a pouty face and tsked loudly to emphasize what a shame it was.

I nodded. "Everything's going to be updated—new floors, quartz countertops, new appliances, light fixtures. When it's all finished I plan to run the house as a bed-and-breakfast."

"A bed-and-breakfast, eh? Well, you've certainly got your work cut out for you." Her hands punctuated her words with animated gestures.

Jared eyed the basket on the counter with interest. "What did you bring us?"

Wendy's wide grin sprang back. "I didn't know if you'd had breakfast yet," she gushed, "or even if you were able to use this horrid old kitchen, so I brought you some coffee and fresh baked cinnamon rolls, just to tide you over."

"That's very nice of you," I said, awed by this unexpected demonstration of kindness.

"Did you say *coffee?*" Jared's face lit up.

I winced as I explained to Wendy. "I brought a box full of food and supplies, but somehow forgot the coffee. I was just leaving to go get some in town."

Wendy gave a nasally laugh which set her springy mass of curls to jiggling. She said to Jared, "Help yourself then, by all means. It's in the thermos." Turning back to me, she asked, "Will your husband be joining you later?"

"No," I said. "I'm divorced."

"Kids?" she persisted.

Her round, inquisitive face leaned in and her eyes shone bright. It dawned on me that her visit might actually be motivated more by a desire to snoop than by simple neighborliness. I let it go. Wendy seemed good-natured and harmless. Maybe I could glean some information from her as well.

"My daughter's staying with my mother until I get the place livable," I said.

Jared poured himself some coffee. Wendy looked him up and down like a hungry lion weighing a gazelle. I'd seen that expression on women's faces before.

Mentally, I rolled my eyes, then changed the subject. "Wendy, you live in the white house next door? Did you know the lady who lived here?"

"Blossom? Of course. Poor thing. All alone in this creaky old house. I'm the one who found her, you know. Dead in her bed. It was awful. No telling how long she'd been lying there."

I repressed a shudder at the gruesome image this evoked. "I thought the police found her."

"Well, who do you think called them? I knew something was wrong when I hadn't seen her for a week." Warming to her grisly tale, she continued with undisguised zeal. "I have a perfect view of the back yard from my bedroom window. Blossom used to walk around her garden every morning, rain or shine."

Wendy lowered her voice and leaned closer, clutching her hands theatrically to her chest. "Some say she still haunts this place, waiting for her long lost love to return."

I started, swallowing hard as an image of the ghostly woman I'd seen at the piano rose abruptly in my mind. I quashed it. *It had only been a dream.* This spooky old house had been playing havoc with my imagination lately.

Jared gave me a look of barely concealed mirth. "Why do they say that?" he asked Wendy.

"Because of the odd noises and strange lights that flicker on and off around the house at all hours of the night." She laughed nervously. "Of course, I don't believe in that sort of thing."

"Of course not," Jared said, struggling to keep a straight face.

I shot him a frown. "With the house standing empty for so long, I imagine there was a problem with kids breaking in. That *has* to be the cause of the lights and noise."

Wendy shook her head. "Huh-uh. Kids around here won't come within a mile of this place. They all think it's haunted."

My lips gave a wry twist and I shrugged. "Well, I'm sure there's a rational explanation. Besides, now that we're here, it won't be happening anymore."

Wendy's plump face crinkled merrily as she chortled and fluttered a hand in the air. "Of course not," she said, grinning and clucking her tongue in amusement. "You're certainly not ghosts, are you."

"Did Blossom ever tell you about her family?" I asked, keen to steer the conversation away from ghosts. I was curious to find out if she knew anything about Dillon Thatcher or his parents in Ohio.

"Not really. She told me once she had a brother, but she never talked about him. She wasn't much for socializing, you know. She was friendly enough but mostly kept to herself. Didn't talk much. She preferred to spend her days playing the piano."

"She must have had friends in town," said Jared.

"I suppose, but I don't think they came out here much, especially the last few years or so, except maybe the church minister once in a while."

"Why is that?" I asked. My sympathy for the poor old woman was growing.

"Well, she could be a little . . ." Wendy whirled her index finger next to her ear.

"What do you mean?"

"Well, sometimes I'd come over, you know, just to check on her because she was all alone in this big house, and she'd act all spacey and far away. She'd sing this same song over and over. It was unnerving. When she got like that, there was no talking to her."

"What song?"

"An old World War II song. My grandmother used to sing it." Wendy started in, slightly off key: *"Don't sit under the apple tree with anyone else but me . . ."*

I stared, unable to speak as icy fingers gripped my throat. That song. It was the same song the woman in my dream had sung. But how could I have dreamed the song? It *had* been a dream, *hadn't it?* I didn't believe in ghosts. *Did I?*

Jared said, "Sounds to me like Miss Thatcher was just a lonely old lady living in the past."

"Oh, don't misunderstand," Wendy continued. "She was always very nice, and she loved my two kids. When they were little she'd bake them cookies at Christmas, and she'd make them little things for their birthdays. They called her Grandma Blossom. But, other times, she'd act real nervous and tense like something dreadful was about to happen. She'd pace and wring her hands, then go and stare out the window for the longest time. I was afraid she'd give herself a stroke."

"Do you know what she was afraid of?" I asked, forcing my voice to remain steady.

"No, but I'm pretty sure it had something to do with the man who jilted her a long time ago. They were supposed to be married and he just left her in the lurch." Wendy lowered her voice. "Some sort of scandal." With a dramatic sigh, she added, "Poor thing never got over it."

"How sad," I managed, recalling the glistening tear on the cheek of the specter.

"She probably should have been put in a nursing home," Wendy said with a sanctimonious air that I found a trifle offensive, "for her own good."

It occurred to me that Wendy was probably one of those people who relished gossip and hearsay, trading in it as her chief source of entertainment. I'd met the type before, among the wives of Daniel's colleagues.

Jared decided he'd had enough. "If you ladies will excuse me, I've got things to do. Thanks again for breakfast, Wendy." He turned and strode off to resume work in the depths of the basement.

I took a quick glance at my watch. It was after nine. "Yipes, look at the time. Wendy, it was awfully nice to meet you—and thank you so much for the goodies—but the workmen will be arriving any minute." I began surreptitiously nudging her toward the back door.

"Oh, sure, I understand." She bobbed her head agreeably. "Come over any time you need anything. Just through the gate."

As she bustled out the door, I called after her. "I'll bring the empty basket over later."

The contractor and his crew arrived shortly thereafter to begin work. I retreated to my room and dropped cross-legged on my sleeping bag, pulling out my cell phone to scan the internet for information on Blossom Thatcher. It didn't take long to find the obituary in the local paper. It included a picture of Blossom taken at a church function in town before she died.

My mouth went dry as I recognized the elderly manifestation of the ghostly woman I had seen in my house last night. I had never laid eyes on her before. How could I have dreamed her? I read the article:

"Blossom Thatcher was the daughter of Washington pioneer Morgan Thatcher who settled in Salmon Falls in 1910, establishing a successful timber industry. Born in 1919, Ms. Thatcher spent her entire life in Salmon Falls and at the time of her death was its oldest resident. A fine pianist and long-time supporter of young local musicians, her presence in the community will be missed. 'Blossom was a gentle soul who loved this town and lived a long full life. I'm glad she's finally at peace,' said Flossie

Gerhardt, president of the Salmon Falls Historical Society.
It is believed that Ms. Thatcher had an older brother, but nothing is known of any living relatives today. A graveside service will be held Saturday morning at the Salmon Falls Cemetery where Thatcher will be interred in the family plot."

I read the obituary a couple of times, then searched for anything having to do with the history of Salmon Falls. The Historical Society had a web page filled with various articles and pictures. I regretted not bringing my laptop, but I had feared leaving it in my room with all the different workers coming and going throughout the house and the doors being left unlocked all day. So I made do with the screen on my phone.

Most of the photos were black and white and grainy: images of loggers, horses and wagons, and various people and locales around the vicinity over the last hundred years. It was nearly impossible to make out any individual faces.

I read with interest a short piece on Morgan Thatcher. He had been one of the early founders of Salmon Falls, and a dominant figure in the region. Over the course of the country's worst depression, the Thatcher timber industry had supported the local economy. Most of the people in the surrounding valley had depended on Thatcher for their livelihood. According to the writer, Thatcher had been a financial genius, rising from obscurity to establish a wealthy empire.

But Blossom Thatcher had died alone and impoverished. Wendy had mentioned some sort of scandal and a long lost love who had left Blossom at the altar. What had happened? A prickle of mystery ran through me. Clearly Blossom's spirit remained in the house. But *why?* Why linger here in this sad ghostly existence? Was she still waiting for her fiancé to return as Wendy had suggested?

I recalled the two visions. The first had appeared elderly, wrinkled and gaunt as Blossom would have been at the end of her life. But then she had changed, becoming a younger version of herself, smooth and beautiful. It was as if Blossom's spirit had reverted to the form her mysterious lover had known before he purportedly left her.

Did this mean that Blossom would remain eternally heartbroken waiting for him? Would the house be forever haunted? I stopped as I listened to myself. With a sigh, I kneaded my forehead with my fingertips. It all sounded so preposterous.

Chapter Nine

At three o'clock the dark blue Bronco pulled up, parking beneath the two tall maple trees that flanked the driveway. Dillon exited the vehicle and strode toward the veranda steps. He moved with the fluid stride of a big cat, his tight jeans enhancing the symmetry of his slim, athletic figure. He wore the same fawn-colored sports jacket over a navy polo shirt. I met him on the porch.

"Hi, Kate," he purred, gazing around. "So, this is it. Grandpa didn't exaggerate. He said it was big, but I had no idea." His smile broadened as his eyes met mine. "I want you to know how much this means to me."

Before I could say anything, my brother's voice broke in behind me. "I'm Jared Thorson, Kate's brother. You must be Dillon Thatcher." Jared reached between us and gripped Dillon's hand, squeezing it just a second longer than I thought necessary.

For an instant, my mind envisioned two male dogs squaring off, stiff-legged with hackles raised. I wanted to kick my brother but settled for slipping him a quick look of annoyance.

He ignored me and continued. "We were under the impression Blossom didn't have any relatives."

If Dillon noticed anything amiss, he made no sign. His smile was still firmly in place as he answered. "Not surprising. My family lives in Dayton, Ohio. Kate probably told you my grandfather was Blossom's brother. He left Washington State right before World War II, and as far as I know, he never came back. Our families didn't keep in touch."

Introductions complete, such as they were, I led the way inside just as loud pounding erupted overhead. "You'll have to excuse the noise," I said, cringing. "They've just started working on the new bathrooms upstairs. The whole house is getting a complete makeover."

Dillon nodded absently as he walked slowly through the entry hall and into the expansive living area, taking in the opulent features and sheer size of the rooms. "Awesome," he said finally. "It must have been really grand at one time. I'm glad you're restoring it."

I felt a sudden twinge of guilt. Had I unwittingly appropriated his family's heritage? Despite what he'd said at the cemetery, did Dillon regret losing the house?

He seemed to read what I was thinking and hurried to put me at ease. "When the letter first came from the lawyer telling my dad his aunt had died and left him her house, my dad thought he could sell it and make a fortune. After all, my grandfather had been telling us for years about this grand old mansion." He laughed. "But then we looked at pictures and realized how much work it needed. When it came right down to it, the house was just too far away and in too bad a condition, plus it came with a pile of debt. After a few years, Dad decided he just didn't have the time or energy, and couldn't afford to keep paying the taxes on it."

He stopped and took a breath, running a hand over his hair. "Then my mother was diagnosed with breast cancer. She's in remission now, thank God, but my parents were left with a stack of medical bills not covered by insurance. Dad finally contacted a Seattle realtor and authorized him to sell the house for whatever he could get and send him the proceeds. Thankfully, even after paying off the taxes and liens, there was enough money left over to take care of Mom's medical bills. I'm not sure what my parents would have done otherwise. You really did my family a huge favor buying the place; the money from the sale was a godsend."

"I'm glad things worked out," I said. "But I do feel bad that your family had to lose the house. Your great-grandfather built it over a hundred years ago."

"Don't feel bad," he said, waving a dismissive hand in the air. "What would we have done with it? Far better for someone to have it who appreciates it."

"So what brings you to Salmon Falls now?" Jared asked.

Dillon shrugged. "Curiosity. When I was a kid, my grandfather always used to talk about this big old house his father had built. He made me promise I'd come here some-day and see it. But you know how it is. When you're young, you're always too busy. You think you have all the time in the world. But things didn't turn out that way. Grandpa died when I was fourteen, and right after high school I went into the military for a couple of years. When I got out, I went to college and then right to work."

"And now?" I prompted.

"I don't know. It just seemed like now or never. I guess I was afraid the new owner would tear it down before I ever got a chance to see it."

"It's too bad you never got to meet your great-aunt Blossom," I said.

He gave a quick shrug. "Maybe I can pick up a memento or two to take back with me." Glancing around, he added, "Looks like some of her stuff is still here."

At that point, Jared excused himself. "You guys go ahead. I want to get back to my project in the basement." He shook Dillon's hand once more and departed.

"What project is he working on?" Dillon asked curiously.

"Cleaning," I said with a scoffing laugh. "Goes completely against his nature. But he wants to turn the basement into a workshop and I'm not about to do it for him."

I led the way through the living and dining rooms, pointing out the great marble-tiled fireplace with its carved oak mantle, the rich wainscoting, and patterned tin ceilings— all original, classic Victorian features.

"Really," I said, "for all the dust and cobwebs, the house is in remarkably good condition. The electrician thinks the wiring was updated some time in the seventies which helps. A lot of new plumbing pipe has to be run, of course, but, overall, it just needs a bit of spit and polish and a few modern conveniences."

Dillon nodded, craning his neck in every direction, trying to take it all in.

"It reminds me of Miss Havisham's mansion in *Great Expectations*," I said.

"Is that a book?"

"Charles Dickens. Yeah . . . never mind." *Am I the only one who's ever read it?*

I took him through the door into the kitchen where two workers in coveralls and goggles were busily attacking the cabinets with electric sanders. Sawdust swirled thickly in the air. The men saw us watching and switched off the sanders.

I gazed around at the work they'd accomplished. "Looks great," I said. "At this rate, you'll have the old place fixed up in no time. Do you need anything?"

One of the men lowered his dust mask to answer. "Nope, everything's under control. We'll be taking out that set of drawers there next to the sink for the new dishwasher. The plumber will be here tomorrow to hook it up. The new appliances should be installed in a few days."

"Sounds good," I said, smiling appreciatively.

Dillon looked around, then pointed to the stairway by the back door. "Where does that go?"

"That's the way to the second and third floors for the maids and children so they could come and go unnoticed—seen but not heard, you know."

He peered curiously up the narrow passage.

"There's really nothing up there but a lot of bona fide junk," I said. "Old clothes, magazines, broken toys, musty furniture, that sort of thing."

"That's okay. I want to see it. I'll bet there's a great view from up there." With a roguish grin, he headed up.

I had no alternative but to follow, resigned to the inevitability of getting dirty. Behind me I heard the sanders kick back on as the carpenters resumed their work.

The third floor of the house had deteriorated badly. The wallpaper was yellowed and peeling, and there were cracks in the plaster. A thick layer of dust and cobwebs lay over everything. It seemed strange to think of Blossom Thatcher playing up here as a child a century ago, perhaps under the watchful eye of a governess.

Dillon moved deftly through the clutter, looking this way and that like an excited child in a candy store. Occasionally, he would pick something up and examine it, only to put it down and move on.

"Would you do me a favor?" he asked. "When you're cleaning, if you come across any old letters, pictures, or documents, would you save them for me? I'm thinking of putting together a family history scrapbook."

"Of course. If I find anything, I promise I'll save it for you. In fact, I have something for you already. Jared found an old family Bible that belonged to Blossom. It had a photograph in it of her when she was a baby with your great-grandparents. It's downstairs. Remind me later and I'll give it to you."

"Awesome. Thank you."

Spiders scurried in all directions as I stepped past an ancient dollhouse and around an old rocking chair. Objects strewn across the floor created a virtual obstacle course in the dusky room. Despite my caution, I managed to trip and lose my balance, stumbling backward. The next thing I knew, Dillon had his arms around me.

"Careful," he said as he set me back on my feet. A tiny smile played on his lips.

"Thank you," I mumbled. My heart fluttered shamelessly. It had been a long time since a man had held me.

Knock it off, I admonished myself sternly. *Do you want him thinking you purposely threw yourself at him?*

I forced myself to act as though nothing had happened. Keeping my eyes averted, I moved ahead. I lifted the corner of a cardboard box and let out a squeal as a surprised mouse darted out and ran between my feet. Revolted, I watched as the tiny creature disappeared into a crack in the wall.

"Don't worry," Dillon laughed. "He's probably more scared of you than you are of him."

I shuddered. "Why does everybody always say that? I don't believe it for one minute." Maybe I should get a cat. Maybe two or three. I hated mice.

"You know," Dillon continued, the teasing smile still on his face, "they say for every mouse you *see*, there's a dozen more you *don't* see."

"Quit trying to make me feel better," I snapped.

Just to show him I wasn't a complete coward, though I vowed to get some more traps as soon as possible, I grabbed ahold of the box and yanked it upright. Broken glass tinkled as the remains of a crystal vase, a small hand mirror, and an old picture frame fell out on the floor.

"Careful," Dillon said. "Don't cut yourself."

Gingerly, I picked through the fragments. The glass in the frame was cracked and smudged. I picked it up and attempted to wipe off some of the grime with the corner of a moldy rag that may once have passed for lingerie.

"Hey, look at this," I said excitedly.

Dillon hurried over and peered at the black and white photo of an attractive, dark-haired young woman in a skirt and blouse sitting at a piano.

"Is that Blossom?"

"Must be." I stared at the face in the picture—the same youthful face that had materialized the night before in the moon-shrouded music salon. My pulse began to race. I was convinced now that I hadn't merely dreamed it.

"That has to be the piano downstairs," I said. "I read that Blossom was once quite a pianist."

"I'll bet she loved that piano," Dillon mused.

"I'm going to take the picture out of the frame and see if it says anything on the back."

"Good idea," Dillon said, watching with interest.

I loosened the back of the frame and carefully slid the photograph out. Turning it over, I saw that someone had written in a faint curving hand, *Blossom 1941.*

All at once, an icy gust hit my face and goose bumps ran up my arms. The light dimmed. Movement over Dillon's shoulder drew my eye as a faint thready voice like a sigh wafted across the room: "*Mind the apple blossoms.*" I felt a rush of blood in my head as the eerie specter of young Blossom Thatcher appeared, translucent in the recessed shadows. She reached a hand out to me.

Dillon looked at me curiously. "What's the matter? You okay?"

The ghost faded and was gone as fleetingly as she'd come.

I took a tremulous gulp. "Yeah, sorry. I . . . I thought I saw another mouse."

He laughed. "Seriously, Kate, they can't hurt you."

I nodded, adding my nervous laugh to his. "You're right, I know, but I'm ready to get out of here. Didn't you say something about dinner? I'm starved. We can finish the tour later."

I hurried downstairs and slipped into my room, ostensibly to freshen up. My breathing was ragged and my heart hammered in my chest. My hands shook. Why had Blossom appeared to me? What did she want?

That's when I realized I was still holding the photo. I decided to put it away in the old nightstand in my room for safe keeping. I slid it into the drawer with the other picture we had found. I wanted to make copies before giving them to Dillon.

After that, I went into the bathroom and splashed cold water on my face, pulling in deep lungfuls of air to calm myself. I began to brush my hair—even, rhythmic strokes as my nerves relaxed. Slowly, my breathing returned to normal.

I gazed at myself in the mirror. After ten years of marriage and a child, my body still maintained its trim, shapely figure. My blond hair shone with sleek highlights, curving in natural waves around my face. I touched up my mascara, added a hint of lipstick, and declared myself ready to go.

Dillon gave me an appreciative smile as he looked me up and down. "You look great."

At the front door, Jared appeared out of nowhere and strode forward with hand extended. His six-foot-two-inch frame towered over Dillon's as he gripped his hand.

"Take care of my sister," Jared intoned. His demeanor was vaguely threatening.

"I will," Dillon said. "Don't worry."

"Jared . . ." I frowned.

He turned to me then and stuck his finger in my face, uttering in a serious voice, "And as for you, young lady—no *drinking*, no *hanky-panky*, and home by *ten*."

I gave him a sisterly smack in the arm.

"Owww!" He staggered back, breaking into a grin and grabbing his arm as if mortally wounded.

"Thanks, *Dad*," I drawled, "but I think I can take care of myself."

He waggled his eyebrows at me. "Don't do anything I wouldn't do."

Dillon looked on in amazement.

I put on my jacket and grabbed him by the arm. "Come on, let's go, before he gets *really* annoying."

* * *

Dillon took me to a Chinese restaurant he'd discovered near his hotel. He was a great listener as I prattled on about the hurdles and pitfalls inherent in renovating an old house. Through all my droning tales of permits, outdated plumbing, and refinishing hardwood floors, he smiled and managed to look thoroughly engrossed.

Suddenly I stopped, embarrassed, realizing that I had done most of the talking. I laughed. "Forgive me. I'm not usually this self-absorbed. I guess lately that old house has been addling my brain."

"That's okay, it's really fascinating."

I laughed again. "Right—like a root canal."

He responded with a look of amused indulgence as a good-natured smile tugged at the corners of his mouth.

"Your turn," I entreated. "Tell me about yourself. You come from Dayton, right? What do you do there?"

"Well," he said, "at the moment I'm between jobs, taking a sort of sabbatical. My degree is in psychology and up until a couple of months ago I worked as a school counselor. But I've also done some HR work, and even spent a year managing a restaurant."

"Siblings? Wife? Kids?"

"None of the above. I'm an only child and I've always been too busy to settle down. Not that I'm opposed to the idea if the right girl came along." He peered at me provocatively. "What about you? I know you have at least one very *large* brother."

"Don't mind Jared," I said with a careless wave of my hand. "He's the original gentle giant. He doesn't even kill spiders."

"Uh-huh." He said it like he didn't believe it for one moment. "I take it you're not married?"

"Divorced," I said. "And I have a daughter, Amy. She's eight years old, and the only good thing to come out of my marriage. She's staying at my mom's while I work on the house, and I miss her like crazy. As soon as school's out, I'm going to bring her here to live with me."

"What about your ex-husband?"

"The original workaholic. He lives in Seattle. I'm sure he'd keep Amy if I asked him, but he's so busy all the time he would just hire a nanny and that would defeat the whole purpose. Amy's better off with my mother. She lavishes her with attention. Daniel prefers to keep to his weekend schedule so he can plan for Amy's visits and not be too inconvenienced."

"Do I sense some hostility?"

"Don't even get me started. When I think about our marriage the only word that comes to mind is betrayal."

Dillon leaned toward me, his face creased with sympathy. "He cheated?"

"No, nothing like that. I mean it was like he married me under false pretenses." I looked at my hands, playing absently with my fork as I recalled those early days. "We met in college. Our first date was a benefit concert to aid victims of land mines. We hit it off right away, and afterwards we spent all night in a corner booth at the local diner talking and drinking coffee. I thought he was wonderful, so smart and charismatic. After that, we did a three-day march for breast cancer. We were so idealistic." I blew sharply through my nose. "At least I was. I thought he was, too. We even talked about joining the Peace Corps together."

"What happened?"

"We got married and he changed, showed his true colors." I shrugged. "I was so naïve."

Pausing, I looked up and remembered who I was talking to. I rolled my eyes. "Oh, man, there I go again. I'm sorry. You don't want to hear all this stuff."

He smiled. "Well, I am a psychologist."

"Believe me, I've seen my share of therapists in the last few years—probably the only reason I'm still sane."

"Sounds like you've had a rough time, but I can tell you're strong. You'll make it just fine."

I let out a laugh. "If that old house doesn't do me in first."

I don't know why I felt so free discussing my personal life with him. He seemed like such a willing listener that I found myself opening up and talking for hours.

Chapter Ten

April 1940

"You'll never believe it," Blossom said to her friend Helen. "Father bought me a new sewing machine." They emerged from the Salmon Falls dry goods store where they had been shopping, and stopped for a moment to re-juggle their packages.

Helen gave an incredulous laugh. "Whatever for? You hate to sew."

"I know," Blossom groaned. "I couldn't sew a straight line if my life depended on it, but I think Martha talked him into it. She thinks sewing is one of those things all girls are supposed to know."

Helen swallowed a giggle. "Well, it's not a bad idea."

The corners of Blossom's mouth turned down. "You're just saying that because you can sew."

Helen had always been a gifted seamstress, and had just purchased several bundles of soft flannel to make new outfits for her chubby baby boy. Having married Albert Pike right after high school, her new role as wife and mother kept her pretty busy these days. "I would think that if you could play a piano, you ought to be able to operate a sewing machine."

Blossom huffed. "The piano doesn't fight back. Anyway, I've tried. All I manage to do is make a mess. My stitches pucker, the thread gets all tangled, and I always manage to stab more holes in my fingers than in the fabric."

"What kind of sewing machine is it?"

"All I know is it's a Singer, it's electric, and it's mounted to a fancy wooden table. I'm scared to touch it. Of course, Martha still swears by her old treadle machine."

Helen sucked in her breath, her eyes lit up. "I can't wait to see it. I've been using my mother's portable. It's awful."

"Well, you'll just have to come over and try it out. You can sew Harold's baby clothes on it."

Blossom loved helping Helen with the baby. He was so soft and smelled so sweet, like shampoo and talcum powder. It gave Blossom an excuse to get away from the mansion. While little Harold napped, the two friends often spent mornings together, giggling and gossiping companionably in Helen's cozy cottage.

To everyone's surprise, Morgan Thatcher had shown uncharacteristic generosity after the wedding by offering Albert a job at the mill and a house nearby with a small patch of land for a garden. Blossom didn't kid herself as to her father's motives. While Albert and Helen gushed with gratitude, Blossom knew her father's purpose had been to keep her friend close by, forestalling any notion his daughter might have of moving away from home. Considering her father's jealous, over-protective nature, Blossom had resigned herself to spinsterhood for as long as he lived. The thought didn't bother her much; she was young and had yet to meet a man with whom she would seriously consider spending the rest of her life.

"Who's that with Clay?" Helen asked, pointing across the street.

Blossom turned and looked. Coming toward them on the opposite side of the street, Clayton Thatcher was deep in conversation with a dark-haired young man in a sheepskin jacket and short-brimmed fedora set at a rakish angle over his eyes.

"I don't know," Blossom said. She waved, calling out to her brother.

The two men stopped and Clay waved back. He said something to his companion and they both trotted across the street to where Blossom and Helen stood waiting.

"Tommy O'Connell," Clay said, drawing close, "this is my kid sister, Blossom, and her friend, Helen Pike."

"How do you do," Blossom said.

The stranger extended his hand and dazzled Blossom with a smile that left her breathless. His riveting brown eyes seemed at once guileless and beguiling, and she was instantly captivated. Not as tall as Clay, he had a straight nose, square jaw, and dimpled chin, and carried himself with an air of panache seldom encountered in the rural town of Salmon Falls. Doffing his hat, he revealed a thick mass of dark wavy hair combed back from his face in Cary Grant style. He gave Helen a polite nod, then appraised Blossom from head to toe and smiled approvingly.

"Clay," he said, eyes never leaving Blossom's face, "when you told me you had a little sister, I was imagining a girl with pigtails and knobby knees, not a woman to rival Venus herself."

Blossom blushed, self-conscious in her plain cotton dress, shapeless wool coat, and black laced shoes. She was unsettled by this man's admiring gaze, yet surprisingly pleased. Under her father's constant watch, men in this town knew better than to show her any interest, let alone speak to her in such familiar terms.

"Back off, jack," Clay warned. "Blossom is off limits. Morgan would kill you if he heard you talking like that."

"Good thing he can't hear me then." Tommy grinned and gave Blossom a wink.

Helen stepped forward. "We haven't seen you around here before, have we, Mr. O'Connell? Where did you and Clay meet?"

"Please, call me Tommy. We met over a card game in Seattle. Clay had run out of luck and I was feeling benevolent."

"Oh, you were benevolent, all right," Clay snorted. "You nearly got me killed."

"I gave you my gold watch to cover your bet."

"Which turned out to be *phony*."

"How did I know Pierce would take it so personally?" The two men laughed at the shared memory of their unsavory exploit.

How carelessly Clayton lives his life, thought Blossom. *How narrowly he balances the line between nerve and recklessness.*

"Clay," she said, "I wish you wouldn't gamble." She would have liked to say more but held her tongue. If anyone knew the dangers of gambling, it was Clay. She knew he still resented being so abruptly removed from the life he had known. Only his feelings for Hiram Decker had made him agree to stay with Morgan in exchange for payment of Decker's gambling debt. Without the money, Clay's foster father would surely have been killed. Once payment was made, Decker had fled the state and not been heard from since. Blossom could not understand her brother's inclination to follow down the same sordid path.

Tommy gave her a mischievous smile. "Don't worry. I won't let him lose much."

"He shouldn't lose any," she scolded.

Clay interposed. "Let's go before she lets slip what a sinner I am."

"Too late," Tommy said. "That secret is out."

Clay spun as if to walk away, then turned back and asked, "Do you girls want a ride? I've got the car."

Tommy inclined his head at Blossom, his expression enticing.

Unnerved, Blossom decided she was in no mood to be crammed into the roadster with this obvious scallywag. She shook her head. "No, thanks, we've got more shopping to do. We'll walk."

Once the men were out of earshot, Helen leaned toward Blossom. "I think he's stuck on you."

Blossom jerked back as though stung. "Don't be ridiculous."

"Why not? You're a nice-looking girl and he's . . ." Helen grinned, lifting an eyebrow suggestively.

Blossom rolled her eyes in protest. "In the first place, guys like that never go for the quiet country types—"

"Huh-uh. What about *Scarlett O'Hara?*"

"—except in the movies."

Helen turned her face heavenward and her voice swooned. "Clark Gable and Vivien Leigh . . ." She sighed. "They don't come any dreamier."

Blossom ignored her. "In the second place, my father would throw a fit."

That brought Helen up short. She looked around to make sure no one was listening, then leaned forward and said sternly, "When are you going to stand up to your father? You're not a kid anymore, you're twenty years old. He has to let you go out sometime. Not all men are mashers."

"You don't understand."

"Does he want you to stay an old maid forever? Doesn't he want to see his grandchildren? There are lots of nice, hard-working men out there. Look at Albert."

"It's not that."

"Well, what is it then?"

Blossom took a deep breath. "He's afraid of being alone, of being abandoned in his old age. Everyone he's ever loved has abandoned him in one way or another. His parents left him at a foundling home when he was eight years old. He had to fight just to survive. Then his first wife, Clay's mother, ran off and took Clay with her. I told you about that."

"But your mother never ran off."

"No, but she died after they'd only been married a few years. That was a kind of abandonment in his eyes. She left him to raise me all by himself."

"Still . . ."

"Don't you see? Our roles are becoming reversed. He's getting older. He *needs* me. He needs me more than I need him. He knows it and it scares him. That's why he's so cross. He's afraid I'll meet someone and leave him alone to fend for himself in his old age."

"He's got Clay," Helen pointed out.

Blossom snorted. "Does Clay strike you as the kind who will stay home and take care of his aging father?"

"It just doesn't seem right." Helen's eyes held concern for her friend.

"Oh, twaddle," Blossom said briskly. "I'll be fine. Don't be such a mother hen." She stepped toward the curb. "Let's run over to the drug store. I promised Martha I would pick up a bottle of tincture of iodine."

"Then we'd better get back." Helen smiled. "Albert likes to have dinner on the table the minute he gets home from the mill."

* * *

To Blossom's surprise, Clay brought his friend to the house that evening, leading him through the grand foyer and into the front room where Blossom sat reading a book. Tommy strode in with that same self-assurance that had so intrigued and unnerved her. He gazed around in admiration at the elegance of the room with its polished oak and mahogany woodwork, imported Persian rugs, and extravagant furnishings.

When his eyes lit on Blossom, he broke into a wide grin. "Nice little place you've got here, Miss Thatcher."

Blossom stood and set her book on the small table beside her chair, secretly pleased that she'd changed her clothes upon returning from town. This dress with its tight waist and pink floral pattern was most becoming. "It's nice to see you again, Mr. O'Connell."

"Please, call me Tommy," he entreated.

"All right, and you must call me Blossom." She knew nothing would ever come of the flirtation, but it was flattering and there was no harm in enjoying it while it lasted. "How long will you be in Salmon Falls?"

"I haven't decided yet. Clay invited me out here to see the wonders of the countryside, but he didn't tell me that the most wondrous thing was right here in his own house."

"You shouldn't talk that way," Blossom demurred. "We hardly know each other."

"I'd like to change that."

Clay cleared his throat. "I thought maybe we'd go hunting tomorrow."

At that moment, a deep voice interjected. "Just what does your friend intend to hunt, Clayton?"

They turned to see Morgan Thatcher scowling at them from the archway leading to the hall. His imposing figure towered like a great Goliath in the shadows.

After the space of a heartbeat, Clay spoke. "Allow me to introduce my friend, Tommy O'Connell. Tommy, this is my . . . father . . . Morgan Thatcher."

Blossom noticed the hesitation as Clay made the introduction. Clay never called his father by anything but his first name. Blossom looked away sadly. The two men had been at odds since the day Clay arrived.

Tommy strode toward the older man, hand extended. "A pleasure, sir. You have a fine home here. You must be very proud."

Morgan grudgingly took the proffered hand, his scowl unabated.

Clay continued. "Tommy and I met in Seattle. He helped me out of a jam and we've been pals ever since. I invited him to stay for a few days—thought maybe I'd take him hunting and fishing, show him what country life is like."

Tommy said, "Clay tells me you're quite the hunter, Mr. Thatcher. He says you killed a bear with one shot."

Morgan was not so easily mollified. He glowered at the intruder with suspicion, barely deigning to grunt in response.

"He sure did," Clay said. "Shot it right in the gullet as it was charging. Isn't that right? You shot it right in the gullet?"

Blossom thought her brother's exhortations sounded almost pleading, and she feared their father would interpret his posturing as weakness. She knew her father despised weakness above all else. She had once overheard him muttering to Jed Hawkins about Clay's cowardly demeanor, and how he blamed Hiram Decker for bringing the boy up in gambling halls and sleazy hotels.

"Tell us about it, father," Blossom coaxed. She had heard the story many times but knew that her father liked to tell it. She thought it might help ease the tension.

Morgan gave a grumbling sigh and ambled into the room, eventually stopping to lean against the fireplace mantle. He began, "I was hunting elk with my thirty-aught-six in the mountains just east of here." Morgan's scowl faded as he warmed to his story. "I'd built me a blind in this big maple, see, about fifteen feet up or so, and I'd climbed up to wait for the elk to come by. It was near a well-worn game trail and I'd hunted there before. I had a round in the chamber all ready to go, when suddenly this big black bear comes along and decides he's going to climb up into that tree after me."

"*Whoa*—that must have been quite a surprise," Tommy exclaimed.

Encouraged by his guest's enthusiasm, Morgan continued with a vigorous nod. "I've met bears in the woods before. Usually, the damn things scare off pretty easily but not this guy. He was determined to get me. So when he got close and opened his big slavering maw, I just shoved the rifle down his throat and fired point blank. He fell like a stone and never moved."

"Ha! That's great," Tommy said. "So, what'd you do with the bear's carcass?"

"Had it stuffed. It's in my den. C'mon, I'll show you."

As they started toward the hall, Morgan turned to Blossom and frowned. "Why don't you go help Martha with dinner. It must be nearly ready by now. Tell her we'll be there in a couple of minutes." He didn't wait for her answer but turned and started toward the wide staircase.

As soon as Morgan's back was turned, Tommy shot Blossom a grin and blew her a quick kiss off his fingertips. She smiled back, feeling her heart flutter in a way she'd never felt before. Then she hurried off to the kitchen to find Martha.

Chapter Eleven

April 1940

"What is that delectable aroma?" Tommy exclaimed as Martha entered the dining room carrying a large platter. "Surely, it can be nothing short of ambrosia."

She set the platter on the table in front of him, smiling modestly. "Nothing so fancy, I'm afraid—just roast beef and potatoes."

He closed his eyes and inhaled deeply. "If it tastes half as good as it smells, I will think I've gone to Heaven."

"Don't be silly," Martha said, looking pleased. "It's just simple country fare."

Morgan frowned and cleared his throat. They quieted while Blossom bowed her head and said grace as she had done since childhood.

Martha went back to the kitchen and returned with a large bowl brimming with hot green beans and stewed tomatoes.

"Another triumph," Tommy declared. "Green beans are my favorite."

Clay snickered. "Laying it on a little thick, aren't you, chum?"

"Martha grows and cans the vegetables herself," Blossom said, aiming a kick at her brother under the table. "She has a real knack for gardening."

Tommy loaded his plate with fervor while the matronly housekeeper tittered and offered him another ladle of gravy. "Yes, thank you," he said. "The gravy is divine. My own mother doesn't make gravy this good."

"Oh, go on," Martha demurred coquettishly.

Martha is thoroughly charmed, Blossom thought with a smile. It was nice seeing the older woman revel in the well-deserved compliments.

"I'd like some more gravy," Clay said, holding out his plate.

Martha turned her back as though she hadn't heard him and bustled off to the kitchen. Tommy stifled a grin as Clay sputtered his indignation.

Blossom glared at her brother. *Serves you right. It wouldn't hurt you to show a little courtesy once in a while.*

Moments later, Martha brought in a loaf of warm bread she had baked that afternoon, along with a bowl of freshly churned butter. She set them on the table near Tommy's right hand.

"Mmm, I do love fresh bread," Tommy said, taking two slices before passing the plate to Blossom. "It looks wonderful."

Martha beamed at him appreciatively. "You have a touch of the blarney, haven't you, Mr. O'Connell?"

Tommy winked. "Not at all. Just giving credit where it's due."

Clay glowered reproachfully.

"Everyone needs to be told they're appreciated from time to time," Blossom interjected. She looked at the housekeeper. "Everything is delicious, Martha. Thank you."

The older woman smiled. "You're welcome, dear."

Blossom saw Clay cast a meaningful glance at his father, but Morgan paid him no heed. He was absorbed in helping himself to the beef and showed no interest in the discourse. Blossom sighed, and busied herself with buttering a piece of bread.

She noted that the foreman was absent and she wondered whether it was coincidence, or if Clay had waited to invite his friend until he knew Jed would be busy elsewhere on estate business. The two men made no bones about disliking each other. Jed made it clear he thought Clay was beneath him and only tolerated him for Morgan's sake. Blossom suspected Jed was jealous of Clay and saw him as an interloper.

"So, Mr. Thatcher," Tommy said, slicing into the generous slabs of roast beef piled on his plate. "What do you think of the situation in Europe? Will the United States join the fray?"

"Hard to say," Morgan muttered. He barely raised his head as he stabbed at a chunk of boiled potato.

"My father thinks the war will boost the American economy," Blossom said. "He says it will get people working and building again."

"I can speak for myself," Morgan growled, shooting her a censorious look. "No sane man wants war. It's a terrible thing. The last war cost millions of lives. But it's a cold hard fact that a war would get this country off its collective butt and back to work."

"I see your point," Tommy said.

"But at what price?" Blossom protested.

Tommy gave her a warm smile and nodded. "You also have a point."

Morgan scowled openly.

Clay hastened to change the subject. "Morgan used to do a bit of gold mining in the mountains around here."

"No kidding?" Tommy said. "Where 'bouts?" His steady gaze showed real interest. Blossom knew her father admired a man with a forthright countenance.

"Northeast of here," Morgan said. "But that was a long time ago. Most of the mining companies have packed up and left."

"But there's still plenty of gold out there," Clay asserted. "Prospectors are staking claims all the time."

Morgan snorted derisively. "There's a big difference between staking a claim and striking it rich. You seem to think a person can just walk into the mountains and find nuggets lying around for the taking. It don't work that way, believe me. It's a lot of hard work and sweat." He jabbed a piece of meat for emphasis.

For a moment they ate in silence, then Tommy spoke up again. "So Blossom, tell me, what do people in this town do for fun?"

"People work," Morgan interjected gruffly. "They don't have time for fun."

"Sometimes the church has a social," Blossom suggested.

"There's the movie theater in town," Clay said.

"That sounds like fun," Tommy said, smiling boldly at Blossom.

"Don't get any ideas, Mr. O'Connell," Morgan said in a low, threatening voice. "My daughter doesn't go out with drinkers and gamblers. She has standards and they don't include men like you. Now, I suggest you finish up your dinner and Clayton will show you to the guest room."

Blossom bit her lip. Only her father's long-studied decorum as a man of wealth and position restrained him now from throwing Tommy out of the house. He had agreed to put Clay's friend up for a few days and he would not go back on his word.

* * *

"Good morning, Blossom."

Startled, Blossom halted and glanced around. She had been strolling down the lane to Helen's cottage listening to the birds and enjoying the brilliant spring sunshine. The way was so familiar, she hadn't been paying particular attention to the surroundings. Over one arm she bore a basket covered with a checkered cloth.

To her surprise, Tommy O'Connell emerged from the shade of a large alder tree growing beside the path. Even in the same fedora and sheepskin jacket he'd had on yesterday, Blossom thought he exuded an air of sophistication. *Some people must be born that way.*

Tipping his hat, he gave her a genial smile. "May I carry that for you?"

She returned the smile, pleased to see him and grateful no one else was around. She felt less awkward speaking to him outdoors like this, just the two of them.

"No, thank you," she said. "I can manage—it's not heavy."

"Where are you off to this morning?" He matched his step to hers, walking comfortably beside her.

His nearness filled Blossom with an unaccustomed exhilaration. The twinkle in his eye, the way his shirt opened at the neck revealing a hint of dark hair, the firm line of his jaw, and the dimple on his chin—accentuated when he smiled—all heightened her senses and gave her a jittery feeling of excitement she couldn't explain. But his cheery, lighthearted manner quickly put her at ease.

"I'm going to visit my friend Helen. You met her yesterday, remember? We were shopping together in town."

"Yes, I remember but, in truth, I was only looking at you."

His gaze was bold and playful. She looked away shyly, feeling the blush rise to her cheeks.

"Where's Clay?" she asked, reaching for something to say.

Tommy laughed. "Still in bed as far as I know. I guess he's not an early riser like his sister."

Blossom adjusted the basket on her arm, saying nothing. She had no wish to speak ill of her brother. Clay still held on to many of the old habits he had acquired living with his mother and Hiram Decker in the hotels and gambling halls of the big city. He liked to stay up late, drinking and playing cards, then loiter in bed the next day until noon. Even Morgan's disgusted tirades had had little effect.

"What have you got in the basket?" he asked curiously.

"Oh, just a few things for Helen." She looked away, unable to meet his eye. The basket was filled with delicacies for her friend—costly items Helen couldn't easily afford on her frugal budget: a pound of bacon, a tin of coffee, a bag of sugar, a jar of raspberry preserves, a small smoked ham, and four ounces of baking chocolate.

His eyes narrowed in mock reproof. "You haven't been raiding Martha's larder, have you?" He reached across to lift the corner of the checkered cloth to spy the contents for himself.

Blossom yanked it away, then confessed with a guilty laugh, "Martha will never miss it. We have more than we need and Helen has so little. I like to help her out when I can."

Tommy gave a soft chuckle. Blossom loved the way his head tilted and the corners of his eyes crinkled when he laughed.

"I'm sure Helen appreciates it," he said.

"Besides," Blossom said. "I'm pretty sure Martha knows. As long as I don't take too much, she doesn't mind looking the other way." She knew Martha harbored an affection for Helen. As Blossom's best friend and childhood companion, Helen had spent many carefree days with Blossom in Martha's homey kitchen. Under the housekeeper's watchful eye, the two girls had studied and played and learned the finer points of canning and baking.

"Martha seems like a wonderful lady."

"She is," Blossom said, reflecting on the lifetime of kindness shown her by the feisty older woman. "I had a nanny when I was young, just until I started school. But I was never as fond of her as I am of Martha. She's always been like a mother to me. My own mother died of influenza when I was small."

"I'm sorry," Tommy said.

Blossom shrugged. "I was two years old. I don't remember her. My father doesn't speak of her much, but I know he loved her. He still keeps her picture on the table beside his bed."

"I wonder that he never remarried. Your father is wealthy and good-looking. There must be scores of ladies who would jump at the chance."

"I used to wonder that myself," Blossom said. "When I was younger I used to dream of having a new mother. I asked Martha about it one day, and she told me she didn't think his heart was in it. She thought he'd had so much heartache in his life, he just wasn't willing to risk any more. So he buried himself in his work and it became his whole life." Wistfully, she added, "Sometimes I think he forgets about the rest of us."

She quieted abruptly, embarrassed that she had revealed so much. Despite his gracious attentions, Tommy was still a stranger. He wasn't interested in hearing intimate details of her family's lives.

For a while they walked in silence, then Tommy said, "How do you like living way out here in the middle of nowhere?"

Blossom bristled. "It's *not* the middle of nowhere. It may not be the big, bustling city you're used to, but Salmon Falls is a lively community in its own way, filled with good, brave, hard working people."

Her voice rose in defense of all the things she loved about her home. With a sweep of her arm, she encompassed the surrounding landscape, the fields, forested hills, and majestic mountains, embracing all the natural sights and sounds. "It's beautiful here—peaceful and full of life. Just look around and listen. Do you hear the woodpecker? Or that squirrel scolding us from the branch over there? Have you ever seen grass so green or a sky so blue?" She put a finger to her lips and pointed. "Look there, in the orchard, two young does. You won't see that in the city."

He smiled. "It *is* beautiful, especially through your eyes."

"I've been to Seattle a couple of times," Blossom went on. "My father took me with him when he went there on business. He thought I needed the experience. But I hated it. It was noisy and crowded. Nothing but big ugly buildings, with cars rushing in all directions, and people pushing and shoving, always in a hurry to get somewhere. It even smelled dirty, like oil and soot and rotten fish."

"I wish I could take you there," Tommy said. "I would show you a different side of the city—theaters, restaurants, shops and salons, all catering to the whims of fashionable young ladies."

Blossom snorted derisively and shook her head. "Doesn't sound like me." Then she brightened. "Oh, here we are. There's Helen on the front porch."

The cottage was a cozy one-story bungalow painted white with green shutters and window boxes, nestled between a grove of hazelnut bushes and several newly planted fruit trees. Three fat hens clucked and scratched in a coop constructed in one corner of the yard. Daffodils and hyacinths bloomed in profusion in a flower bed along the front of a covered porch, and the rich loam in a vegetable patch beside the fence showed evidence of having recently been planted.

Helen tripped lightly down the steps and met them as they turned off the lane onto the path to the cottage. "Shhh," she warned them. "I just got the baby down for a nap." Her eyes darted curiously from Blossom to Tommy, then her face broke into a wide welcoming grin. "Tommy, how nice to see you again. Won't you come and sit on the porch while I fix us some coffee?" She caught Blossom's eye with a furtive look of approval.

Oh dear, Blossom thought as she passed the basket to her friend. *Helen will have us married and settled down with three children before lunch.* A serious talk was obviously in order. Helen would have to accept that Tommy was just passing through. He was a drifter, a gambler—someone Clay had met and befriended in a poker game. He was certainly not looking to put roots down here in Salmon Falls. Strangely, the thought filled Blossom with regret.

"I can't stay," Tommy said to Helen. "I enjoyed the walk, but it's time I got back. I think Clay has something planned for us this morning."

He turned to Blossom. "Thank you for the pleasure of your company." With a chivalrous air, he took her hand and drew it to his lips. His eyes shone. "I'm sure I'll see you again later."

He turned to go, then paused and turned back, his eyes fixed on Helen. "What's that?" he asked, reaching toward her left ear.

Startled, she froze and waited fearfully as he plucked something from her hair. Blossom leaned forward to get a better look.

Clasped between his thumb and forefinger, Tommy held up a shiny silver dollar. He extended it to Helen and placed it in her hand. She gasped in surprise.

"I can't take this," she exclaimed. "A whole dollar!"

"Of course you can take it," Tommy said. "It's not mine. I found it behind your ear. A funny place to keep money, I must say."

As Helen uttered her thanks, Blossom stared at Tommy with a mixture of delight and gratitude. Such generosity. With careful spending, a dollar could buy a substantial number of groceries. Blossom felt her heart swell. *If only he . . .* She pushed the thought away. She had no illusions. She would accept the friendship he offered and demand nothing more.

He gave her an inscrutable smile, doffed his hat, and strode back to the lane, heading toward the mansion. Soon he was lost from sight behind a thicket of alder and elderberry.

Chapter Twelve

The next morning I found Jared already up as usual, making coffee on the card table in the dining room. The kitchen remodel was ongoing.

"How was your date with Dillon goo-goo-eyes Thatcher?" He made a sarcastic face.

I frowned. "Jared . . ."

He threw up his hands. "I know, I know. It's none of my business."

"Why don't you like him?"

He shrugged. "It's not that I don't like him, exactly. He just seems too—I don't know—perfect. I always get suspicious of guys like that."

"You're just jealous."

"You're right. My life would be totally different if I had teeth like that."

"Well, just don't be rude."

"*Moi?*" He feigned a shocked expression.

I blew out my breath in disgust. "Fine. And for your information, I had a great time. He was a perfect gentleman."

He reached for the coffee pot, then stopped. "Kate, I just don't want you to lose your focus, okay? After everything you've been through lately . . . you just got *rid* of one guy."

"Don't worry," I said. "I'm a big girl. Look—"

I stopped when I heard a knock at the back door.

"Guess who?" Jared said with a smirk.

I made a shushing noise then went into the kitchen. "Hi, Wendy," I called. "Come on in."

Without hesitation, our buxom neighbor bustled in, springy hair all aquiver. She carried the familiar wicker basket on her arm. This morning her over-sized t-shirt loudly displayed the words, *Hand Over The Chocolate and Nobody Gets Hurt.* I wondered how many of these t-shirts she owned.

"Mmm," Jared said. "What have you made today?"

She gave him a flirtatious grin. "Banana bread. My own recipe."

As Jared helped himself, I waited for Wendy to get to the crux of her visit. I didn't have to wait long.

"I've been dying of curiosity all night," she said. "Who was that gorgeous hunk in the blue Bronco I saw here yesterday. Your *ex?*"

Jared guffawed loudly, nearly choking on the huge chunk of banana bread he had stuffed into his mouth.

Does she keep binoculars by her kitchen window?

"No," I said, scowling at my brother. "His name is Dillon Thatcher. He's Blossom's grandnephew. Blossom's brother was his grandfather. He came here from Ohio. He's staying at the Salmon Falls Hotel."

Wendy sucked in her breath. "No kidding! What does he want?"

"Just to see the old house. He seems rather sentimental about it."

She leaned forward eagerly. "How long will he be here?"

"I don't know."

She gave me a coy look. "He took you out, though, didn't he? What's he like?"

"He's very nice," I said, irked at the nosy questions. "He took me to dinner to thank me for showing him around the house, and that's all there is to it."

I knew she craved more information, but my patience was wearing thin.

Unabashed, she grinned again and nodded. "Well, I know you're busy so I'll run along." She disappeared out the back door with surprising alacrity.

I suspected she could hardly wait to get home and start making phone calls. Soon the whole town would be talking.

Jared's gleeful smirk threatened to split his face in half as he went to get the coffee pot.

The sun had come out and it promised to be a glorious day, so I took my cup and went out the back door. The air was cool but it felt good. Without thinking about it, I strolled off the porch and made my way across the grass to a knoll where a gnarled old apple tree stood. I gazed up into the branches and tried to imagine a bower of fragrant pink and white apple blossoms. How delightful it must have been with bumble bees humming from bloom to bloom and sunlight dappling the lush green carpet underneath.

I thought of Blossom Thatcher and her long lost beau. This would have made a perfect setting for a wedding—eighty years ago. Now the apple tree was well beyond its fruit-bearing years. The bright morning sunshine did little to enhance the black peeling bark and brittle misshapen limbs. Only a few meager blossoms sprouted at the tip of one scraggly branch.

I jumped suddenly when something brushed my leg. My eyes had been turned upward and I hadn't noticed the arrival of a large yellow dog beside me. Its tongue lolled out the side of its mouth and its tail wagged vigorously.

"Well, hello there," I said. "Where did you come from?"

The dog gave his tail one more enthusiastic wag and then proceeded to run snuffling through the long grass until he located a foot-long stick which he promptly presented at my feet. I gathered by the way he dropped it and stepped back that I was supposed to throw it. I obliged, and he dashed headlong through the weeds to retrieve it.

I looked around for the dog's owner, expecting to see some youngster struggling through the tangled woods growing beyond the fence to the south. Instead, a crotchety-looking older man in worn slacks and heavy wool coat shoved his way through the broken section of fence. The nearest house on that side lay nearly a quarter mile away across a tiny brook and through a thick copse of cedar, hemlock, and vine maple which provided a natural screen.

"Come 'ere, you stupid dog," the man shouted.

The dog, a Lab, bounded toward him, heedless of the man's foul mood. I feared the man might strike the dog in anger, but instead he merely grabbed it and attached a long leash to its collar. The dog turned clownish eyes up to his master's face and happily wagged his tail. The old man tousled the retriever's ears and then turned to me. "Sorry to bother you, ma'am. He saw a rabbit in the brush and took off before I could stop him."

"Oh, it's no bother at all," I said. "He's a beautiful dog. What's his name?"

"Freddy," the old man muttered, his voice low and grating. "Damn foolish name if you ask me. My grandkids named him when he was a pup. Belongs to them, really, but he grew into more dog than they could handle and my daughter dropped him off on me. Thought he oughta live in the country, but he's turned into a real nuisance."

They say that people often resemble their pets, but, if that were the case, this man should have owned a bulldog. His head was large and heavy-jowled with a thick, furrowed brow that implied a gruff demeanor. Short and stocky, he had wide shoulders and a barrel chest. On his head he wore an old tweed deerstalker. Watching him stroke the dog's head, I doubted the ire in his words, despite the bluster.

He peered at me from under a hedge of gray, bristly eyebrows. "You the new owner?" He tilted his head toward the house.

"Yes. My name is Kate Ecklund. My brother Jared and I are working to refurbish the place and turn it into a bed-and-breakfast."

"Harold Pike," he said. "I live just down the road a piece." We shook hands. His were knobbed and rough, like a bear's paw. My slender fingers disappeared in his brawny grip.

He gave me a skeptical look. "A bed-and-breakfast, eh? This here's a grand ol' house. I hope yer not plannin' on making too many changes."

"No, not at all. In fact, I'm hoping to restore it as closely as possible to its original splendor."

"Blossom loved this old house," he said wistfully.

"Were you good friends?"

"You could say that. I knew her all my life." His gaze drifted to the horizon where a distant ridge of trees reflected the morning sun. "It's hard to believe so many years have passed."

For a moment, neither of us spoke. I wondered awkwardly what I should say next. But then he sniffed loudly and continued. "My mother used to be Blossom's best friend. 'Course that was ages ago. My mother's been gone nearly thirty years now."

He paused again as if sorting his thoughts. "Blossom was always such a beautiful lady. You might say I had a crush on her my whole life. My poor wife never could get over her jealousy. She left me after eighteen years." He snorted humorlessly. "Not that I ever had a chance with Blossom, of course. She was older'n me by twenty years. She used to sit with me when I was little. To her I was never anything more'n a snot-nosed kid. Her heart lay elsewhere."

"I heard she was jilted by the man she was supposed to marry. Did you know him? Do you know what happened?" Here was someone who had known Blossom most of her life. Perhaps he could fill in some of the blanks regarding what had happened all those years ago, perhaps explain the fear and reclusive behavior Wendy had mentioned.

"No, I don't know nothing about him 'cept what my mother told me. Tommy O'Connell was his name. She said he was good lookin', but kind of mysterious. Nobody really knew much about him or where he came from. He took off when I was small. My mother told me Tommy used to pal around with Blossom's brother—and before you ask, I didn't know him neither. That was all before my time."

"I understand Blossom waited her whole life for Tommy to come back. I can't help feeling sorry for her."

"Yeah," Pike growled. "Blossom had it bad for him. She'd never look at anybody else, though heaven knows, she had other suitors. But when Tommy left, I guess something went out of her. My mother said Blossom was never the same."

"And nobody knows where he went?"

Pike shook his head. "Not that I ever heard."

"Is it possible Tommy joined the army and was killed in World War II? It was about that time, wasn't it?"

He shrugged. "Could be. I don't know. I only know what my mother told me. I was pretty small when all this happened. But my mother always said that when Blossom's father died, it was the beginning of the end for this place. Blossom didn't know enough about the business to keep the operation going. Over my lifetime, I've watched what was once a huge property get sold off in bits and pieces. The saw mill closed and the company collapsed. This old house is about all that's left."

Before I had a chance to digest this statement, the kitchen door opened and Jared stepped onto the porch, hollering, "*Kate!* Gary's here with his truck. We're leaving to take a load to the dump, and the guys are here to work on the plumbing."

"That's my brother," I said apologetically. "I guess I'd better go in."

The old man chuckled. "And I better get this dog home. It was nice meetin' you."

"Can I give you a ride to your house, Mr. Pike? It'll only take me a minute to run in and get my car keys."

"Call me Harold. *Naw*, sounds like you're busy. We'll walk back. Been walkin' it my whole life." He gave a little tug on the leash as he turned to go, then added, "Come on down and visit sometime. You can throw tennis balls for Freddy. He'll be your best friend for life." He put his hand up in a stiff little wave.

I laughed and waved back. Guess he wasn't as crotchety as he looked.

For a moment, I stood gazing after the old man as he disappeared back the way he had come through the broken fence. There must be a well-worn path that way. One day, I would have to go exploring. If the woods were crisscrossed with good hiking trails, I ought to install a gate for easy access when I repaired the fence. There was nothing like a tranquil walk in the forest to clear the cobwebs after a chaotic day. I chuckled to myself. Probably should find out who owned the property before I got too carried away.

My mind drifted back to Blossom Thatcher. It was a shame Mr. Pike hadn't been able to shed more light on what had happened to her, or the fate of her mysterious fiancé. But at least now I had a name: Tommy O'Connell. Maybe I could look him up. *Everything* was on the internet now, wasn't it?

As I prepared to go back to the house, a chill wind swept over me and the sky grew curiously dark as though a brooding cloud had covered the sun. I turned, and a lump like cold lead thudded in my stomach as I stared toward the hillock where the old apple tree grew. Standing there was the same darked haired young woman I'd seen in the attic.

Blossom Thatcher. I knew her immediately. Slowly she glided across the grass in my direction, her white gown trailing along the ground behind her. I held my breath, unable to move.

Chapter Thirteen

"*Mind the apple blossoms . . .*" The words echoed inside my head, perceived intangibly, like thought.

She drifted past me and faded away. I was left staring at nothing. My knees felt weak. With a gasp, I remembered to breathe. No sign remained of the ghost, but the oppressive atmosphere lingered. The air itself felt heavy. Even the birds were subdued.

As I gathered my wits, the sun gradually re-emerged and the day regained its warmth. One by one, the birds resumed chirping among the trees.

Why had Blossom appeared to me? What did she want? What had she meant? Mind the apple blossoms? *What* apple blossoms? Did she mean the old tree here in the yard?

The kitchen door opened and a man stepped out onto the porch. "Ms. Ecklund? Do you have a minute?"

I jumped, then realized it was the contractor. I inhaled deeply a couple of times and waited for my heart to quit pounding, then went inside. The rest of the morning was spent conferring with the builder and plumber. They agreed to scope out the basement for the purpose of installing a bathroom. After that I made phone calls. I set up an appointment for an estimate on a new roof, found an inspector to look at the chimneys, and called a couple of places to get bids to replace all the windows. I was dying to do an internet search for Tommy O'Connell but wanted to wait till I had more time.

Not long after noon, Jared returned and Gary left. The workmen were occupied on various projects around the house so my brother joined me at the card table in the dining room where I made sandwiches.

"By the way," I remarked, "I've seen Blossom's ghost again—*twice.*" I girded myself for the ribbing I knew I was going to get.

"*What?* Kate . . ." He buried his face in his hands and began vigorously massaging his temples as though trying to rub out a colossal headache. "There's no such thing—"

"I'm not kidding," I said, cutting him off. "I saw her yesterday upstairs when I was showing Dillon around, and then again this morning in the back yard. You saw me. I was talking to Harold Pike. He's another neighbor who lives down the road. Blossom came floating right past me toward the house. It was broad daylight and I wasn't sleeping."

"Did *they* see her too?"

I squared my shoulders, preparing to stand my ground. "No, but I am *not* making it up. For some reason, she only appears to me."

Jared pulled his mouth sideways in a dubious frown. Finally, he puffed up his cheeks and blew them out again. Cracking a grin, he threw his hands in the air. "Fine. I give up. Have it your way. The house is haunted. It'll look great in the brochure." He took a huge bite of his sandwich, chortling to himself as he chewed.

"She said the same thing both times," I went on, ignoring his cynical retort. "*Mind the apple blossoms.*' I'm sure she must be trying to tell me something. I just can't figure out what. The only apple blossoms I'm aware of are on that old tree in the back yard. There must be something significant about it."

Jared bobbed his head noncommittally. I knew he was humoring me. I could hardly blame him. It sounded ludicrous.

"Well," he said at last, "if you're smart you'll keep this to yourself." He motioned with his head toward the staircase where we could hear the contractor barking instructions to the men on the second floor. "There's a good chance you'll lose your crew if they find out they're working in a haunted house." He let go a hearty laugh. Apparently, the idea struck him as hilarious.

I rose and took my sandwich through the kitchen and out the back door, gazing thoughtfully across the yard to where the withered old apple tree stood. Despite the ghost's obsession with apple blossoms, I knew the tree would have to be cut down. It was essentially dead and an eyesore. I couldn't risk any children injuring themselves climbing on it, or a branch breaking and falling on a guest. In its place I would plant a new, young apple tree in Blossom's honor.

Jared joined me, stretching his back and shoulder muscles. "It's barely April but it feels like June, doesn't it? I wonder how long it'll last?"

"Not long," I said. "The weather report says it's supposed to start clouding up tonight."

He looked around the yard. "Maybe you should look into buying a lawn mower. The way this grass is growing, if it's not cut pretty soon it's going to take a scythe to get through it."

I pointed my chin in the direction of the weathered old garage sitting by itself at the end of the gravel drive. "Check in there. I think I saw an old blade mower when I first looked at the place."

He started to make a rude comment about old lawn mowers, but we were interrupted unexpectedly by the sound of tires coming up the driveway. We turned to see a gray van pull up alongside the house. A short, thickset man dressed in jeans and a garish plaid coat jumped out and approached us with a wide, friendly grin. He was built like a small refrigerator, with a high domed forehead and a neatly trimmed beard.

"*Halloo,*" he called. "You the owners? I'm Slade Borello, your local picker." He strode up to Jared and vigorously shook his hand. "I deal in the old and collectible. I heard around town that you just bought yourself this venerable old piece of history chock full of odds and ends left by the previous owner. Wondered if you might consider selling anything? Here's my card."

Jared took the card and glanced at it briefly before handing it to me. It said: "*Slade Borello, dealer in antiquities and collectibles, your junk may be someone else's treasure.*"

We introduced ourselves and Borello continued, his grin never slacking. "If you've got a few minutes, I wonder if I might take a quick look around. You never know what sorts of treasures lurk in the closets and attics of these old houses. I'm sure I can make you some good deals." As he spoke, he sidled up to the back door. "What d'you say? Quick peek? I've got *cash.*"

Amused, Jared said, "Well, I've got it on good authority that there's an old lawn mower in that garage over there. How much will you give me for it?"

Borello let loose a belly laugh. "Power tools aren't my usual shtick, but I'll consider anything if it gets me in the front door."

I thought about all the random objects I'd discovered in the house, not to mention the stuff stored in the basement and on the third floor. Most had struck me as castoffs, discarded items that were worn out or broken. Jared had once joked about having a garage sale to dispose of the clutter. But I knew there were also many genuine antiques mixed in with the junk. Until I had an opportunity to look everything over carefully, I wasn't ready to just start giving things away.

I regarded the man. His round, cheerful face seemed earnest. I relented. What was the harm in letting him look? He was just trying to make a living like everyone else. There were undoubtedly one or two items in the house I could let loose of.

"Okay," I said. "I'll take you inside and you can look around a bit, but I have to warn you, I'm not sure I'm ready to sell anything. We'll have to see."

"Fair enough," he said happily, then turned and pushed open the kitchen door.

As we went inside, Jared leaned toward me and whispered in my ear, "Don't take your eyes off him."

The antiques dealer didn't waste any time. He went around oohing and ahhing at all the dust-clad objects amassed in the old mansion, picking his way through areas where the carpenters were working, stepping over tools and around stacks of lumber, ignoring the hammering and sawdust, as well as several irritated glances. He searched through desk drawers and end tables, opened cupboards, inspected shelves, and peered into closets. He examined with interest a cracked porcelain vase, a ceramic beer stein, an oaken chest, and a brass umbrella stand.

In a room upstairs, we came across a hideous, moth-eaten taxidermied bear. Repulsed, I turned to Borello. "Here, you can have this for nothing. You'll save us having to haul it to the dump."

He eyed the poor beast up and down then broke into laughter. "Sold. Might be worth a hundred bucks to some local hunter to put in his man cave. But I don't think it'll fit in my van so I'll have to come back and get it later."

Jared followed as we continued from room to room, his expression a mixture of curiosity, amusement, and wariness. "Is there anything in particular you're looking for?"

"Oh, no, nothing in particular," Borello said, wiping his brow with a handkerchief pulled from his pocket. "I'm always on the lookout for unusual, one of a kind pieces. You'd be amazed at what people collect. Ahh, like this antique humidor. Looks like Spanish cedar and carved jade. Very nice. I'll give you fifty dollars for it."

It seemed like a fair price to me, especially since I didn't know anyone who smoked cigars. I glanced at Jared who merely shrugged.

We shook hands and Borello gave me the cash.

Just then, someone knocked at the front door. I ran to open it and was pleased to find Dillon Thatcher smiling back at me.

"Hi," he said, his crooked grin as captivating as ever. "I just happened to be in the neighborhood and thought I'd stop by. Do you have plans for dinner?"

"Just happened to be in the neighborhood, eh?" I smiled at his flimsy ruse and invited him in, then looked at my watch. "I didn't realize it was so late."

Behind us, heavy footsteps came down the main staircase and we were joined by Jared and Slade Borello.

"Thanks for your time, Ms. Ecklund," Borello said. "I'll just take this humidor and get out of your hair. I appreciate your letting me look around. Maybe I'll come by again another time when you're not so busy."

"Who's this?" Dillon asked suspiciously.

I made introductions. "Dillon Thatcher, I'd like you to meet Slade Borello. He's an antiques dealer. He was just looking over some of the old things left in the house."

Dillon's smile vanished. "You're selling Aunt Blossom's things? You know they have sentimental value to me and my family. To him, they're nothing but commodities to be bought and sold to strangers."

"He only bought an old humidor," I said. "It's a box for holding cigars, not a valuable keepsake. I told you I'd save anything personal I found."

Borello took a step forward and extended his hand to Dillon. "Do I understand you're a relative of the previous owner?"

Dillon grudgingly shook his hand. "Her brother was my grandfather."

"I see," Borello said. "Nice to meet you. Didn't mean to step on your toes. I'm not interested in your family heirlooms, just the odd collectible, like this old humidor. It's a nice piece. I'm sure someone will buy it who really appreciates its unique value."

"Is your store nearby?" I asked, hoping to deflect tensions.

"Nope," Borello said with a chuckle. "It's down in Monroe, but I also have a lot of things stored in my garage at home and do a good portion of business online. My inventory comes from estate sales, garage sales, and word of mouth."

I escorted him through the kitchen to the back porch and waved as he drove off in the gray van. That's when I noticed Wendy watching from her yard wearing a straw hat and cotton gloves, presumably working in her garden. I decided to take a moment to talk to her now and save her the trouble of inventing an excuse to come over later.

"Hi," I called, giving her a little wave.

"Who was that?" she asked as I approached the fence.

"Slade Borello. Says he's an antiques dealer." I fished the business card out of my pocket and handed it to her. "He has a store in Monroe but mostly sells stuff online. Said he heard we were renovating this place and came to see if we'd sell him anything. Do you know him?"

She studied the card then shook her head and gave it back.

"Well, I'd better get back. Dillon Thatcher is inside with my brother. That's like leaving the fox alone with the hound."

She grinned, showing teeth like a Cheshire cat.

When I went back inside, the builders and plumbers were gathering up their things and preparing to leave for the night. My first impulse was to find Dillon and apologize for selling one of his great-aunt's possessions. The humidor must have belonged to Blossom's father.

Then I stopped. I had no reason to apologize. The house and its contents were mine to do with as I saw fit. These latent feelings of guilt had to be remnants of my years kowtowing to Daniel. Angrily, I shook them off. I would not be reprimanded. Dillon Thatcher and his family had had ample opportunity to come to Salmon Falls and visit Blossom while she lived.

In fact, I mused, if Dillon was so sentimental, why had he not asked about the photographs we had found among her things on the third floor? Those pictures were certainly more precious than some stupid old cigar box.

I found Jared and Dillon in the music salon examining something Dillon held in his hands. I was surprised and pleased that they seemed to be getting along.

"What have you got there?" I asked curiously.

Dillon looked up. "I was thinking about how Blossom must have loved this piano and how much time she must have spent playing it, so I decided to take a closer look."

"We found this in the piano bench among the sheet music," Jared said.

Dillon placed a framed five-by-seven-inch photograph in my hands. It wasn't a studio print, but a black and white snapshot blown up to resemble a portrait. The face was that of a handsome young man with dark hair slicked back under a jaunty hat. The tilt of his head and bold smile suggested an air of urbane self-confidence.

"Tommy," I breathed. "It has to be."

"Who?" Jared and Dillon asked simultaneously.

"Tommy O'Connell. Blossom's lost love. They were supposed to be married, but, for some reason, he disappeared. No one seems to know what happened to him."

Just to be sure, I removed the picture from the frame and turned it over. Handwritten on the back were the words, *"Love always, Tommy. 1941."*

Somewhere in the distance, I heard the sound of soft weeping. Looking around, I saw nothing and the men seemed oblivious. I remained silent, but I knew it was Blossom and my heart ached for her.

Chapter Fourteen

Dinner that night was casual. Jared tactfully declined Dillon's invitation to join us, saying that he'd rather stay in, eat leftovers, and practice his guitar. So Dillon and I went into town, choosing to sample the local fare. The options were limited, but ultimately we settled on an unobtrusive Thai restaurant which, while not fancy, turned out to be surprisingly good.

Salmon Falls was a town about five blocks long, an eclectic mix of old and new. The clean, modern lines of the grade school and public library attested to the town's dedication to its children, while the imposing brick buildings containing the post office, bank, and city hall were clearly evidence of an earlier era.

It was past ten by the time Dillon brought me home. I noted with some amusement that the porch light had been repaired in my absence and now shone brightly beside the door. Several of the old floorboards squeaked and flexed as Dillon walked me up onto the veranda.

The night was cold, the moon obscured by dark clouds; a chill wind rustled the tree tops and whirled around the eaves. "Feels like a storm," I observed with a shiver.

"Too bad you don't have a porch swing," he said in a low voice. "There's nothing like a porch swing during a storm."

Then he leaned in and kissed me softly on the lips. It startled me. I hadn't been kissed by anyone but Daniel in the last ten years. The nearness and warmth of his body were unsettling, the spicy scent of his cologne intoxicating. I wondered if he could hear my heart beating. Terrified and exhilarated at the same time, my flummoxed brain couldn't think what to say.

"Good night," he whispered. "See you soon." He kissed me again, then turned and trotted to his car. Raindrops began to fall as he waved through the window and slowly backed the Bronco down the driveway.

I remained on the porch for a moment, leaning against the door while I regained my composure. With a short self-deprecating laugh I realized that I hadn't dated in so long I'd forgotten how. I smiled as a wicked thought popped into my head—*if only Daniel could see me now*. What sweet revenge that would be.

Later, as I lay curled up in my sleeping bag, I listened to the rain beat down in torrents while the wind wailed outside my window like an enraged banshee. I thought of the two towering maple trees in the front yard and fervently prayed that their roots were well fastened to the ground. At intervals, lightning flashed, illuminating the room in shocking brilliance. These were followed by ear-shattering booms of thunder that shook the house.

I slept fitfully through the night, as each new clap of thunder and howling gust jarred me awake. Woefully, I wondered how much of the aging roof would be left by morning. I had arranged next week for a couple of estimates to replace it, but wished now I'd acted sooner.

In the morning, I stumbled down the hall into the bathroom and discovered that the power was out. Nothing worked and the house was freezing. I washed my face with cold water then dressed in jeans and my warmest sweater. Gray light filtered in through the window and soft pattering outside told me it was still raining.

Why, oh, why hadn't I gotten around to having the chimneys cleaned? Power outages were an aspect of country living I hadn't anticipated. Was this going to happen every time we had a storm?

Jared came into the kitchen a moment later, his sleeping bag wrapped around his shoulders. "Wow, that was a hell of a storm last night, wasn't it? Get the coffee on, I'm freezing."

I gave him a patient look. "Jared, the coffee maker's electric, remember? No power, no coffee."

His face fell.

"Look," I said, "the minute the new kitchen appliances are installed, I promise I will make you eggs and pancakes. But, in the meantime, how does a peanut butter sandwich sound?"

He made a face. Then his eyes roved to the brick hearth set in the wall.

"Let's make a little fire," he said. "What's the worst that could happen?"

I frowned and rolled my eyes. "Well, let's see. The kitchen could fill with black smoke and soot, and ruin all the work that's been done—or, better yet, it could start a chimney fire and burn the whole place down. You want to risk it?"

"No," he grumbled, "but may I suggest a generator as your next major purchase?"

I only half heard. I was looking past him to the back door which stood open about four inches. I blew hard in exasperation. "You know, it would stay a lot warmer in here if you'd remember to shut the door at night."

He looked wounded. "I did. I'm sure I did." He strode to the door and pushed it shut. It hit the frame and bounced back. Puzzled, he hunched down to examine the lock. "It's been jimmied. The latch is broken."

A shiver ran up my spine and goose bumps prickled the hairs on my arms. "Someone must have broken in during the night. I heard noises, but I just thought it was the old house creaking in the storm." I glanced around, fearful someone might be lurking in a corner. "Do you think they're still in the house?"

"*Naw*, I'm sure they're long gone by now." Jared stood up, rubbing his chin thoughtfully. "Maybe it was your ghost."

"Ghosts don't need to jimmy locks," I retorted in a huff. From the window, I could see over the fence to the Hilliards' house. Their lights were off too. "I should probably get a battery-powered radio to keep on hand for emergencies."

"At least your phone should work," Jared said.

I chewed my lower lip. "Yeah, depending on how much charge it got before the power went out."

At that moment, a deep rumbling rose from the basement as the oil furnace kicked on.

"Ah-ha!" Jared said, his eyebrows shooting up. "We have power. Disaster averted." He flipped the switch on the wall. The kitchen blazed with light. He scanned the room. "Now, about that jimmied lock . . ."

"But what would a burglar want here?" I asked, looking about. "There's nothing in the house but dusty old furniture and a lot of junk."

"And some expensive power tools," Jared said, glancing around the kitchen at the various drills and saws left lying about by the workers.

"And some valuable antiques," I blurted. "*Darn!* I should have made an inventory."

Jared wasn't listening. He knelt at the base of the back staircase. "Kate, come look at this. There's fresh mud on the steps."

A cold knot tightened around my insides. "Do you think he went up there?"

"Looks like it."

I stared over Jared's shoulder at the tell-tale evidence, suppressing a shudder at the thought of a burglar prowling around the house during the night while we slept. "But the second floor is just empty bedrooms in the middle of renovation, and the third floor is mostly stuff to go to the dump."

He nodded. "A good place to search if you were looking for something."

"Looking for what? You think Blossom stashed money under the floor boards?"

"Old people have been known to do that."

I peered up the narrow stairwell. Even with the light on, it seemed dim and foreboding.

Jared got to his feet and began to ascend the stairs.

"Wait," I called after him. "Shouldn't we call the police first?"

"Go ahead—I just want to take a look."

Jared and his infuriating bravado. I took a few steps up and hesitated. He had reached the second floor. A few more steps and Jared would disappear from view.

I waited, listening, wondering if I should run and fetch my phone. No sounds of a scuffle, no shouts of surprise. "Jared?" I called, poised to make a dash for it.

A moment passed. "*Jared!*" I called louder. "Is everything okay?"

"Yeah, come on up." He stuck his head around the door at the top of the steps. "What are you waiting for?"

I clenched my teeth. Sometimes I could just throttle him.

The few times I'd been to the top floor I hadn't seen anything of value—just an accumulation of damaged or worn out personal items. I particularly remembered a mounted moose head, a decaying dollhouse, and an old sewing machine. There were also numerous cardboard boxes thickly covered with dust and cobwebs. Inspection of the contents had revealed nothing more than mothballed clothing, discarded household gadgets, and mouse-chewed magazines.

But now as I stepped through the door, I gasped in shock. The place had been ransacked, every box opened, the contents dumped out and strewn around. Pillows and rugs had been heaved aside, things knocked over and broken apart. Even the upholstery on an old chair had been slashed, the stuffing pulled out and flung carelessly about. Had all this taken place last night? I had heard nothing over the crashing of the storm.

"Don't touch anything," Jared said. "It's time to call the cops."

Fifteen minutes later, a uniformed police officer arrived. His expression remained stolid as I detailed our discovery of an intruder in the house. He made a cursory inspection of the broken lock, the mud on the stairs, and the ransacked upper floor, poking around and taking notes.

"Any idea what they were looking for?" he asked.

I shook my head. "Not a clue."

"What about that junk dealer?" Jared suggested.

"Mr. Borello?" I crooked my lips sideways as I considered. "I doubt it. He seemed harmless to me. Besides, he didn't really look built for stealth, did he?"

Jared just shrugged.

The policeman arched an eyebrow curiously.

"A picker," I explained. "An antiques dealer, Slade Borello. Said he had a shop in Monroe."

He jotted a note in his book.

Suddenly, I remembered something. "Wait—last Sunday as I was leaving, there was a man standing on the shoulder of the road in front of the house taking pictures."

Jared pivoted, drilling me with an accusing look. "Why didn't you mention this sooner?"

"I forgot about it till just now," I snapped back. "I've been kind of busy lately."

The officer asked, "Can you describe him?"

"Uh . . ." I gnawed my lower lip as I tried to recall the stranger. "He was tall, good looking, brown hair . . . oh, and he drove a yellow VW bug."

"Did you get the license number?"

I shook my head, chagrined at my lack of foresight. But I hadn't suspected the man of anything at the time.

"Did you actually see him taking pictures of your house?"

"Not exactly," I said. "But he was standing there holding a cell phone."

"Did he do anything threatening or malicious?" the officer continued. "Do you have any reason to believe he was engaged in criminal activity?"

"No," I said, picking nervously at a fingernail. "I thought he was just interested in photographing the house. Its history and architecture do make it something of an attraction."

"That's probably all it was," he said, making a final notation. "Okay, I'll file a report. Chances are the culprits were local teenagers. In the meantime, you might want to think about installing deadbolts on all your doors."

I got the distinct impression that this investigation would not figure highly on the department's list of priorities. Well, what had I expected? Since nothing appeared to be stolen and nobody was hurt, there wasn't much the police could do. I thanked him and he left. Now I would have to add a new lock for the back door to my list of things to buy.

Suddenly, I heard my cell phone ring. I ran back to my room where I'd left my phone on the charger. It could be my mother or Amy. No such luck. It was Daniel.

"Just checking to see if you survived the storm," he said.

I assumed he was attempting to be sarcastic. "Sorry to disappoint you, but everything's fine." I certainly was not going to tell him about the break-in and give him fuel for further disparaging remarks.

"That's good. Wouldn't want the boogeyman to get you during the night."

What a curious thing to say. I hung up and went back to the kitchen to find Jared and relate the conversation.

"You don't suppose . . . ?" I said, glancing toward the staircase.

"What? That your ex-husband snuck out here in the middle of the night during the worst storm of the season, jimmied the back door, and ransacked the attic?" His mouth gave a wry twist. "Sounds pretty far-fetched, don't you think?"

"Okay, but what about that guy I saw out in front of the house? Daniel could have hired him to break in and trash the place hoping to scare me." My hands clenched. "I wouldn't put it past him."

Jared shrugged. "Well, he didn't succeed, right? And no real damage was done. There's nothing upstairs but useless junk. The sooner we haul it off to the dump, the better."

"What if he was some sort of private eye?" I persisted, a frightening new thought emerging. "That's why he was taking pictures. Maybe Daniel sent him to get evidence to build a custody case against me. He hates this place. He doesn't think it's safe for Amy to live here."

I began to pace.

"Kate, *stop*." Jared gripped my shoulders and looked me full in the face. "You're starting to sound paranoid. Let it go. The guy taking pictures was probably just some innocent dude out bird watching or something." His voice softened. "You know there's no way Daniel's going to take

Amy away from you. He knows what a wonderful mother you are."

I let out an audible sigh. "Thank you. You're probably right. This whole thing has just got me freaked out."

Then Jared frowned. He rubbed his chin slowly and said, "There's one other possibility I don't think you've considered."

I looked up sharply. "What's that?"

"Your neighbors. Maybe someone doesn't like the idea of a bed-and-breakfast in their back yard."

For a moment, I just stared at him. "But it'll be good for the town's economy," I protested finally. "Bring in tourists and their money. The local realtor thought it was a great idea. Wendy didn't seem bothered by it. Neither did Mr. Pike."

"I don't know," Jared said with a shrug. "Just sayin'. But hey, you can't drive yourself crazy over stuff you can't control. You don't see *me* worrying, do you? Meanwhile, let me see if I can jury-rig this lock till we get it replaced."

He left the room and returned moments later with a screwdriver and some duct tape.

As Jared squatted by the back door, I suddenly noticed a shadow looming in the window. I gasped as the door was thrust open. Jared fell back on his rear.

"*Yoo hoo . . .*" The piercing voice was followed by a familiar shaggy head peering around the door frame. "Jared? What are you doing on the floor?"

"Sit-ups."

Wendy gave him a huge grin and pushed on inside, as usual not waiting for an invitation. She set her dripping umbrella by the door. Over her left arm she carried her wicker basket. Whenever she got the urge to visit she brought us something fresh-baked from her kitchen. Her hunger for gossip seemed limitless.

"I saw the police car," she blurted out. "Is everything all right?"

"Someone broke the lock on the back door during the night," I said. "Looks like we may have had company."

Wendy pressed her right hand to her ample bosom and gasped loudly. "Burglars?"

"Maybe," Jared said, "or vandals."

"The top floor was tossed," I said. "But it doesn't look like anything was taken."

"What is this world coming to?" Wendy exclaimed with dramatic vigor. Her tangle of short dark curls jiggled in cadence with the bobbing of her head.

Jared ignored the remark but fastened his eyes hungrily on the wicker basket. "What did you bring us this morning?"

Wendy proudly extended the basket. "I made raspberry turnovers. I had the best crop of raspberries last summer. Here, they're still warm. Good thing the power came back on when it did."

Stuffing a turnover into his mouth, Jared looked at me and mumbled, "You should get Wendy to teach you how to bake."

I scowled at my brother. "As soon as the house is finished and we start running the bed-and-breakfast, you'll see how well I can bake."

"Oh, by the way," Wendy said, "Rick wanted me to ask if you'd like to borrow his chainsaw."

Jared glanced at me. I shrugged.

"Okay," he said, "I'll bite. Why would I want to borrow your husband's chainsaw?"

"Well, for the tree of course. You're not going to just leave it lying there in the yard, are you?"

"Tree?" I asked. *Uh-oh, this doesn't sound good.*

"Haven't you been outside? That little wind storm we had last night blew it right over. It was virtually dead so I'm not surprised . . ."

Jared and I nearly knocked each other down in our haste to get outside. Thankfully, the rain had subsided. Sure enough, the apple tree on the knoll had toppled over, limbs shattering and roots pulled from the earth in a tangled mass of mud, like the head of Medusa.

Chapter Fifteen

I stared into the gaping hole left by the root ball, not certain what I expected to see. My mind provided a number of outlandish possibilities. A forgotten cache of money? The bleached bones of the long vanished Tommy O'Connell? All I could make out was mud.

Jared was more pragmatic. As he walked around the fallen trunk, he said, "Well, if we ever get the chimneys cleaned, at least now we'll have something to burn."

Wendy came up behind us, clucking her tongue. "I'm glad it waited to fall down until after Blossom died."

"Yes," I said sadly. "I'm sure she loved this old tree. It would have broken her heart."

"Well, I don't know about *that*. I was thinking of the mess. She probably would have expected Rick to come over and cut and stack it for her."

I didn't know how to respond to this. It struck me as heartless somehow.

Jared had also heard. He caught my attention with a wry look and a roll of his eyes.

"Of course, I'm sure it was a marvelous tree at one time," Wendy continued. "Old as it was, it was still producing a fair number of cherries."

I blinked. "You mean *apples*."

She gave me a curious look. "No, I mean *cherries*."

"But . . . but . . . I thought it was an apple tree."

She shook her head. "Nope. Trust me, it's a cherry tree."

Jared suddenly burst out laughing. He laughed so hard, he tottered backwards and sat down hard in the soggy grass, gasping for air.

I stared stupidly from Wendy to the tree and back. This didn't make sense. It *had* to be an apple tree!

Confused, Wendy eyed us both suspiciously as if we'd slipped some joke past her.

"What's so funny?" she demanded.

I wasn't about to tell her the truth, so I merely scowled at my brother and said, "We had a bet on what kind of tree it was, that's all. Now I'll never hear the end of it."

"Oh," she said, grinning broadly. "Why didn't you just ask me?"

I was trying to think of a snappy comeback when the Labrador retriever I recognized as Freddy appeared out of nowhere, prancing about happily with a stick dangling from his mouth. He galloped up to me and leaned against my leg, begging to be petted. I looked around and sure enough, Harold Pike, the elderly neighbor, wearing the same shapeless wool coat, came clambering through the broken section of fence, muttering irritably.

"Sorry, ma'am," he growled. "We were out for our morning walk in the woods when that stupid dog heard all the activity and just had to come check it out for hisself. We're not used to hearing voices up here."

"It's all right, Mr. Pike. I don't mind. He's a nice dog. And please, call me Kate." Freddy immediately went to sidle up to his master and was rewarded with a rough caress.

Pike flashed his bulldog grin, exposing yellowed, uneven teeth. "I'll do that if you call me Harold." He aimed a cordial nod at Wendy so I assumed they were acquainted.

Motioning Jared to come over, I said, "Harold, I'd like you to meet my brother, Jared Thorson. Jared, this is Harold Pike. He lives just down the road. And that's his dog, Freddy."

"Nice to meet you," Jared said, shaking the old man's hand.

"Likewise," Pike said. He ambled over for a closer look at the uprooted tree. "So this ol' thing finally came down, did it? Not surprised. It's been looking pretty sad lately."

"Kate thought it was an apple tree," Wendy interjected with a delighted little chuckle, happy to pass on the joke at my expense.

The old man gave me a sideways glance, shaking his head. "Nope. Cherry. Jed Hawkins planted it a long time ago."

"Who's Jed Hawkins?" I asked.

"He used to be foreman at the mill years ago. He helped Blossom run it after her father died, but my mother always said he was more lumberjack than salesman; he knew timber not dollars. He just didn't have the business sense to keep the operation going. I was about fourteen when he passed away, but I remember him. He was a mountain of a man."

"So Blossom didn't plant it," I said, more to myself than the others. Another notion shot down. I'd fostered images of a fair young Blossom lovingly planting this tree with her own hands, an apple tree in memory of her lost love. But if that wasn't the case, what was the obsession with apple blossoms?

"Nope," Pike said. "As I recall, Jed planted a couple of cherry trees out here, plus a small vegetable garden. I think he even had a few rabbits and some chickens. There used to be an apple orchard over thataway on the other side of those trees there, but it's long gone. There's a couple of houses on that property now."

I stared in the direction he pointed and was able to make out the backs of two houses on a low hill a hundred yards beyond the fence through a screen of trees.

Jared was ignoring this byplay. He'd found a broken branch, and was poking at the root ball with it. Freddy cavorted around him hoping the stick would be thrown.

"Whatcha lookin' for?" the old man inquired, angling for a better view.

"Oh, I don't know," Jared said, aiming a sly grin in my direction. "Buried treasure maybe, or a body . . ."

It was scary how we thought alike.

Wendy hurried over to look.

I let out a deep sigh. "Wendy, he was joking."

"Oh, I know," she said sheepishly, but continued to watch as Jared pried chunks of sticky mud away from the roots.

Exasperated, I finally said to Jared, "Are you about done playing in the mud?"

Reluctantly, he nodded and tossed the branch away. "Yeah, let's get this thing cut up and stacked out of the way." He laughed as the retriever dashed after the stick and brought it back.

Harold muttered, "Yeah, I should be goin' too. Nice to see you again, Kate. You too, Wendy. Nice to meet you, Jared." He fastened a leash to Freddy's collar, then gave us a wave and started down the driveway toward the road, pulling the dog with him.

* * *

Wendy's husband Rick was only too happy to loan us his chainsaw, though he didn't offer to stay and help, saying he had to leave shortly for the office. I had never asked Wendy what her husband did for a living, but, somehow, he struck me as the stereotypical banker or accountant. Round and flabby, he didn't look particularly suited to physical labor. Frankly, I was surprised he even owned a chainsaw.

It took about an hour for Jared to cut up the remains of the cherry tree while I stacked the pieces inside the old garage. To my surprise, Wendy hung around and even helped me carry a few of the heavier chunks of wood. I thought at first I might have misjudged her, but then I realized her insatiable thirst for gossip hadn't yet been satisfied. There was still the matter of our burglary.

When he had finished with the chainsaw, Jared returned it to the neighbor's garage, then joined Wendy and me in the kitchen. He gulped down an entire bottle of water, then trudged once more up the narrow back staircase. Wendy and I followed.

"I'm going to haul all this junk down to the dumpster," he said. "The sooner we get rid of it, the sooner we eliminate any reason for burglars to come back."

"Or maybe you'll find what they were looking for," Wendy said eagerly, puffing as she climbed the stairs.

Personally, I thought it unlikely that Blossom had kept her valuables hidden among her castoffs in the attic. But I was happy to have the clutter cleared out, so I didn't argue.

"What did the policeman say?" Wendy asked. "Did he find any clues? Did he have any idea who it might have been?"

"He just assumed it was teenagers," I said. "He told us to get deadbolts for the locks."

Wendy digested this but made no reply. When we emerged finally on the top floor, she spun around in awe, forgetting the burglary as she sized up the cavernous attic story. "I've never been up here," she exclaimed. "It's huge! I never realized there was so much room." She ran to the front and peered out the turret windows. "Wow! You can see clear to the lake from up here."

"Wendy," I said. "You knew Blossom for quite a while. You don't really think she hid anything valuable up here, do you?"

Wendy turned and fixed me with wide eyes. "You mean like in a secret compartment behind the wall?"

I laughed. "You've been watching too many spy movies. I was thinking more like in a shoe box or something."

She shook her head. "I doubt it. From everything I've heard, she was flat broke when she died."

"That's what I thought." I looked around again at the scattered junk. "I can't imagine there's anything up here worth stealing, other than maybe a few antiques. But I don't see anyone sneaking out of here with a sewing machine or a rocking horse under their coat."

So why would someone break in? Just to vandalize the place? Was it simply teenagers as the police surmised, regardless of the rumors in town that the house is haunted? Or was it something more sinister? Was there indeed something valuable hidden in the attic?

I suppressed a shudder. Obviously, I'd been reading too many gothic mysteries. A wry smile tugged at the corner of my lips. My imagination was working overtime again. If I didn't get a handle on it, I would soon have ghouls and vampires lurking around every corner.

Time for a reality check.

I glanced at my watch. It was nearly noon. Maybe I should go over to Mom's and see Amy. I could also do some work on my laptop. I had been keeping a spreadsheet of my expenditures so far, with notations of estimated expenses yet to come. The contractor and his crew were at another job site today so this seemed like a good opportunity to go catch up on my accounting. Daniel had always kept the books during our marriage, telling me "not to worry my pretty head" over such matters, but now I derived immense satisfaction in exercising control over my own money.

I said to Jared, "I think I'll go over to Mom's this afternoon. I want to see Amy before the weekend and do a little bookkeeping. Do you want to come? This stuff can wait."

Jared was filling a box with old magazines. He paused and looked at me. "I'd love to, but some of the guys are getting together at Gary's later to jam. I thought I'd go hang out there tonight."

"Are you sure? You haven't had a hot home-cooked meal in awhile."

"Maybe next time. I already told Gary I'd be there." He hefted the box to his shoulder and strode down the stairs.

Wendy was poking through some of the discarded clothing strewn on the floor. "You know, you ought to save some of these," she said. "They might actually be worth something if they were cleaned."

"You're right," I said. "I meant to tell Jared not to throw away the clothes. I'm sure we can sell them to a vintage clothing store. In fact," I paused, surveying the mess, "I really should go through all this stuff before we throw it away. I promised Dillon I'd keep an eye out for family pictures and heirlooms."

Wendy's eyebrows rose and a suggestive little smile played on her lips. "Sounds like you two are getting cozy."

"For heaven's sake, Wendy. He's Blossom's grand-nephew. He only came here because of his grandfather."

"Is he married?"

I gave her a disgusted look. "No, but that's irrel-evant." Even as I said it, I remembered Dillon's goodnight kiss and felt a warm flush creep up my neck. "He's just here searching for mementos to take back with him. That's it. Nothing else."

"Uh-huh," she said. The smile persisted on her face.

* * *

It was nearly one thirty by the time I got to my mother's house in Seattle. Between bites of grilled cheese, I recounted the progress we had made on our renovations, and how Jared was hard at work clearing out rubbish left behind by the previous owner. Then I launched into my plans for decorating the rooms behind the kitchen for Amy and me, including stripping the old wallpaper.

Mom grimaced. "Ugh. Sounds like a tedious job. You couldn't pay me enough to do that."

"I know, but it's got to get done. I'm going to rent a steamer and see how far I get. I can't put the new paper up till I get the old stuff off." I gave a woeful smile. "And after that, I've got the whole rest of the house to do. Blossom, the previous owner, must have really loved wallpaper. It's everywhere."

"In the old days," Mom said, "I think they would just paper over the old wallpaper rather than tear it down each time."

"Tell me about it. I did some scraping in one corner just to see what kind of job I was getting into. There must have been five layers."

"You couldn't just put your new paper over the old?"

"No." I shook my head. "Most of the old paper is cracked and peeling. It really needs to be removed."

At three o'clock I left to pick Amy up at school. When she saw me waiting, she came flying to greet me. I enveloped her in a bear hug that lifted her clear off her feet. The sweet smell of her hair filled my nostrils as I covered her face with kisses.

"Mmmm," I exclaimed. "I could just eat you up, I missed you so much."

She squealed in delight and returned my kisses, wrapping her arms around my neck. "I missed you too, Mommy!"

In the car, Amy talked nonstop about school, her teacher, and classmates. She seemed to enjoy it so much. I felt a twinge of remorse at having to switch her to another school next year, but I was certain she would adjust and eventually come to love Salmon Falls.

The conversation continued at my mom's. I told them both about meeting Dillon Thatcher, the previous owner's grandnephew from Ohio, but left off how good-looking he was and that I'd gone out with him. I wasn't sure how Amy would react, and I really did not want to deal with my mother's third degree. I merely said that Dillon was here at the behest of his late grandfather, and that he hoped to take back one or two keepsakes. Besides, Dillon was simply a passing flirtation, a pleasant diversion, and nothing more than that. As for the break-in and trashing of the third floor, I decided not to mention that either. No need for them to worry.

As the afternoon wore on, the sun shone brighter and Amy took me for a walk around the yard. The forsythia and camellia were blooming now, adding long-awaited color to the dreary Northwest springtime. Amy showed me where clusters of purple crocuses flourished in the flower beds, and where daffodils bloomed among crowds of blue hyacinths. Finger to lips, she led me on tiptoe to where she had discovered a bird's nest on the limb of her grandmother's pink flowering plum tree.

As I watched her, I remembered Daniel's reaction when I had told him I was pregnant. He had exploded. Children weren't part of his plan, not yet anyway. They were expensive and time consuming. He had wanted to establish his career first, ensconce himself in society, make his first million.

His father had pulled some strings and gotten Daniel hired into one of the most prestigious brokerage firms in Seattle. Then had come the Jaguar, followed by Italian suits, a diamond-studded Rolex, season tickets to the Symphony, and a brilliant stock portfolio. Before my eyes, the man I had met in college, the man with high ideals, the man I had loved and married, metamorphosed into something I abhorred: a cold-hearted, moneycentric executive bent on getting ahead at any cost. He had even had the gall to say he was doing it for me.

He had been a success all right, in everything but marriage. My thoughts and feelings had meant nothing to him, and he had often become angry when I ventured to assert an opinion. It had taken ten long years to finally admit to myself that I was nothing more than a showpiece, a stylish wife to hang on his arm and hostess the elaborate corporate parties he threw. I had mustered my courage, gotten an attorney, and walked out with half of a considerable fortune, exuberant at the prospect of being on my own.

Suddenly, an image of the stranger taking pictures intruded on my thoughts. Was it possible that Daniel was after custody of Amy? Had he hired a private investigator?

Considering my ex-husband's penchant for the high life, it seemed doubtful. Daniel liked to mix with the movers and shakers; he liked to stay out all night at their sumptuous parties, or jet off to exotic locales for weekend getaways. Caring for a young child would definitely put a crimp in such activities.

On the other hand, the divorce had caused him to lose face. He had been humiliated. He wasn't above payback. *But at Amy's expense?* I didn't want to believe he could be so callous. Despite everything, he wasn't uncaring. He loved Amy, and a drawn-out tug of war would only hurt her.

Amy tugged at my arm. "Mommy, look what I found." She extended her hand and showed me a small, pearly white pebble she had found in the garden. "It's a magic stone," she breathed.

I bent to examine it. "Yes, it is. You must keep it for a special occasion."

She put the pebble in her coat pocket and skipped happily away. How different my life would be without her, I thought. How empty.

Chapter Sixteen

May 1940

Blossom sat at the piano warming up with some easy chords and scales. It was a perfect spring morning, unseasonably warm for May; the chickadees and juncos flitted about outside the turret window chirping in syncopated harmony as she began a lively toccata. She should practice more, she thought meditatively. It wasn't like she was too busy.

Presently, she let her mind wander as she settled into the soft familiar notes of Beethoven's *Moonlight Sonata*. Her fingers moved fluidly over the keys as the melody slowly unfurled. Unbidden, thoughts of Tommy O'Connell drifted into her daydreams like wispy clouds in a blue sky, adding texture and interest to an otherwise plain existence.

She hardly knew him—no more, really, than she knew her own half-brother—but he excited her in a way no one ever had. He was good-looking, of course, and she warmed inwardly as she imagined his deep brown eyes gazing into hers, his strong arms pulling her close, but she knew it was more than simply physical attraction. He paid attention to her, teasing her one minute, making her laugh and engaging her in thoughtful conversation the next, treating her like he found her interesting and worth listening to.

He had moved into town, taking a room at the Salmon Falls Hotel, but continued to be a frequent visitor at the house, purportedly to meet with Clay. But, in her secret mind, Blossom liked to imagine that this was just an excuse to spend more time in her company. A happy smile played on her lips, even as she realized it was only a fantasy. He was older, worldly and experienced, certainly not the type of man to settle down to a quiet life in the country.

Behind her, a floorboard squeaked interrupting her thoughts. She turned to find the subject of her musings leaning against the doorway watching her. He was dressed casually for a day outdoors in denim trousers, plaid shirt, and leather boots. Blossom thought he looked more striking than ever. The usual fedora was replaced by a wide oilskin hat pushed back on his head allowing his wavy brown hair to fall carelessly over his brow. A red bandana hung loosely around his neck and his sheepskin jacket was slung over his shoulder.

Blossom instantly stopped playing and swiveled on the bench to face him, embarrassed that he might have read her thoughts. "I didn't hear you come in."

"Don't stop," Tommy urged. "It sounded great. You're very talented."

Blossom smiled and shrugged, masking her pleasure. "I used to get lessons from one of Seattle's foremost pianists until the day he told my father I ought to study at some east coast conservatory." She laughed. "That was the last time I saw him. I don't think my father was keen on his putting crazy notions into my head."

"You should be the one giving lessons," Tommy said.

She gave a short laugh. "Yes, it would give me a career to fall back on in case I ever find myself destitute."

His eyes twinkled as he grinned.

"Clay's upstairs," Blossom said, "but I expect he'll be down soon. Are you going hunting?"

Tommy shook his head. "No, but we *are* going exploring up in the hills. Clay's got his mind set on finding gold in some old mine around here. He's bringing the gear and I'm going along for the ride."

Blossom's brow creased in concern. What was her brother up to? She immediately thought of all the hazards of gold mining she had heard her father rage about over the years. She wondered if Clay had even consulted him.

Tommy must have sensed her thoughts because he hurried to set her mind at ease. "Don't worry, I doubt anything will come of this. At best, we'll get a lot of exercise and a healthy tan."

"And at worst?"

"We'll be eaten by a bear."

She gave him a scathing look and he laughed out loud.

"Is your father here?" Tommy asked.

"No, he left early for the saw mill. I think he'll be there most of the day."

Tommy's grin widened. "Perfect. I won't have to keep looking over my shoulder when I talk to you. Would you like to take a walk around the garden while we wait for Clay?"

"I'd love to, but Helen will be here any minute with her little boy. I promised to watch him for her while she goes to see the doctor. She thinks baby number two might be on the way."

"Then we can sit on the veranda while we wait for her." Tommy offered his arm, and Blossom placed her hand lightly in the crook of his elbow as he led her outside to the porch swing. He sat down beside her, then leaned back and casually laid his arm across the back of the seat. A mild breeze ruffled the leaves of the azaleas planted along the front of the veranda while a large robin hopped across the lawn in determined pursuit of a worm.

"It's a beautiful day, isn't it?" Blossom said as she smoothed the front of her skirt. She was very aware of his arm behind her shoulders. She didn't know what to say, she'd had so little practice at this sort of thing.

"Yes, very beautiful," Tommy agreed.

"I like to watch the birds as they flit around in the bushes," Blossom said self-consciously.

"I like to watch you."

"They're nesting now and feeding their young."

"I like the way your hair frames your face, accenting your eyes." He reached over and gently caressed a curl that hung loosely in front of her ear. "You have beautiful eyes."

Blossom stood suddenly and stepped toward the porch rail out of reach. "There's a robin's nest in the maple tree over there. You can just see it through the leaves." She spoke too quickly, her heart beating erratically in her chest. This was her daydream come true, but now she didn't know what to do. It scared her.

"Do I make you uncomfortable, Blossom?" He leaned forward, his hands resting on his knees.

"No . . . I mean . . . yes. Look, I know you probably know lots of women and this all comes naturally to you, but I'm not like that. I'm a country girl. I haven't had many beaus . . ."

Tommy reached out a hand, his expression earnest. "Blossom, I'm sorry."

"If you're looking for a date . . ." she said, "one of those women who . . . someone who likes . . . I'm sure Clay can help you." She was getting angry—at him, at her naïveté, at herself for being so awkward, at the situation for falling apart. He must think her terribly silly and foolish.

"Blossom, stop." He grabbed her hand and pulled her toward him. "That's not what I want. Believe it or not, this is new to me too. *You're* new to me. I hardly know what to make of you."

Blossom exhaled softly through parted lips, feeling flustered and confused. She sat back down on the porch swing, leaving a generous few inches between them.

"My father warned me about men like you," she said with a shy smile.

Tommy laughed. "I'll bet he did."

At that moment, Helen appeared on the lane approaching the house. She was walking and pushing a baby stroller. She and Albert didn't own a car; cars were expensive and they didn't need one since they could walk almost everywhere in town.

As she neared the veranda, Helen waved and called out, "Hi, Tommy, nice to see you again."

"Good morning," Tommy said, standing and touching the brim of his hat.

Blossom hurried down the steps and lifted little Harold out of the stroller. He cooed and grinned as she bounced him on her hip a couple of times. "My, he's getting big."

"Yes," Helen replied, "and he's walking now so you'll have to watch him like a hawk or he'll be into everything the instant you turn your back. I promise I'll be back just as soon as I can. Everything you'll need is in this bag." She hoisted a large diaper bag off her shoulder and set it on the porch steps. "You can give him a bottle if he starts to act fussy, then with luck he'll sleep until I get back."

"Don't worry," Blossom said. "We'll get along fine. Harold and I are best friends. It's a lovely day so we'll probably just sit out here in the grass and watch the birds.

Won't we, sweetheart?" She chucked the toddler under his chin causing him to chortle and wave his arms happily.

Helen gave her son a quick kiss, then turned and hurried down the driveway toward town. Blossom carried the baby up the veranda steps and sat down once more on the porch swing, placing little Harold in the middle between her and Tommy. The baby grinned and babbled at Tommy who looked down at him with an amused smile.

"So, you're Harold," said Tommy, addressing the one-year-old. "That's a pretty grown-up name for such a little guy. They ought to call you Harry."

To Blossom's astonishment, Tommy placed his hat on the baby's head, tilting it back so it wouldn't flop down and cover his face. Harold immediately reached up with both chubby hands and dragged the hat into his lap where he could more easily get his mouth on it, gnawing vigorously on the brim with his new baby teeth.

Blossom feared the hat might be ruined, but she knew that taking it abruptly away would result in a torrent of tears so she quickly removed her wristwatch and enticed the baby with a trade. Soon he was busily fingering the shiny watch, cooing happily as he played with the new toy while Tommy wiped his hat clean with his handkerchief and set it back on his own head.

Tommy smiled at Blossom as she stroked the baby's downy head. "You're very good with babies," he said. "You look very natural playing with him. You'll make a wonderful mother someday."

Blossom felt her cheeks flush. Was he teasing her? More likely this was his subtle way of saying that she'd make a wonderful mother someday married to *someone else*. He was trying to warn her not to make too much of his attentions. Of course, she chided herself, he was a gambler, a drifter, a lothario; the thought of him settling down and bouncing babies on his knee was absurd.

Abruptly, she stood and picked up the baby. "Let me go and see what's keeping Clay."

She turned and reached for the door, but at that moment Clay emerged, clenching something in his hand. He was also dressed for the outdoors in a pair of sturdy dungarees, a red flannel shirt and wool coat. A gray tweed newsboy cap was pulled down over his unkempt mop of sandy-colored hair.

As the door slammed behind him, Clay said eagerly, "Tommy, *look*—I found it. The map I was telling you about." He held out a rolled up piece of paper. "The mine's in the mountains not far from here. Shouldn't take us more than a couple of hours to get there. I've got the truck all loaded with everything we'll need."

"Clay," Blossom exclaimed. "Where did you get that? It belongs to Father. You can't just take it."

Her brother rounded on her. "Know where I found it? Jammed into the back of the bottom drawer of his desk, that's where." His voice rose angrily. "You know perfectly well Morgan doesn't want it."

Tommy stepped between them. "Take it easy, chum."

"My father . . . my *other* father," Clay corrected vehemently, "set a lot of store by this map. He swore it was legit. He spent years mining and he knew the real thing when he saw it. He always believed this map led to a rich untapped gold mine. It cost him everything to hand it over to Morgan."

"Clay," Blossom began in a conciliatory tone, "I just don't think you should go off in the mountains by yourself. Gold mining is hard, dangerous work, and the mountains can be treacherous. What will you do if one of you is injured? Have you spoken to Father about your plans? He might be able to help you."

"I don't want his help," Clay growled. His cheeks were flushed with crimson blotches. "He don't ever give me credit for nothin'. I'm a grown man and he treats me like a child. This time it's gonna be different. Tommy and me are gonna find this mine and get all the gold for ourselves. Now quit yer worrying, we'll be fine."

Blossom turned to Tommy. "Can't you talk some sense into him?"

Tommy arched his eyebrows and laughed helplessly, stepping back. He raised his palms in a defensive posture and said with a shrug, "Sorry, I make it a point never to get involved in sibling disputes."

The angry voices were upsetting the toddler in Blossom's arms causing him to whimper and squirm. She tried whispering shushing noises in his ear as she rocked him, but he refused to be consoled and began to cry in earnest.

Surrendering at last, she said, "Fine. I've got to go inside and take care of Harold, just *please* be careful—and if you get eaten by a bear, don't say I didn't warn you." With that, she turned, grabbed the diaper bag off the porch, and stalked into the house.

Tommy grinned as he watched Blossom disappear through the door. "I like your sister," he said to Clay as the door banged shut.

"Yeah, well, don't get too attached," Clay said in exasperation. "Morgan'd shoot you dead and drop your carcass in the river before he'd see her with the likes of you."

Tommy turned to him defiantly. "Why? What's wrong with me? I'm no worse than the next guy. She's a grown woman, isn't she? She can make her own decisions. He can't keep her isolated forever. He's got to let her marry someday, hasn't he?"

"*Marry?*" Clay cocked an eyebrow at Tommy. "Since when did you start thinking marriage?"

"Well," Tommy stammered. "You know . . . I mean . . . someday." He cleared his throat awkwardly. "Come on, are we going or not?" He removed his hat and slapped a bit of imaginary dust off the brim.

Clay faced his friend with a sober expression. "Look, you're right. He will let her marry someday, but it'll be to some wealthy blue blood who can take care of her in the manner he feels she deserves, not some traveling grifter with less than two bucks in his pocket."

Tommy stood staring at the ground, deep in thought. *Marriage?* Where had that come from? He'd known plenty of gorgeous women and never once had marriage crossed his mind. But Blossom was different. She was beautiful, but she was also pure and kind and intelligent. She was unlike any woman he'd ever known.

"So," Clay continued, rubbing his hands together, "let's go get rich. This map is our ticket to the big time. All we have to do is go get the gold. I've loaded the pickup with all the gear we'll need. Are you ready?"

Tommy had his doubts, but suddenly felt it was worth a shot. If he ever hoped to pursue a serious courtship with Blossom, he would have to improve his image, be respectable, and prove to her father that he was worthy of her and could take care of her. If this mine turned out to be as rich as Clay promised, then perhaps he'd have a chance after all.

When Morgan returned home later that evening, Blossom met him at the door. "Father, I'm worried about Clay." Her voice was high and rapid, revealing the frayed state of her nerves. "He found that map—the one to the gold mine Mr. Decker gave you. He and Tommy have gone up into the mountains to find it. I'm afraid they'll get lost or hurt or—"

"Hold on, girl," Morgan said gruffly. "Give me a chance to get in the door." He shucked off his coat and hung it on a rack in the hall.

"But, Father," she said, following him into the front room, "they don't know anything about mining or how to survive in the mountains."

He poured himself a Scotch and took an unhurried sip before settling himself into a chair by the fireplace. "Okay, now tell me what fool thing your brother has done."

Frustrated, Blossom dragged in a deep breath and started again. "Clay found that map in the desk drawer in your study—the one to the gold mine that Mr. Decker gave you. He and Tommy loaded up the truck and drove into the mountains this morning, determined to locate the mine. Clay thinks they'll find gold and strike it rich."

Morgan frowned but said nothing. He reached for a cigar from the humidor on the table beside his chair and proceeded to light it, taking several puffs and blowing out the smoke.

"Father," Blossom said, "aren't you concerned? They could get hurt." Both Clay and Tommy were raised in the city. What did they know about hiking in the mountains? Her half-brother had only lived in Salmon Falls for a few years. In that time, her father had taken Clay hunting and fishing several times in an attempt to instill in him some enthusiasm for the outdoors, but Clay had shown no real aptitude, complaining incessantly about insects, cold, and fatigue.

"I'm more concerned that Clay felt free to rummage in my desk," Morgan growled.

"But what if they meet a bear, or get into something poisonous, or fall and break a leg? What if there's a rock slide?" She gave him a pointed look. "Aren't you the one who's always saying how dangerous mining is in the mountains if you don't know what you're doing?"

Her father blew out a cloud of cigar smoke. "Blossom, honey, don't worry. They're grown men, they'll be all right. Worst case, they'll come home tired, sore, and discouraged. And even if they *should* happen to stumble onto the mine—which I doubt—they're going to find it ain't no easy task diggin' ore outta the side of a mountain."

"But Clay seems so determined."

"Look, I took a gander at that map before I stashed it in my desk. I know the area. It's rugged terrain up there—granite cliffs and heavy forest. And that ain't no placer mine they're lookin' for where the gold's just lying around in some alluvial stream waiting to be panned. No, what they've got there is a hard rock mine, which translates into hard *work*." He snorted. "They're welcome to it. I give 'em two days at the most." He leaned back and took a deep pull on his cigar, looking smug.

Blossom knew her father found Clay a disappointment. The years of separation had created differences too great to reconcile. Instead of the dutiful son he'd hoped for—a man strong and capable—Morgan had found himself saddled with an embittered, intractable antagonist, an indolent young man spoiled and unaccustomed to physical exertion.

"You could help them," Blossom said, her eyes beseeching. *Just make the gesture, Father. Show Clay that you care.*

Just then, Martha came in and announced that dinner was ready. The aroma of roast chicken wafted in from the kitchen. Morgan downed his Scotch and stood up. He gave Blossom a grim look. "If Clayton wants my help, he can damn well ask for it."

Two hours later, as twilight was setting in, Clay came bursting triumphantly through the front door. His hair and clothes were disheveled, but his dirt-streaked face beamed. "We found it!"

With a cry of relief, Blossom ran to embrace her brother. Morgan glanced up with a look of cool indifference.

He shook his head and smirked, muttering something low under his breath, then dropped his eyes back to the newspaper he was reading.

Chapter Seventeen

I stayed over Thursday night at my mother's, and headed back to Salmon Falls the next morning after dropping Amy at school. Daniel would be coming in the evening to pick Amy up for the weekend. I debated staying to confront him about his boogeyman comment but then decided against it.

I wasn't eager to see him. The more I thought about him hiring someone to spy on me or to break in and vandalize my house just to scare me, the more unlikely it seemed. It just wasn't his style. And if he *had*, I didn't want to give him the satisfaction of seeing how shaken I'd been. I was done letting him get to me. No, I decided to keep my cool and let it go, at least until I knew more.

Then there was Jared. He still didn't have a working phone and I didn't have any way to let him know I would be late. I assumed he would figure out I stayed at Mom's overnight on Thursday, but I thought he might get concerned if I didn't show up after another whole day.

On the way home, I stopped at the mall to buy a couple of new tops. I didn't have a decent thing to wear. Jeans were one thing, but my work shirts were looking pretty sorry. Most of my good clothes were crammed away in boxes in my mom's basement. Rinsing things in the sink only went so far. Jared had disconnected the old washer and dryer, and I had yet to purchase new ones. I needed to sit down and peruse the internet for good deals on commercial-grade washers and dryers for the bed-and-breakfast.

Next, I stopped off at the John Deere dealership, and after much soul searching, decided on a brand new 18-horse riding mower. It was a little more than I had wanted to spend, but the salesman assured me it was just what I needed and would last forever. It would be delivered tomorrow. I could hardly wait to see Jared's reaction. I only hoped he would continue working inside the house. What was it with men and machines? I still remembered the look of rapture on Daniel's face when he purchased his new Jaguar.

It was noon by the time I got home. I recognized the contractor's van parked at an angle across the yard as usual, and several other crew members' vehicles parked on the shoulder in front of the house. As I turned into the driveway, a red pickup arrived and pulled in behind me. Jared and a husky man in washed-out jeans and faded gray t-shirt got out of the truck. The latter had stringy brown hair and a bushy mustache.

"Hi, Gary," I called, getting out of the Subaru with my shopping bag. "Sorry I'm late getting home," I said to my brother. "I stayed over at Mom's and didn't have any way to get ahold of you."

He shrugged. "No problem. I figured you might stay. Besides, what could I have done? If you'd been killed on the way home, I'm sure someone would have let me know eventually."

I gave him a disgusted look which only made him laugh.

"So, how's Amy?" he asked.

"She's fine. She misses me."

"Of course she does, but she'll be okay. I'm sure Mom's doting on her."

"Yeah, I know." I sighed, then glanced around. "So, what are you guys up to?"

"We just took the old fridge and water heater to the recycling center," Jared said. "But we still have the stove and washer and dryer. It'll probably take us most of the day."

I nodded. That was fine with me. I had projects of my own. I needed to touch base with the plumber about the second floor bathroom renovations, and I wanted to check out places to rent a wallpaper steamer so I could start work on the rooms behind the kitchen.

"And, um . . ." Jared started to mumble something but stopped when a frantic, high-pitched voice called his name.

Surprised, we turned to see Wendy Hilliard dashing from her front porch toward the gate that opened between our two properties. By the time she reached us, she was huffing and puffing for breath.

Something terrible must have happened, I thought—or at least something terribly newsworthy. I wasn't certain yet whether it was a boon or a bother to have a busybody living next door.

"I thought you'd never get home," Wendy gasped. "There was a man here prowling around, looking in the windows."

"A man?" I echoed. "One of the men working on the house?"

"I don't think so. He was wearing a brown suit."

"A suit?" Jared said. "Not one of *my* friends."

Gary chortled.

Could it have been Dillon Thatcher? No, Wendy would have recognized him. Who else—? I gulped. "Was he driving a silver Jaguar?"

"No." She shook her head emphatically. "It was a beat up old Volkswagen Beetle, yellow with a big rusty patch on the driver's door."

My mouth fell open and I let out a gasp. I turned sharply to look at Jared, but he avoided my eye.

"Couldn't have been Daniel then," he quipped, making a great show of nonchalance. "He wouldn't be caught dead in a V-dub."

I saw the inquisitive look on Wendy's face.

"Kate's ex," Jared explained.

Wendy nodded, and I could see her filing that tidbit away as she went on. "Do you think it was the burglar again?"

Jared shook his head. "Not in broad daylight with the house full of carpenters and plumbers. It was probably just a nosy salesman. Don't worry about it."

"Thanks for looking out for the place, Wendy," I said, forcing a composure into my voice that I didn't feel. "I'm sure it was nothing. Maybe a Jehovah's Witness or someone looking at the house who doesn't know it was sold."

Wendy's shoulders drooped. "You're probably right. Oh well, you never can be too careful." She plodded back to her house with decidedly less vigor.

Had she hoped it was the burglar back for a second try?

Once Wendy was out of earshot, I rounded on Jared. "Do you *still* think he was some innocent bird watcher?"

"No, but I don't think Daniel hired him, either. I have a new theory."

I folded my arms across my chest. "What's that?"

"I think he was probably from the county assessor's office. Now that the house is under new ownership and being renovated, you can probably expect a whopping increase in your property taxes."

My eyebrows shot up. That was the last thing I had expected, but it made sense in a vexing sort of way. "Oh, great."

"Yeah. A run-of-the-mill burglar would probably have cost you less in the long run."

I gave a sigh. Just one more gaping hole to throw money into. Well, I didn't have time to worry about it now. I began mulling over my plans for the day.

Jared continued to hover. He exchanged a glance with Gary who waited nearby.

"Something else?" I asked.

His face executed a series of contortions before settling on an uneasy grimace. He rubbed a hand over the back of his neck. "You're not going to like it."

I looked at him impatiently. "What?"

"Remember that storm the other night? Well, it caused a major leak in the basement. I think there may be some damage to the foundation."

"*What?*" I should have known something would go wrong. The renovations were going too smoothly.

"Take it easy," Jared said. "I already showed Perry and he's on it. He called a mason and they're in there right now looking at it."

"Why didn't you say something sooner?" I growled, clenching my fist around the handle of my shopping bag. I hurried up to the house dreading what I might find.

I had a lot of faith in Perry Shackelford, my building contractor; he'd come highly recommended, and his knowledge of historic home renovation seemed limitless. I knew he was capable of fixing nearly any problem that might arise, but it was the cost that worried me. I had sunk a large portion of my divorce settlement into the house already, plus taken out a couple of loans to complete the restoration. The new roof alone was going to set me back somewhere in the neighborhood of thirty thousand. I had no idea what a new foundation would cost, but I was certain it wouldn't be cheap.

I have got to get this place up and running as soon as possible, I thought miserably.

The last time I had been in the basement was when I'd taken Jared down there the day he first moved in. It was as vast as an underground cavern, cool all year round, with thick stone walls that reminded me of a medieval stronghold. The enormous old oil furnace sat hunched in one corner while a network of pipes and ducts extended across the ceiling like the arms of some ancient petrified octopus. Half a dozen dirt-caked windows set at ground level yielded a modicum of light.

Complete with plumbing and electricity, I figured the basement had been more than just a cellar. A small fireplace built into the wall shared a chimney with the music salon directly above, and gave me reason to think it had once served as a servants quarters or perhaps a workshop of some kind. But that was long before the spiders and mice had moved in.

I found the contractor and another man conferring near the center of the northern wall. The space was illuminated by an electric trouble light hung on a nail pounded into one of the ceiling joists. They turned when they heard me.

"Ah, Kate, glad you're here." The wiry old builder was gray at the temples and hindered by a limp from some long ago accident, but his diligent manner and authoritative voice always had a way of instilling me with confidence.

"Jared tells me there might be a problem with the foundation," I said, my eyes roving the walls nervously for signs of imminent collapse.

"Yeah, that heavy rain we had seeped through the foundation in this area and caused some erosion in the mortar joints." He indicated a portion of the foundation where the smooth cement-like veneer on the wall had crumbled away to reveal a section of large stacked stones. He nodded toward the other man. "Mike here is a stone mason I've worked with before. He can explain what needs to be done."

I smiled and we shook hands. The mason was a brawny man in his mid-forties wearing a faded blue coverall. He said, "Fortunately, the damage isn't extensive. These old stone foundations were built like castles, made to endure for centuries. I just need to clean out the old mortar and dirt in this area"—he reached out and swept a handful of loose debris from between two stones for emphasis—"then re-point the gaps."

"Do what?" I stared in confusion at the massive rock wall. Above this ran a heavy wooden sill and a framework of weighty beams that supported the entire house.

He chuckled. "Slap new mortar in the spaces between the stones. Once it's hardened, I'll re-coat the surface with a mortar plaster to blend with the rest of the wall. This old plaster does tend to flake off over time, but it's typically an easy repair. If you want, I can start work on Monday."

I heaved a sigh of relief. That didn't sound too bad. Thank God I didn't have to replace the whole foundation. "Thank you," I said gratefully, shaking his hand again.

He continued. "It'd be a good idea to go around and check the rest of the walls. You've got a lot of stuff stored down here you probably don't want getting wet. Moisture invites all sorts of problems—mold, dry rot, termites. Might want to think about coating these walls with a permanent moisture sealant for just a couple of thousand more."

I swallowed. "I'll think about it."

At this point, Perry interjected. "You've got plans to replace the roof, right?"

"Yes," I said, glad to change the subject. "I've got someone scheduled to give me an estimate next week. I want to get that done as soon as possible."

"Good. I went outside to see where all the water was coming from, and it looks like a section of gutter is missing right over this spot, letting water pour down right against the outside of the foundation. If that's not rectified soon, you'll be in for a heap more trouble. I'll have one of the guys stretch some tarp over it in the meantime in case it rains again."

"Great," I said. "Thanks, I appreciate it."

"That'll go a long way toward keeping it dry down here," Perry said.

I thanked them both and went to find Jared. He and Gary were busy loading the old stove into the back of Gary's truck. I related what Perry had told me.

"Doesn't sound too awful," Jared said. "Good to know the house isn't going to fall down any time soon. Look, I know you've got stuff to do this afternoon, so why don't you go ahead. When Gary and I get back from taking this load to recycling, we'll do a quick check around the rest of the foundation. Sounds like the sooner we get that basement cleaned out, the better."

Chapter Eighteen

After lunch and a few phone calls, I headed for Monroe, a few miles away. I had located a wallpaper steamer and wanted to pick it up today so that I could start work in the morning. Before I left, I warned Jared I might be late getting home. Dillon Thatcher had called and asked me to have dinner with him. I had agreed and told him I'd meet him at the Salmon Falls Hotel once I finished my shopping.

When I arrived, he greeted me with enthusiasm. "There's a little Italian bistro just down the street I've been wanting to try."

The evening was clear and warm so we walked to the restaurant. It was small and quaint, replete with traditional Italian décor, including checkered tablecloths, a rustic stone fireplace, and moody landscape paintings on the walls. Music in the background and soft lighting enhanced the charming ambiance.

The hostess sat us at a cozy table by the window and left menus. She was followed by a busboy who filled our water glasses and left a basket of warm bread and butter. When the waitress arrived to take our order, Dillon folded his menu. "We'll have the special and a bottle of Zinfandel."

Without a glance at me, she replied, "Very good, sir." Then she pivoted and walked away, taking the menus with her.

For moment I sat there, speechless. What, were we back in the *Fifties?* I didn't even know what the special *was*, let alone whether I liked it or not. Shades of my ex-husband.

No, don't go there. Dillon probably thought he was being gallant. I just needed to gently set him straight.

"What did you order for us?" I asked sweetly.

"The house special—spaghetti and meatballs. Is that all right? I figured everybody likes spaghetti and meatballs."

"Luckily for you, I do. But, in the future, please allow me to decide for myself, okay?"

He looked surprised. "Sure. I'm sorry. My dad always told me that a gentleman should order for a lady in a nice restaurant. I thought you'd find it chivalrous."

I gave him an incredulous look. "Dillon, that sort of thinking went out decades ago, along with pillbox hats and smoking jackets."

"Fine. I *said* I was sorry. It won't happen again. Here, have some bread." He thrust the basket at me and turned his attention to his napkin, unfolding it with deliberate care and laying it across his lap.

This peevish response was uncalled-for and put a damper on my feelings. My brother's words suddenly came back to me: " . . . after everything you've been through lately . . . you just got *rid* of one guy."

But soon the spaghetti arrived and the mood lightened. The food was delicious and Dillon reverted to his amiable self. I decided to give him the benefit of the doubt and dismissed the incident as a misunderstanding.

The sun had gone down by the time we finished, but the town was lit up by street lights, illuminated signs, and shop windows. When we arrived back at Dillon's hotel, he leaned close and whispered, "Would you like to come up?"

I had expected this, perhaps even wanted it on some level, but now that we were here my feelings were mixed and I hesitated. I liked him a lot and enjoyed his company, but this was a complication I didn't need, and it wasn't fair to lead him on. After my divorce, I had relished the thought of being on my own, doing what I pleased, making my own decisions. I didn't want to lose sight of that.

I gave him a wan smile. "Not tonight. It's been a long day and I'm tired. Let's call it a night, okay? Thank you so much for dinner. I'll be working at the house all day tomorrow. You can come by if you want."

He sighed and nodded. I knew he was disappointed, but he had the good grace not to pursue it. He escorted me to my car and said in parting, "Maybe I'll see you tomorrow. Good night, Kate."

Driving home, I reflected again on my determination to make it on my own and resolved not to let myself get sidetracked.

* * *

Early the next morning, I set about the arduous task of stripping off the old wallpaper in my bedroom. The steamer created a sauna-like atmosphere and droplets of scalding water kept running down my left arm as I pointed the apparatus toward the top of the wall. Standing on a stepladder, I used my other hand to scrape the paper with a putty knife, being careful not to gouge the plaster underneath. With a groan, I realized it would take forever to remove all five layers of old wallpaper.

Dillon arrived a little before noon with an offer to take me to lunch. I was chagrined when I realized what I must look like. With an embarrassed laugh, I ran a hand through my damp, bedraggled hair. "I don't think I'm fit to go out in public. I've been steaming and scraping wallpaper all morning."

His smile was tantalizing. "You look fine."

Uh-huh. Like something the cat dragged in.

I considered stopping work and getting cleaned up, but I was pleased with the progress I'd made and was not anxious to stop. I really wanted to finish the downstairs bedrooms today. Jared was holed up in the basement, cleaning and moving things around in preparation for the stone mason. I hadn't seen him all morning. He would probably appreciate a break.

"I have an idea," I said to Dillon. "Why don't I make sandwiches for the three of us to eat here. Then we can all get better acquainted. Afterwards, if you're up for it, you can help me tear down wallpaper."

His face flinched in a fleeting look of distaste, but then he grinned and nodded agreeably. "Sure. Anything I can do to help."

I laughed. "I should warn you, it's tedious work and won't be much fun. You may regret your decision."

About the time we finished lunch, the unexpected sound of heavy tires could be heard outside as a large vehicle pulled up the driveway. Jared went out the back door to investigate.

Moments later, he stuck his head back in and cried, "You bought a riding lawn mower!"

Dillon and I followed Jared outside and watched as the delivery man unloaded the mower. My brother bounced from one foot to the other like an excited kid getting his first bike. I signed the papers while the man explained the operating procedures and added some gas as part of the customer service. The truck left and Jared hopped enthuse-astically aboard the mower and started it up.

I laughed and looked at Dillon. "Well, we won't see *him* for the rest of the day."

He gave me a sly look. "Pity."

"Wallpaper," I reminded him in mock reproof.

"Lead the way."

I took him down the hall to the rooms behind the kitchen where I had left the steamer, the stepladder, a pile of plastic garbage bags, and my scraping tools. I had nearly finished my bedroom and still had Amy's to do. There was more than enough to keep us busy the rest of the day.

He took off his good shirt and laid it aside to keep it from getting wilted in the steam. My breath caught as muscular, well-defined pecs showed under his tight-fitting white t-shirt. I tried not to stare.

"Where do we start?" he asked, surveying the disarray.

I handed him the working end of the steamer—a flat device on the end of a hose—then turned it on, and explained how to use it. "When it gets hot, you run this back and forth over the wallpaper to loosen the glue, then I'll scrape it off. Simple as pie. We'll start along the ceiling and work our way down. Just be careful, it can get a little drippy."

I positioned the ladder, grabbed the scraper, and climbed up.

His eyebrows drew together in a look of concern. "Maybe *I* should get up on the ladder. I'd hate for you to fall off and get hurt."

I snorted. "What do you think I was doing all morning before you got here? Don't worry, I'll be fine."

"Still . . ." He didn't look convinced. "This is a pretty big job for—"

"If you say '*for a girl,*' I swear I'll come down there and punch you right in the middle of your pretty face!"

He laughed.

"Don't go getting all macho on me," I said. "There's not a ladder in the world I can't ride. Now, let's get started. I think it's hot. It's starting to steam."

We worked late into the afternoon, successfully scraping all the old wallpaper from both bedrooms. With a heavy sigh, I dropped the last piece of soggy paper into the bulging garbage bag.

"*Whew*," I said. "Glad that's done. Thank you so much for all your help. Let's call it quits. I'm exhausted."

As we washed at the bathroom sink, I smiled apologetically. "Not exactly what you bargained for when you came today, is it? I'm a lousy hostess."

Dillon reached for the towel. "Hey, I asked for it, didn't I? Besides, I got to spend the whole day with you."

He gave me a seductive look, gazing playfully at me with his dark, luscious eyes. His damp t-shirt clung to his chest and his nearness was unsettling.

I looked down at my hands pretending to wipe off some imaginary grime. I took a deep breath. "You need to stop."

He narrowed his eyes. "What's wrong?"

What should I say? How could I explain? It was all so complicated. How could I tell him that I wasn't interested in starting something, that I was enjoying my independence. He had to understand that I had a goal and I couldn't let myself get distracted. There was so much work to be done if I was going to get the house finished and the bed-and-breakfast opened by summer.

"Things are just moving too fast," I said, struggling to keep my voice even.

He stepped back. "I'm sorry."

"I just went through a bad divorce and I'm trying to get my life back on track. I need to stay focused. I hope you understand. I just don't have the`time or energy right now for a new relationship."

"I guess I should have known after last night." His lips quirked in a fatalistic smile.

"Dillon," I said. "I'm sorry. Really, it's not you."

"That's okay. I get it."

I gave him a grateful look. "Just friends for now, okay?"

Just then, Jared hollered and we both jumped. "Hey, are you guys hungry? I'm going to order a pizza."

"I guess he's done mowing the grass." My flustered brain seemed unable to come up with anything intelligent to say.

Amorous advances curtailed, Dillon said, "What are you doing tomorrow?"

"More of the same, I'm afraid. Once the old wallpaper's off, I need to paint the ceilings and moldings, then put primer on the walls before I put the new paper up. I want to get these rooms livable by summer so I can bring my daughter here to live with me. Oh, and I've also got roofers coming to give me an estimate and—"

He placed a finger to my lips, stopping the torrent. "I get the picture. I'll see you in the morning."

The next few days disappeared in a flurry of activity. New doors and windows were installed on the ground floor, the chimneys were cleaned, and the mortar in the stone foundation was repaired. I barely saw my brother as he attacked various jobs around the house and continued to sort through the hoards of junk amassed in the basement.

One morning when Dillon stopped by on one of his frequent visits and heard that Jared was working in the basement, he showed an unexpected enthusiasm for checking it out himself.

"Come on, Kate," he urged. "It'll be fun. I've never seen the basement. Who knows what sort of cool stuff might be stored down there."

I made a face. "I know what's down there." I ticked them off on my fingers: "Junk, mice, dirt, cobwebs, more junk, spiders, and—did I mention?—*mice!*"

He laughed, the corners of his eyes crinkling. "They're not going to hurt you. To them you're a giant. Remember, they're a lot more afraid of *you* than—"

"Don't say it!" I flung a hand up, putting a fast halt to his assurances. "I don't believe it for one minute."

He pulled open the door, a heavy wooden portal just off the kitchen, and peered down into the gloomy stairwell. "Come on. If nothing else, I'm sure your brother would appreciate the help."

That was probably true. It was also a good way to get the two of them to interact. If Jared accepted Dillon's help, then working together would only aid in improving their friendship. I turned on the light at the top of the stairs and led the way.

Chapter Nineteen

Jared had replaced all the burned out lightbulbs so the space wasn't as dim and foreboding as I remembered. I explained to Dillon how we planned to remodel the basement into an apartment and workshop for Jared once we'd cleaned it out. The architect had drawn up plans to include a kitchenette, a den, and a bathroom, as well as a dedicated laundry room with space for a freezer and pantry for the bed-and-breakfast.

Dillon seemed intrigued by it all, looking into every corner and curiously examining each object as it was dragged into the open and the top layer of grime swept off. I took several boxes of old canning jars upstairs to be rinsed and recycled.

Jared unearthed a sturdy old workbench from beneath a pile of old paint cans, herbicides, and plastic tarps. "I think I can use this," he said. "And look, here's a complete set of antique iron tools."

As he pulled a large box away from the workbench, he suddenly reared back with a yelp. "There's a snake under there!"

"How'd a snake get in here?" I whirled around to look.

"The back door's been propped open all week while I've hauled stuff out of here." He began yanking randomly at objects in his way as he tried to reach the hapless reptile.

Dillon grabbed a shovel he found leaning against the wall. "*Here*," he said, "chase it this way and I'll kill it."

"*No*," I cried. "Don't *kill* it. Just shoo it outside."

"What if it's poisonous?"

"There are no venomous snakes in western Washington," I said. "It's just a garter snake. They eat mice and slugs, and therefore have my full protection."

Jared gave a loud grunt as he leaned over and attempted to pull a large metal bucket out from beneath the workbench. "*Ow! Shit!* Not only did she hoard newspapers," he grumbled, "she hoarded rocks too. There must be half a dozen buckets under here full of rocks."

"There it goes," Dillon yelled suddenly as the snake slithered out from under the bench and across the floor. He chased it into the center of the room.

"Don't let it get behind the furnace," Jared warned.

Holding a flat piece of cardboard in front of me, I steered the reptile toward the back door. Dillon traded the shovel for a lawn rake, and Jared grabbed a broom. After a bit of fancy maneuvering, the three of us finally guided the snake out the door, up the concrete stairwell, and away into the tall grass outside.

"*Phew!*" Jared said. "He was good sized for a garter snake—two feet at least."

I exhaled in a rush. "Yeah. Glad we got him outside. Poor thing. I'd have hated for him to die down here."

"Yuck, no kidding," Dillon said, making a face. "He probably would've stunk something awful."

My lips tightened. *Not an animal lover, I guess.*

Dillon didn't seem to notice my disapproval. He strode over to the workbench and began to examine the buckets of rocks Jared had pulled out.

"Why would an old lady save a bunch of rocks?" Jared said. "She must have been some sort of rock hound."

"Might not have been Blossom," I said. "Remember, her father and brother lived here too, a long time ago. Maybe it was one of them."

"Some of these are real interesting," Dillon mused. "Colorful, kind of shiny. Do you mind if I take a couple?"

"Of course not," I said. "Help yourself." I picked up a baseball-sized stone and examined it in the light. It glistened in shades of green and orange, and had a ribbon of white quartz running through it. "These would look nice in the garden in front of the house where the sun can shine on them."

Jared tossed the rock he was holding back into the bucket. "Come on, we're wasting time. We can look at these later. There's still a ton of junk to go through."

Dillon stuffed several pieces of the colorful stones into the pockets of his jacket, then rubbed his hands briskly together and said, "Great. What's next?"

Following Jared's lead, we dove once more into the mounds of clutter piled up around the basement, attempting to separate useful items from obvious rubbish. In our search, we discovered a treasure trove of discarded antiques: an old wringer washing machine, a butter churn, a treadle sewing machine, a set of enamel dishware, a couple of old-style telephones, a kerosene lamp, and a number of other antiquated oddities we couldn't identify. From a large box, I pulled a tangle of leather straps and buckles I thought might once have been part of a horse harness. Obviously, Blossom never threw anything away.

At last, Jared straightened and flexed his shoulder muscles. "I'll bet the Historical Society would love to get their hands on some of this stuff." He surveyed the piles he'd been sorting through then swiped a sleeve across his damp forehead, leaving a dirty smear.

"You're probably right," I agreed, "but I might actually use some of these things to decorate the bed-and-breakfast. I especially love the treadle sewing machine. Blossom must have been quite a seamstress back in the day. There's a newer electric model up in the attic."

As evening approached, Dillon wiped his hands on his jeans and declared that he should be going. I walked him to the front door, grateful for the absence of pounding and sawing upstairs; the work crew had gone home too. He gave me a peck on the cheek and I waved as he backed the Bronco down the driveway. It had been a long day, but I was cheered at the thought of all we'd accomplished.

I rejoined Jared in the basement where he was eyeing the furnace. "I wonder how old this monstrosity is?" he muttered. "You ought to think about replacing it and having all the ducts cleaned."

"I know," I said. "It's on the list."

"I was just thinking that every time the furnace comes on it just blows dust and crap all over the house through these filthy old air ducts."

"You're right, okay? I get the message. But, for now, we'll just put in a new filter." I changed the subject. "It was nice of Dillon to help out today, don't you think?"

Jared gave me a reluctant shrug. "Yeah, I guess so."

The good mood I'd been clinging to suddenly slipped. "What's that supposed to mean?"

"I don't know," he said. "I just keep wondering *why?* What's he after?"

I bristled. "What do you mean? What makes you think he's *after* something?" So much for hoping the two could be friends.

Jared fidgeted uncomfortably, running a hand over his hair. "It's hard to put a finger on. I mean, most guys try to impress women by being cool—buying expensive presents and taking them out to fancy restaurants—not by getting all dirty cleaning their basements." His mouth gave a wry twist. "That doesn't come until after the wedding."

I jammed my hands onto my hips and nailed him with as fierce a look as I could muster. "First of all, he probably can't afford expensive gifts, and *second*, forget about weddings. That's not going to happen. I told him I just wanted to be friends, and that's what he's doing—trying to be a friend. I'm sure that's why he offered to help. He's trying to get you to like him because he knows it's important to me."

"Maybe. But it's more than that. Did you see how he had his nose into everything? I swear he inspected every nook and cranny in this entire basement. Almost like he was looking for something."

"He *is* looking for something," I spouted angrily, throwing my hands up. "Have you forgotten? He's Blossom's long lost grandnephew, the great-grandson of the man who built this house. He's looking for mementos of his past, sentimental keepsakes."

Jared snorted. "Sounds like a girl thing."

"See what I mean?" I almost shouted. "He's probably afraid you'll just throw everything in the trash without a second thought."

"Hey, wasn't it me who set aside those old things we found? Didn't I say they ought to be preserved for the Historical Society? What do you take me for, a Neanderthal? Don't you think I know the difference between garbage and keepsakes? *Geez*, Kate, give me some credit."

"I just don't see why you don't like him."

"I'm not sure why, either. Maybe he reminds me of Daniel." His mouth slanted cynically and he gave a shrug.

"Maybe I'm afraid you'll run off and get married again, then sell the house and toss me out on my ear. I don't have any place else to go, you know."

"Oh, for heaven's sake." I rolled my eyes. "I have no intention of marrying Dillon. I barely know him. And even if I did, I would never sell the house. I've worked far too long and hard for this. No, he's just a nice guy, someone fun to hang out with. Besides, I'm sure he plans to go right back to Ohio once he's found what he's looking for."

* * *

Driving into Salmon Falls a couple of days later, I happened to glance toward the library. Parked in the lot was a yellow VW bug with a rusty patch on the driver's door. I gave a little start and my heart did a sudden somersault. There couldn't be more than one like it in Salmon Falls. It had to belong to the mysterious stranger I had seen in front of my house. The same man Wendy had seen prowling around.

For a moment I debated. Jared had suggested a tax assessor. But wouldn't he be driving an official vehicle? And what was he doing parked outside the Salmon Falls public library? Perhaps he was a salesman after all—one who enjoyed a good book. Or the meter reader. Or just about anyone.

This was getting me nowhere. If I wanted an answer I would have to go inside and confront him. What was the worst that could happen? I could make a fool of myself. Wouldn't be the first time. I went around the block, then pulled into the lot and parked. Before going in, I dug my phone out of my purse and snapped a picture of the license plate, then stuffed the phone into the pocket of my jacket.

Inside, an efficient-looking middle-aged woman stood behind a long counter. Remembering Mrs. Attila-the-Hun, my old high school librarian, I half expected her to frown, lay a finger against her lips, and warn me with a severe *shhhh*.

Instead, she merely looked up, smiled pleasantly, and went back to her work.

The room was not large; banks of shelves lined the perimeter walls, and more shelves stood in parallel rows down the middle. To one side, three work tables held computers, and to the far right was a small alcove with brightly painted miniature tables and chairs where a mother sat showing a picture book to her toddler. To the left, a gray-haired woman in a loose-fitting lavender dress perused the biographies. There remained only one other person.

He sat at the first table surrounded by a stack of books, newspapers, and periodicals. He was tall and thin, just as I remembered. His brown suede jacket hung on the back of the chair beside him. He appeared thoroughly engrossed in whatever he was reading.

I realized I was staring when the librarian discreetly cleared her throat and asked, "May I help you find something?"

"No, thank you," I replied. "I've found what I came in for."

Taking a deep breath, I strode up to the table where the man sat. In a curt voice I asked, "Who are you, and why have you been poking around my house?"

The other patrons glanced over in disapproval, but I didn't care. I had every right to be upset. This man had barged into my life, rattled my nerves, and shattered my peace of mind. I intended to find out why.

Startled, he looked up, but when he saw me his face broke into an unabashed grin.

"Busted," he said cheerfully. He displayed all the characteristics of a rascal caught red-handed snitching cookies from the cookie jar. He motioned to the empty seat opposite him at the table. "The Thatcher house, right? Won't you sit down?"

I plunked unceremoniously into the chair and studied his features more closely. While I wouldn't have described him as handsome exactly, he certainly was not *bad* looking. His face and nose were long, his ears a little too big, but these were balanced by a pair of arresting brown eyes and a strong masculine chin. He had broad shoulders and was well proportioned. Indeed, his was a case of the sum being greater than the individual parts. In need of a haircut, his shaggy chestnut mane stuck out at unruly angles.

"So, who are you?" I repeated, mindful to keep my voice at a tolerable level. "What were you doing at my house? Did my ex-husband send you?" I drummed my fingers on the table.

Instead of replying, he turned the newspaper that was spread on the table toward me so I could get a better look. It was a *Seattle Times* Sunday pictorial article about aging historic buildings in the city. "Here, this is me. I wrote this."

Perplexed, I read aloud the name under the title. "*Nathan Powell.*"

"Yep." He grinned again. "Nathan Powell, at your service."

"Kate Ecklund," I said hesitantly, shaking his proffered hand. "You're a journalist?"

"Uh-huh. Freelance, mostly—articles for newspapers and magazines. Local stuff, you know—history, interesting people and places. Pam over there will vouch for me.

He directed this last to the librarian who responded with a nod. I noticed the woman in the lavender dress had apparently also overheard, for she paused long enough to glance our way and smile her own assurances.

So, he's known in town. I suppose that counts for something.

I still felt unsettled, but at least he wasn't a tax assessor or a private detective. "That doesn't explain what you were doing snooping around my house."

"I was doing research for something I'm writing. I had hoped to talk to you, but each time I went out there you were either just leaving or not at home. I did take a couple of pictures, though. Hope you don't mind."

My mouth tightened in annoyance. Yet despite my vexation, I was curious. I glanced at the books on the table: *A History of Gold Mining in the Cascade Mountains* and *Pioneers of Western Washington*. A magazine with colorful pages was open to a feature titled *Salmon Falls: Early Lumber Capital of the West*. He was obviously reading up on the area. How much did he know about the Thatcher family?

Chapter Twenty

He saw me reading the titles. "Interested in local history?"

"You could say that." I gave a little snort. "I did just buy a historical landmark, you know."

"And I understand you're working to restore it."

I smiled and nodded. "It's quite a project."

He gave me a warm, approving look. "There are a lot of folks in this town who will thank you for it, especially those who remember Blossom. That old house is more than a mere landmark to the people around here. You could almost call it a monument to the past. It represents a bygone era, a time when this town was important."

I thought of the elderly ladies I had met at the cemetery. They all had cherished memories of the long defunct mill and the once great estate.

"So, what are you writing?" I asked, my opinion of him improving. "Something to do with the Thatcher mansion? I've been meaning to do some research on it myself."

"Not specifically. Actually, I'm doing a favor for another town landmark, Flossie Gerhardt. If you haven't met her yet, you will. She's sort of a fixture in this town."

I shook my head, drawing a blank. The name sounded familiar, but I couldn't place it.

"She's president of the Salmon Falls Historical Society."

"Oh, right," I said, remembering. "She was mentioned in Blossom Thatcher's obituary. I read it online the other day. But you still haven't answered my question."

He leaned back. "Currently, the Historical Society is using a small room set aside in the Senior Center, but they've been trying to acquire a place of their own. They'd like to open a sort of museum. Now they have an option on the old grange hall, but they still have to raise $50,000 by the end of the year to clinch the deal. So I offered to do a book, a history of the town—biographies of longtime residents, details of historical events, things like that—and donate the proceeds to the Historical Society."

"Very noble."

"I've been doing interviews with some of the old-timers in the area or their descendents when I can locate them, and I've taken hundreds of pictures. Everyone's been very cooperative. Most people are pretty excited about the idea. Take your house, for instance. Did you know that Morgan Thatcher was one of the original founders of this town? He built that house in 1914 from the fortune he made in the timber industry."

"That's fascinating," I said, "but I read all that on the internet. I don't have anything to add. Interviewing me would be a waste of your time, but you're welcome to take all the pictures you need."

"Thanks," he said, then added, "Actually, I was also sort of spying. As soon as word got around that the Thatcher mansion had been sold, Flossie wanted to know who had bought it and what they intended to do with it. As chief historian in town, she felt somewhat protective of the old place." His face settled once more into an easy grin. "But that was over a week ago."

"So?"

"So, in a small town like Salmon Falls a week is more than enough time for the grapevine to ferret out and circulate everything there is to know about a person to just about anyone in town who's interested."

I was galled. "Really? So, what do you know about me?"

"Well, let's see . . ." He sat forward in his chair and flipped open a small notepad. "Kate Ecklund, attractive blond, recently divorced, one young daughter; ex-husband has money and drives a Jaguar; your brother, a tall, good-looking hippy-type is living with you; you're currently renovating the house and planning to turn it into a bed-and-breakfast; and apparently you have a mouse problem."

He must have noticed my astonishment because he laughed suddenly. "You bought several packages of mouse traps. The clerk at the hardware store is my nephew. Don't ever try to keep a secret in a small town."

"Yeah," I said dryly. "I'm learning that. Anything else?"

"Uh-huh." He gave me a devilish wink as he made a show of consulting his notes. "To everyone's surprise, a previously unknown Thatcher has turned up, and apparently you are dating him."

I glared at him in indignation. "Don't tell me, you have a niece who works at the pizza place."

His eyes crinkled merrily as he chuckled. "Close. Second cousin."

"I'm sure I also have my friendly next-door-neighbor to thank for her big mouth. I don't know whether to laugh or be offended."

His expression softened. He set the notepad on the table. "People are curious, that's all. It's human nature.

They don't mean anything by it. Once they get to know you, they'll move on to something else. It's all part of small town living. Better get used to it if you plan to stick around."

"I'll have to be careful what I say to people—no telling who's related to whom!"

"You're catching on."

"Do you live here in Salmon Falls?" I asked.

He nodded. "Just moved back. I lived in Seattle for a year and different places around the world before that. I wanted to get out, have some adventure, and seek my fortune. But I grew up here and I still love the place."

"Did you? Find fortune and adventure, I mean?"

"Well, I haven't found any fortunes yet, but I have had lots of adventure. I did a stint as a news journalist overseas for awhile. I've been to Northern Ireland, Iran, and West Africa. I've covered riots in Israel and the earthquake in Haiti." He whistled softly, shaking his head. "Thousands dead. It's almost inconceivable, that kind of destruction."

I nodded sympathetically. "What a fascinating life you've had. Just the opposite of mine. So what brings you back here to sleepy little Salmon Falls?"

"I had my fill of it, I guess. Wanted to try something else, something less hectic. Now I freelance and teach a class at the community college."

I was about to comment when my cell phone chirped. I apologized and grabbed it out of my pocket. Jared had finally gotten around to buying a new phone and I thought he might need me to get something for him while I was in town.

It was Dillon texting: *Lunch?*

I responded: *Not today. Busy.*

Where are you?

Library. Talk later.

I stashed the phone back into the pocket of my jacket feeling strangely annoyed. I couldn't explain why. Dillon had done nothing more than ask if I wanted to have lunch. Maybe it was the fact that he'd been at the house nearly every minute of the past week, and I was beginning to feel a bit crowded.

At that moment, Pam the librarian cleared her throat meaningfully. "Uh, Nathan . . . I'm sorry to interrupt, but you did say to remind you."

He checked the time on his phone. "Thanks, Pam." He began to gather up his books and papers. "Sorry to run off like this, Kate. I've enjoyed meeting you." He stopped abruptly. "Say, if you're really interested in learning about local history, you should come with me. I'm going over to the Senior Center to meet Flossie. You'd probably enjoy seeing the pictures they've got up on the wall. I'm sure there must be some of Blossom and her father from the old days."

"I've been wanting to do that," I said. "Are you sure I wouldn't be in the way?"

"Of course not. Come on, we can walk. It's just a couple of blocks.

No sooner had we exited the library than my phone chirped again. I heaved a sigh. "Just a second."

Nathan smiled and waited patiently.

It was Jared texting: *Your boyfriend is looking for you.*

Irritated, I jabbed back my reply: *Not my boyfriend. Tell him I'm out. Don't know when I'll be back. Need anything?*

Nope.

I put the phone back into my pocket. "My brother."

"No problem," he said easily.

The Senior Center was a modern building, bright, spacious, and welcoming. Nathan and I were greeted by several smiling women involved in some sort of sewing project laid out on a large table in the middle of the room. Nathan returned the greeting, calling each woman by name. I recognized a couple of the women I'd met at the cemetery

He introduced me. "Ladies, I'd like you to meet Kate Ecklund."

One gray-haired lady spoke up eagerly. "Oh, it's the young woman who bought Blossom's house." She hurried over. "Remember me, dear? Mildred Birch. My grandmother Martha used to be Blossom's housekeeper."

"Yes, of course," I said. "It's nice to see you again."

A tiny, frail-looking woman also came over. "We've met too. I'm Esther Wick."

"Yes, I remember." The thin lady with the reedy voice.

She beamed as she introduced the others. I smiled warmly as she gave me their names, though I knew full well I'd never be able to remember them all.

At last, Nathan said to Mildred Birch, "We're here to see Flossie. Is she in the museum?"

"Yes," Mildred said. "She's waiting for you."

I followed Nathan into an adjoining room where card tables were spread with games and puzzles. A piano stood in one corner. Covering the walls were black and white photos in various sizes and condition.

At one table sat an attractive white-haired woman. Slender and straight-backed, silver hair pinned into a neat French twist, she had a likable face, bright blue eyes, and just a touch of red lipstick.

"Hi, Aunt Flossie," Nathan said, striding over to give her a kiss on the forehead. "I'd like you to meet Kate Ecklund, the new owner of Thatcher mansion."

I shot Nathan a look of surprise as I approached the table.

"Ms. Ecklund," Flossie said. She stood and held her hand out to me. "I'm delighted to make your acquaintance. I heard you went by the cemetery to pay your respects. I was hoping you'd come here one day and have a look at our little display."

I took her hand and was surprised by the firmness of her handshake.

"I'm glad to meet you," I said. "I'm eager to learn more about local history, and especially about the Thatcher house."

"I see you've met my nephew."

"Yes." I looked at him askance. "We met at the library this morning. He told me about the book he's writing for the Historical Society. He didn't tell me he was your nephew."

He grinned and shrugged. "It didn't come up."

The frown she gave him was mildly reproving, but the affection between them was plain.

"We're hoping to raise money to buy the old grange hall for a permanent museum," she said. "We use this space to display pictures, but we have many items in storage that we'd like to put out for people to see. There are so many new families moving into the valley who know nothing about the early settlers or what life was like here a hundred years ago. We want to make it an educational destination, an interesting and interactive place for both children and adults, not just a place to house old things."

"You should see some of the stuff they've collected," Nathan said. "My favorite is the giant buzz saw blade that was used at the lumber mill. That thing must be six feet tall."

Flossie nodded. "Blossom donated that when the mill closed down, as well as many other fascinating items. You probably know that Blossom's father, Morgan Thatcher, was a very important figure in Salmon Falls history. By all accounts, he was a hard man to get along with, tenacious and overbearing, but I believe it was those very traits that made him so successful, even during the worst depression this country has ever known. It was his timber and lumber mill that kept this town afloat. Most of the people around here were dependent on him for their livelihoods."

"Did you know him?" I asked.

"Oh, no. He died before I was born. Mildred Birch might remember him. She's a little older. As a child, she often spent time at the mansion with her grandmother. Some of the other ladies lived on the Thatcher estate when their fathers worked there, but they were just children at the time. Everything they know about Morgan they heard from their parents. None of us were close friends with Blossom as children. She was quite a bit older. In fact, no one Blossom's age is still living. You might have heard that at the time of her death she was the oldest person in Salmon Falls. I think now that honor goes to Opal Johansson—she just turned ninety-four. You met her at the cemetery the other day."

"Yes, I remember." The lady with the white cotton candy hair.

I thought again of the weeping wraith that had appeared to me in the old mansion. I tried to imagine what it must have been like for Blossom Thatcher to grow old watching family and friends die. She had never married, never had children. She really had been alone, and now her spirit seemed doomed to carry on her misery.

Flossie skirted the table and guided me to the black and white photos on the wall. We began at one side of the room and slowly worked our way around. I studied each one with interest. There were many pictures of the early town: simple clapboard buildings, plank sidewalks, dirt roads, horses, and wagons. The oldest pictures showed men with beards wearing boots and heavy clothing, while the women had on long dresses and aprons. Beneath each photo, a small paper placard was taped to the wall describing each picture. Nathan followed along, looking over my shoulder.

I smiled at a photo of six serious-looking children in drab clothing lined up in front of a small one-room schoolhouse. *Salmon Falls Primary School, 1910* read the inscription. How things had changed. A random succession of school pictures with various dates spanning the next several decades showed an ever increasing number of students as the town grew.

Flossie stopped and pointed to a curly-haired little girl in a gingham dress standing with a class of grade schoolers. "I believe this is Blossom," she said. The date on the photograph was 1927.

"What a sweet child," I said. "She looks about the same age as my Amy."

The next picture made me stop. I recognized Morgan Thatcher and his young wife from the picture we'd found in the old Bible in the attic. They stood in front of their grand Victorian mansion in what was undoubtedly their Sunday best; behind them the house rose all bright and new. The description underneath read *Morgan Virgil Thatcher and Angela Rose Thatcher, c. 1917.*

Chapter Twenty-One

"Back at the turn of the twentieth century," Flossie said, "logging was a booming industry, and Thatcher's lumber mill was the backbone of the local economy. He built that house as a sort of testament to his success. All the adjacent land belonged to him, from West Valley Road clear down to Angela Lake, plus of course thousands of acres of timber in the surrounding hills and mountains. The lake was named for Blossom's mother. Did you know that? Angela Rose. She was his second wife. A lovely girl, quite a few years younger than he was. It's tragic she died so young. Blossom was only two or three at the time."

"Do you know how she died?" I asked.

"I'm not sure. Probably flu or pneumonia. Remember, in those days even a cold could be fatal. There were no antibiotics, and medical science was primitive compared to what it is now."

Next was a large photograph of the lumber mill with Morgan Thatcher dressed to kill in a three-piece suit surrounded by a dozen men in work clothes holding various tools of the trade posing beside a huge cedar log.

"There's my father," said a high wispy voice behind me. I turned and was surprised to see that we had been joined by Mildred Birch and Esther Wick. Esther reached up and placed her finger on the image of a scrawny young man in khaki overalls holding a gigantic axe.

I smiled at her. "That axe looks as big as he is."

"He was stronger than he looked," she said proudly.

Studying the picture, Mildred remarked, "My grandmother always said that if Morgan Thatcher had had his way, we'd all be living in Thatchersville." She laughed, her voice like the crackle of brittle twigs. "Luckily, that didn't happen."

"Do you remember him?" I asked.

"No, not really. I mostly remember being afraid of him, but I was just a little girl when my mother took me to visit my grandmother. She lived there in the house, you know, in the rooms behind the kitchen."

I nodded eagerly. "Yes, those are the rooms I'm planning to remodel for myself and my daughter."

"To me," Mildred continued, "Morgan was larger than life—big and gruff and scary. I always hid when I heard him coming." She smiled at the memory. "Of course, my grandmother wasn't afraid of him. She wasn't afraid of anything."

"Everyone always said Morgan acted like he owned the town," Flossie added. "Needless to say, this didn't make him too popular with the local folks."

"His men respected him, though," Esther said. "I know my father did."

"Are there any pictures here of Blossom as a young woman?" I asked, remembering the ghost I had seen.

Flossie moved to a picture of several girls standing in front of a picket fence. She pointed to a pretty dark-haired girl in a white lace pinafore. "This is Blossom. I think she was thirteen or fourteen in this picture. It was taken at the church picnic the year the new minister came to town."

Mildred said, "None of us really knew Blossom in those days. She was older. I saw her now and again at the mansion when I visited my grandmother—my father ran the dry goods store in town—but I was just a child and spent most of my time in the kitchen. Blossom would smile at me, but we didn't become true friends until much later after we were grown."

Esther said, "My older sister, Charlotte—rest her soul—was close to Blossom's age. She always used to say that Blossom was a nice girl but thoroughly cowed by her tyrant of a father. He was very jealous and possessive. He hardly allowed Blossom any social life at all. He wouldn't let her date or go to school dances."

"Why not?" I asked, thinking what a lonely girl Blossom must have been.

"Probably because of Morgan's first wife," Flossie declared. "It wasn't generally known at the time, but it eventually came out that she'd taken their son Clayton when he was small and run off with Morgan's old partner."

"That's right," Mildred agreed. "Most people figure that's what turned Morgan sour. He never got over his wife's leaving him and taking his son."

"And then," Esther added, eager to keep her two cents in, "his second wife died and left him to raise Blossom all by himself in that great big house. People always said he was afraid Blossom would run off and leave him too."

"She had everything money could buy," Mildred said somberly. "Position, private tutors, beautiful clothes—but she was always under her father's thumb. He was so controlling and over-protective."

"What about Blossom's half-brother?" Nathan asked. He'd been following along, listening attentively. "He eventually came back, didn't he?"

"Yes, that's right—and what a surprise!" Mildred exclaimed. "I remember visiting my grandmother one day, and there he was. Of course, I was just a little girl then. Nobody told me anything, but I overheard things."

Esther nodded eagerly. "Everybody was talking about it. My father said that Morgan's old partner—the one who ran off with Morgan's wife—came back in desperate need of money. He agreed to return the boy in exchange for Morgan's paying off his gambling debts."

"That's awful," I said indignantly. "It's like he sold him."

I could just imagine the gossip, given my experience so far living in a small town.

"It's funny," Mildred said, puckering her mouth thoughtfully, "In later years, Blossom hardly ever talked about her brother."

Nathan turned to his aunt, "Is there a picture of Clayton here someplace?"

"Yes," Flossie said, tapping a finger lightly against her lip. "I know there's at least one. Blossom told me she took it herself. Let me see . . ."

She moved along the wall studying each photo carefully. Automobiles replaced horses in the pictures, and stately homes replaced one-room cabins. Photographs of the main street evolved, gradually displaying rows of businesses, a church, and an impressive new high school. Clothing and hair styles also changed with the times.

"Oh yes, here it is." She stopped in front of a grainy, slightly under-exposed shot of a tall young man with sandy hair leaning against an old coupe. The caption underneath read *Clayton Thatcher, c. 1941*.

As I studied the picture, Nathan leaned toward me and asked, "Any resemblance to the grandson?"

It took me a second to make the connection between the figure in this aging photograph to the handsome stranger who had appeared in Salmon Falls announcing he was

Blossom Thatcher's grandnephew. "Hmm, a little," I said. "I don't think Dillon's quite as tall."

Suddenly, the phone in my pocket chirped. I snatched it out and saw that it was Dillon texting again: *Your car is at the library but you are not. Where are you?*

I frowned. "Speaking of Dillon . . ."

Nathan cocked an eyebrow curiously. "Problem?"

I shook my head and texted back: *Walked to Senior Center to meet Blossom's old friends. Come on over. Ladies would love to meet you.*

I turned to Nathan and the waiting women. "That was Dillon Thatcher, Blossom's grandnephew. You've probably heard he's visiting here from Ohio. I invited him to join us."

The ladies crowded around upon hearing Dillon's name. With amusement, I predicted a shift in the focus of local gossip from me to him.

Dillon responded: *I'll pass. See you later?*

I texted back: *OK*

"Is he coming here?" Esther asked, her thin voice reminding me of a tin whistle. Anticipation made it even more shrill than usual. "Blossom's nephew?"

"No," I said regretfully. "I guess he had something else to do." *Put off by the thought of talking to a bunch of old women, more likely.* I felt affronted on their behalf.

I did not want to dwell on Dillon. I pointed once more to the picture on the wall and directed my question to Mildred. "Do you remember Blossom's brother?"

She shook her head, her brow furrowing as she answered. "Not really. My Grandmother always told me to stay away from him. I don't think she liked him. She used to say he was 'shiftless.'"

"What do you mean?" I asked.

"Oh, you know—a rascal, a layabout. She disapproved of him. He liked to drink and gamble and run with a tough crowd."

Esther eagerly joined in. "It created quite a stir when Clay first appeared in town as a young man. Few people remembered him. His mother had taken him and run off so long ago. Most never even knew Clay existed—certainly Blossom didn't. She was in high school by that time. I heard all about it from my sister Charlotte, and of course the whole town was talking."

What a bombshell it must have been for Blossom to find out she had a half-brother.

"That's probably why he moved away again," I said. "It had to be hard for him here."

The women's faces suddenly turned serious.

Mildred spoke. "No. Something happened. Something awful. Some sort of gun fight. I don't know the details. Blossom would never talk about it, but a number of men were killed, including Morgan Thatcher."

"What?" I gasped. "I had no idea."

"That's when Clay ran off," Mildred continued, her voice harsh as gravel, "like the coward he was—and left Blossom to deal with the aftermath. Grandmother always said it was too much for Blossom to cope with. The men at the sawmill helped her for a while, but after a few years production slacked off and eventually she had to sell it. She just didn't have the business acumen her father had. There are apartments on that property now, down by the river. She was forced to sell off the timberland too—several thousand acres—and then most of the estate surrounding the mansion. She lived off the proceeds for many years. She had no other income except for what she made giving piano lessons."

This seemed like the right time to pose the question that had been burning in the back of my mind. "What about Tommy O'Connell? The man Blossom was supposed to marry? You haven't mentioned him. I know he disappeared—left her in the lurch I was told. Is it possible he was among the men who were killed?"

Flossie pursed her lips, then spoke slowly and deliberately. "Tommy O'Connell has always been a mystery."

"My grandmother liked him," Mildred interjected, her face lighting up once more. "Even as a little girl I thought he was charming. So witty and handsome—just like Clark Gable."

"No one knew where he came from," Esther said eagerly. "The story is that he just appeared in town with Clayton one day. It was right before the war. Everyone said he was a gambler and con artist. He and Clay used to go into Seattle and get into all sorts of mischief."

Flossie put up a cautioning finger. "Remember," she said, "it was eighty years ago. Most of that is hearsay." She paused for a moment as though gathering her thoughts, then continued. "As you probably heard, Blossom fell madly in love with him. She was quite beautiful in those days. Of course, Morgan flew into a rage, convinced Tommy wasn't good enough for her. Maybe he thought Tommy only wanted her for the money she would inherit. I don't know, but the next thing anyone knew Tommy was gone— disappeared without a trace. Some said good riddance, but Blossom never got over him. She waited her whole life for him to return."

I put my palms together and pressed them thoughtfully against my lower lip. "You don't suppose Morgan . . ."

Flossie picked up my thought. "Did away with him?" She shrugged. "Nobody knows. I'm sure he was capable of it, but there was never any evidence, and Blossom refused to believe it. The whole story has become like a local legend, told and embellished over the years until it's hard to know what's true and what isn't."

Nathan had gone back to inspecting the photographs hung up around the room. "Do you have a picture of Tommy here somewhere?"

"I think so," Flossie said. "Blossom donated a whole stack of pictures and I'm pretty sure there was a picture of Tommy O'Connell among them. She once told me she got a camera for her twenty-first birthday and ran around taking everyone's picture. Of course, that was before her father died and Clay moved away."

She moved slowly along the wall, peering carefully at each image.

"Yes, here it is," she said finally. She pointed to a time-worn snapshot of a handsome young man in a plaid shirt, boots, and trousers, grinning jauntily as he leaned on a shovel. He had a wide-brimmed hat pushed back on his head, revealing a shock of dark wavy hair. I recognized him from the picture we had found in the piano bench. I tried to conjure an image of him romancing the impressionable young woman Blossom must have been in those days.

I felt myself being swept up in the story as if it had happened only last week instead of eighty-odd years ago. "Wasn't there an investigation? Didn't anyone try to find out what happened to him? Blossom must have been beside herself."

Mildred shook her head. "Nobody was thinking about Tommy then because it was just about that time the gangsters attacked the Thatcher home and shot up the place. Morgan and several of the men from the mill were killed. It was dreadful. Even my poor grandmother was injured and spent a night in the hospital. I was just a little girl at the time, but I'll never forget how terrified I was at the prospect of losing my grandma. After the shooting, the police were too busy tracking down the culprits to worry about the disappearance of some itinerant con man."

"What prompted the attack?" I asked. "What did Morgan have to do with gangsters?"

"Most people thought it involved Clay's gambling," Esther said. "That was the story that went around."

"And he left town shortly after," Mildred stated with a firm nod of her head as though that were proof enough. "Didn't even stay long enough for his father's funeral."

"Do you suppose Tommy was involved?" I asked. "Didn't you say he was also a gambler?"

Flossie shrugged. "It's possible. Maybe Clay and Tommy rendezvoused at some prearranged location after the shooting. Maybe they'd made some big gambling score and the gangsters came to get revenge. Lots of rumors went around and the stories got crazier with each telling, but, the truth is, no one really knows."

"All we *do* know," Mildred murmured, "is that Tommy swept Blossom off her feet—"

"—and then left her," Esther finished with a huff in her voice.

My mind reeled. So, was Tommy nothing more than a scoundrel? A gambler and a gigolo who seduced Blossom as part of a get-rich scheme? When it failed, had he then callously left her and never come back? He could have at least written Blossom a letter to let her down easily.

"What about the men who murdered Morgan Thatcher?" Nathan asked, inserting himself once more into the conversation. "Were they caught?"

"Oh, yes," Flossie said. "It was in all the newspapers at the time. Here, we have a scrapbook."

Eagerly, she directed us to a table on which sat a large book stuffed with newspaper clippings. She opened it to the first page. There was the yellowed front page of the *Times* emblazoned with the headline: *Murder and Mayhem in Salmon Falls.* Further articles chronicled the police investigation and ultimate capture and conviction of the notorious Seattle gangster, Vince Logan, who allegedly had familial ties with the infamous Al Capone of Chicago.

What had Clay and Tommy been mixed up in?

Chapter Twenty-Two

"You like Mexican?" Nathan asked as we exited the Senior Center. "There's a great place here in town we can walk to."

"Sounds good. Lead the way."

A few minutes later, we were devouring chicken chimichangas with freshly made salsa and guacamole. Judging by the crowd, this restaurant was a popular lunch destination.

"So," Nathan said, "what did you think?"

"Well, this town has an interesting history . . ."

He nodded expectantly, his face hinting at a smile.

" . . . with a lingering mystery that I find intriguing."

"Tommy O'Connell," he said.

"Right." I leaned forward, gesturing with my fork for emphasis. "Why doesn't anyone know what happened to him? Poor Blossom apparently spent her entire life waiting for him, always believing he would return. It's just so heartbreaking."

"You're an incurable romantic," he said, not unkindly. "But remember, this happened almost eighty years ago. Most of the women at the Senior Center were children back then. They barely remember him, if they knew him at all."

"I know." I shook my head and took a sip of my iced tea. "I just can't stand loose ends. I mean, given what we know, he was either a romantic figure who disappeared under tragic circumstances, or he was a heartless, self-seeking cad who ran off and purposely broke Blossom's heart and destroyed her life. I want to believe the former, but evidence seems to point to the latter."

Instead of laughing and telling me I was being silly, which is what Daniel would have done, Nathan leaned toward me intently. "Let's look at this logically. We know that Clay and Tommy were friends, right? That's a known fact. By all accounts, Clay invited Tommy to Salmon Falls and introduced him to Blossom. Therefore, I think the real question is, how much did Clay love his sister? Would he have let Tommy court her if he knew Tommy was a fraud? Would he have allowed Blossom to become engaged to someone he knew was only in it for her money?"

He let me ponder that while he put away another bite of his chimichanga. After a moment, he continued. "And what about her father? It's common knowledge that Morgan Thatcher was extremely protective of his daughter, and yet he apparently gave Tommy permission to marry Blossom. In researching the Thatcher family for my book, I came across the engagement announcement published in the local paper at the time. Seems everything was all done very formal and proper. According to the article, they were to have a June wedding."

How romantic. I felt strangely relieved. I had so wanted to believe that Tommy and Blossom had truly loved each other. Nathan was right, I was a romantic at heart.

I gave a wistful sigh, pushing a piece of chicken around the plate with my fork. "So, we'll never know what really happened to him."

"Probably not," Nathan agreed with a shrug. He scooped salsa onto a chip and tossed it into his mouth.

"We found a picture of Tommy at the house," I said. "It's a close-up portrait, the kind lovers give to each other. On the back it says '*Love always, Tommy.*' It was in the piano bench."

"She probably placed it on the piano so she could look at it when she played."

I narrowed my eyes at him. "I suspect you're a romantic too."

He chuckled good-naturedly.

He has a nice laugh. The thought came unbidden, surprising me.

Suddenly, my cell phone rang. I started, then dragged the offending instrument from my coat pocket. It was Jared.

"When are you coming home?" my brother blurted without preamble.

"I'm having lunch in town with a friend. I'll be home in thirty minutes. Why? If it's the roofers, just point them in the direction of the roof. I'm sure they can find it."

He snorted. "They got here about an hour ago. No, it's that antiques buyer, Borello. He's here again and wants to show you something he thinks you'll find interesting."

"What is it?" I asked impatiently.

"Just get back here, will ya?"

"Okay, okay. I'm on my way." I frowned as I thrust the phone back into my pocket. What could Borello have to show me that was so important? Oh well, I had been gone a lot longer than I intended. I probably should get back in case the roofers had any questions.

"Trouble in paradise?" Nathan asked.

"Oh, no, just a minor annoyance I have to take care of."

Nathan signaled the waiter to bring the check.

A thought occurred to me. "Hey, after we pick up the cars, why don't you follow me back to the house? I'll give you a tour. You can take a couple of pictures for your book."

"That'd be great. I'd love to see the inside. If the interior is half as grand as the exterior, it must be impressive indeed."

"Well, we *have* managed to sweep out most of the dust and cobwebs by now, but we're still in the middle of refurbishing and updating. There's still a lot of work to be done, but I've always thought it was an awesome house, full of potential, regardless of its age and condition. They just don't make houses with that kind of character anymore."

"I completely agree," he said, placing some bills on the table for the waiter. "It feels like it should be the setting for some sort of romantic mystery."

Tentatively, I asked, "Have you ever read *Great Expectations?*"

"Yes, of course. I hadn't thought of that, but you're right. Blossom Thatcher is Miss Havisham to a tee: a wealthy spinster jilted by her lover, left to mourn alone in a dusty old mansion for the rest of her life."

An elated grin spread across my face. "I think you're the first person I've met since college who's read it."

"Let me guess. English Lit?" He tilted his head provocatively.

"Guilty as charged." I laughed. "I used to dream of writing The Great American Novel, but real life always seems to get in the way."

He fixed me with an earnest gaze. "It's not too late, is it?" His deep brown eyes seemed to bore directly into my soul.

I flashed back to a time a few years ago when I had tried my hand at writing. Daniel had teased me and called it my little hobby. He had refused to take my writing seriously. Eventually his patronizing comments had eroded my self-confidence, and I had abandoned my fledgling novel. It hadn't helped that Amy was a toddler and required a lot of attention. Without Daniel's support, the effort just hadn't seemed worth it.

"I don't know," I said, "maybe someday when I'm not so busy." Discomfited by the personal delving, I rubbed my palms together briskly and stood. "As much as I'd love to continue this conversation, I think I'd better get back and see what all the fuss is about."

Fifteen minutes later, I pulled my Subaru into the driveway and stopped. Nathan halted his yellow VW directly behind me. In my mind's eye, I saw my neighbor at her kitchen window with a pair of binoculars, taking notes. I shook my head, blowing my breath out in a sigh that was somewhere between amusement and exasperation.

The place was a flurry of activity. Men with ropes and harnesses swarmed across the roof like a high wire act. A huge metal garbage receptacle had been moved in close to the side of the house to collect debris pitched down by the workers as they tore off the old shingles. The air was filled with the din of shouting, tearing, and pounding.

Besides Jared's old Toyota and Borello's gray van, two large trucks belonging to the roofers were parked in the yard adding to the confusion. As I emerged from my car, one of the roofing contractors hurried over for a consultation.

Nathan got out of his car and leaned against the fender, absorbing the hubbub with a tolerant smile. Finally, he came up beside me and said, "Let's do this another time. Looks like you're busy today."

Flustered, I had to agree. "Okay, but promise me you'll come back another day."

He nodded amiably, then pulled a business card out of his wallet and handed it to me. "Call me when things calm down."

He gave me a quick wave as he got back into his car. Watching him pull away, I felt a twinge of regret. He hadn't been a boogeyman after all.

Chapter Twenty-Three

December 1940

"Happy birthday, Blossom," Tommy O'Connell said, stepping into the foyer as Blossom held the front door open. He pressed a small, gaily wrapped package into her hand. "Here, I brought you a little something."

"Oh, Tommy, you shouldn't have," she gushed, exceedingly pleased that he had.

"Well, one doesn't turn twenty-one every day," he said with a wink. He was dressed in a dark gray suit with a bold silver and blue silk tie that Blossom thought accentuated the twinkle in his luminous brown eyes. His thick wavy hair lay meticulously brushed back under his fedora, but when he removed the hat a stray wisp fell forward as though in protest of upper-class conformity. Blossom thought it perfectly defined his independent personality, and her heart swelled.

"Quick, come inside. It looks like it's starting to snow." She swung the door closed against the frigid night then hastened to unwrap the palm-sized gift in her hand.

With a little gasp of pleasure, she lifted the lid of the small white box to reveal a delicate gold brooch shaped like a cluster of apple blossoms inlaid with pink and white enamel.

"It's beautiful," she breathed, carefully lifting the brooch and admiring the exquisite craftsmanship of the tiny petals.

"Blossoms for my Blossom," Tommy said.

My Blossom.

Her face warmed as she leaned forward and gave him a kiss on the cheek. "It's perfect. I love it."

She hurried to the hall mirror and affixed the pin to the bodice of her dress, pleased with how it glistened in the light of the overhead chandelier. The pink and white enamel blossoms made a stunning complement to the mauve taffeta of her evening dress.

Finally, she said, "Father and Clay are in the parlor. We should join them. Dinner will be ready in a few minutes." They linked arms and Blossom led the way, her full skirt swishing as she walked.

Her father and Jed Hawkins sat conversing in chairs by the fire, nursing glasses of Scotch. In the background, a cheery jazz ensemble played over the radio. Morgan looked up as they entered and scarcely gave Tommy a nod. Blossom's father had grown accustomed to seeing Tommy with Clay these days, but he still resented the attention the young man gave his daughter.

Jed looked ill at ease in a tweed coat and tie, his bushy hair and beard stuffed into his collar like straw shoved into a scarecrow. He kept surreptitiously scratching at his neck and pulling on his tie till it was all askew. Blossom had to suppress a smile. *You can put a suit on a bull but it's still a bull.* She assumed her father had insisted Jed dress appropriately for her birthday. The foreman looked up and gave her a nod, lifting his glass in a genial salute. She wasn't sure whether to feel honored by his effort or sorry for his obvious misery.

Tommy sauntered over to where Clay slouched in a wingback chair near the window. Seeing his friend, Clay downed his drink with one swallow and jumped up to give Tommy an enthusiastic slap on the back. "Hey, partner, glad you could make it."

Blossom leaned close to show off the new brooch. "See what Tommy gave me?"

"Nice," Clay said. "Little apple blossoms."

Blossom thought she caught a look and a wink pass between them but couldn't be sure so she said nothing.

She could hardly wait to show the brooch to her friend Helen. Blossom knew what her friend's reaction would be. Helen was hopelessly idealistic and harbored wishes for a match between Blossom and Tommy. Earlier that day, Helen had given Blossom her birthday present: hand-embroidered towels and pillow cases. "For your hope chest," Helen had whispered conspiratorially.

While Blossom loved her friend's optimism, Tommy had been reticent in declaring his feelings, so despite the growing longing in her heart, Blossom hesitated to pin her hopes on what she feared was nothing more than a simple dalliance. In the meantime, she resolved to enjoy his friendship and attention for as long as it lasted.

"Let me get you a drink," Clay said.

"No, thanks," Tommy said. "I'll wait till after dinner."

"Suit yourself." Clay poured himself another Scotch.

Blossom wished Clay wouldn't drink so much, then chided herself for being insensitive. *He worked hard all summer. He certainly doesn't need me criticizing him. Heaven knows, he gets enough of that from Father.*

All summer and into the fall, Clay and Tommy had labored in the mountains at the mysterious gold mine marked on the map given to Blossom's father by Hiram Decker. *Four and a half years ago*, she thought. The night she had first learned she had a brother. *How my life has changed since that day.*

Blossom had never been to the mine and didn't know exactly what Clay and Tommy did there, but she did know that after spending days at the excavation, they always came home dirty, sore, and exhausted. In response to her questions, Clay would only mutter about how things would soon be different around there, while Tommy would wink and tell her she should just be patient.

She looked over at her father still talking to Jed, effectively ignoring his son. If only her father would show some interest, offer some help and encouragement. He never thought they'd last this long. *At least he hasn't tried to stop them.* She suspected her father found the whole undertaking foolish, perhaps even reckless, given his years of experience against their youth and ignorance.

She knew he underestimated them. *Can't you see how hard they've worked, Father? How determined they are to succeed? Can't you manage even one word of praise? It would take so little effort and mean so much to Clay.* She looked down to hide the pain in her eyes.

Blossom had been delighted to discover she had a brother, but it hadn't taken long to realize that father and son had been estranged for too long. Feelings between them had been strained since the day Clay arrived.

With the mine snowed in, Blossom had looked forward to a long, congenial winter with the whole family. Now she feared it would become a quagmire of tempers and resentments through which she would have to carefully pick her way.

Martha appeared in the doorway then, clutching a pot holder. "Dinner's on the table," she announced. Her eyes were moist with love and pride as she turned to Blossom. "I've cooked a pot roast with potatoes and all the trimmings for your birthday, honey, and your favorite peach cobbler for dessert."

As they moved to the dining room, Blossom saw that Martha had made a special fuss for the occasion, setting the table with all the best china and silver, even putting candles on the cobbler for Blossom to blow out. She knew the cobbler was made with peaches Martha had canned herself earlier that fall.

"Everything looks wonderful," Blossom said. She wrapped Martha in a warm embrace and, looking over the stout housekeeper's shoulder, smiled at the woman's four-year-old granddaughter peeking shyly around the door.

Morgan presented Blossom with a new Kodak Brownie camera for her twenty-first birthday, Jed gave her a pink scarf, and even Martha gave her a small book of verses. Blossom thanked them all with happy smiles and pronounced this the best birthday ever.

All through the meal, Clay and Tommy recounted tales of their struggles working at the mine, beginning with their original effort to cut through the thick undergrowth and search along a rocky hillside to locate the spot indicated on the map.

"Lucky for us it's not too far off the forestry road," Clay said. "The original prospector'd hacked out a sort of mule track that we managed to widen enough to drive the truck on."

"Then it's just a little ways up the slope of this outcropping on the side of the mountain," Tommy continued, "kind of hidden behind a grove of big fir trees."

"Good thing it weren't no further or I'd a had to carry Tommy, delicate as he was," Clay said.

"As I recall," Tommy retorted, "it was you who had blisters on your feet so big your boots wouldn't fit for a week."

Clay snorted. "And I had to show you how to use a shovel. Would you believe this poor fella had never done a lick of physical work in his entire life?"

Blossom interrupted their good-natured sparring. "How big is the mine? Is it a cave?"

"It's more like a deep crack that runs way back into the mountain," Clay said. "You can see all these veins of gold and quartz and different colored minerals running all through the rocks."

"We've widened it with our picks and shovels enough to get inside maybe twenty feet," Tommy added. "We had to carve a trail wide enough to haul our wheelbarrows up to the entrance. We've been filling up buckets of ore and bringing them back by the truckload."

"We're going to be *rich*," Clay proclaimed with a passion.

"Oh, Clay, that's wonderful," Blossom exclaimed, truly happy for her brother.

"Next summer we might try some dynamite," Tommy said.

"Yeah," Clay agreed, "then we can really make some headway."

"God help us," Jed muttered, shaking his head.

Suddenly fearful, Blossom said, "Are you sure that's safe? You don't know anything about using dynamite."

Tommy hastened to put her at ease. "Don't worry. If we do, we'll hire someone who knows what he's doing."

Blossom looked at him gratefully.

"Yeah," Clay added, "it's not like we'd do anything *stupid*." He angled a glance at his father.

Morgan had kept quiet until then, but as Martha cleared away the dessert dishes, he roused, lit a cigar, and in his slow gravelly voice said, "So, you think you've discovered the mother lode, eh? You ever going to let us see a sample of these hard earned riches?"

Clay nodded and jumped to his feet. "Meet me in the parlor—I'll be right there." With that he tore out of the room and made for the basement stairs.

Filled with anticipation and ignoring her father's scowl, Blossom took Tommy's arm and went into the front room as instructed. Behind her, she heard her father mutter something to Jed but couldn't make it out. She sat on the small brocade sofa in the middle of the room and pulled Tommy down beside her. It was her twenty-first birthday after all, and she would sit beside whomever she pleased. Jed resumed his seat by the fire while Morgan remained standing, leaning against the mantle and puffing on his cigar. Blossom looked at Tommy, but he only smiled.

Within minutes, Clay burst into the room looking slightly disheveled. "Happy birthday, Sis." He strode toward Blossom and deposited a hat-sized box into her lap.

Blossom wondered briefly if he'd sneaked another drink before coming in, but she said nothing and, instead, thanked him profusely, opening the box to reveal a large multicolored stone wrapped in brown paper.

As she lifted the stone and held it up to the light, it began to sparkle and glisten. Golden crystals erupted from the stone's surface in glittering patches mixed with white quartz and other ores of various colors, reds and greens, creating an object of extraordinary beauty. Blossom held it up proudly for her father and Jed to see.

"Oh, Clay, it's wonderful," she exclaimed. "This is from your mine? I've never seen anything so beautiful."

She set the stone on the coffee table in front of her, then caught Tommy's hand and gave it a squeeze. She could barely contain her excitement. *Perhaps if the mine is successful, Tommy will stay in Salmon Falls and settle down.* She hardly dared to hope.

For a moment, nobody spoke. The fire crackled warmly on the hearth as Clay stood triumphantly looking from one face to another. On the radio, a spirited piano piece kept the mood lively. Blossom and Tommy exchanged happy glances as he continued to hold her hand, oblivious to her father's glower.

At last, Morgan crossed the room and picked up the stone, examining it closely under the light of a nearby table lamp. "Real purty," he said. "What you've got here is a real nice piece of quartz and iron pyrite."

Jed snickered.

"Iron pyrite?" Clay asked suspiciously.

Blossom's heart froze. She'd heard her father tell enough stories from his mining days to know what that meant. Tears welled in her eyes.

"Some call it *fool's gold*," Morgan said. "Beginners fall for it every time."

Tommy dropped Blossom's hand. He stood and walked dejectedly to the other side of the room, keeping his eyes averted from her sorrowful gaze. He looked completely disheartened.

"*No*," Clay cried. "You're wrong—*this is gold!*"

"Now, son . . ." Morgan set the glittering stone back on the table.

"Don't *son* me," Clay screamed. "You may have been responsible for my birth, but you weren't never no father to me! You *wanted* the mine to fail just simply 'cause it came from Hiram—*who was a far better father to me than you've ever been.*"

"Will you listen to me?" Morgan said angrily. "Maybe I *was* jealous of Hiram, and maybe I should have helped you, but . . ."

"I don't *need* your help!" Clay pivoted and stormed out of the room. A minute later the front door slammed. A draft of cold air blew in from the hallway. Outside, they heard a car engine rev and roar away into the night.

With a disgusted snarl, Morgan stalked out of the room with Jed on his heels. As they went, Blossom heard Jed say, "He'll be back, boss. He's got no place else to go."

Blossom sat on the sofa staring at her hands in her lap. What would happen now? Clay would go back to drinking and gambling, getting into trouble and wasting his life away; Tommy would leave town, resuming his life of carefree independence; and she would die a sad old spinster in her father's house. Without thinking, her hand strayed to the brooch pinned to her breast. A tear rolled down her cheek.

Chapter Twenty-Four

December 1940

"Blossom?"

She looked up. Tommy stood in front of her, his outstretched hand offering her a handkerchief. She took it with a murmur of thanks and wiped her eyes. In her misery, she could find no words to say.

"Will you come out on the veranda with me?" he asked. "I'd like to talk to you."

She sniffed and nodded. "Let me get my coat."

Outside, he motioned her to the porch swing and sat down beside her. He pulled a lap robe over their legs to ward off the chill. It had quit snowing, but a thin blanket of white covered the lawn and surrounding trees, creating a peaceful winter scene.

Blossom waited, fearing the inevitable words of farewell.

Tommy took her hands. "Blossom, I love you."

She looked at him, confused. His eyes met hers with an earnestness she had never seen before. There was longing in them but also an overpowering sorrow.

He said, "I had hoped the mine would produce enough money to make me a worthy suitor in your father's eyes. I know he only wants the best for you—which is what you deserve. A penniless drifter like me doesn't stand a chance." He smiled. "I can't believe he hasn't run me off already."

"Oh, Tommy. I love you too." Tears streamed down her face. "I thought you brought me out here to tell me you were leaving. I thought you'd go and I'd never see you again."

Tenderly, he wiped the tears from her cheeks. "Do you think you could ever be happy with a poor chap like me? I don't have a lot of skills, but I'm willing to learn—and I *have* recently learned how to handle a shovel."

Blossom laughed and threw her arms around him. Music from the radio could be heard playing softly in the background, but, at that moment, it sounded like a choir of angels. The world was once again a glorious place. "Oh, yes. I don't care about gold or riches. All I want is to spend my life with you."

"What about your father?" Tommy asked apprehensively. "He won't be happy, and he's a powerful man in these parts."

"Let me worry about my father," Blossom said. "If I give him the choice between a wedding and a life where I stay nearby, or an elopement where he never sees me again, I think he'll choose the wedding."

"Maybe he can put me to work on the estate digging ditches."

Blossom sniffed and smiled through the joyful tears glistening in her eyes. "I think he can arrange something better than that."

Tommy smiled and pulled her into a passionate embrace. At last, he said, "We should get married in the spring in the orchard under the apple trees."

"That's perfect," Blossom murmured. Despite the winter chill, she felt warm all over. She loved the feel of his strong arms around her, his ardent lips pressed against hers. Never had she been so completely content. She was his Blossom and he was her Tommy. Forever.

Suddenly, heavy footsteps pounded up behind them and large hands gripped Tommy's shoulders, wrenching him bodily off the swing and down the front steps of the veranda into the wet snow. Jed Hawkins glowered angrily at him from the top of the porch steps. "Keep your mitts off the boss's daughter, you no-account woman chaser."

"Jed, *no!*" Blossom screamed, flying at the foreman and grabbing his arm.

He shook her off like a mosquito and stomped down the stairs to face off with Tommy who had leaped to his feet to meet him, a wiry mongrel against a charging bull. Jed's tweed coat and tie had been abandoned in favor of a more flexible leather jacket.

Blossom would have thrown herself into the fight to stop Jed, but a strong hand on her shoulder prevented her. "Hold on, girl," her father said into her ear. "Let's see what kind of man this fellow is."

"But *Father*," Blossom cried, struggling to get free of his hold, "Jed will kill him."

"Maybe not," Morgan replied. "Let's wait and see."

Tommy's fine suit was soaked with snow, and his hair fell in wet strands over his face as he stood with fists clenched waiting for Jed to strike. He didn't have long to wait. The big man lunged forward throwing all his weight into his meaty fist as he swung for Tommy's jaw—but empty air was all he met as the younger man dodged and leaped nimbly aside.   Jed staggered forward, momentarily off balance. Tommy's fist connected with a sharp blow to the foreman's cheekbone. He reeled back.

Blossom gasped. Then it occurred to her that Tommy had spent the last five months swinging a pick and carrying heavy buckets of rock down from the mountain. He was no longer the dandy who had come to Salmon Falls that spring. He was now a limber, well-muscled man in his prime. Behind her, she heard her father grunt in grudging admiration. Had he expected this? Had he deliberately set up this fight to test Tommy? But *why?*

Enraged, Jed threw his fist once more, intending to bash the smaller man senseless. Again Tommy danced out of the way.   His quick jab connected solidly with his opponent's protuberant nose. There was a sickening crunch and a spurt of blood. Jed howled and lunged, but Tommy refused to stand still. He dodged and weaved, punching as the bigger man threw himself around, wasting energy and growing increasingly exhausted.

Finally, Jed's foot slipped in the snow.   He fell backwards and didn't get up. Tommy stood over him. "Had enough?"

Jed glanced at his boss, then looked up at Tommy. "Yeah." He got to his feet, clamped a handkerchief to his bleeding nose, and trudged away toward his own cabin.

"You fight pretty well," Morgan said.

Tommy ran a hand through his hair, straightened his tie, and smoothed the front of his rumpled suit. He looked Morgan in the eye. "Gentlemen don't brawl, they box. I learned that from my grandfather when I was a kid. He worked in a gym in Chicago and even sparred once with Jack Dempsey. Taught me everything I know."

He came up on the porch and put his arm around Blossom, drawing her close. She looked at him with adoring eyes.

"And by the way," Tommy said, "I'm going to marry your daughter."

"I figured," Morgan said, a wry smile pulling at the corners of his mouth. "Sorry about the fight. I just had to know what kind of man you were. Can't have my best girl marrying some pantywaist milksop who can't take care of her."

"Father!" Blossom scolded. "We love each other and that's all that's important, not whether he can beat other men in a fight."

"It's important in this business," Morgan stated. "A boss has to earn his men's respect. I won't be around forever and I need someone strong I can count on to take over."

"Take over?" Tommy said. "What about Clay? Isn't he the one who'll take over someday? He's your son."

Morgan snorted. "He's my son in name, but he takes after his mother and that fool who raised him. Neither was any good. They were losers, both of 'em—greedy, devious, and untrustworthy."

"But, father," Blossom protested. She had come to love her brother despite his faults. "I don't think you're being fair. Surely, with some guidance . . ."

"Oh, he'll be taken care of," Morgan assured her. "I just can't trust him with the operation of this outfit. There's too much at stake."

"I'm just sorry the mine didn't work out," Tommy said regretfully. "That gold would have been a great help in this economy."

Morgan looked around. "Come inside. There's more you should know about that mine. Clay didn't let me finish."

Curious, Tommy and Blossom followed him back inside to the sitting room where the large piece of ore still sat sparkling on the table in the lamplight. The fire had died and the room had cooled considerably. Morgan picked up the stone and turned it this way and that, examing its different aspects.

"This here sparkly stuff is fool's gold, iron pyrite, like I said. It's worthless. You can chip it and crush it. It's brittle. Gold ain't brittle, it's soft. You can pound it with a hammer and it won't break. But pyrite don't necessarily mean there's no gold. In fact, it ain't unusual to find pyrite with gold. This here white quartz is another good indicator, along with these other colored ores."

"You mean there might be gold in the mine after all?" Blossom asked. She glanced at Tommy and saw that he also looked hopeful.

"I'd say there's a good chance," her father answered. "The trick is to break it all down and get rid of the impurities. There's a couple of ways to do it. I can show you how. Then we'll take it to the assayer's office for analysis, but I've got a pretty good hunch about this."

"But you purposely let Clay think the mine is worthless. Why?"

"Gold fever. I could see he's got it bad and needed to be reined in. I've seen a lot of good men destroyed by gold fever."

"We need to find him," Blossom said. "He and Tommy are partners. He deserves to hear this."

Morgan frowned, then said, "Yeah, you're right. Somebody'd better find him before he goes and does something stupid."

Blossom looked at Tommy. "Do you know where he might be?"

Tommy thought for a moment. "I have an idea where to look, and I'd better find him quick. I think he's got the map with him."

"One more thing," Morgan said. "Any chance either of you thought to file your claim legally with the Bureau of Land Management?"

Tommy looked confused, then shook his head. "I don't think so. I've never heard him mention it."

"I mighta known," Morgan growled. "There's laws about these things, you know. Paperwork that has to be filed. You need a land description and a location certificate filed with the BLM. You can't just waltz into the mountains and start digging without going through proper channels."

"Well, it's not too late, is it?" Blossom asked. "They can still file a claim, can't they?"

"Sure, they can file a claim—but so can anyone else in possession of that map. So, you'd better hope Clay doesn't lose it."

Chapter Twenty-Five

December 1940

Tommy was fairly certain he knew where Clay had gone. They had first met at an all-night clandestine poker game held in the back room of the Four Dragons Restaurant in one of Seattle's seamier neighborhoods. The game took place nightly and continued until dawn, players coming and going at all hours. Word of the game had circulated among Seattle's gambling population and was typically frequented by a circle of regulars and their guests, though the occasional newcomer was not unheard of. A ready wad of cash was seldom turned away.

The local police seemed to be aware of the game, but tended to look the other way provided no overt drunkenness or public disorderliness broke out in the neighborhood. As long as the game remained hidden and drew no attention to

itself, they were content to ignore it.   The likelihood of
stumbling onto a random city official at the game may have
been a factor in this uncharacteristic broad-mindedness.

The restaurant's proprietor was suspected of being
involved with several nefarious characters in the local
underworld who dealt mainly in gambling and loan sharking.
This was a world all too familiar to Tommy. He headed
there now.

Tommy had grown up in Al Capone's Chicago
during Prohibition.   This had presented him with
opportunities for a different sort of education than most.
While his mother was a teacher and saw to it that Tommy
mastered the academics, his father's occupation was more
ambiguous, and seemed to be divided between serving as
maître d' at a swanky restaurant during the day and dealing
cards at a notorious speakeasy at night.

Under his father's tutelage, Tommy had mastered the
shell game by ten years old. By eleven, he could pull a penny
from the ear of an amazed bystander, and by twelve was
nimbly dealing cards off the bottom of the deck. Much of his
early life was spent refining his card playing skills, honing his
dexterity, and learning to read the tells of other players. As
he got older, he also learned that by playing on his good
looks and boyish charm he could insinuate himself into all
manner of wealthy circles, hustling and conning his way to a
very comfortable living.

Eventually, Tommy became bored with Chicago and
decided to take his game elsewhere, desiring to see more of
the country and expand his horizons. He had no goals other
than to have a good time and make some fast money.
Eventually, he made his way to Seattle. Clayton Thatcher,
the son of a wealthy lumber baron, had seemed a likely mark.

Tommy had not counted on meeting Blossom.

He parked on a deserted side street a block away and
walked toward the back of the restaurant. In the alley, he
encountered Clay savagely throwing stones at an empty tin
can. Tommy grabbed him by the arm and spun him around.

"Clay, do you have the map?"

"No, I got rid of it. I'm done with mining and I'm done with Morgan Thatcher."

"What do you mean you got rid of it? Where is it?"

"What difference does it make?" Clay snarled drunkenly. "It's just a worthless piece of paper."

Tommy glanced quickly around. Several nasty-looking goons lounged nearby, smoking cigarettes and eyeing them with interest. He put a hand on Clay's shoulder. "Keep it down, chum."

He pulled him out of the alley and down the sidewalk, out of earshot. "Listen, there's something you need to know. You took off before Morgan had a chance to finish. The truth is, he thinks it's possible we *have* struck gold. All those different ores are good indicators, he says."

Clay looked suspicious. "*Bullshit*. What about the fool's gold? He seemed pretty certain of that too."

"I know. But turns out that's just a type of iron ore. He says it's not unusual to find it along with the gold—same with the quartz and all those other ores, copper and such. It needs to be processed and analyzed by an assayer."

For a moment, Clay just stood and stared. He seemed to be having trouble comprehending this new information. Finally, he shook his head. "Well, it's too late. I bet the mine in a poker game and lost. The map's gone."

Tommy chewed his lip thoughtfully. "How did you get them to accept the wager? What value did you put on it? Surely they didn't just take your word for it."

"I threw in some of them 'gold nuggets' I had in my pocket as proof." He snorted. "They didn't know the difference any more'n I did. Logan's eyes lit up like headlights when he saw that fool's gold—just like mine did that first time. I didn't have any trouble convincing him the map was legit."

"Vince Logan?" Tommy asked with a sick feeling in his gut. Vince Logan was a notorious crime boss in the Northwest, dealing in everything from drugs to gambling to prostitution. Rumor had it he was distantly related to Al Capone himself, and definitely not someone to trifle with.

"Yeah," Clay muttered, kicking at a bottle lying on the sidewalk. It skittered off the curb and rolled into the street with a resonant clink. "You don't suppose he'd give it back if I asked him, do you?"

"Oh sure. Why don't you just march in there and tell Mr. Logan you made a mistake. Tell him you meant to defraud him by tricking him into accepting a wager on a gold mine you knew to be worthless, only to find out it *wasn't* worthless after all and now you'd like him to give it back. Sounds perfectly reasonable. I can't imagine why he'd be anything but agreeable."

Clay remained silent, glaring sullenly at his feet.

"And then he'd have your throat cut," Tommy continued, "and your body dumped in Puget Sound."

"All right, all right," Clay blurted angrily. "I get it. But so what? So what if we don't have the map? We don't need it anymore. We know where the mine is. We can still get all the gold we need to get rich."

Tommy struggled to stay patient. No wonder Morgan didn't want to leave the management of his lumber empire to his son. Clay seemed incapable of grasping anything beyond the immediate.

"There's something else," Tommy said. "Did you ever actually file the claim?"

"What?" Clay stared at him blankly.

"I'll take that as a 'no,'" Tommy said with a sigh. "According to Morgan, just because you are in possession of a map doesn't mean you own the mine or whatever minerals come out of it. You have to file the claim with the Bureau of Land Management. If Logan files before we do, then we can be prosecuted for claim jumping."

"*What?*" Clay said again.

"Only the person with a legitimate certificate on record can legally claim ownership in a dispute. There's all kinds of paperwork involved."

"*Goddamnit.* This is all Morgan's fault," Clay snarled, kicking out at a lamppost. "Why didn't he ever tell us this before? None of this would've happened if he had just helped us from the start."

Tommy bit his tongue, deciding for the sake of expediency not to remind Clay of his insistence that they do everything themselves, and of his adamant refusal to go to his father for advice.

"Water under the bridge," Tommy said. "Right now we need to keep cool heads and figure out a plan to get the map back."

"Well, why don't we just go in first thing Monday morning and file the claim ourselves?" Clay's smug expression clearly showed that he thought the solution obvious.

"So, you want to go back to business as usual knowing that Vince Logan has a map to the mine's location? Do you plan to dig with one eye looking over your shoulder all the time? Or were you planning to hire a battalion of armed guards? Don't you think Logan will want to go up and see this wealth of gold for himself? What will keep him from simply killing us while we work, burying our bodies on the mountain where they'll never be found, and taking the gold for himself?"

"So what do we do?" Clay clenched his fists in despair.

"We make a plan," Tommy said. "I'll need a sheet of paper and a cigarette."

* * *

Tommy entered the gambling den in the back of the Four Dragons through the alley behind the restaurant minutes after Clay. It was late on a Saturday night and the place was hopping. Originally intended as a banquet room, the space had fallen into disrepair and eventually converted to storage. Shelves containing restaurant supplies ran along one wall, while the rear had been relegated to cleaning implements. The restaurant staff did a cursory cleaning of the dining area every morning and a thorough scrubbing of the kitchen every night. The resultant greasy rags were dumped out of the way in bins in the back corner until Monday morning when they were hauled out to the alley for pickup by the city's sanitation department.

For the purpose of gambling, two circular tables had been set up in the center of the room, each accommodating six players. A shabby sofa and a couple of mismatched chairs crammed in along the third wall allowed a modicum of comfort for guests awaiting their turn at the tables. Several bottles of liquor were set out on a makeshift bar, while a phonograph on an adjacent table spewed loud jazz, adding to the noise and confusion.

The atmosphere was suffocating; a thick blue haze of cigarette smoke hung over the room mingling with the acrid stench of sweat, kitchen grease, and caustic chemicals. Lighting was dim, consistent with the secretive nature of the establishment. Men conversed in shadowy corners or leaned against the walls smoking and drinking and making lascivious advances to the half dozen tawdry women who hung about, laughing raucously, flirting, and plying their dubious trade. One or two couples attempted to dance.

Vince Logan held court at the first table, hunkered over his cards and surrounded by his winnings. With satisfaction, Tommy noted the map rolled up and lying on the table among the stacks of cash at Logan's right elbow. Armed thugs skulked strategically around the room, keeping order and ensuring the security of the large amounts of money exchanging hands at the tables.

As instructed, Clay engaged himself in an argument with Vince Logan, brashly demanding to be let back into the game for a chance to win back his treasure map. He begged, he argued, he appealed to Logan's sense of fair play, creating a scene and drawing attention to himself.

With all eyes on Clay, Tommy moved nonchalantly to the back of the room where the bins of used cleaning rags were stored. Casually, he lit a cigarette and tossed the match into one of the bins. He took two or three deep pulls on the cigarette, making sure it was well ignited, then threw it into another bin. Before ambling off, he made certain that a coil of smoke rose from the greasy rags, ensuring the onset of a nice smoky fire.

Clay's voice was becoming more strident while Logan grew increasingly irritated. When Tommy heard Clay offer to wager his new car, that was Tommy's signal to intervene. He came up behind his friend and laid a hand on his shoulder. As he did, Tommy heard his father's voice in the back of his head: *"Finesse, my boy, finesse. Never lose your cool, no matter what game you're playing. Smile, and they'll never know what you're thinking."*

"Come on, chum," Tommy said in a calming voice. "You don't want to do that. Why don't you go have yourself a drink and cool off."

Clay seemed to come to his senses and straightened up, looking around. One of Logan's thugs approached the table with a hand on his gun.

"That won't be necessary," Tommy said. "Clay, why don't you go wait for me at the bar."

Clay hung his head, the very picture of contrition. "Sorry, Mr. Logan," he murmured, then shuffled off to the bar.

"Drunken shithead," Logan muttered. He waved off the goon.

Tommy nodded congenially. "I'm sorry, Mr. Logan. I should have gotten here sooner. I'm afraid my friend has had too much to drink. I hope he didn't cause you too much inconvenience. May I sit down?"

Logan looked him up and down then motioned to the man at the table to his right. Without a word, the man picked up his meager winnings and withdrew. Tommy took his place.

"Have I seen you here before?" Logan asked, shuffling the cards.

"Maybe. I've been here once or twice. O'Connell's the name. I moved here last spring from Chicago."

"Chicago, eh?" He eyed Tommy with interest. "What brings you way out here?"

Tommy shrugged and gave him a crooked smile as he added his ante to the kitty in the middle of the table. "I don't know. Guess I just needed a change of scenery."

Logan smirked and nodded like he understood. He began to deal the cards.

Suddenly, a shout cut through the din.

"*Fire!*"

Everyone turned to look. At that moment, the lights went out and the room was plunged into darkness. Chaos ensued. Women screamed and chairs fell over. Men jumped to their feet in panic. Flames shot from the trash bins at the back of the room. Clouds of oily black smoke poured into the air. Grotesque shadows writhed on the walls as people pushed toward the exit.

"*Get the lights back on!*" Logan roared above the clamor.

Two of Login's security guards began beating at the flames with their coats. Another soon joined them with a fire extinguisher hauled in from the restaurant kitchen. Seconds later, the lights blinked back on and the fire was quickly subdued.

"Sorry, Mr. Logan," a loud voice called out. "Someone must have bumped the light switch."

The room was a mess of fallen chairs, spilled drinks, broken bottles, and strewn cash. Men and women stumbled about, disheveled and disorientated. Poker players made hurried grabs to recover their winnings. Fist fights broke out. Brazen hookers ruined their stockings crawling on the floor, hastily snatching at fallen coins. Sounds of coughing and retching competed with the cacophonous jazz music still blaring from the phonograph. Someone hurried to prop open the back door into the alley to help dissipate the smoke.

Vince Logan had remained in his seat during the commotion, loath to abandon his considerable stacks of money. Tommy leaned toward him and said urgently, "You should probably scram, Mr. Logan. You can be sure the police and fire departments are on their way. Best not be caught in the middle of all this."

No sooner had he said this than a faint siren could be heard wailing in the distance, growing nearer. Tommy stood and motioned to one of Logan's henchmen. "Help Mr. Logan get his things together and get out of here before the cops arrive. Hurry."

The man brought a leather bag and began to stuff it with the piles of cash on the table, along with the rolled up map. Then Logan and his men hustled out the back door and into a car waiting in the alley. It roared away into the night.

Tommy let out a sigh, then turned and hurried to find Clay. He was pacing nervously on the sidewalk half a block from the restaurant's entrance.

"Did you get it?"

Tommy grinned. "I did. A little sleight of hand and—*presto!*" He pulled a worn, rolled up piece of paper from the sleeve of his coat. "Perfect timing on the lights, by the way."

"Thanks. Now let's get out of here!"

Chapter Twenty-Six

December 1940

Weeks passed. The events of that night in Seattle were batted about at length, with Clay and Tommy congratulating each other on a plan well executed. Tommy explained to Blossom and her father how they had obtained a cheap white paper placemat from an all-night diner around the corner. They had hurriedly sketched on it a crude facsimile of the map, changing or leaving off crucial details such as road names, landmarks, compass coordinates, and distance measurements. They made sure to scuff it and smear it with a bit of dirt like the original before rolling it up and making the swap.

"We took a chance that Logan wouldn't bother to examine it during all the hurry and confusion," Tommy said. "That's the beauty of a great distraction."

Blossom wrapped him in her arms, resting her head against his chest. "I'm just relieved you both made it home all right. I care a lot more about you than I do that old map."

The Christmas holidays came and went in a festive gala of lights and music with Morgan Thatcher hosting a banquet and barn dance for all his employees. Gifts were exchanged and a cheerful atmosphere lingered about the estate for days. Even more thrilling were the plans developing for Blossom's wedding to Tommy. They had decided on a June wedding. The apple orchard would be lush and green by then, the gardens bursting with flowers.

How will I ever be able to wait? Blossom's heart beat faster just thinking about it. Alone in her room, she hummed a lively tune, dancing and twirling in barely restrained joy.

Then early one morning, several days after Christmas, a large black car pulled up the driveway. Blossom heard it from her bedroom and ran to the window at the end of the upstairs hall overlooking the front of the house. Four men exited the car and marched up the front porch steps.

Who can they be? she thought fearfully. She'd never seen anyone like them in Salmon Falls. Dressed in dark trench coats with hats pulled low over their faces, the men had a disreputable look about them. Downstairs, she heard pounding at the door. Blossom knew her father and Jed were in the dining room eating breakfast, and Martha was in the kitchen. She hurried to the top of the landing and nearly ran headlong into Clay charging up the stairs in a panic.

"They found me," he gasped. "I've gotta hide."

"*Who?*" Blossom cried. "Who *are* they? What do they want?"

"Logan," was all he said as he pushed past her and lunged down the dark hallway.

Logan! The man Tommy and Clay had tricked. Her mouth went dry and her chest felt tight, making it hard to breathe. What kind of man was this Logan? What did he want? The map? Revenge? Thank goodness Tommy had not arrived yet this morning. He still kept a room at the hotel, but came to the house almost every day to see her.

Undecided what to do, Blossom stood at the top of the stairs listening as angry voices erupted at the front door. She strained to hear what was being said. Her father sounded heated and intimidating. He could be a fearsome man when riled, and he was used to getting his way. She knew he kept a loaded rifle on a hook over the kitchen door, and a shotgun in a cabinet in the front foyer. Jed often carried a handgun in a holster on his hip.

Without warning, a hand touched Blossom's shoulder and she whirled around in alarm. The clamorous pounding of her heart threatened to overwhelm her. She had forgotten the back stairs leading up from the kitchen.

"You nearly scared me to death," she whispered reproachfully to Martha.

The housekeeper put a cautioning finger to her lips.

"*Shhh,* don't you worry, honey," she whispered. "Your father's more than capable of handling a few thugs."

Moments later, the voices downstairs went quiet. Blossom exhaled and relaxed her grip on the balustrade as the front door banged shut. This was soon followed by the sound of a car revving its engine and roaring down the drive. She ran to the window in time to see it disappear through the trees heading away from Salmon Falls.

Then she saw something else. Seven or eight of her father's lumberjacks, big muscular men carrying hunting rifles, axes, and sledgehammers stood around the yard in a menacing tableau. As she watched, her father strode out and shook each man's hand, clapping him on the shoulder in a comradely fashion. The men were unfailingly loyal, and a kind of pride filled Blossom's heart. Would they feel the same way about Tommy if circumstances demanded he take over operation of the mill someday?

When her father came back inside, Blossom ran down the stairs and threw her arms around him. He seemed startled by this show of affection, but gave her a pat on the back and a crooked smile.

Jed stood nearby. Blossom noticed he carried her father's shotgun.

"I don't think we have to worry about Mr. Logan any more," Morgan said gruffly. "I warned the men weeks ago to be on guard for strangers. They set up a sort of security watch, and today they really came through. I think now Mr. Logan appreciates as how it ain't worth pokin' a stick into this here hornets' nest. He may be a big deal in the city, but out here in the country he ain't nothing more than a bug to be squashed."

Blossom smiled. She hoped he was right.

"By the way," her father said, "what happened to Clay?"

"I think he's upstairs in his room," Blossom said.

"Under the bed, no doubt," Jed muttered, putting the shotgun back into the hall cabinet.

Morgan grumbled in disgust. "Martha!" he shouted. "I need some more coffee." With that, he and Jed headed back to the dining room.

Later that day, Blossom confronted Tommy on the veranda, cornering him when he came to visit. Quickly, she told him about the morning's events, how Mr. Logan and three of his henchmen had arrived on their doorstep, and how her father and his men had driven them off, and how terrified she had been.

"Tell me the truth," she said. "Do you think he'll come back?"

"Your father is a formidable man. You shouldn't worry."

She stamped her foot. "Don't you tell me not to worry, Tommy O'Connell. Tell me what you really think."

He broke into a grin and leaned forward to give her a kiss. "That's what I love about you. You're beautiful and feisty."

"Don't change the subject."

He glanced around, then guided her to the porch swing. It was becoming their habitual place to have serious conversations. The sun had broken through the clouds with the promise of a clear afternoon ahead, but it was cold. Blossom wore wool slacks and a heavy sweater under her winter coat, while Tommy had on a warm overcoat and his usual fedora. He tried to draw her into an embrace, but she pulled back, giving him a stern frown.

"Well?" she demanded.

"Vince Logan," Tommy said finally, "is not a nice man. He was cheated and he's angry. He came here looking for reparation."

"He wants the map." Fear crept into her voice.

"Sure, but after meeting your father, he may feel it's not worth it. Logan may decide he's met his match and won't want to tangle with him again, especially here on your father's turf. Like I said, your father is formidable, and every bit as powerful as Logan in these parts."

"Clay's scared of him. He thought they came for him."

"With good reason," Tommy said with a wry smile. "I don't know what he was thinking, cheating a man like Logan."

"But Logan doesn't know who you are, does he? He won't be looking for you."

"He might not know me personally, but he knows my name, and he knows Clay. Remember, Clay grew up in Seattle's gambling community. Lots of people know who he is. I'm sure that's how Logan tracked him here. He also knows Clay and I were together that night."

"But didn't you slip him a phony map? How did he know the difference?"

"It wouldn't have taken much. I swapped the real treasure map for a rolled up paper placemat with a lot of meaningless scribbles on it. At a glance it might have passed as a map, but anyone looking closely would have seen it was just pencil scratchings with no coherent logic to it."

"But would he know you'd switched it?" Growing fear was making her desperate. "Mightn't he think it was the original, the one he won from Clay in the bet?"

Tommy shrugged. "How is that any better? He'd think Clay purposely put one over on him with a fake map to a gold mine. But I don't think that's the case. Clay had to originally convince Logan the map was legitimate. He would have examined it closely before accepting the wager, maybe even had several people look at it. And now, seeing how hard Clay and I worked to get it back, I'm sure Logan's more convinced than ever that the map is the real thing, and that's why he wants it back."

"*No!*" Blossom said. "After all the work you've put in on the mine, you can't just give it away. Can't the police do something?"

"Well, so far no crime has been committed. But your father is taking precautions—which is why you shouldn't worry. He'll handle it."

Tommy wrapped his arms around her and pulled her close. He made Blossom feel warm and safe. She thought about her father and what a strong, commanding presence he had always been in her life. No one had ever been able to stand up to him. Maybe Tommy was right, maybe she shouldn't worry. Morgan Thatcher always had things under control.

Chapter Twenty-Seven

When I walked into the house, I found the antiques dealer, Slade Borello, sitting in one of my folding chairs in the dining room. A wide smile broke across his face as he leaped to his feet and rushed to shake my hand.

"Ms. Ecklund," he exclaimed. "So nice to see you again. I do hope I haven't inconvenienced you too much, but I just had to talk to you. You see, I came across something recently among my great-grandmother's things that I think you'll find interesting."

Just then, Jared entered from the kitchen holding something metallic about the size and shape of a small soup can which he appeared to be polishing with an oily rag.

"Is that it?" I eyed the odd gadget curiously.

"No," Borello said. "That's something your brother found downstairs, but, in a way, it's related. It sort of confirms what I want to show you."

Jared placed the object on the card table.

It reminded me a little of the old-fashioned camera our Grandpa Thorson used to have many years ago.

Grandpa's camera had had a shiny round disk attached, concave like a cereal bowl, with a small flashbulb screwed into the center. He had called the dish a reflector because it reflected the light from the bulb and made it seem brighter. The object on the table also had a reflector, about five inches across, but I was pretty certain it wasn't a camera. This reflector was attached to the front of a small brass canister, squeezed slightly in the middle, with some odd nobs and hooks on it. I turned the thing over a couple of times trying to decipher its use, and finally set it back on the table.

"I give up. What is it?"

"It's a carbide lamp," Jared said. "I used to have one when I was in Scouts years ago. The bottom part screws off and you fill it with carbide." He picked it up and struggled to unscrew it. "It's pretty corroded."

"What's carbide?"

"Let's see, if I remember my chemistry, it's a hard rocky compound made from lime and coke."

"Lime and *Coke?*" My lips quirked sideways. "Sounds like a drink."

"Not *cola*. This kind of coke comes from *coal*. And lime is an alkaline calcium compound. Believe me, you wouldn't want to drink it."

I looked at him sideways. "When did *you* get so smart?"

"For your information," he retorted, "you're not the *only* one who reads."

Who knew?

"Anyway," he continued, ignoring the arch smile I gave him, "when you add water to carbide it gives off acetylene gas which is highly flammable. So, for the lamp to work, you lift this cap here on top and fill it with water. The water drips slowly into the carbide chamber creating the gas which comes out a tiny opening in the front of the reflector. You light it by turning this little flint wheel in front, creating a very bright light. See these little hooks? They're used to attach the lamp to a miner's helmet or belt."

"Miners?" I asked, confused. "But what has this got to do with Mr. Borello's great-grandmother?" I looked at the stout antiques dealer. He was practically dancing with excitement.

"It proves they were mining," Borello blurted. "Clay Thatcher had a gold mine."

I stared, speechless, from Borello to Jared. I was having a hard time making sense of any of this.

A loud knock at the front door made us turn. Dillon Thatcher swung the door open and shouted to be heard over the noise outside. "*Kate? Jared?*"

"In here," I called.

Dillon strode across the wood floor and joined us in the dining room, stopping abruptly when he saw Borello. "What's *he* doing here?"

"Apparently," I said, "he and Jared were about to reveal how they somehow know that Clay Thatcher, your grandfather, had been gold mining."

"*What?*" Dillon cried. "Did you find the *map?*"

"Map?" I said. "*What* map?"

The smile vanished from Borello's face. "How did you know about the map?" he growled. "I never said a word about a map."

Dillon stood stone-faced, his features taut.

"That's why you're really here, isn't it?" Borello accused, his broad face flushing in anger. "All that talk about family keepsakes was just a ruse—a ruse to get into the house and search it."

"What about *you?*" Dillon threw the accusation right back. "Rummaging all over the house for knickknacks and antiques? Playing all innocent. You were scoping out the place, searching for the map yourself, weren't you?" His hands closed into fists. "Just who are you, anyway? How do you know about the gold mine?"

I looked from one to the other, dumbfounded. What the hell was going on here?

Jared stepped between them, his Viking physique a formidable deterrent. His voice brooked no argument. "One at a time. What do you know about this so-called gold mine?" He gave Dillon a piercing look. "You first."

Dillon turned to me, his dark eyes earnest. "When I was a kid, my grandfather used to tell me stories about how he had once found a gold mine high in the hills of Washington State. It was like his mantra. He loved to tell me, over and over, how he could have been rich if things had been different. To me it was like a fairy tale, a bedtime story. I never put any stock in it—not until he lay dying. He begged me to come back here and find it. He said there had been a map, but he didn't know what had happened to it. He thought his old partner had it, or his sister. He thought they might have hidden it in the house for safekeeping. He made me promise to return one day and look for it. It was his deathbed wish. What was I supposed to do? I was curious, but after all these years I never really figured on finding it."

"Why didn't you just tell me this from the start?" I demanded. "All those times you came over to help—to supposedly spend time with me—you were really just searching for your grandfather's hidden map."

"*No.*" He looked stricken. "Well, maybe at first, but later . . ."

"In fact," I continued, "I'll bet it was you who broke into the house and ransacked the upper floor. It happened right after I took you up there and showed you around." I laughed bitterly. "I can't believe I was so stupid."

I thought he would deny it, but instead he said, "I should have told you. I see that now. But you said you were going to throw it all away. It was just junk. I needed the chance to look. I *swear* if I could go back and do things differently, I would. Kate, I'm *sorry*—"

I turned away, cutting off his plea. I picked up the small brass lamp once more, examining it, turning it over in my hands, keeping my eyes averted.

I turned to Jared. "You think this little gadget here proves there was a gold mine? It all sounds pretty hard to believe." I set the lamp back on the table.

Jared shrugged. "Remember those buckets of rocks we found shoved under the old workbench? I took another look. I think it's ore. Copper and iron, maybe. I'm no geologist. We'd need an assayer to tell us if there's gold in them, but it's not unreasonable. I also found picks and shovels stashed out in the garage. There has always been a lot of mining in the Cascade mountains around here. In fact, there was quite a boom in the 1870s. There's also Borello's great-grandmother's journal."

I spun to face the antiques dealer. "That's right," I said. "What was it you were going to show me? A journal?"

Until then, I hadn't noticed that he held something in his hand. Now he placed a worn, dog-eared book on the card table next to the carbide miner's lamp.

"Yes," Borello said. "It's a journal kept by my great-grandmother. Much of it concerns the time my great-grandfather spent in prison."

"Prison?" A sudden appalling thought rose in the back of my mind: the *gangster*, the one who had killed Blossom's father and caused the ultimate wreck of her entire life. *This* was Borello's connection? But how did the gold mine figure in?

Borello nodded, his face guarded. "Now, don't kill the messenger," he said. "I had nothing to do with it, but," he paused and took a deep breath, "my great-grandfather was convicted of murdering Morgan Thatcher, and spent the last years of his life in prison. He confided everything to my great-grandmother, and she wrote it all down in this journal. I found it recently in a trunk stored in my parents' attic. I'm sure it hasn't been read in over fifty years."

This was astonishing. Just that morning, I had scanned the newspaper accounts of the arrest, trial, and conviction of Morgan Thatcher's killer in the scrapbook kept by the Salmon Falls Historical Society. To have both great-grandsons here in the house built by Morgan Thatcher was almost too uncanny to fathom.

"What has any of this got to do with my grandfather's gold mine?" Dillon demanded, voicing my own question.

"According to the journal," Borello said, "Clay Thatcher bet the gold mine in a poker game with my great-grandfather. Thatcher convinced everyone at the table of the map's authenticity and placed it in the kitty with the other wagers. According to the journal, Thatcher lost the bet, fair and square. But later that night, Thatcher and his partner managed to pull a fast one and stole the map right out from under my great-grandfather's nose. Naturally, he was angry."

"That didn't give him the right to murder *my great-grandfather!*" Dillon snarled.

"And he *paid* for it, didn't he? He spent the rest of his life in prison." Borello turned to face me. "It's no excuse, I know, but you have to understand. My great-grandfather was a powerful man in those days, and he wasn't used to being *swindled.*" His eyes narrowed, darting back to Dillon. "He took his revenge the only way he knew how."

The temperature in the house began to plummet. I noticed Jared shiver.

I licked my lips. "Your great-grandfather was . . . ?" I had to ask, though I knew the answer.

The lights flickered. My heart beat faster as I glanced hastily around. Malevolent shadows seemed to swell up and expand from the dark, murky depths of the old house. The very air became heavy and my skin began to prickle as I sensed a peculiar presence all around me.

" . . . Vince Logan," Borello finished.

All at once, a high keening wail rent the air, rising to an ear-splitting shriek of anguish.

"*Good god*," Jared gasped. He whirled, searching for the source of the scream.

"What was *that?*" Dillon cried, cowering back. The color drained from his face.

Borello cringed. His eyes probed the dim recesses of the sprawling room.

"*Blossom*," I whispered as the eerie sound echoed throughout the mansion.

Jared gave me a sharp look. "Had to be the roofers," he said. "One of them must have fallen."

"Oh, no," I said. I had forgotten about the roofers.

As one, we dashed out the front door. I pulled my phone from my pocket in case I needed to make an emergency 911 call. Adrenaline pumping, I silently pleaded, *please, don't let anyone be dead.*

Outside, everything appeared normal. The sun shone bright in a clear afternoon sky. There were no cries of panic, no signs that anything was wrong. I searched around the house and found nothing.

Finally, Jared hailed a worker walking to the house from his truck. "Hey, is everything okay out here? We thought we heard a scream."

The roofer, dressed in white coveralls, looked surprised. "I didn't hear anything," he said. "Let me check."

He unclipped a walkie-talkie from his belt and proceeded to talk with someone on the roof. After a moment, he shrugged. "Nope. Everyone's accounted for. There's nothing to worry about. We all wear safety harnesses." He gave the tool belt on his hip a quick adjustment. "Well, I'd better get back to work." He bobbed his head politely, then strode to an extension ladder leaning against the house and scrambled up.

"Well, that's a relief," Jared said. "All we need is for someone to get hurt on the property. Of course, they probably have insurance for that sort of thing."

"Seriously?" I gave my brother a scathing look. My hands were still shaking. I went back inside and collapsed into one of the folding chairs in the dining room. The others followed.

"But what was that scream we heard?" Dillon persisted. "Sounded like it was right here in this room."

I swiped a strand of hair off my face and tried to downplay the whole thing. "Who knows? These old houses make lots of strange noises. The carpenters upstairs might have pulled out a big nail. Sometimes they sound like that when you pry them out of the wood."

"That's true," Borello agreed. "I once yanked a sinker out of a floor joist and it squealed like a stuck pig."

Dillon didn't appear convinced, but he gave in with a resigned look as he turned to me once more. "Kate—"

I cut him off with a cool glance. "Not now. We can talk about it later when I'm not so angry."

He nodded dismally. "Okay, I understand. Call me when you want to talk. I'll be around. And Kate, I *am* sorry." He headed for the front door and slipped quietly out. Just for a moment, the afternoon sun illuminated the front hall as the door opened, then closed again.

Borello stood watching Dillon's departure, a smug expression on his face. Jared cleared his throat noisily and gave the stout antiques dealer a pointed look.

He got the hint. "Yeah, well I guess I ought to go too." He picked up his great-grandmother's journal. "But hey, you should keep an eye out for that map while you're working on the house. It may be lost for good after all these years, but who knows, right?" He let loose a jovial laugh, the earlier incident forgotten. "You have my card. Feel free to give me a call if you come across anything else you'd like to sell. As they say, one man's junk . . ."

"Sure thing," Jared said, maneuvering Borello toward the door.

I remained where I was in the dining room, my thoughts in turmoil. *A gold mine? A hidden map?* I ran a hand through my hair. It was all too much to take in. No wonder Dillon had been so attentive. He was here on a treasure hunt. I felt like a fool.

Jared returned and I laid into him. "You heard that scream, didn't you?"

He shuffled his feet uneasily. "Yeah."

"It wasn't the roofers. Nobody fell off the roof. And it wasn't a nail being pulled, or a screech owl, or the neighbor's radio turned up loud, *was* it?" I asserted this as a statement, not a question. My tolerance for duplicity was all used up. I glared at my brother, daring him to attempt a fabrication.

He stared at his hands. "No," he said finally.

"It was Blossom," I stated. "It *had* to be. Did you notice how cold the house got? And how the lights dimmed? Just like all the other times she's appeared."

"Did you see her?"

"No. I didn't have to. I *felt* her."

Jared chewed the inside of his lip, looking pensive.

"So, do you believe me *now?*" I demanded.

He took a deep breath and slowly nodded his head. "It's insane, but, yeah."

I leaned against the card table and cupped my chin in my hands, feeling done in. Jared joined me, and for a moment we just sat together in silence.

"What do you think she wants?" Jared asked finally.

"I don't know. My gut tells me she wants us to find out what happened to Tommy. Blossom stayed in this house her whole life waiting for him to come back and marry her. No one knows what happened to him. I think if we can figure it out, it will give her closure and she can rest in peace."

"And how do you propose we do that?"

"I have no idea." I rubbed my temples. My head felt like an over-inflated balloon ready to burst.

Jared's voice took on a serious tone. "You don't think the ghost is dangerous, do you? Aren't you planning to bring Amy here for Memorial Day weekend? That's next week, isn't it?"

"Yes, I am bringing Amy here, and no, Blossom's ghost is *not* dangerous. Not to *us*, anyway. I'm convinced of that. I've been here working on the house for weeks, and she's never done anything threatening. In fact, until this afternoon, she's never made her existence known to anyone but me. And you've got to admit, it *was* under pretty bizarre circumstances: the great-grandsons of both Morgan Thatcher and his killer under the same roof, *here* in Blossom's house."

Jared gave a sharp laugh. "Yeah, that was weird. The look on their faces . . ."

Chapter Twenty-Eight

That night I slept fitfully, dreaming of ghosts, apple blossoms, and gold mines. By morning, I desperately needed a distraction. My first thought was Nathan Powell. He was interesting, local, and most important, didn't want anything from me. I smiled. He had also read *Great Expectations*. A literate man. I wondered what he would think if I told him about Blossom's ghost.

After breakfast, I retrieved his card from my jacket pocket and gave him a call. He answered on the second ring.

"Hi," I said. "It's Kate Ecklund. Things are quiet here at the moment and I wondered if you were still interested in a tour of the old house."

"You bet. I'll be there in half an hour."

When Nathan arrived, I welcomed him through the front door, furtively admiring his long legs and broad shoulders as he strode confidently into the foyer. I swept my arm in an arc before me. "'Abandon all hope, ye who enter here.'"

He laughed aloud. "Are you likening your renovation project to a *Divine Comedy?* Surely, it's not *that* bad."

I grinned, thrilled that he knew the reference. "Perhaps I should amend that to *A Comedy of Errors.*"

He nodded, giving me a wink. "Yes, Shakespeare is *slightly* less tragic than Dante."

Our footsteps on the bare oak floor echoed like phantom noises in a tomb. The yawning entryway remained as gloomy and cheerless as ever despite all the cleaning that had been done.

"Spooky, isn't it?" I said. "There's still a lot of work to do."

Nathan gazed slowly around, letting out a soft whistle.

"The realtor told me there used to be a huge crystal chandelier here in the foyer," I said, "but it was sold. It must have been worth a fortune. They replaced it with this cheap thing that hardly puts out enough light to see the staircase."

Jared came in then from the direction of the kitchen. "I thought I heard voices."

I made introductions. "Nathan Powell, this is my brother, Jared Thorson. Nathan is a Salmon Falls native and a member in good standing of the 'Small Town Appreciation Society.' He works as a freelance writer and also happens to drive a yellow Volkswagen bug with a rusty patch on the driver's door."

Jared's eyebrows shot up. "You're the one . . ."

"The infamous prowler," Nathan said with a grin, extending his hand.

Jared laughed. "I believe I accused you of being a tax assessor."

"Nothing so dastardly," Nathan said with a chuckle. "I was gathering fodder for a book I'm writing for the Salmon Falls Historical Society."

"The president of which is his aunt," I said, "and a delightful lady. We spent all morning yesterday with her. She's a wealth of information. I'm going to give Nathan a tour of the house and let him take some pictures for his book."

"Well, have fun," said my brother. "If anyone needs me, I'll be in the basement searching for lost gold."

Nathan lifted his eyebrows quizzically as Jared disappeared back the way he had come.

I laughed. "It's a long story. Come on, let me show you the house."

I took him through the music room, the living room, and the library, which Jared was still using as a bedroom. I pointed out the decorative ceiling medallions, extensive crown moldings, and ornately carved mahogany woodwork, pleased by his enthusiastic admiration.

"On this floor we've mostly centered on the kitchen, plus we've replaced all the windows."

"Sounds like you've really made progress," Nathan said.

"Yeah, but there's still a ton of stuff to do. We need to refinish all the floors and woodwork, and remove all the old wallpaper. I'm hoping these original tin ceilings can be cleaned and saved."

I led the way to the kitchen, eager to show off everything that had been accomplished. We encountered one of the workers putting finishing touches on a ceramic tile backsplash above the stove, and stopped for a moment to admire his work.

From there we went into the back hallway. "My personal project has been to re-do the housekeeper's rooms and make them livable for me and my daughter." For a brief moment, a memory of Dillon working beside me, tearing down wallpaper, intruded on my thoughts.

I pushed it away. I did not want to think about Dillon.

After that, we went up to the second floor where the carpenters and plumbers were hard at work. "So far, most of the remodeling has been concentrated up here," I said. "We're converting six bedrooms into four—all with en suite bathrooms."

"Very impressive," Nathan said.

Following a trip to the top floor, we made our way to the basement. Jared heard us and quit working, straightening up and stretching his back with an affected groan. "Is it time for lunch yet?"

"Nope. Get back to work." I cracked an imaginary whip.

Jared looked mournfully at Nathan. "You see how she treats me?"

Nathan grinned and tsked sympathetically. He looked around, his face expressing amazement at the cavernous expanse with its heavy stone walls and massive timbers. Most of the rubbish had been removed, leaving only the various antique items we had uncovered, plus the old workbench, some tools, several buckets, and a stack of scrap lumber.

Judging by the broom in his hand and the piles of dirt here and there, Jared had been sweeping. It looked a lot cleaner than the last time I'd been down here. Again, thoughts of Dillon surfaced and I thrust them away, reminding myself that he'd been here under false pretenses with his own secret agenda.

Nathan gave a low whistle. "This place is incredible. The house just exudes history, doesn't it?"

He strolled over and leaned against the workbench. "You know, I grew up in this town, went to school here. Even back then this place gave all us kids the heebie-jeebies. We thought of Blossom Thatcher as the crazy old lady in the haunted house."

Jared suddenly seemed to choke, giving a sputtering cough and throwing a hand over his mouth.

Nathan looked at him curiously. "You okay?"

I shot a cautionary frown at my brother.

Jared sniffed and nodded. "Yeah, go on."

"It's nothing really," Nathan continued. "I was just reflecting on how long this old house has stood here, neglected and deteriorating, inhabited for decades by an elderly spinster of questionable mental acuity. If you hadn't come along when you did, this place would probably have been bulldozed."

"I don't think so," Jared said, leaning on his broom. "Blossom would never have allowed it."

Nathan gave him another puzzled look.

Here goes nothing, I thought. I set my shoulders, lifted my chin, and girded myself for certain ridicule. Turning to Nathan, I said, "He means the house *is* haunted. Blossom's spirit is still here. I've *seen* her and we've both *heard* her."

Well, there it is. Nathan will either think we're certifiable and run for his life, or he'll assume we're playing some sort of sick prank.

It seemed too much to hope that he'd buy in.

Nathan just looked at us, one corner of his mouth pulled up as though waiting for the punch line. I could tell he hadn't decided yet whether or not we were pulling his leg.

I went on. "It was the middle of the night when I first saw her. The house kept creaking and I couldn't sleep, so I took my flashlight and walked out to the front room. She was sitting at the piano. I thought a strange woman had somehow gotten into the house. Then she started singing. I'll never forget that. It was an old song from the 40s I think, *Don't Sit Under the Apple Tree*. Believe me, I was freaked out."

Nathan continued to listen without erupting into laughter, so I pressed on. "At first, she had her back to me, but then she turned around and saw me and started coming toward me. She was old and haggard, like Blossom would have been when she died, right? Somewhere in her nineties or more? But then she changed. She became young again, like she would have been in her twenties, with dark hair and smooth skin. When Jared came up behind me and turned on the lights, she vanished."

Nathan looked from me to my brother. "You're serious."

Jared raised his shoulders in an exaggerated shrug. "I didn't believe it either, at first. I thought Kate was sleep-walking and had some sort of weird dream."

"But then I saw her again," I said. "Several times. Even outside in the yard in broad daylight. She always says the same thing—*mind the apple blossoms.*"

"What does that mean?"

"No idea," I said, playing idly with my fingers. "I thought at first it must have something to do with the apple tree growing in the back yard—until I found out it was a cherry tree."

"Then yesterday *I* heard her too," Jared said. He shuddered. "We all heard her. She *screamed.* Oh, my god—freakiest damn thing I ever heard. I still get chills when I think about it."

Intrigued, Nathan leaned forward. "Why did she scream?"

Jared said, "Remember when I said I was coming down here to search for lost gold? I was talking about a map to a gold mine that's supposed to be hidden somewhere in the house."

Nathan's eyes widened. "What? You're kidding."

"Get comfortable," I said, "it's a long story. At least you already know the history of the house, and you know about Clay Thatcher and Tommy O'Connell. But what you don't know is that they had a map to a gold mine . . ."

I launched into the story as I knew it, telling how Dillon Thatcher and Slade Borello had both come here in hopes of recovering the map that each thought rightfully belonged to his own great-grandfather.

"Borello's great-grandfather was Vince Logan," I explained, "the Seattle gangster who was convicted of murdering Morgan Thatcher. Remember the scrap book we saw at the Historical Society? The very mention of Logan's name caused Blossom's spirit to scream in anguish."

"This is absolutely fascinating," Nathan said as I finished my account. "It has all the makings of a great mystery novel."

"Sure," I said, "but only if we can give it a happy ending by finding out what happened to Tommy."

"It must have something to do with the mine," Nathan said. He rubbed his chin thoughtfully.

"But why does Blossom always say *mind the apple blossoms?* What have apple blossoms got to do with gold mines?"

"Personally," Jared said, "I think Vince Logan murdered him. It makes sense. He knew Clay and Tommy were partners. Maybe Logan buried his body under an apple tree somewhere."

"*Or,*" Nathan said, "Tommy got wind of Logan's murdering rampage and took off to save his own skin."

He looked at me and his face softened. "I know you want a more romantic ending and you don't want to believe that Tommy left Blossom in the lurch, but sometimes reality is harsh. It may be that Tommy wasn't the romantic hero you wish he was."

Smiling bleakly, I shrugged. "I'm pretty much resigned to never knowing. I doubt we'll ever find the map, either. Too many years have gone by and too much stuff in the house has been changed or removed."

Jared gave a humorless laugh. "I guess we'll just have to get used to living in this great big house with an unhappy ghost. Who knows? Might be kind of cool in a creepy sort of way."

I made a face. "On that note, why don't we go upstairs and have lunch. Then I've got things to do. Amy's coming to stay for a few days next week and I still have to get ready."

* * *

No sooner had Nathan's yellow VW pulled out of the driveway than my nosy neighbor came rushing over. *Right on schedule.*

"Nathan Powell—a *reporter?*" Wendy snorted incredulously when I told her the identity of the mysterious owner of the yellow Volkswagen. "What did he want?"

"Do you know Flossie Gerhardt—tall, thin lady in her seventies? President of the Historical Society?"

"Sure. Everybody knows Flossie."

"Well, he's her nephew, and he's helping her write a book to raise money for a museum."

A light dawned. "Oh, *that* Nathan. Kind of tall? Big ears?" She nodded, her dark curls bouncing wildly. "I know who you mean. I've met him a couple of times at church and at the Senior Center. He volunteers there sometimes. Nice guy." She grinned. "But the guy in the Bronco's a better catch. What a hunk."

I exhaled in disgust. "His name is Dillon Thatcher, remember? And I am *not* out to catch either one. In fact, I am *through* with Dillon."

She perked up at that, her gossip radar on maximum. "*Why?* What happened?"

"I don't want to go into it. Let's just say he's not who I thought he was."

Chapter Twenty-Nine

I spent the afternoon shopping for bedroom furnishings. The antique iron bedstead in the housekeeper's room had been given a fresh coat of white paint, and the fine old oaken dresser and nightstand had been refinished. I still needed to get a mattress, bedding, curtains, and a rug. The soft rose-colored wallpaper I had put up, along with the new window and painted trim, really gave the room a neat, fresh look. The wood floors still needed refinishing, but that could wait.

My mother had volunteered to bring Amy out on Friday afternoon for the three-day weekend. I had thought Daniel would put up a fuss, but, surprisingly, he'd been fine with the arrangement, saying he had plans of his own for the holiday.

I knew Mom and Amy were both dying to see the progress we'd made. The remodeling upstairs wouldn't be finished, but enough progress had been made to show off what we'd accomplished so far. My plan was for Amy to share the larger housekeeper's bedroom with me, while together we made plans to decorate the attached sitting room for her. It was smaller but just the right size for a child's bedroom.

For now, my goal was to create a warm, welcoming home where my daughter would be happy to live. I rearranged the sparse furniture in the living room and added a little antique desk to the entry hall. I planned to place fresh flowers around the first floor to add color to the otherwise dreary rooms. The new windows helped, but I hadn't had time yet to replace the faded old wallpaper or heavy velvet curtains. I was grateful to Jared for spending a day sanding and refinishing the opulent carved oak and tile fireplace in the living room. The chimneys had been cleaned and I hoped to keep a cheery fire going while Amy was here.

By evening I was ready for a break. After dinner, I retreated to my room and sat down on the bed with my laptop; I had brought it back with me from my mom's the last time I visited. It had just been too inconvenient to drive back and forth every time I needed to use it. Now, I wanted to search the web for any reference to Tommy O'Connell. Plenty of hits came up on the name but none for a man who had lived in Salmon Falls in 1940.

Disappointed but not surprised, I put away the computer and pulled a novel from my box of books, determined to relax and read for an hour before going to sleep. I leaned comfortably back on my new pillows and tried to concentrate.

Two sentences were all I managed before my mind began to wander. I kept thinking about Nathan, wondering what he thought about the strange story we'd hit him with that morning. At least he'd been kind enough not to laugh outright, but it must have been a hard thing to swallow. Most people didn't believe in ghosts. *I* didn't believe in ghosts. Or I *hadn't* until a couple of weeks ago.

Nathan said that all the kids in town had called this a haunted house, even when Blossom was still living in it. *What is it about a house that induces people to call it haunted?* Age, isolation, a certain degree of dilapidation, and our human predilection for terrifying ourselves? Years ago, when my friends and I used to walk to grade school in the old neighborhood, there had been an empty, run-down house along the way that everyone said was haunted. After all these years, I could still remember the delicious shivers and childish screams evoked by the yawning black windows as we ran past.

Any old edifice in a remote location seemed a likely setting for ghosts and vampires. Stephen King made a living taking advantage of people's love affair with all things terrifying. The haunted hotel in *The Shining* still gave me goosebumps. *But everyone knows it's make-believe. Nobody believes those stories are real.*

I looked at the time. A few minutes after eight. Not too late to call Nathan. I didn't know what I was going to say. I just didn't want to leave things as they were—with him thinking Jared and I were a couple of crackpots. I sat cross-legged on my bed as I punched in his number. My tongue ran back and forth over my dry lips.

He answered on the first ring. "Hi, Kate. I was just thinking about you."

I cringed. "In a good way, I hope."

"Of course. Why wouldn't I?"

"Oh, maybe because I told you I live in a haunted house with the ghost of Blossom Thatcher, and you think I'm a certifiable nut case."

"Oh, *that.* Hey, I don't mind. If anything, it just makes you that much more interesting."

Flooded with relief, I said, "That's very magnanimous of you. I was afraid maybe you'd run for the hills, or at the very least, change your phone number."

"Not at all. I'm intrigued by the idea of ghosts. Some of the best classic literature involves ghosts. Shakespeare is rife with them. What kind of tragedies would Hamlet and Macbeth be without ghosts?"

"Well, *sure* but—"

"And then there are your classic haunted romances. *The Ghost and Mrs. Muir* and *Portrait of Jennie,* for instance— two great novels from the 40s."

"Yes, I loved those," I said. His passion for these timeless works was refreshing. I hadn't discussed real literature with anyone since college. Daniel hadn't been interested in books unless they involved making money, and Jared's idea of classic literature was *Conan The Barbarian.*

"How about *The Canterville Ghost?*" he continued. "The short story, I mean, not the movie versions. Have you read it? It's the quintessential English castle ghost—with just the right amount of spooky clichéd chain-rattling and snarky humor. My favorite ghost story without question."

"Yes," I said, more than a little impressed that he'd read Oscar Wilde. "It's a great story. I especially like how it ends on a poignant theme of love and redemption."

"You've read it," he said, apparently just as pleased.

"Of course," I laughed. "English Lit major, remember?"

He chuckled. "Right."

"But seriously," I said. "I'm not talking about a make-believe ghost, something out of a story or movie. I actually *saw* an apparition of Blossom Thatcher's spirit and heard her voice. I didn't make it up. I know it sounds crazy. Sometimes I don't believe it myself."

"Kate, I don't think you're crazy. If you say you saw a ghost, then I believe you. We could get into a whole philosophical discussion on souls and the afterlife, but personally I like to simply chalk it up to accepting that there are things in this world we don't understand. I happen to believe in life on other planets too. Some people think *that's* crazy. Truth is, I'm jealous that you've seen a ghost and I haven't. What do you think the chances are of Blossom appearing to *me?*"

"I have no idea. I guess you'll just have to come hang around for awhile and see." I smiled happily at the prospect.

"According to common lore," Nathan said, "when spirits don't move on it means they are trapped on earth for some reason—unfinished business or revenge, for example."

"Could be both, I suppose. Revenge for her father's murder, plus the unsolved disappearance of Tommy O'Connell. Whenever Blossom's spirit appears, she always seems sad. I'm beginning to think she may be stuck here forever unless someone discovers what happened to him."

"That won't be easy," Nathan said.

"Jared thinks having a ghost in the house would be a great draw for the bed-and-breakfast. He wants me to put it in a pamphlet advertising the place, but I'm not sure I like the idea. Some people might be put off. But worse than that, I really don't want to encourage the kind of melodramatics that go along with haunted houses." I snorted disdainfully. "All I need are TV cameras on the front lawn."

"Well, you *could* simply think of it as free publicity. Good way to get your new venture off the ground."

"I just wonder what my ex-husband would think. He's already touchy about our daughter staying here. For some reason, he seems to think old houses are unhealthy." I unfolded my legs and dropped my feet to the floor, pacing as I continued. "He has the money and power to make real trouble for me if he gets it in his head that Amy isn't safe living in this house with me." My voice rose with my growing anger. "Like I'd bring her here if it wasn't safe."

"Kate, whatever threats he's made, I'm sure he's done it just to get you riled. He knows—as does everyone else— that you're not going to do anything to endanger your daughter. Don't let him get under your skin."

I blew out a hot lungful of air. "That's what Jared says. Sorry. I tend to get emotional when it comes to Amy."

"That's okay, you're supposed to. I hope I can meet her one day. If she's anything like her mother, she must be a remarkable child."

A pleasing warmth spread over my face. I sat back down on the edge of the bed. "She'll be staying with me over the Memorial Day weekend. Maybe you can come and meet her."

"I'd love to," Nathan replied. He sounded sincere and I made a mental note to arrange a lunch date when Amy was here. I was eager that they should hit it off.

"Also," I said, changing the subject, "I was wondering if you and your Aunt Flossie would like to come over one day this week to look at some of the antiques we've unearthed in the basement. I was thinking of donating some of them to the future Salmon Falls Museum if she's interested."

"Sounds awesome. Let me give her a call and I'll let you know."

* * *

They came the next afternoon. I opened the front door and my breath did a little catch. Nathan stood there looking dapper in jeans and a casual blue shirt. His eyes met mine with an expression that was both lively and self-assured. He exuded a sort of natural sexiness I felt unexpectedly drawn to.

"Hi, Kate," he said. His voice brought back the rush of feelings our phone conversation had roused the night before; his candor and sincerity had been so heartening.

"Hi, Nathan." I swallowed. "Come in."

Flossie cleared her throat discreetly, and I suddenly remembered myself. I turned to face her and grasped her hand with a welcoming squeeze. "I'm so glad you could come."

She looked from me to Nathan and back again, her mouth curving in a discerning little smile. "Thank you so much for inviting me," she said. "Nathan tells me you've found all sorts of interesting antiques in the basement. I can't wait to see."

She strolled across the foyer into the living room. "It's such a lovely old house," she said wistfully. "I have so many pleasant memories of visiting Blossom here when we were younger, before she became so . . . ill."

I recalled Wendy describing Blossom as nervous and tense, living a paranoid, reclusive existence. Considering what I'd learned since then of Blossom's history, it didn't seem so shocking now. I nodded. "She had a lot of pain in her life."

Flossie gazed toward the music salon and clasped her hands together. "If only you could have heard her play. She had such a talent." Her eyes lingered for a moment on the piano as she reminisced.

I remembered the mysterious music Jared and I had heard that first day he arrived. I realized now that it must have been Blossom. Strange how the thought no longer disturbed me. My lips curved into an easy smile. If the ghost found peace in playing the piano, she was welcome to it.

"I'm so glad you're restoring the house," Flossie continued. "Blossom would be happy knowing someone's taking care of it."

That made me think of something Jared had said awhile ago. Tentatively, I asked, "You're not opposed to my opening it as a bed-and-breakfast, are you? My brother thought there might be people in town who would object."

Flossie looked surprised. "No, not at all. Everyone I've talked to thinks it's a marvelous idea."

"Most people were afraid some developer would knock it down to build apartments, or worse, a strip mall," Nathan said.

I smiled, relieved, and agreed that would have been a tragedy. Then I led the way to the basement. Jared wasn't home. He'd taken the day to go hang out with Gary and his friends. One of them had bought a new truck which apparently called for a lot of high-fiving and beer drinking to commemorate the occasion.

Just as well, I thought. *Jared needs a break and antiques aren't really his thing.*

I flipped the switch at the bottom of the stairs, flooding the expansive space with light. At the same time, the old oil furnace kicked on, emitting a low rumble like some great beast nudged out of a sound sleep.

"Ahh, *The Awakening*," I murmured, glancing at Nathan. I wondered if he would pick up on this classic nineteenth-century novel and resume the book title Ping-Pong we had played on his previous visit.

He narrowed his eyes and gave me a shrewd smile. "Hmm, or perhaps *The Ghost in the Machine?*"

I clapped a hand over my mouth to quash an eruption of giggles. I looked quickly in Flossie's direction, but she was oblivious, hurrying to examine the numerous objects we had laid out in the basement.

"That's awful . . ." I said, still sputtering.

He waggled his eyebrows.

" . . . but then, I do live in something of a *Bleak House.*"

His face broke into a wide, appreciative grin.

"Kate?" Flossie had turned and was looking at us curiously. She waited beside the workbench where Jared and I had set out some of the odd implements we'd found.

I shushed Nathan and went to join Flossie. "I was hoping you could identify one or two of these more unusual items. I worked for seven years in an antique shop in Seattle, but the store dealt mainly in furniture and high-end china and silver, plus some jewelry and art. We didn't get many old kitchen gadgets.

"I know this is a washer," I continued, pointing to the old wringer appliance, "and that's a sewing machine and that's a butter churn, but over here on this table are some things we found that I have no idea what they are." I picked up an ungainly cast iron object about fourteen inches long with a hand-crank on one end. "This looks like a torture device."

Flossie laughed, her eyes twinkling. "Not quite. It's a cherry pitter. The bottom part is like a vise for clamping to the edge of the kitchen counter. Then you put the cherries in the top and turn the handle. The pits come out the bottom. Here, it's similar to this meat grinder." She picked up another cast iron object from the table. "Same principle only you put pieces of meat into the top and grind it up like hamburger. Every kitchen used to have one of these."

"Huh, I would never have guessed." I turned the cherry pitter over in my hands, trying to envision how it worked.

Nathan took it from me and peered at it closely. "I don't know," he said, "I think torture device isn't too far off the mark."

"What about *these?*" I held up two long wooden paddles held together at the top with a metal ring.

"Oh, for goodness sake," Flossie said. "I haven't seen one of those in ages. It's a lard press, very old."

I exchanged a glance with Nathan. "*Yuck,*" we said simultaneously, then broke out laughing.

Flossie continued studying the things on the tabletop. She was as excited as a kid at Christmas. "This is a butter press, and, *oh look*, this is a bacon press. And here's a food mill—great for making applesauce." She also pointed out a ceramic bed warmer and an old iron that was heated by placing it on top of the stove. "You really had to be careful with these not to scorch the shirts." She said it in a way that made me think she had done that very thing at some point in the past. "Thank goodness for electric irons," she added.

I laughed. "Thank goodness for permanent press."

Nathan snorted and made a wry face. "Be honest, Kate. You've never ironed a shirt in your life."

"Not true. My mother made me iron a couple of shirts once when I was in high school just so I'd learn how."

He smirked, then picked up another item off the table. "Hey, look at this. It's pretty cool." He held up a long, thin object of tarnished silver about eight inches long. It was vaguely shaped like the handle of a butter knife with a small hole on one end and a sort of trigger on the side. It was covered with ornate engraving.

"What is it?" I asked.

"It's a cigar cutter," he said. "A nice one."

I wrinkled my nose. "You don't smoke, do you?" *Ugh.* For me, that was a deal breaker.

He gave his head a firm shake. "Cigarettes, never. But I do like to enjoy a fine cigar once a year at Christmastime. My father smoked them regularly, but I never picked up the habit."

Flossie smiled. "A cigar at the holidays has been a tradition among the men in our family for generations. I don't care for cigarettes—a nasty habit—but I think a good cigar once in a while lends a man a touch of class. I always thought my Herbert looked so dashing in his smoking jacket with a glass of sherry in one hand and a cigar in the other."

How romantic, I thought. A different era.

Nathan gave me a sly wink and struck a debonair pose, miming a drink in his left hand and a cigar in his right. "You should see me in a smoking jacket."

His mimicry was so comical, I had to laugh.

"The cigar cutter is yours," I said. "A gift."

Flossie pursed her lips, frowning at her nephew's mockery. "Nathan, your Uncle Herbert was a wonderful man, a distinguished gentleman."

"I know he was, Auntie," Nathan said, all contrite. "I was just teasing." He leaned over and gave her a kiss on the cheek. "I'm sorry." Then he grinned. "But you know, I *would* look good in a smoking jacket."

She chortled and gave him an affectionate cuff on the arm. "Yes, you would, you rascal. You've always looked just like him."

Their fond interaction was touching. I considered Nathan: tall and thin, ears too big, nose too long, in need of a haircut but well-balanced, masculine, and good-looking in his own way. He was literate and well-traveled but grounded in family and tradition, and he made me laugh.

Dillon Thatcher was Calvin Klein gorgeous. His striking features, deep brown eyes and athletic build, presented an almost perfect Adonis. He could be romantic and amusing—but lately I thought he had become shallow, clingy, and deceitful. Wendy liked to call him a hunk. Which one would I rather spend time with? I smiled at Nathan. He saw and smiled back. Molten heat rushed through my body clear to the tips of my toes. *No contest.*

Chapter Thirty

Friday afternoon arrived, and with growing excitement, I hurried outside to watch as my mother's car turned up the driveway. She passed between the guardian maples—as I'd come to think of them—and approached the front of the house, stopping finally beside the walk leading to the veranda.

Amy leaped out of the back seat and ran to me. We embraced in a big bear hug.

"It sure is *big*," my mother said, mouth agape as she gazed upward at the turret. "I can see why you've been so busy."

"You should have seen it two months ago," I said.

"Mommy," Amy cried. "You got a new door. It's not broken anymore."

"Very observant," I said, giving her an approving smile.

The front door opened and Jared joined us, straightening his shirt and running a hand over his hair. "Hi,

Mom." Then he turned to Amy. "Hey, Squirt. How ya been? Wait'll you see all the work we've done."

"So, Jared," Mom asked, "how do you like it way out here in the toolies? Kate tells me you'll be living in the basement?"

He hung his head as one suffering grave mistreatment. "Yeah, she wants to keep me in the dungeon and only let me out when there's heavy labor to be done."

"Uh-huh." I screwed my lips sideways. "You're so abused."

His eyes crinkled and his mouth snapped back into its usual easygoing grin. "Actually, the basement is perfect. Lots of space for a workshop."

Mom turned to admire the rural landscape, the woods, and the mountains beyond. "It's so peaceful out here. So nice and quiet."

"Most of the time," Jared said. He caught my eye with a wry glance.

Right. When Blossom's ghost wasn't playing the piano or shrieking in anguish.

"He means it can get pretty loud sometimes when the crew is working." I cast a warning glance in my brother's direction. "Fortunately, they've all gone home now for the long weekend."

"Great," Mom said. "Let's start the tour. I can't wait to see inside."

"Sounds good," I said. "Come on, Amy, you can lead the way."

The next hour was spent exploring the mansion, stepping over tools and around construction supplies. We looked into all the rooms, wandered the maze of stairways and passages, and nosed through all the nooks and crannies. I was heartened by my mother's unending flow of oohs and ahhs and positive comments.

It was nearly June and the days were getting longer. The sun shone brightly in the evening sky, and masses of crimson rhododendrons bloomed in every corner of the yard.

Other than a patch of dirt on top of the knoll, there remained no evidence of the withered cherry tree that had once stood there. The weather was clear and warm so I decided to set up the card table in the back yard for a picnic dinner. My mother had brought chocolate chip cookies that she and Amy had baked the day before.

"I can't wait for summer so I can move here," Amy cried, putting a voice to my own thoughts.

"Me, neither," I replied. "What this house needs is a little girl to live in it."

My mother looked up and remarked, "It'll look a lot better too, once it's painted."

I turned a critical eye to the weather-worn clapboard and peeling white paint faded gray with age. Here and there an unpainted board stood out in stark contrast, indicating a repair made to the old siding. Many of the classic Victorian adornments, patterned shingles, dentils, and finials, were broken or missing and still needed to be replaced.

"Will you paint it white again?" Mom asked.

"I don't know. White's kind of boring. I've been looking at pictures of old Victorian houses in San Francisco, trying to decide. You should see some of those."

Amy spoke up. "Paint it pink."

"Pink?" I asked, surprised. "I was thinking maybe light blue, like the sky. Wouldn't that be pretty?"

She shook her head, her lips puckered like a rosebud. "I think it should be pink. Like a valentine."

"Hmm, maybe we could paint it pink *and* blue." I wondered how the neighbors would react to having a huge pink house in their midst. Of course, I thought with amusement, it would sure make giving directions easy: *You can't miss it, it's the big pink house on Angela Lake Road—there's not another one like it in the county!*

When we had finished eating, Mom and I gathered up the things while Amy taught Jared a nonsensical song she'd learned at school. Then Jared showed Amy how to weave clover into a garland for her hair. Watching the patient way my brother interacted with his niece, it occurred to me that he was the type of man who ought to be a father.

Before long, Jared produced his guitar and began to regale us with song while my mother played an imaginary drum, beating two sticks against a rock. To Amy's delight, Jared pulled a harmonica out of his shirt pocket and handed it to her, entreating her to join him in a duet. This she did with all the uninhibited enthusiasm of an eight-year-old, blowing with such zeal that all I could do was cheer and applaud.

"You've been taking lessons," Jared said with a wink.

"No, I haven't," Amy giggled, "this is my first time." She reveled in her uncle's praise.

The hours passed quickly. When it was time for Mom to leave, we all hugged and briefly discussed plans for the following week. After that, Jared, Amy and I went inside, and I helped Amy get ready for bed.

"I'm too excited to sleep," she said, bounding onto the newly refurbished bed with its thick down comforter.

"I have just the thing," I said. "Get comfortable."

I dug into my box of books and pulled out a worn copy of *Pippi Longstocking*. It had been my favorite childhood story, and I'd been saving it for just such an occasion. Amy snuggled back into her pillow while I sat on the edge of the bed and started reading the tale of the adventurous little girl who kept a horse on her front porch. I hadn't finished three pages before Amy was sound asleep.

The next day, Nathan came to lunch. Any anxiety I might have had about his initial meeting with Amy was quickly dispelled when he arrived at the front door with a red foam ball stuck Rudolph-like over his nose.

"That's a new look for you," I said, holding back my laughter as I ushered him through the front door.

He drew himself up in a dignified manner. "I have no idea what you're talking about."

As Nathan followed me into the living room, Amy peered shyly from behind one of the big overstuffed chairs. I motioned her to come closer. "Amy, I'd like you to meet my friend, Nathan Powell. He lives here in Salmon Falls."

She stared, her impulse to laugh obviously at odds with what she'd been taught about not pointing at people's disabilities.

"Would you like to meet my dog?" Nathan asked.

Amy nodded, eyes wide.

"He's right here in my pocket." He pulled out a limp, deflated yellow balloon. "Hold on, looks like he's gone to sleep."

As Amy watched transfixed, Nathan blew air into the long, narrow balloon then deftly twisted it into the shape of a puppy. He pulled a marker from another pocket and drew eyes on its face.

When he handed it to Amy, she squealed in delight. "Do another one!"

I shook my head in disbelief. "Mr. Powell, you are full of surprises."

He shrugged, giving me a wink. "Twelve nieces and nephews."

By the time Nathan announced that he had to be going, Amy was thoroughly captivated. Cradling an armload of balloon animals, she escorted him to the door all smiles and giggles, making him promise to come back another day.

This couldn't have gone any better if I'd choreographed it myself, I thought. What a wonderful knack Nathan has with kids. Twelve nieces and nephews? No wonder.

The rest of the weekend I devoted to Amy. We played games, we baked a cake, and we planted flowers in the garden. On Monday, the weather changed and the sky opened up, reminding us that it was still springtime in western Washington.

Looking for something to do inside, Amy asked if she could play the piano. I readily agreed. While I worked in the newly finished kitchen organizing dishes and cookware, Amy plinked happily away in the music salon. I hummed contentedly. I'd have to look into getting her piano lessons.

I was about to stop and fix lunch when Amy came strolling into the kitchen singing to herself. "Mommy, do you want to hear a new song I learned?"

"Of course." I turned and gave her my full attention.

She began in her soft, sweet voice, *"Don't sit under the apple tree . . ."*

I froze. My heartbeat quickened.

" *. . . with anyone else but me—*"

"Amy," I interrupted, trying to keep the tension out of my voice, "where did you learn that song? Did Grandma teach it to you?"

"No, it was the lady in the white dress in the music room. She's pretty."

I heard the blood rushing in my ears. *Stay calm,* I commanded myself. *Don't upset Amy.* I inhaled slowly. "Did she say anything else?"

"She said to mind the apple blossoms." Amy said this in such a matter-of-fact way that somehow it seemed perfectly reasonable.

Obviously, my daughter hadn't been frightened by the apparition. I took another breath, regaining some of my composure. Venturing cautiously, I said, "I wonder which apple blossoms she means."

Without batting an eye, Amy replied, "She means the apple blossoms on the wall in the music room."

I frowned, concentrating. I hadn't spent much time in there, having focused most of my energies in other parts of the house. Though everything but the piano had been removed, I had always thought it was a beautiful room with its high ceiling, stately brick fireplace, and tall, narrow windows in the circular turret alcove. The only detraction had been the dull, faded wallpaper. The floral wallpaper.

I nearly laughed out loud. Not flowers, *apple blossoms*. With Amy in tow, I hurried to the music salon. I couldn't believe I had never noticed before. It made so much sense. A woman named Blossom would naturally have an affinity for flower blossoms, and why not *apple* blossoms? Being a pianist, she had probably spent a lot of time in this room. It would have been her special retreat. She had even kept a picture of Tommy, the man she loved, in the piano bench with her music.

Leave it to a child to see what a houseful of grown-ups had missed.

As Amy watched, I began to examine the walls, running my hands back and forth over the wallpaper. It was old and rough and peeling in places but mostly intact and firmly stuck on.

Suddenly my fingers encountered a slight bulge about twelve inches wide where the paper was only loosely adhered. It was on the wall opposite the room's entry, and situated at a level even with the enormous grand piano, ingeniously placed so as to be concealed from casual view behind the body of the great instrument.

"Amy," I breathed, "I think we've discovered the hidden treasure map."

She didn't understand, but she grinned happily, gratified to be a part of something important.

"Wait here while I go get something to cut it loose," I said.

A moment later, I returned with a kitchen knife and knelt beside the wall, making a careful incision around the edges of the loosely glued area of wallpaper. I was almost giddy as I pulled back the wallpaper and removed two stiff sheets of wax paper, fused together with the map sandwiched in between. Painstakingly, I slit the wax paper apart and released the map, a dingy, yellowed piece of paper with writing all over it.

"Come on," I said to Amy. "We have to go show Uncle Jared. He'll be so surprised."

Gingerly, I carried the map as we hurried down the stairs to the basement. Our footsteps echoed in the hollow space. We found my brother hunched over the workbench, concentrating on the architect's proposed layout for the basement renovation.

"Jared," I called, motioning him to come over. "We found something you have to see."

He tightened his lips in a look of annoyance, then straightened up and joined Amy and me in the laundry room. "What?"

I laid the map out on top of the newly purchased washing machine and stood back. Jared leaned in for a closer look. His eyes bulged as he realized what it was.

"Where did you find it?" he asked in amazement.

"*I* found it, Uncle Jared," Amy said proudly. "It was behind the wallpaper in the piano room. The lady in the white dress showed me."

He gaped stupidly, then looked at me for my reaction.

"That's right," I said with a crooked smile.

Jared seemed at a loss for words. Finally, he managed to stammer, "*Wow*, Amy. That's great. I didn't think we'd ever find this. Behind the wallpaper, eh? I never would have looked there." He gave her a pat on the shoulder. "Good job."

She grinned from ear to ear, basking in the praise.

He turned back to me. "Why don't you put this someplace for now and we'll talk about it later, okay?"

"Sounds good," I said. "Come on, Amy, back upstairs. Let's see what we can rustle up for lunch."

* * *

I had planned to drive Amy back to my mother's sometime in the afternoon, but, to my surprise, my ex-husband called.

"If it's okay with you," he said, "I'm going to come and get Amy and take her back to your mother's. That'll save you the trip."

"Of course, it's okay," I told him. "But you don't have to drive all the way out here. I don't mind taking her back."

"Thanks, but I want to come out there. There's someone I want you to meet."

Surprised, all I could manage was a mumbled, "Okay."

Now I was *really* curious.

When I related this conversation to Amy, she grinned. "Oh, he's probably bringing Trisha."

"Who's *Trisha?*" I asked, perplexed.

"Daddy's girlfriend," Amy said simply.

What? How come nobody's ever mentioned her before?

"Do you like her?"

Amy nodded. "Yeah, she's nice. She makes Daddy laugh."

"That's good," I said, getting over my shock. "We want Daddy to be happy." *Well, good for him. A girlfriend is probably just what Daniel needs to mellow out his sour personality.* It occurred to me that this might be some sort of ploy to make me jealous. Well, it wouldn't work. I uttered a sardonic laugh. Good luck to her—she'll need it.

Daniel arrived around four o'clock with a young morsel of a girl who giggled and hung on every word he spoke. She couldn't have been much over twenty-one. Her kinky brown hair hung unrestrained around her shoulders, and her luminous round eyes were caked with too much makeup. She had a guileless, naïve personality, and Daniel seemed smitten.

Of course, I thought. *She probably doesn't have an intellectual thought in her head. As long as the money flows, she'll happily acquiesce to being his cute, pliable plaything.* Ironically, they were perfect for each other.

Amy seemed to like her, and they greeted each other like old friends. I kept my skepticism to myself as introductions were made. *Besides,* I reminded myself, *a happy ex-husband is one who will stay out of my hair and be easier to deal with in the future.*

After a bit of cajoling, Amy convinced her father to take a tour of the house while she led the way, delighted to be playing the hostess. Jared retreated to his room in the library.

Wide-eyed, Trisha blathered continually as she admired the sumptuous features of the old house. At one point, she turned to Daniel and gripped his arm, gushing, "You should get a house like this."

Knowing his mind on this topic, I was barely able to contain my laughter. Somehow, I managed to keep it to a smirk hidden behind my hand.

Daniel scoffed. "This place is a monstrous money pit. Besides, it's *way* too far out." He gave her a patronizing smile. "It would take you over an hour to get to the mall."

She tittered and bobbed her head prettily. "I hadn't thought of that."

I wanted to puke.

At last, they decided it was time to go. I helped Amy gather her belongings, then buckled her into the back seat of the Jaguar and gave her a big kiss. "Don't forget—school tomorrow."

"It was nice meeting you, Trisha," I said, heroically maintaining a polite smile as she slid into the passenger seat.

"Thanks, Kate," Daniel said. He got into the car and leaned out the driver's side window exuding all the charm of a pit viper. "Really, you've done wonders with the place. Keep at it. Maybe someday, it will *almost* be habitable."

With an effort, I bit back a retort, clenching my fists until my nails dug into my palms. I exaggerated my smile into a caricature of civility, then stood watching as the sportscar backed down the driveway. Once it was out of sight, I relaxed my shoulders and blew out a long breath.

When I went back inside, Jared hazarded a peek out of his room. "Are they gone?"

"Yes. *Finally.*" I felt glum seeing Amy leave, but immensely relieved to have Daniel gone. His constant judging wore on me.

"What did you think of Trisha?" Jared couldn't restrain a mocking chuckle.

"What a ditz."

"At least she seems harmless."

"Yeah, I suppose, as long as her ditziness doesn't rub off on Amy."

"*Naw*, Amy's way too smart for that."

I snorted humorlessly. "Well, ditzy or not, if Trisha keeps Daniel too busy to meddle in my affairs, then I'm all for it."

Jared laughed. "I hope they're very happy." Then he rubbed his hands together, eyes all agleam. "Changing the subject, let's look at the map!"

Chapter Thirty-One

I knew Jared had been dying to examine the map ever since his first cursory glance.

"Okay," I said. "Meet me in the kitchen. The light's better there."

Retrieving the map from the nightstand in my room, I took it to the kitchen and spread it out on the smooth new quartz countertop. It was nothing more than a yellowed sheet of paper about twelve inches by sixteen inches scrawled all over with handwritten notes and sketches, some in ink, some in pencil, and in at least two different hands. A dark crooked line running generally left to right across the middle was labeled *Sunset Highway*.

"Where's the Sunset Highway?" I asked, puzzled. I had lived in Washington all my life and had never heard of it.

"Look here," Jared said, pointing out several notations. "Here's North Bend, and here to the east is Snoqualmie Pass with an arrow pointing toward Cle Elum, and this whole area is labeled National Forest. I think Sunset Highway must be what it was called before it became

Interstate 90. It couldn't have been much more than a wagon road across the mountains back at the beginning of the nineteen-hundreds. They didn't *have* freeways then."

I peered closer. "Here's Denny Creek. Didn't Dad take us camping there once?" I recognized a few other place names on the map, as well as a couple of rivers and lakes, all in the western Cascade Mountains—and not all that far from Salmon Falls. I had driven over I-90 at least a hundred times. "It's got to be a lot different now from what it was when this map was first drawn."

Jared rubbed his chin. "Sure, but that area's still pretty rugged. Obviously, when the Sunset Highway was expanded into I-90, it was straightened out and widened, but there are sections of the old historic road that have been preserved and you can still drive on them. In Scouts we did some backpacking in the mountains. I'm pretty sure the Forest Service roads are still there. See here? The map points to a road going off here to the north. I'll bet we could find that. We just need to get a Forest Service map. I wonder if you can download those off the internet. Forest service dot gov, maybe?"

"*Whoa.*" I stopped him in mid-sentence. "Hold on. Who said anything about *finding* it?"

"Why *not?* What's the point of having a map to a gold mine if you don't go get the gold?" He seemed mystified that I didn't see how obvious this was.

"Okay, I get it, but I have a feeling it's a lot more complicated than that. Don't you have to file a claim or something? Are you even allowed to dig for gold in a national forest?"

"Well, I'm sure we can find out."

"And there's something else you're forgetting."

"What's that?"

I glowered impatiently. "Dillon Thatcher and Slade Borello. Remember them? They have as much claim to the map as we do. We have to tell them we found it."

Jared's mouth pursed in a sullen pout. "Possession is nine-tenths of the law."

"Seriously?"

Reluctantly, he relented. "Fine. Call them. See if they can come over tomorrow. Meanwhile"—he rubbed his palms vigorously together—"I'm going to start surfing the net for things to spend my share of the gold on." As he exited the kitchen, he called over his shoulder, "Let me know when dinner's ready."

I rolled my eyes, then took the map and went to my room to make the calls.

I phoned Borello first. His reaction was predictable. "You *found* it? Fantastic. I'll be over first thing tomorrow to pick it up."

"Well, that's fine. I'd like you to come over, but I plan to call Dillon Thatcher too. He has a stake in the map as well. Plus, my brother also thinks *he* deserves a share. I thought maybe we could form some sort of partnership. We'll have to discuss it."

For a moment, he didn't speak. When he did reply, he sounded less friendly. "I see. All right. How's nine o'clock?"

"That's fine. See you then." I hung up and expelled my breath in a rush. Now to call Dillon. I wasn't looking forward to it.

He answered on the first ring. "Kate? I'm so glad you called. I've been wanting to call you, but I knew you had your daughter with you over the weekend and I didn't want to disturb you. We need to talk. I'm sorry about the whole thing with the map and searching your house. I really just wanted to—"

"*We found it!*" I practically shouted into the phone to interrupt his gush of words.

"What?"

"We found the map."

He paused. "You found the *map?* The map to the gold mine?"

"Yes, the map to the gold mine." *How many maps are there?*

"Where was it?"

"Behind the wallpaper in the music room." I wasn't going to tell him *how* we'd found it.

"That's awesome." His voice rose to a lilting pitch. "I can't believe it. My grandfather would be so happy. When can I come and get it? Tomorrow? Then we can talk about our future."

Oh, crap. I raked my fingers through my hair. "Dillon, I'm sorry. I've been doing a lot of thinking, and I just don't think we *have* a future, other than as friends. Okay? You're a really nice guy, but like I told you, I'm not ready for a new relationship and, I'm sorry, even if I *were...*"

"It wouldn't be with me."

"Yeah. I just don't think we have enough in common to make it work."

His voice became stilted. "Okay, I understand. What time shall I come over to get the map?"

Here we go again. I licked my lips and braced myself. "How does nine in the morning sound? But I'm not just going to hand it over to you. I've also called Mr. Borello. He's coming too."

"What did you call *him* for?" He sounded angry. "It's *my* map. It belonged to my grandfather."

"Look, Dillon," I said, "be reasonable. The way I understand it, your grandfather lost it in a poker game to Mr. Borello's great-grandfather and then stole it back again. I think he deserves a share in it, don't you?"

He made a snarly noise in response.

"Besides, it was in my house. Technically, I don't have to share it with *either* of you if I don't want to."

"You wouldn't do that."

"No, I wouldn't. What I'm hoping is that we can all share—form an equal partnership. Frankly, I think the whole thing is a wild goose chase, but Jared has his heart set on finding the mine."

"Fine," he said glumly. "I'll see you in the morning."

He broke the connection and I just sat there for a moment holding my phone. Hunched cross-legged in the middle of my bed, I spread the map out in front of me. What a lot of aggravation and heartbreak this piece of paper had caused.

I decided to call Nathan. I needed to hear a friendly voice and I knew he'd be excited by what we'd found.

* * *

The next morning dawned chilly and overcast, so I decided to light a fire in the living room before our visitors arrived. Since Amy's visit and my arrangement of the mismatched furniture in front of the opulent fireplace, the room didn't seem nearly as dreary as it had before. This morning it was crucial that the ambiance be as friendly as possible.

I got the flames crackling nicely, then stood and faced the room.

Feeling slightly foolish, I said out loud to the empty space, "Blossom, your brother's grandson, Dillon, is coming over this morning. So is Slade Borello, the great-grandson of the man who killed your father. I know you don't like him, but Vince Logan died a long time ago and he can no longer hurt you or Tommy. He's not a threat anymore. Do you understand? You must keep quiet and trust that I would never do anything to hurt you."

I don't know what I expected. Nothing but the crackling and popping of the fire disturbed the deep silence of the room. If the spirit of Blossom Thatcher had heard, she made no sign.

"Well said," Jared remarked, clapping his hands silently as he approached from the library. His expression displayed a mixture of amusement and understanding.

I shook my head. "If you had told me six months ago I would be addressing a ghost in the middle of my living room, I'd have said you were crazy."

Right at nine o'clock a knock sounded at the front door and I opened it to admit Slade Borello. He was cordial, greeting us both with a friendly smile and a handshake. I urged him to take a seat in the living room where I had set out coffee and an assortment of fresh donuts.

Dillon Thatcher arrived moments later. He was aloof and wouldn't meet my eyes. It was awkward, but his immature sulking made me all the more adamant. It was unfortunate that Dillon felt hurt, but what was I supposed to do? He had brought it all on himself with his double-dealing.

I directed him to the living room where he slumped into one of the overstuffed chairs. I pulled up a folding chair from the dining room. Jared did the same, sitting near my elbow.

"So," Borello said, getting right to the point, "where's the map?"

Dillon leaned forward, determined not to be left out.

"I'll bring it out in a minute," I said. "But first, let's talk."

"What is there to talk about?" Dillon demanded, his dark sensuous eyes looking churlish and cold. "The map belonged to my grandfather. The mine was his legacy to me and I should have it." He glared at each of us in turn.

"Your grandfather was a coward and a thief," Borello spat. "He lost the mine in a poker game, fair and square. It should have belonged to *my* grandfather. It should have come to *me*."

"How do we know the game was fair?" Dillon countered venomously, jumping to his feet. "Your great-grandfather was a gangster and a murderer."

Borello sprang up to face him.

"Sit down!" I rounded on them both. "*Sit down!* We're here to discuss a partnership, not start a war."

Grudgingly they sat, sparks kindled in their eyes.

"You're both forgetting something," Jared declared. "Legally, neither one of you has a right to the map. It belongs to my sister. It was found in her house."

"That's very big of you," Borello growled. "Defending your sister's rights. And just where do you think *you* fit in? What makes you think *you're* entitled to anything?"

"We're in it together," Jared retorted. "We take a third and each of you gets a third."

"It's not fair!" Dillon's face contorted in anger. "All my life, my grandfather talked about his gold mine. To his dying day he dreamed that one day I would come back here and find it. And now that I have, you want to steal it away from me."

"You want to talk about *stealing?*" Borello was on his feet again.

"You fat pig!" Dillon screamed. He leaped up, fists poised.

Jared jumped between them, bodily pushing them apart. "Neither one of you deserves the gold," he snarled. "You're both a couple of crooks." He gave Borello a shove.

Dillon swung his fist and hit Jared on the side of his jaw.

"Stop it," I cried desperately. "*Stop!*" This was *not* how I had intended this to go. I had underestimated the power of greed. If a fight broke out, someone was going to get hurt. "We need to talk about this like *adults.*"

Borello charged at Jared like a bull. The two of them crashed across the top of the table, knocking it over and landing in a tangled heap on the floor. They rolled together, each trying to land a punch. Coffee and donuts flew everywhere. Dillon saw his chance and drove a hard kick into Borello's ribs. The older man howled and twisted around, grabbing Dillon by the leg and pulling him down.

Desperately, I ran to my room and yanked the map from the drawer where I had stashed it. I raced back with the map waving in my hand like a white flag. I dangled it in front of the fireplace.

"Here!" I cried. "Here's your stupid map!" Tears of anger and frustration spilled down my face. "Stop fighting!"

Finally, I had their attention. Sprawled on the floor, noses bleeding, knuckles scraped, hair and clothes disheveled, they stopped and stared at me.

For a moment, I held the map before them so they could glimpse what they were fighting over. Then, with a flick of my wrist, I tossed it into the fire. It flared instantly and within seconds had disintegrated into a pile of ashes.

Chapter Thirty-Two

May 1941

Blossom could scarcely believe the world was embroiled in a violent war. She gazed around the tranquil apple orchard all astir with birds and bumblebees. The news on the radio became more disturbing every day as the Nazis stormed across Europe, but here in Salmon Falls life went on as usual, spring awaking from its cold slumber and breathing warm life into the surrounding hills.

She wore a pink cashmere sweater with a simple string of pearls and tan trousers cinched at the waist with a narrow patent leather belt. Her dark hair was brushed back allowing loose curls to fall around her ears and shoulders. On a blanket spread beneath a bower of new green leaves, she and Tommy O'Connell sat enjoying a picnic lunch of cold chicken sandwiches, potato salad, and custard pie. It was Friday and the weather was clear and warm, portending an early summer.

"I wish this day could go on forever," Blossom sighed.

Tommy leaned over to give her a kiss, his hand caressing her cheek. "So do I."

All of Blossom's dreams were coming true. Talk of Logan and his threats had faded, and her wedding day drew near. Her mother's wedding gown had been found in a trunk in the attic and lovingly cleaned and pressed. The exquisite ivory silk and Spanish lace had been stored in tissue paper and kept in perfect condition. It fit Blossom like it was made for her.

She smiled as she thought of Martha and the flurry of activity taking place at the house. The old mansion hadn't had a thorough sprucing up in years. Now, Martha had a whole team busy oiling the woodwork, polishing the crystal, putting up new wallpaper, and scrubbing every nook and cranny. You would have thought the president was coming to the wedding.

Tommy saw her smile. "What are you thinking?"

Blossom looked around the orchard at the sunlight glistening through the leaves. Birds trilled and fluttered among some late blooming apple blossoms. She sighed contentedly. "I'm thinking that everything is perfect, and that by this time next month we'll be married and off on our honeymoon."

He grinned, his eyes twinkling. "I can't wait."

"I only wish you didn't have to go up to the mine today." Worry inflected her voice.

"Now, we've talked about this." He took her hand and kissed it. "I'll be home by tomorrow afternoon or Sunday at the latest. We've had a mild winter and a warm spring. Your father thinks someone should go check on things to see how the road looks and how much of the snow has melted. He says we should build cairns around the mine to mark our claim until we can get all the paperwork filed."

"But is it safe? Will you be warm enough?" Her forehead creased with concern.

"I promise I won't do anything dangerous. I'll just take a quick look, hike around a bit, and come right back. Remember, I've been there a hundred times. I'll be fine. I've got my tent and bedroll all packed in the truck, plus a week's worth of food thanks to Martha."

"I know." Blossom laughed. "I worry too much. I just wish you weren't going alone." She reached over and brushed a stray flower petal from his shoulder. "I wish Clay were going with you."

Tommy snorted and gave her a crooked smile. "Clay says he's busy with 'best man' duties. I'm afraid he's got some mischief up his sleeve."

"Well, I guess I can't complain. Helen threw me a party last week, so it's only fair you should have one too."

"I can only imagine what sort of party he has in mind."

Blossom frowned and said in a mock scolding tone, "Just you be sure to make it to the wedding on time, Mr. O'Connell. No excuses."

"There is nothing in this world that could keep me away, Miss Thatcher. Now, I think it's time I got going."

He stood and gave her his hand, pulling her to her feet and into his arms. She pressed herself against his chest, listening to his heart, feeling her own beating with it, both hearts in rhythm together. A young doe ventured warily into the orchard with a tiny fawn by her side but sprang away upon seeing the lovers.

At last, Tommy stepped back. From his coat pocket he pulled a worn, rolled up piece of paper and held it out to Blossom. "I want you to put this someplace safe."

"The map?" She took it gingerly as though its touch might burn her fingers.

"Yes. It needs to be kept hidden until we return from our honeymoon."

"You don't want to leave it with Clay?"

Tommy laughed and Blossom joined him. No, they wanted no repeat of the last incident. Blossom loved her brother, but he had not shown that he could be relied upon.

"I could probably give it to your father," Tommy said, "but I'm afraid he would just toss it back in his desk. I'd like to feel it was more secure than that."

"Don't worry," Blossom said. "I'll find a place to put it."

Together they walked to the truck which was packed with everything Tommy would need for a couple of days of camping at the mine. He gave her a final kiss, then climbed behind the wheel and started the engine. With a wave, he pulled away and disappeared down the road.

Blossom slipped the map down the front of her sweater then went back to gather up the picnic things, placing them neatly into the wicker basket. Finished, she walked down the hill to the house humming happily to herself. She had a brilliant idea for a hiding place where she knew the map would never be found.

* * *

They came during the night, kicking in the doors and swarming like shadows into the house. Blossom started awake at the sounds of stomping feet on the stairway and shouts of strange men in the hall outside her bedroom door. Overcome with terror, she lurched out of bed, pulling her blankets with her as she huddled in a corner. Gunshots rang out, followed by yelling and the sounds of crashing furniture.

A harsh voice bellowed. "Find that map! Turn the place upside down if you have to!"

The door to Blossom's room crashed open and two large men stormed in. They grabbed her and dragged her bodily into the hall, their rough, merciless fingers digging into her shoulders as they dumped her next to her father who lay bleeding on the floor.

A thickset, evil-looking man confronted her, his foul breath smelling strongly of liquor, his overcoat fetid with the stench of tobacco smoke.

"Where's the map?" he demanded. His face was fearsome, heavily jowled with a pocked, bulbous nose jutting from the center beneath a ponderous brow. On his head he wore a black fedora pulled low to obscure malevolent eyes.

Blossom ignored him and knelt over her father. Thick crimson blood oozed from two holes in his chest; the rank metallic odor gagged her as she tried frantically to stem the flow with her hands. Her nightgown became soaked. Helplessly she watched her father struggle to breathe, her own chest constricting as she heard the air burbling in his ravaged lung.

"*Father*," she sobbed. Hot, burning tears flooded her cheeks. He was dying. Kissing his face, she squeezed his hand to let him know she was there.

Another man emerged from the dark hallway and addressed the other. "He got away—climbed out the window and made it to the ground. I'm pretty sure I winged him though."

Clay, Blossom thought. *He got away. He'll rouse the men and bring the sheriff.*

"What about the other one?" demanded the leader.

"No sign of him. I don't think he's here."

Tommy. They're talking about Tommy. They want him too. Thank God he was up at the mine, far out of harm's way.

From every corner, she could hear her home being ransacked—furniture knocked over, cushions torn, cupboards plundered, personal belongings strewn and broken. A scream rose suddenly from downstairs followed by sounds of a brief scuffle. Sick with dread, Blossom knew that Martha had tried to fight off the intruders.

"Please, don't let them hurt Martha," Blossom pleaded. "She's just the housekeeper. She doesn't know anything."

The mobster sneered at her. "Tell me where the map is. Hand it over and we'll leave."

Morgan stirred where he lay on the floor. Blossom bent over him, pressing her ear close to his trembling lips. "Give it to them . . ." he whispered. "It ain't worth it." Then he closed his eyes and stopped breathing.

"*Father!*" Blossom cried, choking on her tears. *How had this happened?* Her father had always been so strong, so in control. It was unthinkable that he could be dead. Grief engulfed her senses. Terror became like a rope tightening around her throat, strangling her so that she could barely breathe.

"Where's the map?" the thug demanded again.

"I don't know," Blossom wept. "I don't know."

Tommy, her beloved, was at the mine this very night, alone, defenseless. She pictured his face, so virile and full of life. Then she imagined him bloodied and bruised, his cherished features broken, contorted in pain. No, she would die before she would betray his location. She would never tell, and they would never find the map. She had hidden it too well.

"Boss," said one of the henchmen, "we'd better get out of here. The cops'll be showing up any minute."

As if to press the point, gunshots erupted outside. In the distance, a police siren wailed, growing closer.

The man in charge nodded, then turned and addressed Blossom once more in a low, malicious voice. "Tell your boyfriend, Mr. O'Connell, that Vince Logan is looking for him."

She just stared at him, feeling as though she'd fallen into a nightmare with no escape.

"Yes, I know who he is." He smirked. "I've been asking around."

With that, the mobster turned and motioned to his goons. They stormed out the door and disappeared into the night.

Blossom fell to sobbing over her father's lifeless body.

* * *

The town was stunned to learn of the brutal murder of Morgan Thatcher, the powerful patriarch of the community. While not loved, he had certainly been respected and held in grudging esteem for his ability to command men and make money during a time of economic depression. Many wondered what would become of the logging operation and the lumber mill which for years had provided the chief source of employment for the majority of people living in the surrounding valley.

Clay had been wounded in his escape from the house, but the injury had not been severe. The local doctor had bandaged him up and declared he would be fit again in no time. Many expected him to take over for his father and were astonished to learn that he had no such ambition. Unknown to most, the harm done to Clay's nerves had far exceeded the damage done by the bullet wound. When he told Blossom he was leaving Salmon Falls, she had been saddened but not surprised. The real threat to his life had made it impossible for him to stay. He had offered no destination but simply packed up and stole quietly away.

Martha had received a nasty gash on the head when she was knocked down in the kitchen. She had struck the corner of the tiled countertop and was discovered in a groaning heap on the floor by one of the mill workers who had rushed into the house after the gangsters' departure.

"That fellow who attacked me didn't get away easy," Martha had boasted as she was hustled off to the hospital. "I walloped him good with my trusty cast iron skillet. You can bet he's got a lump on his noggin the size of Nebraska." She had underscored this remark with a firm nod—which immediately elicited a painful grimace.

The next day she had come home from the hospital with a dozen stitches, a purple goose egg, and a nagging headache. The doctor had ordered her to take it easy, but, as always, she was determined to get back to work.

Jed Hawkins and several of the men had not fared so well. Jed, who had led a rescue assault, received two gunshot wounds, one to the abdomen and one to the thigh. After hours of surgery, he had managed to survive, but his long-term prognosis remained grim. Four other men had also sustained wounds. Awakened abruptly in the middle of the night, they had rushed toward the house, ill prepared for what they encountered there. Among the injured was Albert Pike, Helen's husband, Blossom's friend. Helen had recently given birth to a baby girl and was filled with terror at the prospect of losing her husband.

Police were everywhere. Two days after the attack, a couple of dark-suited detectives cornered Blossom in the kitchen where she clung to Martha for support. "Can you identify any of the men who were in your home, Miss Thatcher?" asked one of the detectives. He spread an array of photos on the table before her.

Through swollen, tear-fogged eyes, Blossom studied the pictures. Within moments, she recognized the face of the gangster who had terrorized her. "Him," she whispered, trembling uncontrollably as she pointed out the face of the man who had ravaged her home and murdered her father.

The detective nodded to his partner as though confirming what he already knew. "Vince Logan."

"Do you know what they were after?" the second detective asked.

"No," Blossom said. "Money, I think. My brother was involved in some sort of gambling. I don't know anything else." She could barely speak she was quaking so violently. She didn't tell them about the map or the gold mine. *They don't need to know*, she thought. *It won't help them find my father's killer.*

"Leave her alone," Martha said, interposing herself between Blossom and the detectives. "Can't you see she's in shock? What difference does it make what they wanted? They murdered Mr. Thatcher. That's all you need to know." She drew herself up, all five feet, four inches of fighting-mad mother bear. "Now you get out of here and find that Mr. Logan, and you make him pay for what he did."

The detectives thanked the women for their help and departed.

"Why can't they go away and leave me alone?" Blossom sobbed inconsolably. Her father had died in her arms, her brother had deserted her, and many of her friends had been grievously injured. She just couldn't deal with the police right now.

Martha wrapped Blossom in her arms. "They're just doing their job, honey," she said. "They need to gather all the evidence they can to put that evil bastard away."

Blossom gave Martha a look of surprise, smiling through her tears in spite of herself. In all her twenty-one years, she had never once heard Martha use a vulgar word, no matter how dire the circumstances.

Martha snorted self-consciously. "Well, that's what he *is*, isn't he?"

* * *

Morgan Thatcher was buried with ceremony in the Salmon Falls Cemetery, attended by most of the town. Many were there to honor him, but many came merely to gawk. Blossom knew this and resented it. They hadn't known her father. To them he was stern and heartless, a brazen overseer who lorded his power and position over the town. She was glad when the spectacle concluded and she could escape with her private sorrow back to the house.

She longed for Tommy. But after a week, he still had not returned.

Blossom shrank from talking about the gold mine, though Martha knew full well of its existence. Indeed, the housekeeper had helped Blossom hide the map. But Blossom hushed the older woman when she would have brought it up, panicking over the urgency to keep Tommy safe. Daily, Blossom lived in terror that something would happen to her beloved. Simply discussing the map out loud could be dangerous. Someone might overhear.

Logan or his men might be nearby, watching, listening— waiting for me to slip up and lead them to Tommy or the map. That's why Tommy hasn't returned. He's waiting until it's safe. She just had to be patient and trust in Tommy's wisdom. Every day, the police said they were getting closer to arresting Logan.

The lumber operation came to a standstill. Her father's employees looked to her for guidance, but she had none. Blossom couldn't face them, she didn't know what to do. Her father had always shielded her from the day-to-day workings of the business. Finally, some of the older crew took it upon themselves to get work started again.

After another week, Jed returned, weak but on the mend. He depended on a cane to get around and the infirmity made him cross. Only Martha had the forbearance to put up with his impatient outbursts as he struggled to regain his strength.

Helen's husband survived, but two of the other wounded men did not. They were buried in quiet ceremonies. Blossom attended both funerals to express her condolences and was nearly undone by the depth of grief suffered by the families. She made sure they were awarded death benefits in humble gratitude for the men's sacrifice, but felt shame in doing so, knowing that the money could never compensate for their loss.

Eventually, with help from Martha and others, the house was put back in order. Broken items were replaced. Scattered objects were put away. Furniture was set upright, upholstery mended, and floors cleaned.

People worked quietly, speaking in whispers, sensitive to Blossom's fragile state. *What about the wedding?* they asked each other. Where was the groom? Had he been scared off like Clay, or had he been murdered as well? Speculation ran rampant. Morgan's accountants stepped in to handle the business, and Jed recovered enough to run the mill. Life on the estate settled back into a semblance of normalcy.

Still Blossom yearned for Tommy. Where was he? Shouldn't he have returned by now? Logan had been arrested and was awaiting trial. He would surely spend the rest of his life in prison. Was Tommy still afraid Logan's men were looking for him? Was he in hiding? Why hadn't he sent word?

Tommy is clever, she reminded herself. *He knows what he's doing.* She closed her eyes and imagined his arms around her. She remembered his strength, the musky scent of his cologne, and how his chin stubble tickled her cheek. She pictured his face in her mind, his deep brown eyes, the dimple on his chin, the adoring way he looked at her. *He loves me,* she thought. *There must be a reason he hasn't returned. I have to be patient.*

Disturbing dreams assailed her. One night it was evil men with guns hiding in ambush, and the next it was bears and dark unspeakable dangers lurking in the mountains. Terrified, she huddled alone in the darkness, unable to go back to sleep.

Then she began to overhear whispers, rumors that Tommy had run away in fear like Clay—that he had deserted her and would never return. She refused to believe it. *No, Tommy's just waiting for the danger to pass. I know it in my heart.*

Soon he'll return and we'll be married in the orchard under the apple trees as we planned.

Blossom felt numb and exhausted. She'd suffered too much pain already; she hadn't the strength to cope with more. Reality seemed to slip away as each day merged into the next.

Chapter Thirty-Three

"You should have seen the look on their faces," I said, feeling wretched. "I don't know what I was thinking."

Nathan took my hand and gave it a squeeze. "You were trying to save them from killing each other."

I had called him shortly after the incident in my living room and he had suggested I meet him at the coffee shop in Salmon Falls. We had secured a small table in a private corner where I was now trying to drown my sorrows in a tall caramel mocha with extra whipped cream.

"Dillon acted like I'd murdered his grandfather."

"He'll get over it. Eventually you'll see that it was all *Much Ado about Nothing*."

I laughed. Nathan could always make me laugh. He was proving good at this game. Today Shakespeare figured large. "Maybe, but you weren't there—you didn't see *The Tempest*."

He grinned. "Touché."

I took a sip of my mocha and gave my shoulders a careless shrug. "Of course, one good thing to come out of all this is that now they'll both go away and leave me alone."

His brows drew together as his expression turned serious. "I was under the impression you and Dillon were an item."

"I thought we were too"—I crinkled my mouth in disgust—"till I found out he was nothing but a con man using me to get to the map. And even if he wasn't, we didn't have a thing in common. I'll be happy to see him leave."

"Well, then, perhaps we can say *All's Well That Ends Well*." He sounded hopeful.

I looked down at my hands, studying my fingernails. A smile played at the corners of my lips and a fluttery feeling stirred inside me. I took a long pull on my mocha. "There's something else," I said. "Something I haven't even told Jared."

Nathan gave me a curious look, urging me with raised eyebrows to go on.

I glanced quickly around the room. There were two baristas behind the counter busily filling an order for a couple waiting with a small child, plus two separate groups at different tables immersed in lively conversations. A lone teen hunched over his laptop near the window.

I leaned forward and said in a low voice, "I took a picture of the map." I pulled my cell phone out of my pocket and brought up the map. I handed it across to Nathan.

Intrigued, he took the phone and studied the screen, enlarging portions of the image to get a better look. "It's hard to get good details from this, but it looks like it's up by Denny Creek near the pass. It's been a few years, but I used to hike up there every summer with my father."

"There are some handwritten notations too," I said, "but they're hard to read."

"We need a bigger screen. Let's go to my place."

A few minutes later we arrived at Nathan's apartment building, a vintage two-story structure on Salmon Falls' main street. Next to the entry, a bronze plaque stated that the building had been built in 1914—the same year as my house. I gave Nathan a wide grin of approval.

He looked pleased. "I thought you'd like it," he said. "It's one of the few remaining original buildings in town still being used."

There was no elevator so we took the wide wooden staircase. The boards creaked and showed heavy signs of wear, but overall the building was impeccably maintained with fresh paint on the walls and highly polished woodwork. Nathan's unit was a neat one-bedroom on the second floor, appointed with just enough comfortable furniture to make it a welcoming haven. Besides a sofa and big screen TV, the focal point of the ample front room was a large wooden table serving as a desk. On top of this sat a computer, a printer, and an extra-wide monitor nearly engulfed in files, stacks of books, and drifts of paper. Here and there lay random pencils, staplers, letter openers, paperweights, and coffee mugs in capricious disorder.

Nathan immediately switched on the computer. While we waited for it to boot, he asked, "Would you like anything? I'm afraid my kitchen stocks are pretty meager, but I think I might have a couple of beers, or I do make a mean glass of water."

I laughed. "Water's fine."

Some minutes later, we had uploaded the picture of the map from my phone to Nathan's computer. Shoulder to shoulder on kitchen chairs crowded in front of the moniter, we were able to get a much better look at the overall image, as well as home in and enlarge smaller details. We also did some web research on the area: the Sunset Highway specifically, and gold mining in general.

After reading through several comprehensive articles, Nathan said, "Okay, the highway was dedicated in 1915 so we know the map had to be drawn sometime after that, right?—or the original prospector wouldn't have labeled it that way. There are several places where the old road still exists. If we line up your map with a present-day forestry map, we can see that the mine is in the Mt. Baker-Snoqualmie National Forest. It's still pretty rugged wilderness up there once you get away from the freeway, but I don't think the mine would be impossible to find if you're interested. There are lots of old trails and Forest Service roads we can follow."

"Well," I said, chewing my lower lip thoughtfully, "I have to admit I'm curious—and I know Jared's dying to search for it—but most of these articles aren't very encouraging when it comes to small individual mines."

Nathan nodded. "I don't have any illusions about striking it rich if that's what you're thinking. Besides, any serious digging would have to be cleared through the Bureau of Land Management." He paused and the tone of his voice changed, becoming subtly softer. "Frankly, at this point there's just one thing I'm wondering."

He turned to look at me, and all at once I became aware of his close proximity.

"What's that?" I whispered.

"If you would let me kiss you."

Arousal flared. Before I could even think, I was leaning into his embrace, my lips seeking his.

* * *

I got home around seven that evening and found Jared pacing. "Where have you been?" he demanded. "I tried calling you a dozen times."

"Did you? I guess I didn't hear the phone. Have you eaten? I picked up a pizza on my way home—that pepperoni and mushroom you like." I threw the box down on the kitchen counter and reached for plates out of the recently completed cupboards.

"Are you still mad?"

"Mad? Why on earth would I be *mad?* Just because a brawl erupted in the middle of my living room? A brawl *you* had a hand in starting, I might add."

"I didn't start it," Jared cried. "It was that Borello character. He knocked me down, the fat lout."

I gave him a withering look. "All I remember is three rowdy men, who should have known better, in a bloody pile on the floor."

"You didn't have to burn the map," Jared said glumly.

"The three of you would never have worked together. I know that now." I handed him a plate piled with pizza slices. I dished one onto my own plate and took it to the card table in the dining room. My next purchase, I decided, would have to be a table for the kitchen. There was plenty of room for a breakfast nook, and I envisioned an old-fashioned trestle table.

I munched on my pizza. "At least one good thing came out of this. They're both gone. Dillon Thatcher is probably halfway back to Ohio by now, and Slade Borello won't dare show his face here again."

"Yeah," Jared said, looking morose, "but I still think it would have been fun to try to find the gold mine."

"Why? All the reading I've done says it's nearly impossible to find enough gold to make the effort worth it. You need trained geologists and heavy equipment. I don't have the time or the money."

He shrugged, slumping in his seat. "It doesn't matter now anyway, does it?"

I licked pizza sauce off my fingers, then looked him in the eye. "What if I told you I took a picture of the map before I burned it?"

"What?" He sat bolt upright, his face ignited with sudden eagerness.

"I went over to Nathan Powell's apartment this afternoon and we looked at it on his computer. Here, we printed out copies." I reached into my jeans pocket and pulled out two rumpled pieces of folded up paper. "There's also a copy of the National Forest Service roads for reference."

He grabbed the papers and spread them flat on the table.

"Nathan and I did a bunch of online research of the area and he thinks we can find it. He grew up in Salmon Falls and knows the region. He used to hike with his dad in the mountains around here, and he's familiar with a lot of the trails and old forestry roads."

"Did you see these handwritten notes here?" Jared asked. "It says once you get on the forestry road, you head straight for a mile toward a rock formation shaped like an owl, then veer right just past a forked tree, and left around a craggy outcropping. These directions are pretty specific."

"Yes, but just remember how old that map is. Those landmarks might not even be there anymore."

"Why are you so negative?"

I tightened my mouth and looked at him gravely. "I just don't want you getting your hopes up too high. We may not be able to find the mine at all, and even if we do, it may be a total bust."

Ignoring my concerns, he said, "Let's drive up there next Saturday. I'd say let's go tomorrow except they're going to start framing the rooms in the basement this week and I want to be there."

I knew he'd never let it go. With a sigh, I gave in. "Okay, but let me call Nathan and see if he's free. I don't want to go up there without someone along who actually has some experience hiking in the mountains."

"But—" Jared began.

I put up a hand to forestall my brother's protest. "Weren't you, like, *twelve* when you were in Scouts? That was a *long* time ago."

I left my brother to finish the pizza while I went to my room to make the phone call.

"Sorry," Nathan said when I asked him about Saturday. "I've got a family thing in the afternoon that I can't get out of, but how about Sunday?"

"Sunday sounds good—provided Jared doesn't implode before then. I can't believe how invested he's become in this mine. I just hope he's not too disappointed if we don't find it."

"Well, tell Jared the first excursion you guys need to make is to the store to get some good sturdy hiking boots, and a backpack to carry water and a first aid kit. A flashlight and some rope would also be good to bring for emergencies, and maybe a compass. Remember, your cell phone might not work up there."

I laughed. "That's why I want you along, Daniel Boone. You actually know what you're doing, unlike us city-slickers."

"It's just common sense," he said. "You don't ever want to go hiking in the mountains without proper clothes and gear. You could get yourself into real trouble. Remember, there's *bears* in them thar hills. Maybe even rattlesnakes."

"Enough!" I cried. "I get the message."

Jared looked crestfallen when I told him we would have to wait till Sunday—nearly a whole week away. You would have thought it was an eternity. One of the articles I read on Nathan's computer talked about "gold fever." Many a prospecter had lost all sense of reason as greed and over-excitement usurped their judgment. I had to admit my brother sounded like he was in the full throes of the disease. I hoped there was a cure.

"Let's drive up there on Saturday anyway," Jared entreated. "Just as a dry run. You know, to scope out what it looks like—sort of get an idea where to go."

He was so fervent, I finally relented. What would it hurt? "Okay, we'll drive up and have a look around. But that's *all*. Then Sunday, Nathan can come with us and we'll actually go hiking in earnest to search for the mine." I shook my head in mock surrender. "Even if we don't find it, it will be an adventure—not to mention good exercise."

* * *

Saturday dawned cool and cloudy, but there was no rain in the forecast. Armed with the computer printouts, we took my Subaru and headed east on I-90 toward the mountains. Following Nathan's advice, we had each procured a pair of hiking boots and a daypack to carry a couple of water bottles, a sack lunch, some rope, a flashlight, and a first aid kit. Even though our plan today did not include a lot of hiking, my conversation with Nathan had made me wary enough that I also purchased a canister of bear spray which I clipped to a belt loop on my jeans.

For several hours, we drove around the target area just getting the lay of the land, exploring the freeway exits and frontage roads, comparing the old map to the actual terrain. I tried to imagine what it must have looked like a hundred years ago when the current six-lane divided interstate had been nothing more than a narrow gravel road punched through the thick evergreen forest, winding down the rocky cliffsides.

Fortunately for us, the past winter had been unusually warm and dry with a below-average snowfall in the Cascades. I knew that lack of a deep snow pack might pose a water problem later in the year, but today it was a boon to our search. Any other year we might have had to wait till midsummer to go exploring in the mountains. As it was, the snow had receded to higher ground leaving only patches here and there in shaded areas.

Shortly after noon we pulled the car off the arterial onto what we had optimistically identified as the forestry road labeled on the old map. All the signs seemed to line up.

If I'd had a jeep, I might have attempted to drive it. But the roadway looked steep and rocky, and I wasn't prepared to wreck the suspension on my little Subaru. So we ate our lunches in the car, then got out and started walking.

At first the way was clear: bare dirt, potholed and rock-strewn, wide enough for a small truck. Branches of adjacent trees occasionally overhung the road, but no major obstructions blocked our path so we continued to follow it further into the backwoods. Gradually the road narrowed to no more than a rutted jeep track, eroded and uneven, with a thick tangle of weeds and underbrush encroaching along both sides.

After walking for nearly an hour up a steady slope, I began to get nervous. "I wonder if we should turn back. We don't want to get lost up here."

Jared scoffed. "How can we get lost? All we have to do is turn around and walk back the way we came." He stopped and stretched, taking a deep swig of water. Glancing around, he brightened. "Hey, look—the sun's coming out. That's a good omen, right?"

I looked up and gazed at the rocky peaks surrounding us. I had never felt so small. The afternoon sun shone through the parting clouds and reflected off the granite cliffs with a golden shimmer that seemed otherworldly. Above us, a large bird wheeled in a thermal updraft. I hoped it wasn't a vulture. Then something caught my eye. I pointed. "Jared, look at those rocks. Does that look like an owl to you?"

His jaw dropped and his eyes widened. He reached inside his coat for the map and held it out in front of him, mumbling as he read the handwritten scrawls to himself for what must have been the hundredth time.

"We're getting close," he said.

"I think you're right. Let's mark this place so we can find it again, and then come back tomorrow with Nathan. We'll have more time tomorrow because we'll know exactly where we're going and won't waste time driving around in circles."

He paused and thought about it, obsession warring with logic. Obsession won out. "We're so close," he pleaded. "Let's just see if we can find the forked tree, okay? Then I promise we'll turn around."

I looked at my watch: not yet three o'clock. Sunset was around nine, so we probably still had six good hours of daylight left. Plus, I reasoned, it would take less time going back, being downhill all the way.

I drank some water and wiped a hand across my face, brushing back a limp strand of hair. The air was cool, but I was sweating from the unaccustomed exertion. I dragged in a deep lungful of air and readied myself for more hiking. "Okay. It's against my better judgment, but let's keep going. If we find this forked tree after all these years, I'll be amazed."

We trudged onward, keeping our eyes peeled for something resembling a forked tree. The landscape became rockier and the trail more overgrown. Increasingly, I was grateful for my boots as sharp stones and protruding tree roots strove to trip me as we hiked, slogging through mud puddles, climbing across fallen logs, and trampling over patches of thorny blackberry vines. Thank goodness for Nathan's foresight. I would never have made it this far in my canvas tennis shoes.

Then I saw it. Jared saw it too. He halted, his face breaking into an exhilarated grin. The track had leveled out here, and not more than fifty yards ahead leaned a weathered snag. Dead and bleached white from years of exposure, the twin trunks of the old tree diverged like the tines of a great fork emerging from the surrounding undergrowth.

"That's it," Jared said. He jogged ahead and disappeared around a hedge of thick brush.

I sat down on a large boulder to catch my breath and finish the last of my water. I made a mental note to bring more water next time.

"Kate!" came Jared's urgent call. "*Come here! You've got to see this.*"

With a groan, I stood and forced my limbs to move. Rounding the bend on a trail choked with weeds and scrub alders, I stopped short, giving an audible gasp. Nearly buried beneath layers of vegetation, sat the derelict frame of an abandoned old truck. Rusted and decayed, hidden for decades, it had slowly been enveloped by the relentless encroachment of the forest.

Oh, my god. My heart pounded with excitement. There could only be one explanation: Tommy O'Connell. It *had* to be. He had come to the mine and never returned. An eerie feeling of isolation and dread pervaded my thoughts. The towering trees and dense foliage blocked the sunlight here, casting deep shadows and filling me with foreboding.

Suddenly, I desperately wanted to find the mine and search for clues. *This has to be it. We must be on the brink of discovering what happened to Tommy all those years ago. Maybe at last the mystery will be solved, and Blossom's spirit can find peace.* I felt elated and uneasy at the same time.

Jared was already ahead of me, pushing through the brush, past a grove of tall firs, following a trail long unused. We worked our way around a rocky ridge and, all at once, we were there.

A great crack yawned in the side of the granite wall, barely tall enough for a man to stand and extend his arms to either side. The floor was covered with loose rubble, and I could make out heavy timbers placed just inside to fortify the walls and ceiling. Outside the entrance, in a state of ruin, were the remnants of a wheelbarrow, several buckets, and a shovel.

With growing trepidation, I approached the mine. I could only see a few feet inside where the sun's light shone. Beyond that, it was pitch dark.

"Careful," Jared said, putting a hand on my arm. "It may be unstable."

I nodded, then stopped to fish the flashlight out of my daypack. Together, we crept to the entrance and peered inside.

The beam of light revealed a narrow cavern dug maybe twenty feet into the rock. The walls had been roughly hewn with picks and shovels. Moving the light along the wall showed glistening patches of moisture seeping through the rock, and traces of various colored ore exposed here and there.

I drew a rasping breath, but my gulp turned abruptly to a scream as the flashlight's beam lit upon the stark white bones of a human skeleton lying prone on the bare stone floor near the back of the cave.

Jared saw it at the same time. We both started violently and stumbled backward out of the mine. For a moment, we stood there breathing hard, overcome with horror at the shocking discovery. Finally, bolstered by the bright afternoon sunlight, the absurdity of our fear hit us and we looked at each other foolishly.

"You know who that is, don't you?" I asked my brother.

"I can make a guess," he said, adjusting the straps on his pack.

"It's Tommy O'Connell, Blossom's long lost fiancé, the one who vanished and supposedly left her in the lurch."

"Yeah," he agreed. "It's got to be. We can check the remains for ID if you're not squeamish."

I steeled myself and nodded. "Let's go before I change my mind."

Together, we crept back into the mine, edging toward the skeleton, careful not to disturb anything. While the mine appeared to be carved into solid rock, there were several places where slides were evident. Dislodging one stone could prove disastrous.

Reaching the skeleton, we found that just such a collapse appeared to have been its fate. Both legs below the pelvis were crushed beneath a pile of rubble and boulders. Even if the unfortunate man had been able to extricate himself, both legs had surely been broken. *How tragic*, I thought. What a horrible, painful way to die.

The bones had long ago been disturbed by scavengers—picked clean, pulled apart, and left like a pile of pick-up sticks. The skull grimaced into the darkness, a pale orb staring out of empty, yellowed sockets. I imagined poor Tommy lying here, perhaps holding vainly onto hope of being rescued. Instead, he had died alone, a void of eternal heartbreak stretching before him as he realized he would never see Blossom again.

Most of the clothing had disintegrated over time, but Jared was able to dig a wallet out of the loose earth. It had been chewed by vermin, but the drivers license was still readable, confirming what I had already concluded. Indeed, these were the remains of Tommy O'Connell. Digging deeper into the wallet, Jared also found a small snapshot of Blossom, young and smiling, her face radiant with devotion. On the back, in delicate curved handwriting, were the words, *I will love you forever, Blossom.* She had been true to her word.

A timber creaked and several small stones rattled to the floor. I looked up, remembering where we were. Not a safe place to linger.

"We should go," I said softly. "When we get home, I'll contact the authorities to come and remove the bones so that Tommy can have a proper burial. I think he should be laid to rest beside Blossom."

As we exited the mine, a familiar voice greeted us. "You won't be going anywhere."

Chapter Thirty-Four

I whirled to locate the source of the voice. My eyes squinted in the blinding sunshine, but I knew immediately who it was. *"Dillon!"*

The striking young man reclined against a tree opposite the opening to the mine. He wore his usual tight jeans, a nylon parka, and a wide-brimmed bush hat pulled low over his eyes. In his hand, he held a lethal-looking pistol leveled directly at us. *Had I once been attracted to him?* It seemed a lifetime ago.

"Dillon," I said again, still in shock. "What are you doing?"

"You thought you could steal the gold, didn't you? The gold that rightfully belonged to my grandfather."

"That was never my intention," I said in an even voice. "I wanted us all to share, to be partners, remember?"

He laughed venomously. "That was very clever, burning the map in front of us, letting us all think it had been destroyed. But I'm not so easily fooled. I suspected you'd made a copy, and that if I just watched you long enough, you'd eventually lead me to the mine. And I was *right*—it didn't take long."

During this exchange, Jared had inched to the left away from me, perhaps thinking to rush Dillon from the side while he was distracted. But Dillon was ahead of him. He swung the pistol and hissed, "Take another step, Jared. I dare you."

Jared stood still and sneered. "I knew there was something off about you."

"Dillon," I said, "this isn't necessary. You can have the mine. I never wanted it anyway. I just came here out of curiosity."

"And now you'll spend eternity here." His voice was low and menacing.

"Put the gun away," I pleaded. "We're all friends. We can talk about this. There's no reason for anyone to get hurt."

"It's too late for that, isn't it? If I let you go now, you'll be compelled to turn me in to the police." There was a cold, flat look in his eye.

I shook my head, trying to keep my voice calm despite the fear growing in my gut. "No, Dillon. There's no need to get the police involved. We can work things out ourselves, but you have to put the gun away. You don't really want to hurt us, do you?"

My placating smile had no effect.

"Everyone thinks I've gone back to Ohio." He spoke as though commenting on the weather, his face showing no emotion. "By the time anyone realizes you're gone, I will have. My flight leaves in the morning. I'll just lay low for awhile until things cool off. No one else knows about the mine but Borello, and I've already taken care of him. Seems the fat slob had a tall stack of heavy clay pots stored in his garage to sell. Somehow they managed to fall on him, tragically crushing his skull."

I was gripped with terror. Dillon had killed Borello, and now he was going to kill us. At this point, he had nothing to lose. My mind flew to Nathan. He knew about the mine and he had a copy of the map. He had planned to meet us tomorrow to come up here, but by then it would be too late. I couldn't tell Dillon about Nathan without putting Nathan's life in danger too. It was small consolation that Nathan would be able to direct the police to the location of our murder. Then I had a frightening thought: if he did that, what would prevent the police from tagging *him* as a suspect?

"Dillon, it won't work," I said, trying to throw him off balance. "Lots of people in Salmon Falls know about you. They'll connect you to us. If we disappear, they'll immediately suspect you."

"Why? What's my motive?" He straightened, edging away from the tree and moving a half step closer.

Jared spoke up then, a jeer in his voice. "Forget it, Kate. You can't reason with a madman."

Dillon glared at him. "Funny you should say that. That's what they called me at my last job when they fired me. They called me a sociopath, but that's ridiculous. They just didn't like me because I was smarter than all of them."

Jared took another step sideways. I knew what he was doing; he was drawing Dillon's fire away from me. I could see him tense. He was going to lunge, to sacrifice himself to give me a chance, however small, to get away.

Dillon's mouth widened into a horrible, calculating grin. His knuckles turned white as he tightened his grip on the gun.

I wanted to scream.

In that instant, the sky grew dark as though massive black storm clouds had obscured the sun. A cold breeze whipped up the surrounding trees causing branches to bend and sway. An eerie wail, desolate as a lament, assailed us from within the depths of the mountain. I was seized by a quavering dread.

"Stop right there," Dillon shouted over the howling of the wind. He angled the gun slightly to my right, his gaze focused on the mine entrance a few feet behind me. "Stop or I'll shoot!"

Bewildered, I turned to look.

A man had walked out of the cleft in the rock, moving around me and resolutely toward Dillon. Young and ruggedly handsome, the stranger wore a sheepskin jacket; his dark wavy hair was swept back under a short-brimmed fedora.

"*Stop!*" cried Dillon again. He fired the pistol. All his attention was directed at stopping the stranger. The man never flinched.

I leaped out of the way. Dillon fired wildly, again and again, becoming more panicked.

Jared sprang. He knocked Dillon to the ground. They began to wrestle for the gun.

For a moment, I stood petrified with shock and terror. I knew I had to do something, but my brain refused to function. Then it came to me. Swiftly, I unclipped the canister of bear repellent from my belt loop. Bending over the tussling men, I aimed the nozzle directly at Dillon's face and pulled the trigger, releasing the full force of the acrid pepper spray into his eyes.

Jared reared back to avoid the overspray while Dillon screamed, dropped the pistol, and clapped his hands to his face in excruciating pain. Eyes burning, he rolled helplessly on the ground, gasping and sobbing in agony as Jared grabbed the gun and stepped back out of the way.

The sun emerged once more. When I looked up, the clouds had cleared and the sky was again deep blue. The stranger stood near the entrance to the mine. As I watched, he faded away, leaving only the shadows of trees moving rhythmically with the afternoon breeze against the rock face.

"Thank you, Tommy," I whispered. Tears rolled down my face and I let them come.

Suddenly, a voice could be heard calling through the trees. "Kate! *Kate!* Where are you?"

I exchanged a surprised glance with my brother. It sounded like Nathan, and he was close.

"*Nathan!*" I cried in response. "We're *here!*"

Then came the sound of a body pushing through the undergrowth, scrambling over the stones—and the next thing I knew, Nathan was bursting up the path over the ridge. I ran to him and fell into his arms.

"How did you find us?" Jared asked a few minutes later after securing Dillon with a length of rope from his daypack. "We weren't expecting to see you till tomorrow."

"Which begs the question," Nathan admonished, "what are you doing up here? Why didn't you wait?"

"It's my fault," Jared said. "I talked Kate into coming up here just to check things out. Honestly, I never expected to find the mine. We spent hours driving around, checking the map against the trails and forestry roads." He shrugged. "We got lucky."

Nathan lifted an eyebrow. "I'm not sure *lucky* is the word I would have used. When I think about what could have happened . . ."

He glanced at Dillon sniveling on a log, hands tied, looking miserable. Jared had given him some water to rinse his eyes, but they were still brilliant red, weeping and swollen.

Nathan drew me close, his arm encircling my waist.

I gave him a reassuring smile. "We're all right now—thanks to Tommy."

"Another ghost?"

I understood his doubt. "I know it's hard to believe in ghosts when you've never seen one, but Jared and I both know beyond a shadow of a doubt that it was Tommy who saved us."

"That's right," Jared said. "Most amazing thing I've ever seen."

"Then I'm grateful to Tommy." Nathan said it without a shred of condescension, and I loved him for it.

"You *saw* it, didn't you?" Dillon screamed hysterically. "*The ghost!* You saw it too!"

Jared ignored him, still addressing Nathan. "We found his remains inside the mine. Looks like he died pinned under a rock slide. His wallet and drivers license were with him."

"And one of the first things I want to do," I said, "is have his remains brought down and buried next to Blossom in the Salmon Falls Cemetery."

"Always the romantic," Nathan said, giving me a squeeze. "I'm sure that can be arranged."

"Now, answer my question," Jared said. "How did you find us? And how did you even know to come looking?"

I aimed a sidelong glance at Nathan. "You told me you had a family thing this afternoon."

He laughed. "Well, for starters, it didn't take *The Pathfinder* to follow your trail. Your car is parked at the base of the old Forest Service road—and so is Dillon's, by the way. A blind Cub Scout could have followed you."

"Okay, so we're not *Hiawatha*," I said with a shrug.

He snorted. "You were almost *The Last of the Mohicans*."

Jared stared at us, mystified. The glimmer of a smile on his face told me he was catching on that there was something more than friendship between Nathan and me. He folded his arms across his chest and listened with rapt interest to our exchange.

"Go on," I said to Nathan. "What made you come looking for us?"

"Your neighbor. You'll have to thank her for her powers of observation."

"What? *Wendy?* How?"

"She always knows what's going on, doesn't she? She watches everything that happens on your street. Who's coming, who's going, who's parked suspiciously alongside the road for hours, and who appears to be following whom."

My mouth dropped open. Wendy's spying and meddling had sent Nathan to the rescue.

Nathan continued. "I thought I'd surprise you by showing up and taking you to lunch before I left for Seattle. I was disappointed when you weren't home, but not worried. I figured you had gone to the store or something. But as I was getting ready to leave, Wendy came running over, all concerned because she'd seen Dillon's blue Bronco parked around the neighborhood all week. I think her exact words were 'it felt fishy.'"

I gaped. *Why hadn't I noticed?* I'd been busy. Had my head in the clouds.

"When you and Jared left this morning, Wendy saw the Bronco pull slowly out and follow you. Since you had told me about what happened last weekend with the map, I agreed something was up and decided to go after you. I tried to call and text you a couple of times, but I was hours behind you, and by then you were out of range. There's no cell service up here."

That's when I noticed Nathan was dressed in gabardine slacks, a sports jacket, and what had once been good black oxfords.

"You're hardly dressed for hiking," I scolded playfully. "What exactly were you planning to do once you found us?" I narrowed my eyes. "What about all that stuff about being prepared?"

He gave a short laugh. "I don't know. The only thing on my mind was that you might be in danger."

I smiled, brushing a stray twig off his shoulder. "Your clothes are a mess. You should at least have gone home and changed your shoes. I'm afraid they're ruined."

"A small price to pay."

"Will your family be upset that you missed the function? What was it, anyway?"

"Nothing important," he said with a sheepish grin. "Just my birthday party. My mother always goes overboard."

"Your *birthday?* Why didn't you tell me?"

"I didn't want it to be a big deal."

"*A big deal?*"

"Careful," Jared said, canting an eyebrow. "She's dangerous when she gets annoyed."

I fumed at them both.

"Come on," Nathan said, dodging the subject. "We should be going. We don't want to be navigating that trail in the dark."

Jared yanked Dillon up off the log. "On your feet, scum." Then, to no one in particular, he added, "I've always wanted to say that."

Dillon whined piteously as he stumbled forward. Suddenly, he stopped and turned to Jared. "You *saw* it, didn't you? The ghost? I'm not crazy. Tell me you saw it too. *Tell me I'm not crazy.*"

Jared looked at him silently for a moment, then gave a harsh laugh. "Oh, you're crazy, all right. Now, get going."

Epilogue

The fate of the mine was taken out of my hands. A legal claim had never been filed by anyone, and since it was situated on federal land, the U.S. Geological Survey, The Bureau of Land Management, and the National Forest Service all declared jurisdiction. I was happy to walk away and leave it behind; the mine had never brought anything but grief to anyone.

Two weeks later, a group of Salmon Falls residents including Jared and me, Nathan Powell, Harold Pike, Wendy and Rick Hilliard, Flossie Gerhardt, and a large contingent from the Senior Center, gathered in the Salmon Falls Cemetery to pay their last respects to Tommy O'Connell. His remains were finally being laid to rest with proper ceremony beside Blossom.

Most had not known him, but they knew *of* him through stories and rumors told over the years. Now, they would know the facts through the eulogy I would give: that Tommy had loved Blossom and had always intended to marry her, but had been prevented by tragic circumstances. Theirs had been a love for all time, and I knew that now they would rest together forever.

Sunlight sparkled on dewy grass, rhododendrons bloomed in pink profusion, and from the treetops, birds heralded a perfect morning. Then a movement caught my eye and I looked up.

Walking slowly toward each other across the lawn were Blossom Thatcher and Tommy O'Connell, looking as they had in 1941. Blossom's thick brown hair was tied up with ribbons, and she wore a glistening white gown. She extended her hand to Tommy who was dressed in a stunning black satin tuxedo topped off with a jaunty fedora. He took her hand and gently pulled her into his arms. They embraced in a long, passionate kiss.

Making up for eighty years lost time, I thought with a wistful smile. Then I remembered it was June. Perfect. They were getting their June wedding at last.

Beside me, Nathan gave a little start and his breath did a quick intake. Eyes wide, he gave my hand a meaningful squeeze. He had wanted to see a ghost and here were two. Glancing at Jared, I could tell that my brother saw them too, though apparently no one else did. I felt honored that we three had been included in the rapturous reunion of these two tragic souls. With exultant smiles, the spirits of Blossom and Tommy turned toward us and gave a wave of thanks before vanishing together in a nimbus of morning sunlight.

The ceremony was brief. In addition to my informal homage, Mildred Birch spoke a few words about the Tommy O'Connell she remembered as a child: a charming man, kind and full of life, of whom her grandmother had always spoken highly. Flossie, Mildred, and Esther each laid a small bouquet of flowers on Tommy's grave. It was a touching gesture, and a tear welled in my eye. Afterward, I gave everyone my sincere thanks, surprised at how deeply affected I'd been by the final resolution of this heartrending mystery.

"You know what I think?" Nathan said to me as people turned and started walking back to their cars.

I shook my head. "What?"

He took both my hands and looked me in the eye. "I think you should write their story."

I stepped backward, taken off guard. I knew what he meant, but the idea seemed preposterous. *He* was the writer, not me.

"I *couldn't*," I stammered. "I don't have time. The house . . . Amy . . ."

"Excuses," he said, tilting his head in that irresistible way he had. "You told me once that you've always wanted to write. Well, here's the perfect story. It's practically screaming to be told, and who better than you to tell it? You were the one most touched by it, the one to whom Blossom herself chose to reveal the map, the one who found Tommy and brought him home."

"I don't know if I can." But even as I said it, I knew that I wanted to try, *had* to try. A biographical novel recounting the tragic romance and eternal love of Blossom Thatcher and Tommy O'Connell would be the ideal opportunity to test my creative instincts, to prove that my ambition to write was more than just a whimsical hobby. Done well, it would be a lasting tribute, and perhaps the start of a new career.

Impulsively, I drew Nathan toward me and gave him a warm kiss.

"Thank you," I said.

"For what?"

"For believing in me, for supporting me."

He smiled. "Isn't that what people do who care about each other?"

I kissed him again, content in the knowledge that my own happy ending lay before me.

The End

A true denizen of the Pacific Northwest, Kathleen Easley loves deep blue water, tall green trees, and The Seattle Seahawks. She can often be found with her husband on their boat cruising the San Juan Islands of Washington State. She is the author of the *Brenna Wickham Haunted Mystery* series. Set in Seattle, these are contemporary murder mysteries with a paranormal twist and a hint of romantic suspense. Kathleen is a member of the Puget Sound Chapter of Sisters in Crime.

News about upcoming books can be found at www.kathleenjeasley.com